HOURGLASS

HOURGLASS

DANIEL JAMES

Copyright © 2024 Daniel James

Bottled Lightning Press

This is a work of fiction. Names, characters, places, and incidents either are the product of the author's imagination or are used fictitiously. Any resemblance to actual persons, living or dead, events, or locales is entirely coincidental.

All rights reserved. No part of this book may be reproduced or used in any manner without written permission of the copyright owner except for the use of quotations in a book review.

Cover design by Hampton Lamoureux at TS95 Studios Interior design by Olivia M. Hammerman

ISBN: 978-1-7384956-0-3 (paperback)

PROLOGUE

THE ILYUSHIN 76 ASCENDED THROUGH the kingdom of clouds like a steel dragon, powerful and proud. It roared up and away from the private airstrip, leaving in its wake the alpine snowfields of the classified mountain prison installation known as Peklo. Peklo was hidden away high within the Ural mountain range of western Russia. Escape was an impossibility, and even divine intervention would likely not be enough to assist a prisoner in the lethal environs beyond the walls. Peklo, as its Slavic name suggested, was Hell. A specialist prison, where being a political and civil threat was not enough to permit housing. To land on this guest list, the prisoners had to be something more, something... other; something that demanded additional safety measures beyond that of concrete, steel, high voltage, and rifles. And the Kremlin would first conduct hushed conversations in private rooms about the worth of such prisoners, judiciously deeming their fitness before flinging them up to the white rocky glaciers of a mountain where they could rot in obscurity.

The plane thundered upwards to cruising altitude.

Inside, the belly of the beast was cold and anxious. A handful of Russian military police in green uniforms sat on the benches lining the walls of the cargo hold, working hard to maintain their air of uncompromising toughness for the prisoner. Beyond appearances, they were surplus to this particular covert assignment, a mere favor extended from the Russian

Ministry of Defense, and just as interested in seeing the safe return of their loaned aircraft as they were in the disposal of prisoner 415.

The American man in charge of this transportation, along with a small team of black-clad private security, sat in the middle of the starboard bench, the brief file on prisoner 415 open in his lap. He knew the tough expressions of the military policemen were a sham, a brittle façade of composure, but he didn't lose respect for them because of it, for he, too, was currently mired in a bout of unease. And he was paid handsomely by his employers to keep his nerve and oversee the safe arrival of their asset. The Russian contacts knew the American simply as Mr. Collins. A slight, formal man by nature, with a nice liaison's smile, soft hands, and well-manicured fingernails well suited to pen-pushing. Preferring warmer climes, at most a chilly winter in New York, he was kitted out in the expensive snow gear left over from one old skiing/business trip to France and hugging himself tight.

Collins was professional enough not to stare at prisoner 415, currently strapped in the middle of the cargo hold. He could imagine these guards were only too happy to rid their little mountaintop bunker of one more problem, and the other side of the Atlantic was surely as good a destination as any. He didn't envy their jobs at Peklo, and he was a man who dealt with the extraordinary on a daily basis. Like all members of the Cairnwood Society, he'd seen his share of miracles and nightmares.

The liaison continued to furtively stare at the impassive face of prisoner 415, a man of borderline malnutrition, lost in grubby, red prison overalls. Over the prison uniform he wore some unique, eye-catching articles. Bronze gauntlets, heavy but seemingly manageable, forged with bas-relief arcane runes. A crudely forged bronze breastplate, the lower half of which resembled prison bars, each bar embossed with time-lost scripture believed to originate from a forgotten Slavic tribe. Above his shaggy gray beard was a strong nose and a pair of eyes that contained something unknowable behind their gray clouds, some ill intelligence scouring for something, but whether it be in this life or beyond, Mr. Collins wasn't certain. From what Collins had learned, the bronze armaments were not only of the prisoner's own making but had become a necessity that could only be removed for limited periods of time. Apparently, the warden and the staff at Peklo had learned this the hard way but managed to survive the incident with their skin intact. Besides the peculiar armor, Peklo had outfitted the prisoner with some of their own precautions: a set of large iron shackles big enough in circumference to encompass his gauntlets but otherwise ordinary in their craft; a smaller set for his ankles; and an iron collar of gnostic design, engraved with cultish symbols used to control individuals with a knack for communing with the dead. The prisoner was also doped-up with a light sedative.

Mr. Collins allowed the engine's drone to softly carry him away in thought as he continued to review prisoner 415's heavily redacted file, trying to decide which definition suited the prisoner best: miracle or nightmare. Konstantin Kozlov, or "Gulag" as he had been mirthlessly dubbed by the prison authorities at Peklo. An educated mind, once a driven patriot and officer in service of his country's military intelligence, the KGB. Stationed in REDACTED, he was an officer with a deep occult-honed interest of unverified origin who turned his back on his country in search of something greater, being labeled a traitor and a criminal in the process after having violently assaulted his commanding officer, one REDACTED, and dropping off the grid before finally being located in the... another blacked-out line. All in all, hardly a biographer's dream project. But it was the brief unofficial document that had been included in the file that interested Collins, the one that detailed Kozlov's ability. Collins still remained on the fence as to his opinion of the skill. Personally, he thought it seemed like a burden. But if it was what Kozlov had been searching for, he'd certainly found it. And despite his subsequent incarceration, his talent had proved too useful to squander, and now here he was, still bound in mystical chains, but flying towards a second chance, 30,000 feet above a vast landmass of brilliant white and jagged rock. As a company representative low on the totem pole, Mr. Collins frequently operated in general ignorance of his employers' larger schemes. All he really knew was that Kozlov was on his way to serve new masters now, whether he wanted to or not. And that was why Collins was here, to smooth the transition. The carrot, not the stick. The stick would come later if polite discourse proved untenable.

Collins had been largely ignored by Kozlov since their introduction, but the man had been tractable, probably happy to leave the confines of Peklo, since just about anywhere else would be a likely improvement.

And Collins was friendly company during his working hours. He closed the file and looked up into the old, creased face of Kozlov.

'Your ability, I can't decide if it's a joyous or a depressing experience. I suppose I'll never know. Either way, it's fascinating.'

Kozlov was silent. Collins knew he could speak English fluently, and the drugged stupor shouldn't be affecting him by now.

'You'll be taken good care of. My employer treats his guests very well, particularly those he wishes to work with. We'll get you cleaned up, a hot meal, a comfortable bed. You'll forget all about the squalor you've been used to in that place.'

The belly of the plane remained a quiet, metal tomb.

'It's a shame we couldn't fly you commercial. You could have had a few in-flight movies and a strong drink.'

Collins eyed the contingent of armed, black-clad security he had arrived with. Capable-looking men in black thermal gear. These men were Cairnwood payroll. A cut above regular military personnel in terms of their knowledge and exposure to the scary things operating outside of humanity's pitiful purview. Still, Collins looked at their cautious faces with a hint of unease. The Peklo MPs, for their part, continued their own diligent observation of prisoner 415, staring hard at the old iron collar about his pale neck as if expecting it to break, their hands close to their batons or loaded syringes should 415 decide to become unruly; they were less exotic methods of control, but tried and tested. 415, whatever else he had become, was first and foremost only a man.

Collins gave a thin-lipped smile and took his phone from his pocket to check his schedule. His work was never done. An urgent whisper scraped Collins' ear like a cold blade, causing him to twitch sharply. He glanced up from his phone. Nobody else seemed to have reacted to the sound. Had they even heard it? Had he? He stared hard at Kozlov. The man's jaw was clenched slightly, but otherwise he remained quiet. Collins' gaze skimmed across the dead symbolism along the bars of Kozlov's torso, then tried to catch his eye again, but the man was a million miles away, paying scant attention to the doings of the men on this plane. Perhaps he was in contact with his spiritual tenants.

Gulag. Collins had decided that it must in fact be a miserable existence for prisoner 415. Personally, Collins had enough bother with his own thoughts, never mind those of an assorted collective. He was about to return his attention to the schedule on his phone, blaming the whisper on his ear popping from pressure, when Kozlov's mouth suddenly started bleeding, a dark crimson font leaking down his bushy chin. He had chewed a ragged gash along the inside of his cheek. The MPs thought he was experiencing some type of seizure, with one of them reaching for a medical kit, when Kozlov raised his shackled gauntlets, swilled his cheeks, and spat a shower of viscous crimson saliva onto the blocky right fingers, quickly smearing the blood along the inhibiting characters ingrained into the iron band fitted about his neck. A sudden turbulence thrashed the plane, spilling Collins onto the cold floor, the dossier and his phone scattering. The MPs and the Cairnwood help were sent clattering about too; some struck the walls forcefully and remained there as if held by an invisible hand, while others picked themselves up and converged on Kozlov with urgent expressions and commands.

It hadn't been turbulence, at least not the traditional sort. The pocket of shifting air pressure had come from within the plane. Collins knew it had to have been Kozlov, but the damn dossier, all several useless pages of it, didn't disclose anything about the nullifying effects of smearing blood across the prison collar's symbols. How had none of the warden's idiot experts discovered this before discharging him into such meager custody? They should have knocked him out before take-off.

Sharp music began to shimmer within the fuselage, a tremulous vibrato originating from the bars of Gulag's breastplate, steadily becoming a babel of voices, like devils speaking in mortal ears. Collins witnessed ripples in the air, the visual trickery becoming clearer as a sudden rampage of spectral limbs, torsos, and faces emerged from within Gulag. Judging from their monastic dress, they appeared to share history with their keeper. Before security could pounce on Gulag, they were battered up and down the cargo hold, tossed roughly from one wraith to another, their sedative needles and guns slapped away.

Collins was struggling to his feet when a bladder-clenching beep filled the hold. Near the plane's cargo ramp, the red light turned green. Some of the spirits had already screeched into the cockpit, raising merry hell amongst the pilots and their instrument panel. Collins watched with abject terror as the cargo door began to lower, its opening forcefully speeded up by the sheer might of several paroled spirits.

'The hell are you doing?' Collins screamed at Gulag, his voice tiny and childlike. He spotted MPs and Cairnwood shooters grabbing hold of cargo netting hanging from the walls and followed suit, holding on for dear life. 'We're here to help you!'

Gulag watched the door drop with the stoic interest of one who is ready to die. The sudden loss of cabin pressure was like being at the mercy of a tornado. Collins felt the netting bite into his palms and knew he wouldn't be able to hold it for much longer, and almost sobbed as a Cairnwood employee went screaming past him, carried through the air by one of the ghostly antagonists and flown straight out of the back of the aircraft into the cottony mass of clouds. Discarding the screaming man into the freezing air, the ghost sailed through the clouds, leaping and diving through the foamy masses like a dolphin.

Collins' legs were trailing behind him, his cold hands gripping the netting tight in the presence of this heart-stopping mayhem. The plane rocked and bucked, everybody on board still fighting to keep their purchase on netting and bench seats, except Gulag, who appeared to be fixed in place, somehow standing and staring at the clouds from the open cargo door. Collins was beginning to feel lightheaded and tried not to think about what would happen if the pilots were dead, about the cargo plane nose-diving, when he spotted one of the syringes, sedative-loaded and unused, snagged on the back of the bench seat below his whipping body. He would be losing consciousness any moment now, and the idea of being jettisoned into the troposphere willed him into desperate action.

Collins reached down, snatching up the syringe and released his death grip on the cargo net. He thought he was going to miss, that he would be dragged straight out of the back of the plane, when he crashed into the immovable back of Gulag, almost breaking the needle on the prisoner's iron collar before jabbing it into his neck and sinking his thumb down on the plunger. The effect was almost instantaneous. Kozlov shuddered. The wraiths bellowed their fury but were powerless in the face of this chemical exorcism-in-reverse. One by one they were dragged back inside Kozlov. The pilots swiftly corrected the plane's erratic path and sealed the cargo door.

Kozlov's riot had been short-lived, but he was still a former career KGB officer, his discipline a harnessed ball of steel. Now, as the sedatives coursed through him, Kozlov managed a last attack. A pair of hoary arms, dancing like white fire, extended out from between the bars of his breastplate. Before Collins could react, a set of strong, sharp fingers slapped onto his windpipe and squeezed. Collins' eyes bulged as his larynx was crushed like paper. Meanwhile, Kozlov yanked the needle out of his neck, gave it one look of contempt, and dropped it to the floor. Collins, barely alive, said a silent prayer that his imminent death would not leave him as another inmate in Kozlov's personal inner gulag.

A dark shape rushed into his blurry vision: the butt of a service pistol cracking into the back of Kozlov's skull, possibly fatal, but those were the chances that now had to be taken. The chilly fingers around Collins' throat vanished, but the damage had been done. Weak, slumped on his knees, Collins watched as the Cairnwood man who had bludgeoned Kozlov quickly took a syringe from the hand of an MP and shot a second tranquilizer dose into Kozlov's neck.

A second Cairnwood guard floated over Collins like a dark angel, flick knife in hand. Collins felt his consciousness being smothered under layers of gauze. Nothing seemed to matter anymore. Not his oft-neglected personal ambitions, not the demands of his employers, not even his bountiful regrets. The thin blade expertly pierced Collins' throat, slipping beneath the blockage of crushed larynx to ventilate the windpipe, keeping him on this side of the veil. Though he wasn't out of the woods yet. The battlefield stent was only enough to keep him breathing. Lying prone, staring at the cabin ceiling, Collins was dimly aware of noise and hasty activity. Then nothing at all, as he took his last breath.

The Ilyushin 76 maintained its course for a brief refueling stop at a private airstrip in England, before continuing on to Westchester, New York.

1

It was a little past 9 p.m., but the persistent sun was determined to bleed as much light and color into the evening as possible, gilding the brownstones surrounding Herbert von King Park in saccharine peach and blazing orange. The park was unusually quiet for a summer night, even for this late hour, having disgorged most of the public throngs.

Clyde had chosen a spot for him and Kev at the top of the amphitheater's steps, keeping a semi-relaxed vigil as he and Kev shot the shit and Kev discreetly practiced his Skittles shooting. It was fun, just the two of them being able to act normal in a public setting without feeling like they were breaking the law. And it was another chance to test the water and spend time with Kev outside the apartment, though Clyde hated thinking of it in such dependent terms, as though his best friend of twenty years was a house-trained dog needing to be taken outside to drop a steamer on the sidewalk or piss up against a light post.

Still, Clyde kept a keen eye on their surroundings, especially when Kev started to levitate his Skittles before flinging them towards Clyde's open mouth.

'Ow!' Clyde grinned, cupping his mouth. 'Careful, man. Almost chipped my tooth with that one.'

'You think you could do better?' Kev asked with a deep, throaty chuckle.

'I don't think I can do what you do.'

A red candy floated a few inches above Kev's gloved palm and sailed past Clyde, bouncing down the steps. 'I meant that. That one is for the pigeons.'

Clyde nodded, wearing a patronizing smile. He watched his friend focusing on the rest of the Skittles in his palm and thought about how Kev's choice of attire was at odds for the warm evening. It wasn't what Clyde would call incognito. Kev's outfit could have been assembled by Ray Charles: a trapper hat with big, floppy, sheepskin ears, aviator sunglasses from an old *Top Gun*-themed fancy dress party, a fleece-lined brown bomber jacket, a pair of paint-spattered jeans and sneakers, and to really sell the image of a spy who got dressed in the dark, a black scarf wrapped about his face up to the point of his aviators. But options were limited for Kev's condition. He recalled how Kev had walked down the street wearing a bedsheet like a discount Halloween ghost on his first night out after his return before settling on his current go-to outfit.

'This is a nice change of pace, huh?' Kev said. 'I was beginning to think you don't want me around anymore. All you do lately is bust your ass to the Nth.'

Clyde flinched a little, a pang of guilt nestling in his chest. Had he been working harder, spending more time focusing on his comic-book, and less time with Kev? He scratched his scalp, his coffee-and-cream-colored hand becoming momentarily lost in the shaggy freeform topiary growing wildly from his head, and combined with his wispy chin hair, he looked like some urban shaman in board shorts and a Hellboy hoodie.

'You know, it sure would be cool if you took a crack at writing this comic for me.' Clyde tried not to sound too eager. He had already begged and bargained with Kev several times. 'You could be a—' Clyde quickly caught his tongue, unwilling to finish his sentence.

'Ghost writer?' Kev peered up from his Skittles inspection, pushing his slipping aviators back over his spectacles.

Kev was dead. He died two months ago, murdered in a local liquor store hold-up when buying some off-brand cola late one Tuesday night.

'I'm still not convinced ghosts can have a career in the comic-book industry, but don't worry, I'm talking to the union guys, and we might be able to organize a sit-down.'

Clyde attempted a fraction of a smile, but his mouth quickly gave up. 'Funny.' A pause. 'Shit, I'm sorry. It just came out.'

'Pretty insensitive, man.' Kev seemed to take it on the chin, and Clyde knew his pal was just busting his balls. 'Let it go, already. I'm not a writer. Never wanted to be then, don't want to be now.'

To Clyde's knowledge that was true. Kev had never expressed any interest in writing any type of fiction, but behind his slightly gruff and occasionally abrasive front, Kev had a lot more going on upstairs than a casual observer might give him credit for, his current attire notwithstanding. His interests tended to change like the seasons, often straying into surprising areas, and he had always been a voracious reader, so long as the book in question fit into his latest area of interest. So, after working a succession of demeaning and worthless jobs, he had finally decided to give higher education a go, with his good (though previously wasted) high school grades allowing him to enroll at Eugene Lang College, where he had been working towards a BA in Philosophy, of all things. Until he was gunned down shortly after completing his first year.

The quiet voice in the back of Clyde's head kept telling him that this entire thing was weird. More than that, it was insane. Going through the motions. The old routines and banter as though nothing had changed. But everything had changed. Kev was dead, buried in Evergreen on a bright, cloudless morning. And here I am, thought Clyde, offering him another chance to work on my comic-book like we're just some kooky odd couple. But what else could he do?

When Kev first sprang out of thin air that first night after his funeral, almost causing Clyde to soil his drawers, they had talked into the wee hours of the morning about what the hell was happening, after their mutual shock wore off, of course. There was something else under the fear and stupefaction, though. Hope, like a silvery shimmer in the darkness. Neither of them could account for what was happening, but simply knowing that death wasn't the end was strangely reassuring. Thrilling, even. It took the edge off life, and wasted days no longer seemed to matter. Yes, they had talked at great length that night, but beyond reiterating their confused excitement and confirming that neither of them had suffered some type of psychological breakdown, neither came up with any answers as to what the sweet-fucking-Christ was actually going on. And so, their great denial began.

Clyde felt the bag of comic-books—fresh from Mythic Comics & Collectibles, Clyde's refuge, hangout, and place of employment—jostling against his thigh as though it had come alive. Kev reeled the bag of comics towards him and skimmed them with a restless disinterest under the electric wash of the light poles before promptly returning them to the bag and carefully navigating the bundle back to Clyde's step.

'I got one: no need to worry about losing apartment keys.' Kev had picked up the thread of their earlier bus-stop conversation.

Lately he had been checking off his growing list of positive things about being a ghost: no more paying for haircuts, no need to eat, no need to shower. He dropped his voice like he was about to disclose the saucy details of a recent sordid hook-up. 'No need to go to the bathroom.'

'That's a good one,' Clyde had to admit.

'Don't need to sleep. No need to ever worry about taxes. I mean, really, no need to pay for a lot of things.'

Clyde had been watching a pair of dog walkers off in the distance, but he turned to face Kev. 'What?'

'I'm dead. The laws of man don't apply to me.'

Clyde was more than a little stirred by this. Had Kev been secretly descending into a life of petty criminality while Clyde slept? 'But you're still a man. Just a dead one.'

'But do the laws of the living have any bearing on the dead? Because, frankly, I'm not even a citizen anymore. The Constitution no longer applies. I've transcended, baby.'

'That sounds like a slippery slope. You can walk through walls, but you still have your old morals. I mean, you wouldn't go and kill a guy or steal a car just because you're a ghost now ... would you?'

Those aviator cop shades were impenetrable, but Clyde stared into them like they were a pair of black holes swallowing up his sense of security and warmth.

'Depends how much I like the guy. Or the car.'

The moment seemed to freeze, and Clyde could only see two miniature reflections of himself staring back like frightened little boys. Kev pulled his scarf down a few inches, revealing the cool, translucent blue radiance of his jaw cracking into a wide smile.

'I'm only fucking with you.'

Slowly, the tension leaked out of Clyde. Kev replaced the scarf, sniggering like a naughty schoolboy.

Clyde tried to keep the humor from eroding his concern for his friend's behavior, but failed. 'Is this your foray into a life of super-criminality?'

'Baby steps.' The amusement gently faded, and Kev cleared his throat. 'But I err... I stole that video game I've been playing.'

'You serious?'

'A little bit, yeah. Stole it. You know, it's actually therapeutic. No longer having a true physical form, I feel like my spirit now has a much stronger kinship to video game characters.' Kev's focus seemed to become enraptured on the pigeons pecking away at his scattered Skittles, seeing past them as though he was bearing witness to some profound deeper meaning underneath it all. 'Their binary coding not too dissimilar from the arcane matter that now constitutes my being. All of us devised by an indifferent higher being but left lacking any meaningful autonomy. Just echoes.' He waved a glove reverentially across the dusky sky. 'Echoes of practiced, limited movements that provide us no real means of escaping from our sandbox world.'

Clyde frowned. 'Deep. You got any more pop philosophy horseshit you want to drop on me right now?'

'I like to limit it to one nugget a day, my friend.'

'Being serious for a moment, I don't know how much longer I can keep making rent with you no longer being a tax-paying citizen.' Clyde's brow knitted in wonder. He was talking to the ghost of his best friend—living with him—but the mundanities of keeping the landlord off his back still took precedence. 'I can't keep borrowing. And even if I take up Brian's offer of the assistant manager gig at Mythic, the extra pay is a joke.' He had a few commissions that would pay okay: a poster for some convention, and some preliminary designs for a new trading card series, but really it would only elevate him slightly above ramen noodles and caffeine.

'I could rob a bank,' Kev joked. 'No, better, I could start knocking over drug dealers and scumbags. That would be cool, huh? How jealous would you be? You drawing all those little power fantasies while I'm living the real deal.'

Clyde eyeballed him hard. 'Maybe we can find a way to earn extra money that won't lead to you becoming a viral sensation? You'll have government spooks pounding on our door.'

Kev looked away, his posture stiffening a little. 'I was just messing around. Stealing that game, and dumb shit like that... You don't know what it feels like to be so repressed.'

Clyde's frown softened. 'It's cool, man. For now, please just show some restraint. We'll brainstorm some ideas later, you know, think of some safe ways to earn extra, that help you blow off steam. Ways that won't involve a government satellite tracking us.'

Kev went silent for a minute, playing with his Skittles, spinning red, green, and yellow candies about the empty packet like planets circling a misshapen black hole. 'Let me ask you something,' he said. 'Straight answers, no horseshit.'

'Okay, shoot.'

'A normal life is out of the equation for me, and if I'm going to face the possibility of drifting around this big, polluted marble until the end of days like another bad smell, I'm going to need a purpose. I know that frightens you, but I'm not spending eternity hiding away like some criminal. We need to test things further. I mean really push them.' Clyde started to stroke his wispy chin hair, eyes staring through this moment to an uncertain future. Before he could respond, Kev continued, 'We know we're not joined at the hip. I can jump the train as far as the Bronx—shit, I could probably float there if I wanted to—but I *haven't!* Don't have an aneurysm. My point is, we can't become frozen like we're stuck in some fucking time capsule. If you're to have a normal life, you can't be sharing a room with a spook who can't even pay rent.'

Clyde felt a thin sliver of heartache at this, which Kev was astute enough to spot. 'I'm not saying we part ways here and now, and I'm not planning on wandering the Earth like some corny avenging spirit.' Kev cracked the thickening atmosphere with a snarky chuckle. 'You know me, ride or die. But living with ghosts can't be healthy for anyone.'

Clyde nodded in earnest, simultaneously agreeing with his friend but also worried about the larger consequences of a ghost boldly attempting to make a living in this life. 'Does that mean you're going to tell your family, then? They ought to know.' Clyde, slightly delirious at the time, had offered to help Kev with this, offering to mediate an unthinkable reunion between his friend and his parents and sister.

The rotating Skittle planets increased their speed and were dragged into the black hole of the bag's open maw. By the time the invisible forces had twisted the bag closed, Kev had his answer. 'No. It's too much. I wouldn't have burdened you with this if I'd had a say in it. I still wish I knew what's causing all this.' The bag floated over to Clyde; it wasn't like Kev could eat them.

'Don't even think that. You're not a burden. What I will say is that it's good to see you again, and I'm sure your family will feel the same way.' Kev seemed unconvinced. 'Look, I know you pretend everything is a big joke, and that really you're wigging out as much as I am, but is this...' Clyde trailed off, not wanting to put his foot in it. 'Is this a good thing? We've spoken about it a lot, but I can't stop thinking about it, so I know that you can't either, but if ghosts are real, then it isn't too farfetched to believe in an afterlife, right?'

'I told you, all I remember is getting shot, then nothing. Now I'm back.'

'Okay, but that doesn't necessarily mean there isn't more.'

Kev strained for levity. 'Maybe I got mind-wiped by an angel.'

Clyde scoffed. 'Sure, why not? My point is that maybe you're right about coming out of hiding. And your being here gives the rest of us hope of something more. Your parents and sis, they'd like to know that as much as anybody. To know that your death was meaningless and fucked up, but also that there's a flip side to it.'

'I'm not ready yet,' Kev calmly insisted. 'One day, probably...maybe. Right now, I'm only talking about finding a way to, well, live, I guess you could call it.' He took a moment to orient his thoughts. 'Shit, I miss beer. Now there's a big one for the sucks-to-be-a-ghost list. If I could sink a few, I could probably think better.'

Clyde wasn't so sure about that last part. He poured the last handful of Skittles into his mouth and scrunched the packet. 'We'll figure something out.' He started away from the amphitheater. 'You want to head back? Or we could go to the movies, see what's on?'

Kev mumbled something, nodding towards a couple of shady men approaching them from the central path of the park, their hands concealed in jackets with big pockets and their baseball caps pulled low. Clyde saw that the lead guy was squat and thick like a fire hydrant, and the closer he got, the more his face resembled a provoked bulldog. His companion was of a weedier build but looked no less aggravated by his lot in life. Gang ink wound about his corded neck like a noose.

'Yo, got the time?' the bulldog barked, his attempt at civility simply a tactic to close the gap, his hands never leaving his pockets.

Clyde knew what was coming. Only a blind man or the hopelessly naive could fail to smell the danger clinging to this rough pair like bad aftershave. Right on cue, the gun was drawn, polished chrome catching lamplight and drawing the eye.

'Cuz if you do, I wan' it. Watches, wallets, bling. Now!' The bulldog spoke his edict softly.

Clyde managed to keep his voice calm. Growing up in the city, he wasn't a shrinking violet. 'I got like twenty dollars and a shit phone. You can have 'em. Just go easy.' He was gently moving to grab his pathetic haul, careful not to set the round-shouldered mutt off. His partner stood there like he was just queueing up to use the ATM, his hawk eyes scanning the park for any trouble.

'What's in the bag?' Bulldog was practically sniffing the air for something juicy.

'Comic-books, man. I doubt you'll give a shit.'

'You got that right.' Bulldog snickered with contempt. His lookout, however, perked up with idle curiosity.

'Yo, you got any Spider-Man in there?'

Between his cold, slushy stomach and rattled nerves, Clyde couldn't be certain, but he was pretty sure Bulldog's dark eyes rolled about in his fat head at this development. Clyde tried to remember what comics he'd picked up but struggled. 'Uh, yeah... *Amazing Spider-Man*. Take it.'

The lookout didn't need to be told twice and was about to walk over and help himself when Bulldog, not yet through pissing on his territory, shifted his gun towards Kev. 'You think you got a free pass, bitch? Empty your fuckin' pockets. I won't ask again.'

Kev, a man now capable of defying gravity when it suited him, able to pass through walls and, on one morbidly curious occasion, a speeding train, who existed in a state of phasing intangibility, had frozen solid when he saw the gun. The sight of it, that black hole at the end of the barrel, the single image that proliferates so much of global culture, had hollowed him out.

Kev, so consumed by his now superfluous fear of physical harm, hadn't realized his focus had begun to slip a little, causing his trapper hat and jacket to slowly succumb to gravity, submerging into his spiritual form like melting ice cream.

The muggers stared at this in mute disbelief. Two shots rang out before Kev could fix his constitution and his sagging clothing, piercing him like tiny comets passing through a cloud of vapor. All they killed was his jacket. A sudden volcanic rage, dormant since his return, spewed forth and poured over these animals so quick to bully and murder to get their way in life. Clenching a fist at his side and staring hard at the gun, Kev crushed the bulldog's fingers against the pistol grip with a series of snaps and pops. The brute doubled over, his shriek so high in pitch he could have been mistaken for a young lady. The wounded gunman seemed fixed to the spot, glued to invisible supports, unable to run or release the gun from his mangled hand. Then he rose a few inches off the path, his tough veneer dripping off him like melting wax, blubbering in pain and disbelief.

The skinny lookout could have been a statue, a new addition to the amphitheater, staring at his cohort being slowly lifted six feet into the air, then seven, eight, his clothing being viciously ragged and ripped from his bulk. Bare ass in the warm night air, the pink fleshy thug was tied to one of the nearby light posts with his own jeans. Sobbing and hollering, the hoodlum was a broken man, left to dangle. The lookout, with one hand still in his deep pocket and the other holding the bag from Mythic Comics & Collectibles, shook himself out of his disturbed trance, his mouth trying to find the words but failing. He dropped the comic-books—chances are he was only freeing his hands to better slice through the air as he set a new personal best for the hundred-yard dash, but Clyde, who had also watched these events transpire with a quiet dread, didn't want to risk being wrong should the mugger pull a weapon from his pocket; after all,

Kev was clearly beyond bullets, but Clyde knew he certainly wasn't. He grabbed the rangy man's wrist before it left its pocket, and operating from gut reaction, he sprung up onto the balls of his Nikes to thrust his forehead into the slightly taller man's chin, collapsing him like a house of cards. Still swimming with adrenaline and fear, Clyde moved to punt, slamming a shoe into the downed man's ribs. The man grunted and doubled into a fetal position, his groans adding to the continued warbles and pleas from his broken-handed leader tied to the lamppost.

Clyde stared at Kev. His friend had reasserted his sagging wardrobe, but even with his face hidden by scarf and shades, Clyde couldn't mistake the simmering hostility in his posture. Kev's shoulders were tensed, his arms trembling. He looked murderous.

Kev must have felt Clyde's eyes on him and turned. 'You okay?'

Clyde didn't think he was. But he nodded anyway. 'You?' Kev returned the nod. 'Should we call the cops?'

The neck-tatted lookout was trying to crawl back to his feet when he unexpectedly left the ground with a choking, wheezy, 'NO!'

Dangling the thief upside down, Kev shook his pockets empty, creating a rain of dollar bills, a switchblade, some gold jewelry of varying carat, and a few loose joints. After concluding the violent strip search, he hoisted the skinny gangbanger up to the light post opposite his partner's, using the empty jeans to tie the man's ankles to the pole. The lights cast both of their shadows onto the park's path like a couple of giant confused bats.

'You're both lucky I don't kill you,' Kev stated, his voice as lifeless as his body.

Clyde picked up his bag of comic-books, then looked at the muggers' takings, plus their weaponry. He couldn't leave all this here. He scooped up all the cash and jewelry, not bothering to count it out. He stamped on the joints, grinding them into nothing more than paper and crumbled herb, not because he was particularly anti-drug but because he didn't want some passing little kid to pick it up tomorrow.

Maybe if Kev could still draw breath, he would have happily taken the reefers. The gun and knife puzzled Clyde. Take them? Drop them in a storm drain? He sure wasn't about to stroll into the precinct and drop them on the desk sergeant. Or could he? Maybe he could tell them he was walking in the park and found these two dudes dangling up, and hand over the cash and gold too. Hard pragmatism chose for him. A naive person might believe that handing them to the proper authorities would be the right thing to do, too pure to understand that the underpaid and overworked cops would most likely pocket the cash, and as for the gold, maybe it would end up in evidence, or maybe it'd end up in a pawn shop. Screw it, he could debate this later; right now, he just wanted to get out of the park where two gunshots had recently cracked the stillness. Tucking his hands into his sleeves, he grabbed the knife and gun, keeping his fingerprints away from contact, and stowed them inside the pouch of his hoodie.

'C'mon,' Clyde said, walking swiftly away from the steps of the amphitheater. Kev's gaze lingered on the thieves and possible murderers a moment longer. Then he fell in step with Clyde, following the long path out of Herbert von King, the whimpering and pleas of the muggers calling after them.

■ ■ ■

FROM WITHIN A nearby copse of trees, a stationary figure watched them, tracking Clyde and Kev as they shrank from sight and left the park. A few wispy forms materialized around the shadowy watcher, a small team taking form in the brewing urban twilight.

2

CLYDE SCURRIED INTO HIS APARTMENT like a fugitive with the law hot on his tail, almost tripping over Kev's disguise heaped at the bottom of the door. Bundling it all together, he closed the door behind him and found Kev standing there in the clothes he had been killed in. Kev was stubbled and husky, his spectral hue a watery cobalt that made his short, dark, curly hair resemble steel wool, and he had a deep, bluish hole sitting square in his chest that had stained his plaid shirt.

Kev had entered the apartment only moments before Clyde had put the key in the lock, but in his agitation, he must have forgotten that his disguise wasn't immaterial. He pulled the whole bundle from Clyde: the gloves, hat, scarf, aviators, jeans, and shoes, each item floating away towards the couch in the living room as if they were pulled by trained pigeons in a magic act.

Clyde dropped his comic-books on the coffee table, then tucked his hands into his sleeves before handling the weapons—likely murderous in their past deeds—and placed them down next to the MC&C bag. He stared unblinking at the steel and iron, not to mention the small but substantial stash of dollars and valuable items, reconsidering his hasty decision to take them, and now thinking about going straight down to the 83rd on Knickerbocker, which was only several blocks and five minutes away, and handing them over to the cops with his most innocent face.

Hang on a minute: he *was* innocent! The victim of an intended mugging, perhaps worse! He was mentally fried. The event had been bad enough, but once piled on top of the small fact that he was obviously still coming to terms with living with his best friend's ghost, he knew he was probably bordering on psychological collapse.

He turned to Kev, troubled by more than just the mugging they had experienced. Had Kev been thinking about killing that guy back there? Clyde couldn't be sure. And he didn't know what he would have done if Kev had taken that extra step into some truly dark territory. It took Clyde a second to notice, but he saw a slight change in Kev's appearance. He seemed paler than usual, his usual vibrancy now washed out, the bluish aura several shades closer to that of dirty dish water. Clyde initially ascribed it to the light of the standing lamp in the corner of the room but knew that wasn't the cause; he had seen Kev's ghost in every conceivable light in this cramped apartment, but he had never looked this tired before. Did ghosts tire?

'Stupid question, but are you feeling all right?' Clyde asked.

Kev had settled into his usual spot on the couch. 'Now that you mention it, I'm a bit lightheaded.' He nudged his thick glasses further up the bridge of his nose; they might have been considered trendy by some, but Clyde knew how much Kev hated trends and that he had been molesighted since his early teens thanks to astigmatism. According to Kev, he no longer needed them, but since he had died wearing them, they had become an accessory.

Clyde paced around the coffee table, barely able to take his eyes off the stolen goods. He wished he could have just not given a shit about any of this stuff and left it there for whomever to find. Keeping his fingers laced together before his mouth, like he was holding an invisible microphone, he shot a brief appeal to Kev. 'What you did to those guys, that wasn't floating me a bowl of cereal across the apartment. You think you tired yourself out?'

'I don't know. It's not like I have to worry about muscle tone anymore. Mentally straining, though? I guess that could be a thing.'

Clyde nodded along inanely, already bearing down on the larger point. 'You looked like you were ready to kill them. Was that the bullshit you were talking about at the park? You're already dead, so fuck everyone and everything?'

Kev sighed and appeared a little forlorn. 'I never said "fuck everything." I'm not a nihilist yet. But I won't lie, the thought crossed my mind. And so what?' He leaned forward, elbows on knees. 'They weren't a couple of Boy Scouts. That fuck shot me. How many other people you reckon he's shot?' The sickly aftereffects of fear and grief were still present in Kev's manner, and he almost seemed to choke on his next words. 'I looked in his eyes, and you know what I saw? All I saw was the same breed of cowardly cunt that ended my life and left me a damn vapor trail. You think I'd feel bad if I took a few of those stains out of the world?' A layer of cynicism appeared to coat his brief moment of vulnerability. 'Who do I need to worry about, ghost cops? The spectral victims unit?'

'*Me!* What about me? You might be able to vanish through a wall, but I'm still the brother who was with you. Your accomplice.'

'Well, I didn't kill them, did I?'

There came a loud knock at the apartment door.

Clyde jumped and spun around, expecting guns and badges to burst in at any second. Kev was back on his feet, probably deciding if he should blend into the walls or get proactive with home security. Seconds ticked past, and neither Clyde nor Kev had done a damn thing except look indecisive and edgy. Clyde expected stentorian commands to rattle the door, demanding he open up before the caller kicked the door into cheap kindling.

Nothing.

The knock came again. This time a little more solicitous than authoritative.

'Want me to take a look?' Kev asked. He could shift into the walls and maneuver around the building, carefully peeking his head out into the hallway to glimpse the guest.

'No, hide the stuff. I'll see who it is. Might be Carlos.' The idea of Carlos the landlord stopping by for an unscheduled visit probably wouldn't be much more fun than the police, Clyde thought grimly, imagining an increase in rent or the need to bug-bomb the building or some other minor but major domestic disaster.

Kev spirited the loot and weapons into the kitchen, preparing to chuck them under the sink before throwing them in a plastic bag. Clyde watched him open the kitchen window, presumably to take the bag up to the roof. Nobody went up there apart from Kev. Clyde had found him up there a few times, wallowing in a dejected stupor, gazing at the liquor store that had ended his young, largely wasted life.

Free of the contraband, Clyde feigned calm and checked the peephole. It wasn't a uniform, and it certainly wasn't Carlos. He opened the door to a young, attractive woman, her shoulder-length platinum locks tied into a ponytail, her bright eyes alert and cataloguing him and the environment.

'Clyde Williams,' she said, not asked.

Not much point in denying it, Clyde thought. 'Can I help you?'

She proffered her dainty hand, short nails painted silver, taking Clyde's into a surprisingly powerful grip, not intending to hurt, but definitely capable of it if she had wanted to. She was wearing dark pants, an olive bomber jacket, and black boots; even without this attire, Clyde thought there was something distinctly military about her posture and vibe.

'I'm Agent Rose Hadfield. I'm here on behalf of a special government department. I'll skip the silly games because I think we both know the kind of specialties they're interested in.' All through this candid introduction she maintained a pleasant formality. 'I want you to know that you and your friend Kevin Carpenter have nothing to fear from us. We actually want to help. That's why I'm here.'

You have nothing to fear from us. To Clyde that sounded exactly like something a bunch of cloak-and-dagger government killers would say. They'd probably sent her because she had a pretty face and was therefore quite unassuming, disarming with her charms. Still, that hand grip!

'Would it be okay to continue talking inside?' Rose enquired.

Clyde continued to feel the scratchy sensation of distress skittering over him. This was becoming too much. With a little consternation he stepped aside and allowed her entry, very much wanting Kev to be listening in the wings should there be any black-clad spooks with shiny handcuffs and high-caliber toys circling the building. After she entered, he gave a quick glance into the outside hallway and found it empty. He closed the door and turned to her. 'What do you think you know?'

She humored him politely, professionally. 'You're an art school graduate, completed your studies at Parsons with a BFA in illustration several years ago, and have been working freelance for the past year and a half. Younger son of Richard and Corrine Williams, and younger brother to

Stephen. Both your father and brother joined the US Marine Corps, and your mother is a nurse at the military veterans' hospital here in Brooklyn. You work at Mythic Comics & Collectibles in Bed-Stuy, and spend an inordinate amount of your income on comic-books and art supplies.'

Clyde folded his arms, his weight favoring one leg. He didn't ask if they'd checked his internet search history.

'And Kevin Carpenter—' Rose's big almond eyes inspected the short and cramped hallway as if seeking him out, 'high school graduate, bounced around from job to job before enrolling at the undergraduate philosophy program at Eugene Lang College. Parents are Aaron and Sandy Carpenter, a software engineer and IT teacher at Millennium Brooklyn High, and his younger sister Rhianne, who is currently working through a nursing degree at Rory Meyers.'

'Cool. So?'

'And on May sixteenth of this year, Kevin was shot and killed in a liquor store robbery around the corner from here.' Rose's accent wasn't local; it was more Western, and Clyde pegged it as Californian. 'And we know he isn't dead, and he isn't quite alive. Dropping all subtlety, we know he's a ghost.'

Clyde tapped his foot a little too fast. 'Okay, I'm officially creeped out. So are we on some kind of watch list?'

Kev quietly appeared behind Rose, sifting through the wall into the hallway. He looked over her shoulder to address Clyde. 'I think she's alone. Couldn't spot any suspicious cars from the roof, and there's no suits on the street.'

Rose didn't flinch; she turned around promptly with the ease of somebody who routinely converses with dead people. She didn't even bother glancing at his gunshot wound.

Clyde tilted his head, trying to regain her attention. 'Do you carry a badge, or some official ID?'

Agent Hadfield's nose wrinkled in wry amusement. 'You ask me that after you've invited me into your apartment?'

Clyde had no useful follow-up to her logic and felt like a bit of a silly prick.

'We're not the type of department with a publicly known charter, and in all honesty it's best that it stays that way. I work for an outfit called

Hourglass. It's our primary function to collate intel on possible atypical threats, such as PLEs—that's Post-Life Entities—and assess whether they pose a risk to national interests.'

'It's nice to hear my whole existence reduced to an abbreviation,' Kev grumbled.

'No disrespect.'

Clyde had heard her say "department" but couldn't shake her militaristic presence, which he didn't like one little bit. He frowned, trying to keep his head on straight. 'Okay, you obviously know a good deal about us and have just blown up what little tatters of sanity I had left. What do you want? Do we need to dot some i's and cross some t's? Pledge an oath of secrecy under threat of imprisonment and torture?'

Rose didn't look to be in the mood to speed through the process; she pumped the brakes with her hands. 'Do you have any coffee? We can sit down and discuss this.'

Clyde was about to step around her and head towards the kitchen when the sound of water filling the kettle stopped him. Kev, without having moved an inch from his curious analysis of Agent Hadfield, had flicked the switch and set the kettle to boil.

Rose must have sensed the consternation swelling in this boxy hallway and chose a course of action that might bevel the tense edges of her hosts. She turned her head and glimpsed the shrine of artwork in Clyde's bedroom, lit weakly by the hallway's ambient light.

'May I?'

Clyde considered objecting. Maybe by being blunt he'd speed whatever this was along to its conclusion. Instead, he composed himself, said, 'Sure,' and knuckled the light switch.

Rose kept her firm posture, hands laced together behind her back as she respectfully nosed about the mess of illustrations vying for wall space. The place was a shrine to Clyde's love of comic-books: boxes upon boxes of comic-books and graphic novels were stacked against one wall; fighting for real estate with his own illustrations and character designs were posters and signed artwork from veritable saints of the industry, including a Swamp Thing splash page from the late and legendary Bernie Wrightson; and presiding over it all like cherubic witnesses were an assortment of Funko Pop bobble heads. An unnecessary amount of Funko Pop bobble heads.

'You got room to sleep in here?' Rose asked, politely snooping around his desk and laptop. 'I suppose you could always throw your bed out if you need more room.' She found one of his sketch books next to his drawing tablet and carefully skimmed it, showing care for the spine and the pages. 'You got talent,' she said brightly.

Clyde remained in the doorway, hearing the clink of a few chipped cups being set down on the kitchen counter; Kev had left them to it. 'A little. You an artist yourself?'

'Never something I showed any real aptitude for.' She leaned in to examine his drawing board, where the latest pages of his indie comic were in progress. 'You're drawing a comic-book?'

'Is that on my file too, or have you already placed cameras in my apartment?'

Rose gave him an amused appraisal, then went back to studying the drawing board pages.

Despite Clyde's love for all things superhero, his own comic was tapping into a more macabre and supernatural vein, full of undead criminals and supernaturally tainted crime bosses; he wasn't sure how he felt about it, and this frustrated him. On a good day, the gritty noir seemed to have a ring of Ed Brubaker to it, albeit with more monstrous freaks. On the bad days, the whole thing left him swimming in uncertainty and wanting to abandon his project, or at least the writing aspect of it.

'Marvel and DC love rejecting me,' Clyde said, feeling his last response was a little rude. 'I'm hoping I'll have more luck with the indie route, maybe Image. This all Greek to you?'

'A little. I'm just a little surprised,' Rose answered. 'Dad and older brother both being Marines, being a soldier is in your blood. But you took the artistic route.'

'You know my family history, I think you can understand why I chose not to follow their footsteps,' Clyde said, a bitter edge in his tone.

Rose nodded and bopped the Immortal Hulk Funko Pop on its head.

Clyde sighed quietly. 'It was Stephen who got me into comic-books. He collected them with his pocket money, birthday money, and Christmas money from when he was seven years old and only stopped on the day he packed his bags to join the Marine Corps. I still have a lot of them there,' Clyde said, pointing to the stacks of boxes. Stephen had guided

Clyde at first, ushering him like a wide-eyed VIP into the wild and colorful collection of Silver Age comics, a universe that Clyde ravenously tore through, his imagination expanding as he traveled through the successive comic-book years to the drug-fueled adventurous romps of the Bronze Age of the 1970s and '80s. 'They're difficult to part with.'

Rose stopped the Hulk from head bobbing. 'Okay, let's talk.'

Clyde stepped back from the doorway into the hall, still not comfortable with taking his eyes off this averagely tall young lady who seemed to give off distinctly above-average vibes of lethal capability. Maybe her strong grip would choke the life out of him if he turned his back on her. She did the honors of turning the bedroom light off and followed him across the hall to the living room. The thunderous rattle of the M train screeched along its elevated track outside their building.

'Take a seat.' Clyde flicked a loose hand towards the old worn-in couch. He walked into the cramped adjoining kitchen, trading places with Kev, who dispensed with any unnecessary ceremony and walked straight through the countertop—and the couch backed up against it—to flop into his usual seat. His color still looked a bit dull.

Rose removed her jacket and took the armchair. Wearing a black tank top, she revealed the cause of her tight grip. While she was only around 5'5" and couldn't have weighed more than 125 pounds, she had the impressive physique of a weightlifter, bulging legs like a prize racehorse, a trim, strong core, and upper arms and shoulders filled out with the dense natural muscle tone earned from hard work without the aid of steroids. The muscle and shadowy government vibe contrasted wildly with her sweet and innocent face. She leaned forward, elbows on knees, chunky biceps on show.

Kev looked at her arms. 'Does all that protein help with catching ghosts?'

'I was a competitive powerlifter before I joined the service.'

'Was? Kind of looks like you still are.'

A small, enigmatic smile flashed good white teeth, then vanished just as quickly. 'I guess I am.'

The kettle finished its attempts to turn the box kitchen into a low-rent sauna, and Clyde opened the fridge. He'd forgotten to buy milk. Annoyed, he shut the door. 'It'll have to be black. Sugar?' That line played back through his head, and he hoped it didn't sound like come-on dialogue from a porno.

Rose looked above Kev's head to Clyde's enquiring face. 'Two, thanks.'

Clyde brought the two coffees around into the living room and set them down before taking a seat beside Kev. He felt like they were both in a hospital waiting room expecting some huge, life-altering news. Then he realized that in a way, they were. He kept hold of his cup, letting his left fingertips dance along the hot side of his Green Lantern mug. 'Okay then… Hourglass? What do you people want?'

Rose picked up her cup and rolled it around her hands. 'That really depends on both of you. I'm here to make contact, which I've done. Now I'll explain a little about what it is that we do, after which you'll have two options: you can continue as you are, knowing that we will be keeping a record of any pertinent activity you're both involved in, and where you'll be subject to annual reviews—'

'What?!' Outrage bloomed like a diseased flower across Clyde's face. 'What type of Orwellian shit is this?'

Rose stayed cool as a fresh breeze. 'It's not as invasive as you think. It's nothing worse than what the federal government already does to its citizenry. The only extra is the routine interviews, and those will be conducted at a time and place of your own choosing.'

'But why?' Kev pushed.

'I saw what you did in the park.' She allowed that to sink in. 'That would be pertinent activity.'

Clyde felt his world slightly tilt. Despite the agent's pleasant demeanor, that statement couldn't be taken any other way than as a warning.

'I've seen this more than once.' Her eyes found Clyde's, but then bored into Kev's with a measure of sympathy. 'You're both new to this. It's strange, it's crazy, and somewhere in all that muddle you're thinking that maybe this isn't that big of a deal. You'll adapt, right? That's what people do with change. And, hell, I'd agree with you. But this is still a delicate situation that we try to mitigate in order to keep a lid on it. The global intelligence community doesn't need members of the public going haywire should somebody expose any evidence of PLEs, or anything else, for that matter. And, like you demonstrated in the park against those two scumbags, you're dangerous. You might not see it that way, but given time, people in your shoes can change.' She emphasized that last part as though it could be a useful commodity. 'The interviews are to assess how you're coping. Some people start to struggle but ride it out and achieve balance, and some become potential threats.'

Kev sat quietly for a moment, fidgeting with the left arm of his glasses, an old tic of his. 'So, there are others like me.'

Rose sipped her coffee. 'Of course.'

It was hard for Clyde to get a read on Kev as to whether he was jubilant or distressed at this revelation.

'I figured there must be. Good to get some clarity, though.'

Clyde stared at the chipped edge of his coffee table in his cruddy apartment and asked the question he knew Rose was waiting to hear. 'What's the other option?'

'You can join us.'

Textbook answer, Clyde thought. Become another cog in their machine.

'Educate yourselves about your abilities, master them, and most of all, help us.'

'Our abilities?' Clyde was stunned. 'Is it my fault that Kev is here?'

Rose's powerful shoulders rose up an inch. 'I'm only a field agent. You'll have to ask one of the academics in the department. And that's not a company line to lure you in. We do have some of the best experts in the country.'

Clyde was dissatisfied with that answer. 'So you can't explain to me—for example—how I might have pulled Kev back, or why I haven't done the same thing for my brother or my dad?' To Rose's credit, she looked appropriately apologetic, clearly knowing that both Stephen and Richard had died in the line of duty, serving their thankless country. 'Because I'm wondering if you know how it feels to lose half your family to some rich man's war and then be asked if you feel like throwing your life away in another one that only benefits more of the wealthy elite. All because I may or may not have some accidental power to pull my dead friend back from beyond the grave.'

Rose's face was the epitome of patient understanding. She didn't move an inch, made no obvious commanding gesture, but what happened next was clearly triggered by her command. A squad of three ethereal soldiers melted into the apartment, taking up positions around her; their ghostly complexions rendered their army camouflage indecipherable, but Clyde guessed it was desert combat from the lightness of the tones. They were a grisly bunch, each of the three savaged for eternity by the horrors of conflict.

'Sound off,' she said, not quite a drill instructor's sharp decree, but an order, nonetheless.

Standing sternly to Rose's left, his body and face peppered with bits of glinting shrapnel, the first man nodded. 'Sergeant Richard J. Connors.' Connors had been the eldest at point of death, with a commanding presence, steely gaze, and the type of heroic jawline that looked capable of scraping sparks from flint.

The big, husky trooper to Rose's immediate right added, 'Private Lewis Darcy.' He sounded like a Nebraska farm boy, and his boyish looks possessed a lingering innocence, a young man who had wanted to prove something to someone only to find himself out of his depth. His jaw was caked in what must be a gout of blood, looking more like blueberry slush, his intestines looped out before him like sausage links, and a sizable chunk of his chest was missing in a wound that far exceeded Kev's. The product of either heavier caliber ammunition or a lump of hot bombshell.

The third, and certainly the least in some respects, was the blasted and burnt torso hovering beside Darcy. 'Private Savannah Barros.' Barros could have been a quick and lean Hispanic back when she had legs, but now she looked like she had succumbed to a tribe of ravenous cannibals who had charred and eaten most of everything below her waist. But her tough yet humorous countenance remained completely intact.

Clyde didn't exactly jump at the chance to make new friends with these cadaverous GIs standing—and in Barros' case, floating—in his living room, but he managed to stop his jaw from landing in his lap. He noticed Kev was struck dumb too.

'This is what remains of my squad.' Rose's earlier bright and perky expression grew sober. 'I was a private, same as Barros and Darcy. Totally green. Swallowed the whole bit, wanted to help spread freedom, all that rah-rah-rah garbage. We were deployed to carry out a peacekeeping operation in a small town in Rojava, northeastern Syria. The town was not much more than a restaurant and some ramshackle brick hovels, and it had already been the focal point of some truly awful attacks. Our people were helping to train the Syrian Democratic Forces to fight ISIS sleeper cells. I'd only been there three weeks when everything went to shit. We were caught up in a skirmish with one of those cells.' She continued to roll her cup around in her palms, her attention locked onto Clyde and Kev. 'I vividly remember the bomb going off behind me before the gunfire started. I was knocked flat, hearing nothing but the ringing in my ears and my breathing; it sounded like I was underwater. I crawled out of the smoke into the street, barely hearing the building collapse behind me, but I felt it. I was watching bullets fly overhead, trying to clear some sense into myself, when I first saw them. I thought I was imagining things, that maybe I'd hit my head. One by one I spotted these guys in the smoke clouds,' she turned her head an inch towards Sergeant Connors, then back to Clyde and Kev, 'seeing our own troops and the SDF fighters run through them like they weren't there. Like they were just a part of the smoke. I convinced myself it was shellshock and got back into the fight. But once the fighting was contained, and I was dragged before a medic, I was told I was the sole survivor of my squad. Later that night, I still couldn't shake them.'

Darcy gave her shoulder a playful nudge, the motion of which set his coiled guts wobbling slightly; Clyde was worried they'd tumble loose like a giant shit snake. Barros pushed him back in a display of sibling-like irritation, drawing a smile from Rose.

'They'd flicker in and out like a garbled frequency, and I was having conversations with them back at base. Word quickly spread about the camp, and my staff sergeant sent me to a shrink. Part-way through the counselling session, my dead unit unscrambled their signal and popped back into the room clear as day. You should have seen the face on the shrink. I think he's in therapy now. In any case, I was contacted by some suit who wanted me to transfer out of the army into some private department. I think you get the gist now, and I also think you can believe me when I say I know exactly how it feels to lose family to another's war.'

Sergeant Connors clenched his jaw, grinding on some words left unsaid.

Rose drained her lukewarm coffee and placed the mug on the table. 'I don't have the answers you're both looking for, and I'm not here to draft you into another corrupt war. I'm only a messenger, and I've offered you your choices.' She pulled a plain white card out of her black cargo pants. All it contained was an image of an hourglass with a cell phone number on the back. She placed it on the table before Clyde and Kev, who were still taking in the scene before them, flashing glances at the ghost warriors standing to attention around their physical anchor, Rose Hadfield. 'That's my cell. I'll be local for a few days until you come to your decision.' She slid her powerful arms and deltoids into her bomber jacket, shaking her ivory ponytail loose from her collar. 'But know this: if you choose to enlist with us, our fight is waged in the shadows, and it has nothing to do with flags and politics or some asshole's bottom line. Think about your living situation.'

Clyde and Kev had already done a fair bit of that.

'Now take a good look at who are standing in front of you.'

They had been doing quite a bit of that too.

'There are some fights in this world that truly are about the fate and betterment of humanity. Think it over.' Sergeant Connors and Privates Barros and Darcy stepped out of this reality, leaving Rose alone with Clyde and Kev. 'And call me. Thanks for the coffee.' She let herself out while Clyde and Kev sat in awed silence, staring at the card like it was some cursed object ready to invoke their doom. Moments passed.

'This is too much.' It was Clyde who finally broke the silence. 'It's too much.'

Kev remained quiet, lifted a hand languidly, and pulled the card towards his translucent fingers like it was attached to invisible wire. He studied it as though he would find some hidden details.

Clyde stood and started pacing, picked up his cup of coffee, set it back down, circling the small room. 'Would you say something?' Kev was too withdrawn. 'Kev, for fuck's sake, just say it. Spit it out because I know you're thinking it. Let me hear it.'

Kev sighed. 'I need something, man.' He sounded apologetic. 'She's right. How long can we go on pretending that this is normal? Before I died, I didn't even believe in ghosts. What the fuck did I know? Now Agent Hadfield shows up with her dead-soldier buddies, hits us over the head with knowledge that not only are we not that big of a deal, but our options are to be closely monitored for the rest of our days, or get our feet wet in this whole other world that we didn't even know exists. I can't sit here playing video games forever. I have to at least learn about what's going on with me. With us.'

Clyde stopped his caged-hamster impression and folded his arms, watching Kev. 'I fucking knew you'd say that. I get it, though. We talked about this, right? We wanted answers, and I guess this is our chance. But I'm not becoming some fucking ghost buster.' He tried and failed to keep the insanity from cracking his face into a loony grin. 'I don't care what she said. She and whoever these Hourglass people are, they're looking for recruits. And I'm not walking that path. I'm not reducing my life to another statistic some general or politician will gloss over. Fuck that.'

'Not all soldiers are frontline meat. There are other jobs. Maybe this is the same. We could find a different role.'

'A drone is a drone.'

'I wasn't born yesterday. I'm not saying I trust her because she has some ghosts of her own, but I have no reason to doubt that their war is far beyond flag-waving. We have no idea what else is going on all around us. Who in their right mind passes up an opportunity to find out?' Kev grew steadily more animated; even his color had revitalized some by this new sense of purpose.

Clyde didn't reciprocate the enthusiasm and saw how Kev was struggling to hide his disappointment.

'I'm scared.' Clyde finally said it. 'I don't think I want answers. I don't think I want to find out I'm some freak who—' he became jittery, months of unease and enforced fragile normality crumbling all about him, '—who maybe cursed you to this non-life. I don't want to find out that I might be able to bring others back. Because the scariest part is, what if I can? What if I can, and I do, and then I can't stop myself?' The unknown was fertile ground for fear, and he wondered about calling Stephen and his dad back from their resting place, and how it might break him to see them return with their battlefield injuries in place.

'What if I'm upsetting some natural order?' Clyde ran out of steam. 'There are things I'm happy not knowing until it's time for me to know.'

'What if now is that time?'

Clyde stayed quiet.

'Look, I can go. You stay here.'

'What do you mean?' Clyde asked.

'I didn't get around to testing the limits of our separation. Hopping a train to the Bronx didn't cause any problems. For all we know, we could split to opposite sides of the globe and get by just fine. So maybe you could stay here, and I'll see what Agent Hadfield's offering.' Kev sounded keen, but also restless.

Clyde hated the idea of Kev hiding himself away until... until what? Until Clyde died too? Until the sun burned out? Until some afterlife bureaucrat sorted his filing system and placed Kev in the correct retirement home? He thought about the other night when he woke up because he couldn't sleep and found Kev collapsed like rumpled clothes on the couch, staring empty-eyed at the corner of the room, one finger slowly circling his bullet hole.

Clyde might have been Kev's spiritual lightning rod, but he wasn't his keeper. And Kev's suggestion sounded tempting. It would be the healthiest thing for both of them.

And yet Clyde knew he couldn't leave Kev to go it alone. Finally, his guilt trumped his want to remain here, ignorant and inert.

'Shit.' He dropped onto the couch. 'All I wanted was to draw comics.'

3

IT WAS NIGHT WHEN KONSTANTIN arrived at the palatial piece of Westchester real estate. The moon was a white sickle over the painstakingly landscaped clearing, lit up with tasteful recessed lighting. Konstantin wouldn't have been surprised if the private grounds consisted of at least fivescore acres.

Since waking up on the Ilyushin 76 as it touched down at Westchester County Airport, the surviving personnel had been quick to administer him with a steady, diluted concentrate of sedatives to keep him pliant. They had also taken the liberty of cleaning and stitching his chewed-up cheek, and wiping down the blood-sullied bindings of Peklo's amateurish control collar. In his drugged stupor he had watched as the man with the crushed throat was carried down the plane's ramp on a stretcher and loaded into a waiting private medical helicopter, while Konstantin himself had been guided out to a second chopper. Upon arrival at the helipad hidden in the wooded clearing only a short drive from this house, he had been passed from one set of armed babysitters to another. Very professional, very polite.

Konstantin had his suspicions that he had not been sprung from the dark, overlooked depths of the Russian federal penal system just to be courted about these splendid grounds by some charitable benefactor. But his assumptions were promptly tested as his driver and transport guards left him in the hands of some impeccably suited hosts, who quietly greeted him at the mansion's white portico; these guards lacked the heavy armor and weaponry of his previous minders. Interesting.

Still, he didn't trust any of this.

As he was led into the foyer, he viewed the opulence of the sprawling mansion's grand hallway with distaste, his eyes like glazed winter. Expensive vases, ornamental sconces, numerous owl statues, and carved busts and oil paintings of important men. His gaze followed a trail of painted vines and slender tree limbs curving and winding along the walls until they joined together into an exquisite canopy of green and gold that dominated the vaulted ceiling. It came as little surprise to find more even owls painted within the boughs, their wide, distrustful eyes perpetually hungry.

It had been many years since he had been in the presence of such magnificent architecture and prodigal wealth, having spent the last three decades devoting himself to a grand cause within a secret temple of ancient hewn stone and bronze, and then holed away in prison, kneeling on frostbitten rock while his spirit sought to tangle with the forces of death lurking beyond the veil of this blind world. But during his KGB days he had spent a few pleasurable evenings in similar buildings of grand wealth, associating with prime ministers and presidents who rattled sabers with his one-time motherland.

Personally, he found the whole aesthetic stifling. The country manor reeked of old money with its dual wings and wide portico, second-floor verandas, grand staircase, bedrooms and bathrooms that surely numbered into double figures, and gleaming marble flooring.

His escorts led him up the grand staircase and down a long hallway to the double doors of a study. Then quietly, trustingly, the men left his side and retreated back down the hall, their polished shoes clicking past more oil paintings of owls and important men; important to somebody, perhaps, but certainly not to Konstantin.

He regarded his sigil-laden gauntlets, their bronze weight comfortable but also likely to scratch and dent the hand-carved wooden doors should he attempt to knock. With a pleasing click, the right-hand door swung open. A man stood before Konstantin, tall and skeletal in build and countenance, with thinning, lifeless hair and a dead man's sightless white eyes. Upon his wasting features was a smile of civility that bored Konstantin. He had flown halfway around the world, gouged a sizable blood gambit into the inside of his left cheek, instigated a flawed suicide attempt within a Russian transport plane, and then murdered the liaison—among several others—sent to pluck him from obscurity. He wanted answers. Not sycophants. The doorman, loosely termed, was clearly inhuman and made no pretense to hide his abnormalities. The hand dropping away from the doorknob consisted of five long and knuckle-jointed keys, formed of malleable bone and sheathed in a hard, leathery skin. Out of curiosity, Konstantin checked the greeter's right hand and found it similar, though all ten finger keys were of different cuts.

The man was dressed in a long tweed coat, brown and in need of patching up in parts, with the flaps of the coat hanging open over the emaciated torso like stiff coffin doors. Konstantin caught a glimpse of a white dress shirt under the coat. It must have been a real chore to dress himself with such peculiar fingers, he thought.

Silently, with nothing more than a gracious nod, the odd locksmith stepped aside, providing an unobstructed view of the real clout in the bright and airy study. Standing by the open French doors was a fine-suited man, his jacket folded over the back of a studious wingback throne, tie loosened ever so slightly, watching the wood pigeons flock around the balcony. He was feeding them bread crusts from a china plate.

Konstantin entered the large study, paying scant attention to the bookshelves and old-looking knickknacks dotted about the place. He assumed they were all of a very impressive vintage and carried a tale or two, normally involving great murder and/or theft, the type that came so naturally to people such as these, but he cared very little about this ghoulish collection.

His prison boots clomped to a dead stop on the intricately woven rug before a large, dark, wooden battleship of a desk, and he hoped some residual stubborn dirt and scum from Peklo was smearing into the threads.

'Why am I here?' he grumbled, caring not in the slightest about any phony pleasant formalities. He sensed the key maker hovering somewhere behind him, but Konstantin's coterie of spirits was unable to grant him any immediate protection or reconnaissance, still silenced and restrained by lingering chemicals and the washed bas-relief symbols of his prison collar.

The dapper host tossed a few more crumbs from a fine china plate to the jostling pigeons, then turned from the expansive breadth of the manor grounds. 'Straight down to business.' His smile was utterly devoid of warmth and humor, an empty reflex practiced well. 'I admire that.' He was English, upper-crust born and bred; Konstantin knew his silver-spoon breed well. He was young too, or at least he was younger than Konstantin, somewhere in his mid-thirties. A spoilt brat.

'I am led to believe that you are a man of useful talents, Mr. Kozlov. But your skills are a close second to what I am most interested in.' He placed the empty plate on top of an antique cabinet near the doors. 'Your knowledge, specifically in regard to your post-military occupation.'

'I spent much of former life as man known for his intelligence. Someone who sat at a desk in cramped offices, specializing in collating knowledge, arriving at answers, filing reports, and keeping a keen eye on various developments; this I'm sure you know. You know enough about me to dig me out of Peklo. But I confess I've been out of loop for quite some time and have no idea who you are.' Konstantin's throat was dry, and the harsh, flaky dryness of his own blood had left it tasting like a copper mine. 'So... who are you?'

The Englishman strode confidently around the desk until he was facing Konstantin, parked a haunch on the desk, and folded his arms neatly. 'How humbling.' The first traces of genuine humor lifted his handsome dimples. 'It's good to be humbled from time to time, to be reminded of our place.' Konstantin instinctively heard this as a threat and felt utterly unmoved. 'My name is Edward Talbot. This here is my colleague,' he half-extended a hand towards the key maker lurking somewhere at Konstantin's back, 'Acton Mortis.' The introductory hand quickly burrowed back into the fold of his arms. 'We stand before you as representatives of the Cairnwood Society.'

Konstantin's tongue probed at his stitches, his outer cheek rising like a hairy hillock.

'Still not ringing any bells, I see. I suppose your own interests were very linear at the time.' Talbot tapped a heel against the desk. 'Cairnwood's interests are varied, and recently we have been focusing more intently on matters of the afterlife—or lives, I suppose is more apt. Erebus, the last stop for us all. You may not have heard of us, and in truth, I suppose there's no reason you should have unless you were actively looking for trouble. But we are far from an infantile group, and yet despite our distinction in particular arcane fields, safely cracking the barriers that stand between this paltry mortal plane and Erebus' myriad of wonders is much more problematic than the penny-ante occultist posers of yore used to pretend. However, every so often, certain unique individuals, or certain gnostic practices, manage to provide a toehold in this big insurmountable wall. And sometimes the stars align. In you, and Mr. Mortis here, the stars have very much aligned in our favor.'

Konstantin felt like throttling this pompous mudak until he croaked, wet and cartilaginous. Without question he was a member of the British Conservative Party. A filthy, corrupt, penny-pinching worm of a Conservative; assuredly with links to the House of Lords if one were able to look deep enough. Konstantin could choke the life out of the lot of them and feel nothing but pleasure and a great swell of pride.

'Together, with your unique extracurricular education and Acton's own abilities, we have the potential to not only bridge a path into these new frontiers but set up a fascinating importation business. A vast, limitless, and untapped resource. The potential scientific breakthroughs alone would alter the course of all life on this earth, and death too, if you think about it. The periodic table could be inundated with a raft of never-seen-before elements. If this is correct, there could be a slew of new medicinal properties. And that's only the science and pharmaceutical sectors. Think of the other opportunities. What about construction? Communication? Military? The prison industry! New commerce across the board. And what about all those things science can't explain? The applications of forces and beings that would have the religious idiots weeping over their false scriptures?'

Konstantin's lip almost curled in revulsion. 'How depressingly predictable.' He shook his head at the inevitability of all this. Talbot waited for clarification. 'You're all the same, your whole rotten class. There's never enough for you, is there? When it gets to the point where you have more wealth than you could possibly spend in a dozen lifetimes, you think of ways to waste it and hoard it, instead of thinking of ways you could put it to good use. And this is the best your inbred cabal can come up with?' Those finger keys of Mortis' hands flexed in Konstantin's thoughts. 'I assume you've found a way to unlock the doors to places seldom explored, and your primary concern is to immediately set about raping and pillaging them for personal gain.'

Talbot didn't seem offended. 'It's nothing personal, Konstantin. Just opportunity. When Edmund Cartwright created the loom for cotton mills, he upset the Luddites, whose livelihoods were threatened. But there's always a vocal minority decrying progress. That's business. I had assumed your time away—' his hand frittered about, '—praying in drum circles with the monks would have enlightened you, raised you above the lowly squabbles of class politics. Don't tell me a man like you still clings to his outmoded communist roots? You may have spent the last several decades existing like a yeast infection in Peklo, but surely you've heard the Soviet Union dissolved long ago?'

'Da, I'm beyond such political matters,' Konstantin replied. 'While communism has proven itself time and again to be an egalitarian pipe dream at best, or a ravenous dictatorship at worst, your own system of gross, unchecked capitalism is just as diseased. My interests and ambitions for Erebus are of far more importance than bleeding it dry of material.'

'Would you be more interested in our goals if I told you we are heading for the Eidolon Trench?'

Konstantin paused, his tongue playing along his stitches. 'What do you know of such a place?'

'Cairnwood has a wide membership of bibliophiles and curators, but we still have our blind spots. The known writings of the greatest authorities on Erebus' dead kingdoms and the nine ruling Houses of the Order of Terminus are still sparse. Lost over the millennia to wars and disaster, sabotage and misinformation. When your enemies burned you out of that mountain temple, they managed to recover some cultural trinkets, but what was of most significance were the few pieces of parchment that survived the blaze.'

'How did you get hold of these scraps?' Kozlov asked, jaw clenching.

'I'll tell you later. These scraps of parchment were incomplete, but the crux of what was written down was the pilgrimage your sect took every so many years to try and reach the Eidolon Trench in search of something special—the fire ate the last part; isn't that typical?' Konstantin felt Talbot trying to pry the information from him with a heavy pause. 'But, you know, for the moment I have little interest in what you monks were looking for. We can circle back to that later if necessary. It's the Trench itself I'm interested in, and I don't need some half-crisped scroll to tell me what that is. It's a soul repository, the harvest for the first House of the Order of Terminus. And you can lead us there. Be our local guide. You'll be in good company, and it will be of great benefit to you. Lots of rubles.'

Konstantin felt a twinge of panic. What else had they learned from the scrolls? 'What are your intentions with the Trench?'

'Details. We'll get around to that.'

'Does the name Vor Dushi mean anything to you?' The nightmare creature from that pitiless place ambushed Konstantin's memory.

Talbot uncrossed his arms, his hands lightly gripping the edge of the desk, and took a soft breath. 'Vor Dushi. Soul Thief in your native tongue. A servitor whose eternal trade props up the fat cats of the Order of Terminus, ensuring their nine dead kingdoms stay plentiful enough for them to feed, barter, and gamble until the end of time.'

'Spravedlivyy.' *Fair.*

Talbot nodded. 'How much of that is conjecture? How much is stone cold fact? Right now, all I'm interested in is the Trench's goodies. And look, my associates and I are not some debutantes looking to get our jollies because we've grown bored of fox hunting.' Talbot's gaze seemed to be looking for easy prey in Konstantin's eyes but found none.

'Crossing that beast is not something to be done lightly. Yet you're prepared to do it for profit?' Konstantin shook his head. 'Moronic.'

Mortis paced into view, teetering towards the balcony, where a hooting owl had just staked a claim on the balustrade to confidently devour a still twitching mouse. Konstantin kept his attention on Talbot and continued to repress the memories of his encounter with the demon. The blinding dust, the screams, the fire, the blood-chilling physicality of the creature itself. He cared little for financial gain. But fate couldn't be denied, and Konstantin knew it was his to return to the Trench, to face Vor Dushi, and to find the greatest power in this universe and beyond. Perhaps this braggart and his manpower of fools could help with his own agenda with the Soul Thief. His own internal co-conspirators, once more held captive inside his altered husk of a body, chattered back and forth, voices like a wind through the trees. He agreed with their counsel.

Talbot sighed and folded his arms again. 'You're a rogue ex-Russian intel officer with a few handy parlor tricks and a documented suicide risk. You're useful, but this generous offer I'm putting to you is one of basic convenience. If we have to do this the hard way and send in armed caravans to chart every square inch of Erebus until we find the Trench, then we will. But I don't believe you want that. You have already proven to be a pain in the arse with your stunt on the flight over here, killing poor Mr. Collins, who was a diligent sort. So, if you're so keen to renew your pilgrimage to the dead lands, why bother killing yourself when I can simply have Mortis open the door?'

A gentle wind blew through the balcony doors, the fresh fragrance of flowers and night air caressing Konstantin, a passing comfort. 'Of course, if you wish to continue acting the prick, I have no qualms with putting you right back on a plane to that dank mountainous shithole we pulled you from, where you can continue to try and off yourself until the warden loses interest in keeping you alive.'

A single sharp screech came from the balcony. Mortis had twisted the owl's head around one time too many. Strolling in, he tossed the owl to Talbot, who caught it like a football.

Konstantin watched this with grim interest and kept his eyes on Mortis, who took up a position to his right, standing beside a cabinet full of numinous curios. 'Your hands. You can open doors to Erebus?' He couldn't quite hide his fascination. 'All nine kingdoms?'

Mortis finally spoke, his accent proving he was from this side of the Atlantic, though probably old colonial money if the Cairnwood Society were as elitist as they appeared. 'I can. Think of me as a living skeleton key.' He waggled his long fingers. 'But with the exception of our intended destination, we do have a healthy respect for the other eight kingdoms, and as such, are a bit reluctant to venture across their borders.' Mortis twitched, his eyes briefly falling to the floor before coming back to meet Konstantin. 'But this first kingdom, it's kind of like the red-headed stepchild of the Order of Terminus, and as such, we're going to treat it like one.'

Konstantin didn't feel like correcting them on their error. They'd learn soon enough. 'How do your talents work?'

Mortis flexed his key-fingers, then undid a few buttons of his shirt, exposing a large, dull-steel mortise lock housed deep in his fish-belly-white chest, a mound of putrid grayish tissue veined and pulsing around the base of the insertion. The eye of the lock awoke, a coruscating aura of black light and thrumming violet lightning. 'It was the price of my membership.' Then it went cold, and with surprising dexterity the flat and chiseled fingertips buttoned the shirt back up.

Talbot was stroking the ear tufts of the great horned owl like it was a stuffed teddy bear. He regarded it almost affectionately. 'My acting boss likes to keep these. He has sanctuaries in a number of our clubhouses. Hates to have mice running about the place. Pests that they are. You can imagine how he might feel knowing what I've just done to this one,' he said, glancing at the dead owl in his hands. 'Still, what he doesn't know... So, do we have a deal?'

Konstantin made him wait a few seconds longer. 'Remove my restraint collar, and I'll hear what you have to say.'

Talbot snickered and raised one manicured hand. 'All right.' The hand quickly changed, pale pianist fingers turning mottled and damp, more suited to a misty swamp of slithering and needled teeth than an extravagant study. Talbot dug his fingers into the feathers of the dead owl. The feathers lost their luster, and the body of the bird diminished under his touch like a slowly deflating balloon. Soon it was nothing but desiccated bone and dusty feathers. Talbot shuddered as if with a mild chill of ecstasy, and he extended his misshapen hand towards Konstantin. 'Shall we shake on it?'

4

Early morning. Too early. Clyde was sitting in the back of a dark SUV, the type he'd seen in a million TV shows and movies. He couldn't decide if he felt like a criminal or a celebrity. Kev was in the back with him, done up in the same unseasonal anonymity he had worn last night.

Clyde could practically feel the excitement radiating from Kev like vibrations from a struck tuning fork. The joy of potential. Of change.

Clyde only felt nervous.

They arrived at New Jersey's Teterboro Airport, a small and private strip, but very busy, primarily servicing the high rollers of the financial industry and other flyers who could afford to shun the commercial airlines.

Agent Rose Hadfield, silver hair tied back, sunglasses on, cruised the SUV to a stop on the tarmac only a short walk from a waiting private jet. Clyde's heart was beginning to race as he listened to the powerful engines and turbines. He wasn't a huge fan of flying. Add that to the madness from last night and, inevitably, that which was still to come, and he could quite easily see himself throwing the type of embarrassing panic attack that would haunt him for the rest of his days.

'Come on, guys,' Hadfield said, springing from the vehicle. The big, nameless agent riding shotgun, who smelled like a sun-baked hangover, started to wake like a bear from a boozy hibernation. He was dressed in a casual Friday manner: sleeveless denim jacket over a Rush band T-shirt, standard-issue spook shades, a boxer's nose, a mane of dark hair, and a handlebar mustache. Rose led the way to the jet's stairway.

Clyde grabbed his backpack and willed himself to hold it together. He didn't trust Rose, the big guy, Hourglass, any of it—shit, he didn't know any of it even existed until last night!—but options were limited. And he and Kev needed a plan for their future, no matter how unorthodox it might be. He watched Kev practically speed-walk with enthusiasm towards the jet, the ear flaps on his trapper hat flapping in the morning wind. Kev needed this.

'Dude, get a wiggle on,' Kev called over his shoulder. Clyde gripped his backpack tight, loaded with only the bare necessities as instructed by Hadfield, and caught up to Kev, who had paused near the jet's fold-out stairs. Lifting his aviators up, sincerity welling up in his eyes, he said, 'Thank you for this. I know this isn't your first choice.'

'Hey, don't mention it.' Clyde could tell his smile was more of a wince, so he squinted into the early morning sun to try and hide his unease. 'We'll hear what they have to say, maybe get a few of our questions answered.' And yet he couldn't help but add, 'But I meant what I said last night. If they try to pull any of their subliminal propaganda shit, then I'm out. And they can keep all their mysteries of the universe.'

Kev nodded and dropped his shades over his spectacles before bounding up the steps. Clyde had the distinct impression that Kev might be willing to sign along the dotted line at the first available opportunity.

. . .

CLYDE HAD DOWNED two complimentary too-small bottles of vodka and a packet of dry roasted nuts before take-off. Now that they were peacefully cruising at altitude, he felt some semblance of calm. He'd never been to New Mexico. Had no real interest in ever visiting the place before now. Living in New York, he was already smack-bang in the sleepless nerve center of comic-book opportunity, not that geography meant much these days. Kev had slipped out of his disguise, occupying the adjoining aisle seat to Clyde's left, making use of the vast leg room, which he clearly didn't need. Rose sat opposite Clyde, who was wondering whether she was checking off mental boxes, assessing which of them was the talent in this duo. The most valuable for the agency's needs. Was Kev the talent, or was it Clyde? Were they an inseparable package deal? She had removed her bomber jacket pre-flight, exposing those popping muscles again. It still jarred Clyde to see such a young, petite woman own the type of arms that would utterly humiliate him and many other guys on the beach and at the same time possess a face so attractively feminine that he almost felt an innate need to be protective of her. He expunged such nonsense from his foolish head. She was a trained soldier with combat experience who probably knew a few dozen ways to kill him before he could even leave his seat.

'So, what is this place we're going to?' Clyde asked.

'The last place you'll ever see.'

Clyde watched her hazel eyes harden like peach pips. He anxiously looked to Kev, then back to her.

After a tense few seconds, a cruel smile curved the corners of her mouth. 'I'm only fucking with you. God, you're so nervous. You need another vodka?' Clyde tried to play along, being a good sport but not enjoying the role of soft target. 'Indigo Mesa. Hourglass HQ. It's nice, beautiful scenery, secluded.'

Clyde didn't like that "secluded" feature and, despite Rose's harsh attempt at humor, wondered if they were several hours from being permanent guests at this facility. Twenty-three-hour lockdown with an hour for exercise. He'd already talked to Kev about such a possibility last night on the roof of their apartment, but Kev and his damn logic had argued the point that these people, who clearly had more going on than just your standard federal resources, had already had ample opportunity to act against them, but hadn't. Plus, they had tracked them down once and could do it again if necessary, so why fight this right now?

'Unclench your sphincter, Clyde. If we had wanted, we could have put a bag over your head and trapped Kev inside an endoastralis gem. Maybe sniped you or blown your apartment up and made it look like a gas leak.'

'I see you've thought about this. You still fucking with me?' Clyde asked.

'Now you're catching on. Hey, I've been where you are. The nervous new guy, feeling out of place. I was that way when I signed up for boot camp. Being around a lot of testosterone-charged dudes. Being sent to the desert.'

'But you signed up for that.'

'That's true, but I didn't sign up to carry around my dead squad. Life just has a way of surprising you.'

Clyde let the vodka carry him over the hump. 'Last night my only plans for today were to go for a coffee and finish a couple of pages. Start work on one of my commissions.' He realized as he said this that he might have to ask the trading card company for a possible extension if he wasn't back within a day or two. 'Now I'm here, flying to a state I've never been to, to learn the answers to questions I'm still a little uneasy asking.'

'You'll adapt. Trust me.'

'Endoastralis? Like... inner stars?' The inflection in Kev's voice heightened the uncertainty of his translation.

'Sounds sexier than it is. It's a special type of jewel, but really, it's just one of a wide variety of objects in which to can a PLE.'

Kev glanced about the long, spacious cabin, devoid of anybody other than the three of them and Rose's stoic, dozing partner. 'Is that where the rest of your unit is right now? In some "can"? Connors and Barros, and the farm boy—what was his name... Darcy?'

'No, never,' Rose assuaged. 'They were killed in war, but I'll die before I see them become prisoners of some tarot reader's knickknack. They're my guys.'

Kev settled back in his seat, hands resting over his stomach. 'So where are they now?'

'I'm able to tune them in and out of this realm. But I only do it after discussing it with them. It's not like I clap my hands and make them vanish if they start to bug me.' She tapped her armrest, slowly lolling her head to one side, then the other. 'When they're not here, they're in the command center.' She smirked. 'That's what we call our little clubhouse. It's a private place, not really here, not really there, but somewhere.'

'But where?' Kev had his amateur journalist's hat on. 'The same place I was before I came back?'

'Negative, Curly.' Kev and Clyde spun around to see Sergeant Connors coming down the aisle behind them, the shrapnel protruding from his face giving him the appearance of a damaged cyborg.

Clyde then noticed Privates Darcy and Barros materializing into the visible spectrum. The pair perched on the wing of the jet and appeared to be deep in conversation, Barros' legless torso teetering on the edge of the wing, and Darcy's looping guts flopping half in and half out of his abdomen. Clyde shunted his gaze from the window.

'We have our own safe space.' Connors stopped beside Rose's seat and leaned an arm across the top. 'The place you're referring to, the true dead place, it has a heap of names. Officially, it's Erebus. At least, that's what our big-brained people in the intelligence community call it in their correspondence. Sounds classy.'

'We just call it the Null,' Rose added. 'Seems less drama school.'

'Sure does, Private,' Sergeant Connors growled. 'But a turd is still a turd in any language. We'd be out of a job without it, though, and our lives would be a lot less interesting. Anyway, the Null is a discussion for later.'

Less interesting. Clyde was totally cool with that.

'Mediums, necromancers, whatever you want to call us, our abilities can vary wildly,' Rose explained. 'These guys,' she flicked her head up towards Connors, 'don't have telekinetic applications like you do, Kev. That means they can't whip up breakfast from across the room or strip and tie up muggers with their own baggy pants, but they sure upped my game in flexing. I was strong when I thought I was normal. I was a competitive powerlifter before the service, as I mentioned. At my last meet, before I enlisted, my deadlift was 185 kilograms. A personal best. My bench was 81.6 kilograms, and my squat was 143.5 kilograms.'

Connors grinned admirably. 'Don't let the face fool you. This little powerhouse could break Darcy over her knee.'

'Now I look at those PBs and try not to laugh.' Rose seemed to share an in-joke with Connors. Clyde tried to decipher the code of pee-bees and guessed it meant personal best. 'I've had some major gains since then.'

Connors let the good humor bleed slowly from his metallic face. 'Major Gains. That was our company's nickname for this little Amazonian.'

'The general consensus of Mesa's spook think-tank is that some types of necros share a deep empathic bond with their bound PLEs. My official assessment determined that that's my jam. When people die, they release more than a soul and a buffet for the worms. They release a burst of emotional psychic energy.' She gestured towards Barros and Darcy out on the wing. 'I channel theirs and the sarge's: their anger, their pain, and their grief. Crystallizing it. Harnessing it physically.'

'And my ex-wife used to say I was too emotionless. Guess I showed her.' Connors released a chuckle straight from the gallows.

'Because of our link I'm able to draw these handsome sons of guns into me like passengers. Hence the command center.'

Clyde didn't realize he was shaking his head until Connors flicked his wrist up and gave him a lazy finger point. 'Trust me, son, this is about as normal as it's going to get. Shake it loose. How about another drink?'

Clyde no longer wanted any more booze; fuzzing up his faculties further could only make this more problematic. 'I've had enough, it's not even nine A.M. And flying west, it's like being trapped in breakfast time.' Kev gave him a nod of solidarity, which was all he needed. No matter what, they were in this together.

'You'll feel better when we get there,' Rose said.

After a few moments Kev gestured towards the guy who'd been riding with them since their Brooklyn apartment. The one who looked like a scuzzy rock band roadie from the 1980s. 'So, who's the stiff?'

Rose and Connors turned to look at the snoozing lunk, then looked to Clyde. 'That's Ace,' Rose said. 'He's the guy who'll be teaching you how to hit people.'

5

KONSTANTIN ROSE EARLY TO THE bright sounds of bird song, the pale sky still building up its strength outside the windows.

The guest bedroom was larger than it needed to be, preposterously so, adding a crass quality to its smug stateliness. The bed didn't help matters. It was too soft, like one big king-size marshmallow, for he had always been content with the bare necessities, bedding down on cots in the barracks, or cheap hotel beds during his time with the KGB intelligence office, camping in cold, unforgiving terrain during his own quests for enlightenment, finding the hard, sanded benches in his monastery quarters a blessing on his lumbar, and the steel cot in that self-proclaimed hellhole Peklo equally so. This bed, though? Such trappings made one soft. And it wasn't just the bed that irked him. The ceiling was too high, the square footage too excessive, and the décor and hanging paintings of proud owls and lush landscapes too self-important.

Konstantin escaped his restless half-sleep and abandoned the bed with a sense almost of embarrassment. The inside of his mouth ached fiercely, but that was okay. Discomfort was good for the soul. Tiredness dogged him also, but that, too, was okay; sleep-ins had been jettisoned from his body clock early in life, ever since his KGB recruitment upon graduating university. The numbered prisoner overalls from his stay at Peklo had been neatly folded and placed on the generations-old divan squatting beneath the spacious sill of the picture window, the thin, scrappy garbs looking conspicuous next to the bronze breastplate and gauntlets of his necronaut suit. How long had he been out of his armor? A thin slice of panic slashed through him, and he went very still, trying to sense if it was slowly stirring to activity deep inside of him. He couldn't feel anything. He needed to delve deeper, to consult with his wards.

In nothing but his tatty cotton underpants, he crossed the room to the Turkish rug in the center. The dawn light's rosy glow exposed the honeycomb prisms in his sinewy torso that made him a living apiary of souls. His once supple knees cracked with stiffness as he sat cross-legged. His chest rose and fell with a steady rhythm, his eyes closed and his mind dead to this physical world. It took a moment, but the honeycomb cells marking his torso began to sparkle with a lazy luminosity, the houses of his temple coming alive with the inquisitiveness of his brothers and sisters, their spirits freshly roused by his wakefulness. The prisms in his forearms and palms almost yawned with their coruscating blush of stored souls. The voices of the soul hive were internalized, bypassing any outsider's ear and tuned directly to his own vibrant soul.

One by one the clerics spoke up. These were the final vestiges of his family, his sect: the Rising Path.

Konstantin took his duty as their caretaker with great solemnity. It was his curse. Each and every one of them would have gone into death with open arms, for that was the way of their ideology. To confront the next life head-on, in order to change it from within. Change it for the better. But he'd stolen that opportunity from some of them, interceding in their great departure through chaotic chance. And while this was not their desired fate, they bore no hostility towards Konstantin, for he was their brother and would face any trial by god or man to protect their souls from the malevolent infection spoiling a dark corner of his own soul. The spoil of Vor Dushi.

After several minutes of quiet council, his concerns had been laid to rest. Opening his heavy eyes, he slowly unfurled the fingers of his right hand and gazed at the dark and blighted hexagon in the palm, rooted centrally amongst the community of muted lights like a dead battery. It seemed the maggot still slumbered in the pit of his soul. He could forgo the armor for a short while longer. Konstantin restated his oath to his brethren and felt each of the clergy retreat to their respective chambers within his temple of flesh.

Getting up, he approached the large picture window above his necronaut apparel. His hand passed smoothly, almost luxuriously, through the morning light and caressed the finely stitched drapes. Through the spotless panes he watched a few of the suited security entourage complete their perimeter checks while the hired gardeners started to fuss over the already prim and perfect grounds, some setting off to tidy the large owl sanctuary rising out of a copse of mighty oaks that stood like some fairy tale kingdom. His right hand fingered the hollow of his throat, the skin still raw and tender since the release of the prison's iron band. It had been a peasant's protection, but he couldn't deny it had humbled him. Perhaps more time would have favored his own escape attempts from Peklo, either through means of dismantling the iron collar or performing a less futile suicide attempt. The 23-year internment at Peklo had been an inconvenience to his cardinal objective, and being moved from one prison to another—which this place surely was, no matter how gilded its edges—was only prolonging the interruption of the Rising Path's long-sought ambition. As of this moment he couldn't decide if this decadent trap was worth another escape attempt. He and his party were now free to attack and to spy unimpeded, to do what was necessary to continue their stalled holy objective. But the thought of Talbot and Mortis, and their inhumanity, made him consider the unknown security measures that were most certainly installed within this building. It didn't matter how much disdain Konstantin harbored for these people; he couldn't underestimate them and their resources. So why bother becoming a fugitive to these new enemies? He was alone in here for the moment; he could take the shortcut and kill himself right here and now. It was an appealing thought. Appealing but unnecessary. If Talbot's plan was as foolish as he had described, then this would be a free meal, or a banquet. He was getting his wish. He'd be returning to Erebus soon enough, and he'd be leading these idiots with him. Good riddance.

Breaking away from his observation at the window, Konstantin left the small men to their small roles and entered the en suite bathroom.

. . .

THE RAZOR HAD already scraped his long, unkempt hair to its roots, revealing a gray-bristled skull. Now he set about doing the same to his tufts of beard. Without the temple's sacramental oils to keep it nourished, the hairs had grown dry and coarse in the recent tumultuous period, becoming a wild gray brush, tough as wire. Konstantin stared hard at his reflection in the clouded mirror, the hot, scouring mists from the shower drifting from the claw-footed tub and wrapping the sandstone-tiled bathroom in a haze. It felt better having cut his long hair down to the scalp. A practice that he and his brethren had maintained as ritual.

The original inner circle of the Rising Path had been a small band of shamans from Khakassia, southern Siberia. A surprisingly sunny, warmer clime of the nation, and one known amongst certain communities for its esoteric channels of energy. Traditionally, men from this region would grow and braid their hair in a kichege to symbolize their heavenly bond with the spirits and the spiritual world of the Tengri, the predominant deity of Central Asia who, according to lore, created the universe and everything it held. This great being of sun and blue sky cast his rays of tolerance and devotion far across time and space, back when the cultures of the Turkish and the Mongol Empires labored vigorously with bronze. The founding shamans of the Rising Path, however, had found that Tengriism, for all its virtues of finding peace and harmony with the mountain and the sea, the trees and the grass, was just another man-made deception, and so it was on that day that they severed their kichege to symbolically sever their association with the false idol, Tengri.

He rinsed the blade in the sink and angled his chin upwards, smoothly slicing away another patch of beard, his hand practiced and skillful with the straight razor. The veils of warm moisture seemed to alter his perception, a sensory trick of memory, the scents of expensive soap altering and becoming sweet and pungent incense. The tiled bathroom changed too, becoming the hewn ancient stone-and-wood-paneled walls of a once grand hall, the prayer hall of the Khram Bessmertnoy Nadezhdy.

The Temple of the Undying Hope.

He could almost hear the chants of his brothers and sisters, their khai throat singing drawing the ear in with rhythm and melody.

The razor rinsed and cut.

The memories lulled him back further into a spiral, making him a tourist of his own history, back to his days as a foreign intelligence officer for the KGB. The threaded recollections pulled him to a special, formative place in time, in his career and his life. Back to Serbia, and a small, smoky motel room in Belgrade where his commanding officer, a nasty piece of work called Major Morozov, was aggressively berating him. Konstantin had never liked Morozov. He found the man's stance on President Gorbachev's nuclear disarmament agenda to be problematic. Morozov believed a nuclear arsenal would always be a stark necessity in this world, particularly with the US acting as tireless instigator in foreign affairs. Konstantin understood Morozov's opinion up to a point, but he still despised working for a man whose personal ideology undermined that of their General Secretary and added fuel to the pyre of shaky international affairs. But it wasn't their disagreements over international relations that had caused this particular episodic friction; no, it had been Konstantin's lapse in discipline.

Up until this first professional error in judgement, his KGB responsibilities had always focused on aspects of the mundane: liaising with East German Stasi operatives, assisting them in keeping a close eye on their visiting countrymen; maintaining strong relations with Stasi officials and key East German Communist Party members; and on more than one occasion, going undercover to West Germany and England in attempts to subvert political opponents. It was challenging and deeply stressful work, work that then became so much useless nonsense after he had been selected in good faith by Major Morozov for a revelatory new post, a role within an unheard-of sub-department of the KGB: the office of Matryoshka. This new role switched him out from the traditional dealings of the political theater for those involving the sorts of powers not officially recognized by any earthly governments. The old cloak-and-dagger games Konstantin had become so weary of had now become secondary. His eyes had been partially opened, and he had wanted to see more. Craved it. Knowledge that transcended banal human conflict. His new operations had him shifting focus from defecting citizens and government operatives to spying on extraordinary individuals and accumulating intelligence on much older and mysterious forces not of this world.

It was fulfilling work. And before too long Morozov had demanded to know why Lieutenant Konstantin had tried to hide intel from him concerning an East German occultist turned information broker. Konstantin had known at the time that his actions were risky, but the temptation had been too great. He had gotten greedy. The unprecedented nature of his new duties for Matryoshka had quickly changed him, arousing a ravenous spirituality within him that he had neglected long ago with all the rest of his silly boyhood superstitions.

The professional mistake had transpired after he'd infiltrated a diplomat's office at the local British Embassy. He had been assigned to install a listening device in the office of Avalon, the secretive British branch that dealt in paranormal acquisitions, when his perusal found a small sheaf of notes about the East German informant, Jurgen Kross. Konstantin had come across the name a couple of times before in previous investigations. Kross was an itinerant and understandably difficult to track down when he wanted to be, but for the most part he had been drifting around Belgrade. Most pertinently, according to a few sources he was reportedly a failed acolyte of an interesting but unsubstantiated group, the Rising Path. The local underground lore whispered of this sect's ability to pass from the mortal realm to the one beyond, shepherds driven to create a new paradise for all the earthly flocks. A couple of years ago, Konstantin would have chuckled and ruled them out as a crazed suicide cult, but he'd seen too many inexplicable things since then, occurrences that defied known scientific principles. And if the mysterious cult was so conjectural, why was Kross attracting interest from Avalon as well as the KGB's more exotic corners, and quite possibly other national departments affiliated with celestial truths and infernal powers?

Standing over that mahogany desk, riffling through the British diplomat's unkempt stack of local phenomena, Konstantin had fought with his decision, heart pounding, attention glued to the office's closed door. He was tired of only seeing glimpses of a captivating bigger picture, of handing over invaluable information to Morozov and a jangling chain of bureaucrats. He wanted to learn the secrets of the Rising Path for himself: for a greater good, he told himself, and not for more men in different-colored uniforms to squabble and murder each other over. The last thing he needed was the self-serving major to trounce all over this promising lead just to climb the company ladder. Kross was local. Right here in Belgrade, for the moment at least. And so, with the listening devices carefully set within the Avalon office and the Kross file folded away in his coat, Konstantin had calmly and quietly vacated the embassy and walked the several blocks over to his parked car.

Sitting behind the wheel, he had immediately felt the cold fear seizing him through his flimsy sense of elation. It had been a mistake to steal the file. How long would it be before the British witlessly gabbed about the missing report in front of the bugs for Morozov and his staff to overhear, inevitably levelling some of the suspicion at Konstantin?

As it had turned out, not long enough.

Having returned to his motel, he hadn't been there half an hour when he heard the heavy, imperious rap on his door. He recognized that knock instantly. Major Morozov. Konstantin had been preparing to head out to scout for the asset Kross, and suddenly he was trapped. Trying to feign innocence hadn't worked, with a choking apprehension quickly filling the small motel room, leading to accusatory language and caged hostility. Konstantin made the mistake of continuing to feign innocence right up until he simply refused to talk, citing Morozov's accusations as insulting to his proven loyalty to the department. It got violent, regrettably, and ended with Morozov screaming obscenities and hatred with only one eye left in his head as his two-man team lay clutching bullet wounds in the chilly motel room. That was one way to end a promising career. The incident would have guaranteed Konstantin a permanent sentence in the gulag, so the lieutenant fled the motel to the outskirts of town, pushing a stolen car beyond the speed limit for several blocks before composure set in. He knew how to find Kross; he only hoped that the man's last known haunts were still accurate.

Their meeting had been chary to start off with, held within a quiet café on a drizzly, overcast day. Kross was a somber man in his autumn years whose body had seemed to invoke an early winter. Regret clung to him like storm-sodden clothing. Konstantin didn't ask what had precipitated his excommunication from the Rising Path, but Kross had volunteered it anyway. He couldn't handle it, was his simple explanation. The other side: that hell, that purgatory... it was too much for him to bear. But the Path had been both loving and understanding, bidding him a fond farewell with the promise that they would meet again one day. Kross went on to tell Konstantin that if he was serious about seeking out the Path, it would entail traveling nearly five and a half thousand miles east to Novosibirsk, and from there, further east still, to the Kuznetsk Alatau mountains. It would be a journey fraught with risk; after all, he had just spat in the face of his nation's government and was a wanted man, and now he would have to venture deep into the wounded heart of his motherland. And Major Morozov always had been the vindictive type. If Konstantin could have done it all again, he would not have made the mistake of showing Morozov mercy.

After thanking Kross, Konstantin told him to go underground and become a ghost, figuratively, for he had powerful people searching for him. For the next several days Konstantin slept little, on guard from his own shadow as he made his way northeast across the continent, crossing borders with his identity obscured by his set of KGB-forged documents, which had fortunately not been red-flagged this far from home.

. . .

HE LET THE razor sink to the bottom of the basin, the water now a swampy marsh of hair. Before his eyes, a line slowly began to trace a symbol in the steamed-up mirror. He watched its trail complete an ouroboros. Another started to form beside it. Then another. The thick finger of the artist appeared. He was a big, brawny man, his scalp shaven, and his beard brushing the top of his sternum. Brother Kuznetsov. He was Konstantin's rock, but also the biggest source of his regret. Kuznetsov didn't bother to speak. He didn't have to; as usual, his face displayed interminable patience, and the repetitive symbolism was all the incentive Konstantin needed. All about him, in the mirrors of the cabinets and the larger glass wall of the shower stall, the invisible fingers of his other monks joined in, communicating their message, their need, to their vessel and savior. One by one they had all left the soul prisms of Konstantin's aging husk, taking shape amidst the wafting steam, their eyes blazing with zealous light. A sharp stomach cramp, so deep it emanated within the core of Konstantin's soul, doubled him over, knees hitting the damp tiles.

Amidst his brothers and sisters, a darker form tried to gather substance, a dark, featureless shadow, unwelcome but also powerful enough to brace their shared animosity, and also something else... fear.

The Arkhitektor.

The spasm passed, and as quickly as he had appeared, the coal-smudged spirit of their afflicted former elder evaporated within the steam, returning to Konstantin's marrow. Konstantin knew he would have to retreat to his armor and gauntlets shortly to keep the Arkhitektor weak, to repress that which could bring doom to all of them. His eyes addressed the wet finger traces, then the faces of his people, lingering lastly on Kuznetsov.

'I'll find it,' Konstantin vowed. 'The eternity we deserve.'

Konstantin got back to his feet, his hand clasped to the geometric soul hive arranged across his torso, watching as one by one they all phased back into him. Kuznetsov was the last to return home. 'I'll find us our sanctuary. I'll find the Firmament Needle.' How many times had he said that to him, to all of them, over the last twenty-three years?

He couldn't say, but his words hadn't lost any of their original conviction.

6

AFTER RECEIVING AUTHORIZATION TO LAND, the jet touched down on an airstrip at Darnell Air Force Base, situated in the vast, barren open plains of Valencia County. The heat was sweltering, plastering Clyde's The Venture Bros. T-shirt to his back. He could smell warm metal; he figured it was from the accumulation of parked jets and ground vehicles. He didn't feel too much like a welcome guest upon touchdown, but then he was still a civilian, and this wasn't a sightseeing tour. Rose and Ace had a perfunctory word with the waiting Air Force officer, leathery and tanned, with two silver bars on his uniform that Clyde recognized as that of a captain rank.

As the captain broke away, ready to continue his business, Kev nabbed him with a friendly question. 'You fellas keep a nightly vigil for any strange lights passing over the desert?'

The captain—Niles, Clyde saw on his name tag—gave Kev's mishmash of inclement clothing a dubious look, then walked away without comment. Clyde joined Kev in sharing a shrug at the testy officer's lack of people skills.

'I don't think he likes my dress sense,' Kev said. 'Probably thinks I'm weird.'

'Darnell was commissioned in 1948 to work as part of a joint venture with Hourglass,' Rose said. 'Trust me, Captain Niles has seen weirder than you.'

'Is Indigo Mesa nearby?' Clyde asked as Rose and Ace started to march off.

'Not far,' she replied over one shoulder, leading them away from the strip, past several F16s, and towards a waiting jeep parked by the nearest hangar. 'Just a little drive.'

They were many miles from the nearest civilian population centers of Rio Communities and Meadow Lake, so Rose drove with a lead foot, speeding them east across the boiling wastes. Before too long, they had left the rugged plains behind, the jeep bouncing along in the cool and merciful shade of Bosque Peak, one of a series of secluded and topographically varied peaks just over forty miles southeast of Albuquerque, New Mexico. It was just past midday, and the sun was falling from its punishing zenith, its light dappling through a green corridor of Douglas firs, but the forest was beginning to give way to a tall, hardy canyon of red rock walls bathed in light-blue shadow. With the top down, Clyde sipped from the bottle of water Ace had given him and stared up at the sandstone canyon walls, unused to canyons being made of anything other than glass and steel. This certainly wasn't Manhattan.

Leaving a plumage of dust in their wake, they continued east for the best part of five miles towards the imposing impasse of the Manzano Mountains—running north to south—with no discernible trail or road to guide them. Clyde was almost certain Rose was just going to foolhardily challenge the steep, rocky gradient until the jeep received a broken nose or was flipped over onto its back like a tortoise. Then he saw the restricted wooded road, unwelcoming in the shade of a jagged cleft. The large white sign that declared WARNING—NO TRESPASSING—USE OF DEADLY FORCE AUTHORIZED acted as a polite reminder for outsiders to stick to the designated hiking trails within the mountain range.

The effects of the airplane vodkas had all but dissipated now, the alcoholic breakfast leaving Clyde in a state of tired, surreal acceptance of his situation. Kev was sitting with him in the back, still swaddled up in his disguise and lost in thought. Judging from the long chat on the plane, Clyde knew Kev had already confirmed his desire to stay if it meant he could be a part of something again. Clyde wanted to feel betrayed, just a little bit, but how could he? He was still heavily leaning towards listening to the presentation, or job offer, or whatever these guys were selling, smiling politely, and asking for the soonest plane ride back to NYC. But it would be selfish of him to expect Kev to go back with him. For all their talk about moving out into separate apartments, and maybe expanding their link across boroughs, cities, states, countries if necessary, what type of life could Kev expect to have when he would still have to dress up like a blind bank robber to do anything? Kev wouldn't be buying a house, landing a good job, finding the right girl and having kids, and all those other hackneyed society-fed fallacies that are supposed to necessitate happiness. This could be the only home Kev would ever truly know from here on out, and that thought hit Clyde like a punch in the stomach.

He sipped his water, wondering how Ace got the bottle so damn cold in the desert. He didn't see a cooler in the shotgun seat of the jeep. Rose weaved the vehicle along the baking clay of the tracks winding through the deep, cool valley. The sound of tires crunching gravel must have started to bore Ace, so he got his phone out, and the next thing, "Hide Your Heart" by KISS was rocking through the speakers.

Clyde couldn't say he had ever been a fan, but if that big, grizzled bear was apparently going to be teaching him how to fight—a blasé presumption that Clyde would be shutting down as soon as they got to Indigo Mesa—he didn't think it would be a smart move to complain about the guy's taste in music. Instead, he realized his geeky knowledge could help him find a patch of common ground with Ace, and he decided to use it.

He leaned forward, patting the side of Ace's seat. 'Did you know these guys were big fans of Marvel Comics back in the day? They actually mixed some of their blood into the red ink that was used in their very own comic-book. But there's a rumor that their blood donations had been mistakenly added to a copy of *Sports Illustrated* instead.'

Ace, still clearly the worse for wear, his head lolling left a few inches to better hear Clyde's anecdote, stroked his handlebar mustache once, gave a barely perceptible nod, and turned back to continue monitoring his wing mirror. Clyde noticed Rose's embarrassed grin and couldn't help but smirk a little himself. It was worth a try.

The jeep curved up a hard-packed winding trail, passing house-sized boulders and leaving patches of mayweed trembling in its wake like dozens of tiny, cheerful, white-crowned suns snared in tangles of brown grass. For the second time in ten minutes, Clyde was certain Rose was going to smash the jeep into a towering rock wall until she produced a small plastic fob from her pocket and tapped a button. Up ahead, a large wall of the canyon slid apart in two sections. Turning the wheel, she left the wide trail and took the shallow fork that, until only a moment ago, had led to nowhere but a sheer, vertical bluff. The tunnel was air conditioned and sleek, with paved lanes, large air vents, smooth concrete walls, and strip lights lancing off into the distance.

'That's a dope entrance.' Clyde couldn't help but admire the sudden shift into espionage and secret bunkers.

'Yeah, but it's a fucking pain in the cooch when you lose your fob,' Rose said.

Kev's face was unreadable behind his ridiculous disguise, but Clyde knew he was crackling with excitement. He had that same bustling charge about him that Clyde last recalled seeing after he'd been accepted into his college course, an unexplored yearning to try and reach for something outside of his usual passive routine, the spine-tingling sensation of uncertainty.

The arrow-straight tunnel finally led somewhere: a bulletproof guard station manned by a humorless sentry in black tactical gear. Ace turned down the music, just slightly, and handed his ID to Rose, who passed both of their credentials to the guard. He scanned them on a small terminal in his guard box. Passing inspection, the guard was about to hand the credentials back when he paused, running a curious gaze over Clyde and Kev.

Clyde looked away, accidentally glancing up at the security camera above the guard shack, staring right into its clinical little eye. He pictured his face being stored forever on some private server in a sub-basement somewhere. Ace took out a small wad of twenty-dollar bills, leaned past Rose, and moodily passed them to the guard without comment. Pocketing the payment, the guard knuckled the button and lifted the barrier.

'Did you just bribe him to get us in here? I thought this was all legit?' Clyde experienced a swift and unwanted vision of being arrested for sneaking onto a military base and spending the afternoon being waterboarded for information. At least Kev had the option of running through the fucking walls.

'Relax, rookie. I lost a bet, that's all. The Rangers beat the Maple Leafs last night,' Ace grumbled. Actual words. A sentence even. 'Why do you think I'm sweating beer? I'll give you a hint. I wasn't celebrating. I fly all the way to the Garden to watch them get turned over. Bye-bye, Stanley Cup. And then I find out afterwards that since I'm already local I should stick around and babysit you two with little miss dick twister here.'

Clyde didn't care one way or the other about Ace's woes and didn't see any point in pretending. 'I'm not into hockey.'

Ace quietly huffed. 'And the season started off so well.' He turned the volume back up for the last chorus.

The tunnel split off into a junction, and Rose accelerated around a bend, taking them deeper into Indigo Mesa.

. . .

'So this is the grand tour, huh? The cafeteria?' Kev seemed incapable of restraining himself, dying to get into the sexy stuff. A kid in Santa's workshop, foaming at the mouth and overeager to run free and indulge in all the possible magic on offer.

Clyde wished Kev would calm down and try to view things from a mortal perspective. An *objective* perspective.

The cafeteria brought chilled relief to Clyde's sweat-damp skin. The place possessed a high-tech space station aesthetic. A massive sterile vault of aluminum and plastic, with one enormous glass wall offering a stunning elevated platform view of the vast subterranean limestone cavern that had been partially converted into a long, extensive deck of vehicle bays, held up on unshakable industrial stanchions above an underground river flowing off to parts unknown. Other agents were scattered about the sea of tables, eating and talking, the acoustics garbling their collective speech; most of them paid very little attention to Clyde and Kev. Without comment, Ace left them standing there and walked over to the lunch line.

'Ace needs to soak up the beer keg in his stomach,' Rose said. 'You hungry?' she asked Clyde.

He looked at some of the agents eating bacon and eggs, but he couldn't muster an appetite. 'Coffee?'

'Hot and black coming up. Park your asses. I'll get some grub.' She turned to Kev. 'Then we'll show you a few things.' She left them both there in the air-controlled tomb. Clyde parked his ass at the nearest empty table, as commanded, but Kev took a moment, drinking the place in, his scarf down below his vaporous chin, grinning tightly.

'It was a mistake coming here,' Clyde muttered, more anxious than ever. 'They're not going to let me leave. I don't care how many non-disclosure agreements they make me sign. I'm stuck here.' He watched Ace and Rose standing in line with a group of off-duty agents, grabbing a few burgers and coffees from the kitchen staff working the trough.

Kev didn't need to put on a show in here to pretend he was normal, so instead of lifting his leg to straddle the table's bench seat, he lackadaisically phased through it, leaving the physical material of his jeans to drape along the seat behind him. Sitting opposite Clyde, he kept his tone easy and hopeful. 'You need to relax. Nothing's happened that you didn't already agree to. We'll see the experts, hear what they have to say, and if you still don't want any part of this, then I guess it's time for a few more airplane vodkas. But, I mean, come on.' He spiked a thumb over his shoulder towards the giant observation deck overlooking the energetic hustle and bustle of the vehicle docks arranged alongside the wide river. 'Well...?'

'What? It's an underground cave,' Clyde said. 'We have them back home; they're called subways, and they suck.'

'It's a super-secret military base built into an underground cave. Don't play me. I know when you're trying to act cool. Saw you do it enough times when trying to impress some chick at a party.' Clyde scrunched his mouth tight and fired off a dismissive bolt of air. 'I thought somebody who has spent most of his life reading and fantasizing about this type of stuff would be spraying nerd juice everywhere about now.'

Clyde had no comment and continued to feel the slow, sinking certainty that getting out of this place was going to be a lot harder than getting in. Kev turned in his seat to look through the giant glass wall at the tiny agents and mechanics tooling about with armored personnel carriers, jeeps, and even a few swift-looking boats moored at the banks of the river. Clyde knew Kev wasn't bothering with pretenses anymore. No more half-truths about the pair of them flying back home after this. Kev was swan-diving straight into whatever Hourglass was offering. 'You made up your mind already? I thought you'd have at least waited until they gave us the carefully polished presentation of how awesome it is to be an expendable military tool before you fired off a salute and joined them. These fuckers could be up to all kinds of shady shit.'

Kev methodically removed his aviators and hunting cap. Clyde could see the wavering indecision in his eyes. 'I don't know what I'm going to do. And let's not get carried away with what these guys are or aren't up to because until last night, we didn't even know they existed. I'll hold off on making any snap judgements for or against these people, but look about the place, look at me... does this seem like the type of operation pissing about with installing puppet dictators into banana republics or attempting to turn the whole planet into one great big retail park?'

'Yeah, well, so far all I've seen besides Hadfield's dead GI buddies are a bunch of living, breathing GI buddies. Suits, uniforms, makes no difference. This could be any branch of the military or some CIA post. It's just in a more expensive office. And tell me something. Do you really think any government would turn down an opportunity to use ghosts to push their agenda? This whole place could be here to turn you into an assassin. It's the perfect crime.'

'You're pretty sharp, rookie.' Ace was talking with a half-chewed mouthful of burger, stepping over the bench and sliding his tray along the table until he was shoulder to shoulder with Kev. He stared at Clyde with a mean glint in his eyes. Kev drifted a few inches away from Ace out of respect. 'What d'ya think, Rosie? Throw him in the hole now or let him finish his coffee first?'

Clyde turned to see Rose settling in beside him, a tray with two burgers and two coffees: one black, one with cream and sugar. She passed him his coffee mug, barely taking her eyes off the carb load on her tray.

'Let him finish his coffee. It'll be the last luxury he ever has. Maybe on his birthday we'll get somebody else to empty his toilet bucket for him.' Her tone was almost robotic in its factualness. Ace took another bite and glowered at Clyde.

Clyde shot a swift look at Kev, praying that through all their time hanging out over the years, they might share an unspoken telepathy for dire situations like this. Clyde couldn't wait to find out and decided to test the theory.

It was a reckless theory, born of panic.

Springing up from his seat, he drove a wild right cross straight for Ace's already badly set nose, hoping to break it again. Ace caught the fist like a baseball in a catcher's mitt. His other hand didn't even drop his burger. Clyde felt a powerful chill compressing his knuckles; it felt like he'd stuck his hand into an ice bucket. The temperature stole his breath. It all happened so fast that Kev didn't even get around to reacting, which was for the best. All at once Ace and Rose broke out into big smiles, trying not to laugh so hard that they choked on their late breakfast/early lunch.

'Too easy, rook. We're fucking with you. Just some gentle hazing.' Ace released Clyde's fist, the skin stinging and covered with a light coating of frost. 'Gotta hand it to you, though, that took some big, hairy nuts. I'm impressed, but only a little.'

Clyde shook his hand and slapped it into his other palm to generate some heat. 'What the fuck was that?'

Ace sipped his black coffee and swallowed a lump of beef and tomato. 'Not everyone here is a creep who pesters the dead. I've got my own skillset. I'm a living ice box. Good for keeping my beer cold, making snow angels, and if the situation calls it, busting a huge fucking block of ice over somebody's head.'

Staring at Ace's bear paws, Kev's eyes practically melted into mushy acclaim. 'How do you do that? Is it magic?'

Ace seemed a little cheerier with his belly full, splitting his attention between Kev and Clyde. 'Magic comes and magic goes, but what I have is a kind of supernatural performance enhancer in my genes. There's more of us than you might think out there. The paper-shufflers call us Sparks. There's a whole secret history to it, which I'm too tired and too uninterested to get into right now, and it doesn't matter anyway. Indigo Mesa mainly specializes in PLEs, not Sparks. This place is about people like you two: a skinny kid and a four-eyed ghost.'

Rose was starting in on her second burger, pausing just long enough to breathe in between bites, her muscles hungry for fuel. 'You can sit back down, Clyde.' She tore off another bite. 'We're not going to brainwash you or shove some explosive tracker up your ass.' Clyde eased back into his seat, his frown telling of a continued sense of mistrust. 'It seems like you have some real hostility towards the powers-that-be.' She cast a quick glance about her person as if waiting for her patrol of the damned to reappear, but they didn't, and they didn't have to. Her meaning was clear: she wasn't any happier about her dead squad than they were themselves. 'You think I don't?'

'You're the one who signed up to serve in an age where it's impossible not to know how fucked up and hypocritical the entire military machine is. And once you're in, all logic and independent thought gets beaten out of you.'

A warning entered her big brown eyes, which told him to tread carefully. 'Is that what happened to your brother and old man?'

Kev's attention bolted to Clyde, preparing for damage control. Rose didn't look away in shame or apology; she took another bite and awaited his response as if to say, you want to talk shit? Let's talk shit.

Clyde blinked first. He wasn't going to get into personal business with strangers.

Kev smartly provided a quick conversational detour, putting the focus back on Ace. 'What about you? You lifelong military?'

Ace was slouching, leaning his ribs against the table and staring out the observation deck window. He smiled a broad grin, showing his missing front teeth and a few molars, too, from the looks of it. 'Nah, not even close. I was a high school dropout from Mississauga, Ontario, staring down the barrel of a career as a factory worker.'

'That's some career change.'

'I poured everything I had into hockey, trying to break out of the local circuit to the big leagues. I played for the St. Mike's Majors as a junior. I was always a big, sturdy kid, used to the rough stuff. Full-blooded goon on the ice, putting the liquid shits up the opposition. Not too graceful on the ice, but I spent every spare minute at the rink until I glided like a dancer and hit like a caveman. I could score too, though. Make no mistake, I had talent.'

Ace might have once recounted this unfilled dream with an aura of wistful nostalgia, but clearly time had proven itself to be a capable healer. 'In my last season at the OHL, I racked up seventeen goals in thirty-three games and enough scraps to get a rep. But putting one in the net was always a secondary priority for me. Personally, the best moments were seeing that flinch of uncertainty in a rival's eyes.' He seemed to remember a crucial detail. 'And protecting the team, of course. I was with St. Mike's until I was nineteen, just about the time the NHL scouts started sniffing around me for the draft. It was a big home game against the Ottawa 67s at the Hershey Center, and I got into it with number twenty-three, a big, pissed-off yeti named Tillerson. We're throwing bombs at each other, and at some point in that hazy scuffle I realize I'm a fucking ice sculpture with skin slapped over it. I noticed my left hand looked like it was stuck inside a shook-up snow globe, like a mini blizzard was freezing Tillerson's jersey to my hand. I let him go before we needed a salt shaker to separate us, and put him down with a parting shot. I figured if he remembered any of that when he woke up, people would think he was just in need of a lie-down. Thought I got away with it until some suits pulled me up in the parking lot after the game.'

He smiled his imperfect smile again, his rugged looks making up for the gap in his top row of teeth, where his two foremost incisors shold be. 'They were talent scouts, just not the type I was expecting. Fucking typical.'

'You couldn't turn them down?' Clyde found himself asking.

Ace pondered this briefly, but he clearly had his stock answer loaded up. 'I could have, sure. The same way you're eager to. But I wasn't sure how long a career I would get out of hockey. When your hands start acting like snow machines, it's time to think things through. How much longer could I keep that quiet before the wrong type of suits started hounding me?' Ace sipped his coffee. He didn't need to blow on it to cool it down; it was steadily dropping in temperature in his hand. 'But they helped me. I wasn't thrilled at the time. I always thought I'd be watching my highlight reel on TV someday, parked in a big recliner in my huge fuckin' house, some babe waxing my stick. But I did the right thing in signing up with these guys. They trained me to control my stats, and it's more fun punching true assholes and monsters than some other working-class stiff trying to make a crust.'

Something about Ace's story resonated with Clyde, and it bothered him, raising an ire that he had, for the most part, blotted out of his thoughts. What if I got my big break? Clyde thought. What if I made it and found myself haunted by a throng of ghosts, some of whom are less concerned with being low key like Kev? If there's one thing that could derail a burgeoning career in the comics industry, it would be having every meeting, every signing, every working day besieged by angry ghouls. Still, Clyde was determined to keep his front up. He patted his knuckles, feeling his blood slowly warm them up, and was about to continue his suspicious inquest when Rose latched onto the very thing that remained at the top of his interview topics.

'The assassin thing you mentioned? You weren't too far from the mark,' she admitted. 'Yes, we're still operatives with an agenda, and that involves killing if necessary. The big difference is that it isn't for any of that political, big business crap. There are enemies out there far greater than the ones the mass media try to scare you with. You've already met ghosts, and now you know that Ace here has abilities all his own. The war we fight is on the margins, but it's also bigger than anything you can imagine. I've seen things you wouldn't believe, evil of all shapes and sizes, and each and every one of them had to be stopped. Hourglass has a lot of pull. A lot of the military's black budget gets funneled into us because they need us, but all the money and weapons contracts in the world can't compete with specialists like us.'

Clyde tensed under Rose's eyes, which bore down on him like a heavy barbell.

And it wasn't just her eyes that were on him, as Kev's focus had become unwavering as he waited to see how Clyde would take this information. Ace was not as invested, paying more attention to his coffee and the other field agents and admin staff scattered about the place, but Clyde sensed he was playing his role: the gruff, cool guy who didn't give a shit if the rookies made the cut or not.

'That's very rousing and all,' Clyde said, 'but I'm just trying to be a comic-book artist. I'm sorry if that's not heroic or bad-ass or whatever, but that's how it is. I'm humble like that.'

Kev eagerly leaned over the table. 'Jack Kirby, Jim Starlin, Steve Englehart.' He must have had that one chambered for a moment just like this. Had he thought about this one during the ride in the jeep? 'All comic-book artists and writers, and they all . . . ?' He left it open for Clyde to fill in the blanks.

Clyde didn't appreciate Kev's angle, huffing defensively. 'They all served in the military.'

'I'm sorry, you probably regret telling me that now. But they still went on to have great success in comics, and I bet none of them could talk to ghosts.'

Ace was still casually glancing about the room as though bored, fidgeting with a loose thread on his cut-off denim jacket. 'Kirby had a working relationship with us in the fifties.'

'What?' Clyde's eyes popped.

'Can't say any more. Classified.' Ace went straight back to looking like he didn't give a shit about anything.

Clyde continued staring at Ace for a slow three-count before focusing on Kev. 'Look, if you want to stay here . . . it'll suck, it really will, but you have my blessing. Honestly, on my mom's life, I'll understand. In a fucked-up kind of way, this might be the best place for you now. But I can't just turn my whole life around. I'm no soldier, and I can't pretend that losing half my family to someone else's war no longer bothers me just because there's ghosts and goblins involved. And if I die, what about my mom? I'm her only child now. I'm to risk getting killed in some top-secret ghost-hunting bullshit and leave her all alone in the world?'

'If you clean the wax out your ears, you'll have heard me say already that this isn't someone else's war.' Despite her words, Rose was patient, her voice calm, reasonable. 'What we do, it's for everyone the world over.'

'Can I just go see whoever it is I'm here to see, to make sure I'm not about to turn into some ghost magnet? After that I'm gone, and I'll hitch-hike back to New York if I have to.' Clyde hated seeing the disappointment in Kev's eyes. He must have really expected to win him over, to see this thing as some wild adventure. Who knows, maybe Kev was onto something there. If life was no longer finite, if death was only the next step, then was there anything to be scared of? Danger, warfare . . . wouldn't everybody have the chance to find each other again at some point during eternity? Clyde killed the thought quickly.

Kev removed his hat and placed it on the table, quietly dejected. Ace continued to pay scant attention to the discussion.

Rose poured a few brown-sugar sachets into her coffee and whisked it with the spoon. She grabbed the mug and stood up, leaving her empty plate. 'Whatever you want, tough guy.' Her playful, roughhouse demeanor had become a blunt formality. Not so much brusque, merely a cynical acceptance, as though she knew something Clyde didn't.

'Let's go see Spector.'

7

KONSTANTIN WASN'T SURE WHAT HE thought about this modern world. After stepping outside of it for so long, denied a window into its developments, he knew he should be amazed by the stunning technological advancements that had shaped societies since the early 1990s, but for each incredible achievement, he was unsurprised to see the same old rusty mechanisms churning away underneath, the gears and sprockets of tired, ancient machines using these futuristic accomplishments to power the same stubborn systems that this world was forged upon.

Murder. Espionage. Control. Greed.

He stood in the middle of the drawing room of this giant doll's house, so eerie and unlived in; more a collection of timely furniture and tasteful ornaments for stuffy old men to admire over snifters of cognac. A pair of silent guards watched him from beside the glass-paned double doors of the drawing room. His babysitters were back. Or maybe they were simply making sure the fine hanging artwork didn't get defaced or the 17th-century sofas' upholstery were scuffed; though they had provided him with a pair of dark army fatigues to wear under his bronze necronaut armor and a pair of well-fitted boots, it wasn't quite fashionable. But what did you get an ex-military hermetic monk forced to spend huge amounts of his time wrapped in gauntlets and a multi-barred breastplate?

He watched the constant news cycles about international affairs slowly creaking towards Armageddon. Crises and politicians whom he wouldn't be in this world long enough to become invested in.

Blank-faced, he turned off the embarrassingly ostentatious TV.

It made him consider if his species' collective soul truly was worth his sacrifice and those of his deceased brethren.

The voice of Kuznetsov rose up from within, chagrining Konstantin for his momentary lapse in purpose: *Since the Path's inception, their credo had been to find the light for all of humanity, and all living sentient beings. Time and weary judgement should not dishonor the guiding principles of the original priests, brother.*

Konstantin sent a thought back to the peaceable Kuznetsov by way of apology. He hadn't meant his brusque dismissal of the entire human race. It was an emotional response, a mortal's error.

But his apology had quietened Kuznetsov. Konstantin didn't need to earn his trust, even after his poor, costly decision back in Erebus.

He placed the TV's remote control down on the 19th-century European coffee table.

Konstantin was awaiting his summons. Talbot was allegedly preparing himself in the den before their second meeting. Konstantin imagined a green, slithering, sewer-oozed thing slipping into its pale-skinned mansuit. He had been of two minds about sending Kuznetsov or some of his other contingent out as ornery delegates, to carefully slip like wisps by the guards and find Talbot, and demand that he, the imperious little prick, hurry up and initiate the meeting. But the sheer size of the manor would still most likely have his messengers prowling around the wings for twenty minutes before eventually finding Talbot, or maybe the other one, Mortis, shambling about the place like a mausoleum's butler. It was then that Mortis, the big stoop-shouldered cadaver, strolled into the room on a cold, musty breeze. With a chipper nod and a slice of a smile, he led Konstantin from the drawing room and towards the den, nestled away in the northwest corner of the manor, through marble hallways with arch-windowed views of the cloisters and the lush, verdant acres of meadow and forest.

Mortis entered the hideaway without the formality of knocking on the door. Konstantin presumed he had been given prior permission to enter. Den was something of a misnomer. The room wasn't cozy: it was austere.

Konstantin had seen museums with more warmth in his day, and surely this place was exactly that, a museum. All around the room's marble-pillar-supported vastness were wooden, waist-high pedestals, each one glass-topped and housing some type of relic imbued with hexes and not entirely of this limited world. Konstantin personally knew nothing of the surrounding artefacts, but they looked to be an eclectic assortment: a large and desiccated reptilian paw, an old whistle, an old cannonball from the looks of it, a jester's marotte, jeweled ceremonial knives, pendants, rings, a paintbrush that bore a strong resemblance to bone; the inventory was stunning, but Konstantin was too busy following Mortis to the middle of the room to fully appreciate any of the items.

They came to a stop near a very large, very old, and very ugly claw-footed table, adjacent to a wide circle of tall bookcases. The rough tabletop was crudely engraved with ancient symbols. He gingerly ran his brass-covered fingers over the surface, feeling a gentle thrum running through the metal. Whatever curse had been placed upon the black wood, Konstantin was happy to remain ignorant of it.

Hanging over the table from a very long brass chain was a wide, five-tiered chandelier of colored glass, arranged with red, blue, green, orange, and yellow crystals. Konstantin imagined that the huge sky wheel of lights carried an interesting legacy, but he was thankful it wasn't lit up at the moment, knowing it would paint the whole gallery in a garish, numinous light.

'You didn't attempt to commit suicide?' Talbot sounded pleased, but he didn't bother to look up from his place at the table, where he was leaning over, examining a small and loosely assembled gathering of pages, some in much worse condition than others. 'That's reassuring. It tells me you're willing to return to Erebus in a less gruesome manner.' He glanced up from the array of pages, casting a sharp eye over Konstantin's freshly shaved face, the grooming of which only highlighted his gaunt and sallow features. 'Don't you look dapper? Who knew you had a face hiding behind that awful beard.' Konstantin's closely scraped pores were fresh and revitalized after decades of growth. 'The clothing measures up all right, I hope?'

Konstantin grumbled, sounding somewhat satisfied with his clothing. 'You hungry?'

'Nyet.' He would have added thank you, but didn't deem Talbot worthy of basic niceties.

'I see your rest has done little to cheer you up.'

Konstantin exhaled impatiently in reply, his clinical gaze slicing down to the pages on the table. They were maps. Some were torn, some badly singed, and the ink on a few was badly aged, but it was clear that they were not all from a single source.

'You must be great at parties.' Talbot fiddled with his cuff links and huffed politely. 'But you're right. Let's get straight down to brass tacks. After all, that's why we very kindly sprung you from prison.' Konstantin felt nothing from the snipe. Talbot's fingers scuttled spider-like across several pages. 'These articles constitute a crude and patchy geography of Erebus. We used to have a slightly broader collection, with some in better condition—' he passed a hand over the fire-blackened half of one sheet, '—but when a group has been around as long as ours, things can go awry from time to time. Having said that, even when these maps were in their found state, the individuals who drew them were still only providing a glimpse into a fraction of what we believe Erebus to be. Like striking a match in a cave.'

Konstantin caught Talbot searching his eyes for any recognition.

A gruff indignant mumble preceded the monk's words. 'Not familiar with these places. They all from same kingdom?' He heard his fractured syntax reappear ever so slightly, an irregular occurrence that hinged upon his mood.

'Our sources indicate that some may be from different territories. The cartographers each had their own ways and means of navigating to Erebus, and it's possible that they ended up in various territories of different Houses. And we don't yet understand how any of the maps connect. They could each be a million miles apart from each other.' Talbot's brow became a shallow ledge of shadow.

Konstantin leaned over the inked sketches, searching for any thread, any point of interest, to connect into his own remembered passages.

'You're certain you have never been to any of these locations?' Talbot asked.

Like a soaring eagle, Konstantin's stare roved over a wide range of topographical landscapes, the choice of parchments as varied as the environments: sketched and labeled upon the maps were luminous mountains of spectral light, frozen lakes of souls, forests of bone and hungry soil, and misty valleys of dying breaths—populated by death-rattle adders, according to some faded English cursive.

Konstantin straightened up. 'Never,' he answered honestly.

'You sound certain.' Talbot's eyes searched Konstantin's for truth or lies. 'Well, no harm in asking. I was simply trying to fit a jigsaw piece into this great black abyss. Since you're going to be the local guide for the upcoming expedition, I'd like you to produce a map for me and the military leader running it. I don't expect it to be precision mileage in scale, mind you, not from the top of your head. Only a rough draft detailing key points: terrain, wildlife. You get the idea.'

'You never said what your objective is with the Eidolon Trench.'

'The era of crude oil and gas is slogging its way towards the finish line. Cairnwood is enthusiastic in lobbying for alternative energy sources. Not so much green energy, but a source that is nevertheless long term, and you don't get much more long term than eternity.'

Konstantin clenched his jaw, swallowing the words he wanted to spit. Inside he could hear the slow churning rage of his church, incensed by what Talbot was hinting at. 'This planet has been ravaged already. Now you plan on violating souls of the deceased to run power stations?'

'Souls are the untapped energy source we're banking on. But this is uncharted territory, literally and metaphorically. If we find a more palatable and sustainable energy source, we're open to it. The soul agenda is only phase one. If this operation is successful, we are planning on installing a secure pipeline to the Trench, managed by an occupying force. But after that we'll have whole research teams over there. It could be an energy gold mine of unknown minerals, in which instance we'll have no need for souls.'

Konstantin focused on his own agenda. The bigger picture. And wasn't about to let this gloating cockroach ire him.

Talbot gazed at Konstantin's armor or, more specifically, what lay beneath. 'But you have my sworn word that we are not interested in your menagerie. They're your family, and we wouldn't dream of making this personal.'

Konstantin heard Kuznetsov whisper a warning in his thoughts, a soft thrum on a night's breeze. Only a minute ago he had passed through the soles of Konstantin's boots into the marble floor, performed a quick and furtive inspection of the outside corridors, and returned with news. Company was on its way. So it was no surprise for Konstantin when four of the dark suits entered the room, blocking the exits and making a point of showing him their most intimidating expressions and their amusingly ordinary weaponry. Two held 9mm semi-automatic pistols, and two held sub-machine guns. The four of them wouldn't stand a chance under the circumstances. Konstantin was waiting for the catch.

'There is one caveat,' Talbot added. 'Some of the security are not what they once were, in human terms. That might not be enough for a man called Gulag. However, from this point on, each and every member of my personnel will be loaded with a very special type of ammunition,' he clicked his fingers once, then twice at both pairs of gunners, 'capable of forever silencing a spirit. So for your sake, and those of your loved ones, don't get any silly ideas. Do your job, and afterwards, you'll be left to your own devices. Carry on seeking your enlightenment in the land of a billion corpses. I don't care, as long as you don't interfere with my business.'

Konstantin looked over his shoulder to the bulky guard standing ready, his handgun drawn. The guard over by the far doorway to the right was posed the same way. Konstantin eased the tension rising in the ranks of his brothers and sisters. This still didn't change anything.

He would shepherd these greedy parasites to the dead wastes and abandon them to the scavenging beasts.

Konstantin directed his attention to Mortis. 'Maybe these cartographers knew ways to punch deeper into the dead continents. Maybe they survived there for years, traveling deeper and deeper. But the elders of Rising Path could only open doorway to outer limits of Erebus—' again the imperfect syntax, '—along shores of outer kingdom, the House of Fading Light. If you land us there, I can guide us to Eidolon Trench.'

Mortis' right index key wagged reflexively against his leg. 'Shouldn't be a problem. I've opened the door to that mad land several times already. Practice runs. Each time that miserable beach has been the default entry point. I don't know if it's because these door locks have some form of fussy cosmic pin tumblers or because I'm still getting to grips with these,' he explained, raising one rake-shaped hand. 'Or maybe it's the doing of some peculiar force. Whichever, each time I've allowed the door to close behind me upon returning, it resets back to that original entry point. Could be a burglar deterrent designed to drive a man around the bloody bend if he had to make repeat trips.'

Something occurred to Konstantin and, aghast, he reared his head back an inch. 'You don't leave doors open, do you?'

Talbot answered for him. 'We're not idiots.'

'And your nine other keys?'

Mortis again, 'One for each of the other eight dead kingdoms of Erebus.' He gave a right-hand thumbs-up and added, 'And one is a skeleton key for anywhere on this glorious old world of ours.' He appeared to enjoy the attention, though wary of stepping on Talbot's toes. 'I briefly opened one of the other doors. It wasn't long after I first cut these keys. Turned out to be a silly thing to do, really; it had more stringent security than the place where we're going. Maybe security gets tighter the closer people encroach to the crown's domain.' Mortis suddenly seemed a little twitchy, an insect trapped between two competing spiders in Talbot and Konstantin. 'And I don't want the Order of Terminus putting a price on my head.'

'I wouldn't worry. You stick with plot to invade and commit grand larceny against Order's weakest house, I'm sure it won't cause too much trouble.'

Mortis' gray, filmy eyes rolled about in their dark, baggy sockets, sliding from the Russian to the Brit. Talbot relished having the upper hand and was most likely used to the feeling, finding little issue with Konstantin's attempt to instill doubt within Mortis, the walking tool.

'When do we begin?' Konstantin enquired, feeling his restless cargo roam about the hive of his torso.

'You two will be leaving as soon as you have drawn me a map for posterity. So you should get cracking.'

'Imagine my surprise,' Konstantin said. 'You're staying here. Safe.' Typical of industrious snobs in every war, far removed from the violence as they plot atrocities and move lives around their chessboard with delicate hands.

'Don't be a bitter pill.' Talbot knelt down behind the table to bring up two beautifully carved wooden boxes: one the size of a pencil case, the other quite a bit larger. 'To show you I'm not all bad, I got you a couple of gifts.' He placed them on the table, careful not to do further damage to the grid of incomprehensible maps.

Konstantin eyed the boxes wearily, and after a moment he selected the smaller, lighter of the two. Opening the lid, his eyes became distant, looking through the object and to the memories within. It was a seven-headed clay figurine of Vor Dushi. Each microcephalic head guided by a long writhing neck, a gangly-limbed effigy of the terrible guardian of the Eidolon Trench, the attack dog of the House of Fading Light's soul bank.

'Few things of value were recovered from your burning temple,' Talbot said. 'But that was one item. It landed in the hands of a private owner following your sect's misfortune, and I thought it rightfully belonged to you.' He tapped the larger box with a neat and trim fingernail.

Konstantin closed the figurine box with an acrimonious look, happy to never see that thing again until he reached the Trench in person. The lid of the bigger box was carved with owls and tree boughs, and had a brass hasp sealing it shut. He popped the hasp and swung the lid open, being instantly hit by an aroma of velvet and rot.

'The private owner. I'm sure you still recognize him,' Talbot sounded like a macabre auctioneer describing the innate worth of some ghoulish prized object.

Konstantin recognized him. The ragged skin at the base of the neck still looked fresh. And after several ambiguous seconds, he closed the lid on Major Morozov's severed head.

Talbot was done with this. 'Let's get something to eat.' His irises gave a brief shimmer, like two pennies in a reflecting pool, then returned to their normal color. 'And then I'll get you a pen and paper for that map.'

8

CLYDE AND KEV SAT IN the back of an electric cart, whizzing through tunnels past offices, labs, and research wings, with Rose quietly piloting them. Ace had stayed at the cafeteria.

Clyde could practically feel a hand slowly maneuvering him this way and that, a light pressure at the base of his spine nudging him from his own insistent path. Not a ghost's hand per se, but a spirit nonetheless: the spirit of begrudging loyalty. It was wreaking havoc in his head, his thoughts spinning like a fast cycle in a washing machine. He was trying to remain calm, worried he was creating the beginnings of a rift between him and Kev. A rift he didn't want, would never want, but one that may be inevitable if Kev had built up a fantasy in his head, a fantasy in which the pair of them played secret agent for these people. That would never happen, but Clyde wasn't going to let this place cost him their friendship.

It felt like a long ride. Kev had tried a few stupid jokes and observations since leaving the cafeteria to try and lighten the serious mood hanging over Clyde, much like the rain cloud that followed that donkey in *Winnie the Pooh*. Except Clyde wasn't so much morose as he was prickly and untrusting. Clyde smiled at the right times to show Kev he wasn't trying to step on his excitement, but he knew his anemic grins and terse laughs didn't fool him. Kev was cool enough to leave it alone, allowing Clyde to deal with his thoughts.

Rose stopped the cart outside a large set of chamber doors that could have been fitted on a bomb shelter, and once more Clyde set his nerves jangling with thoughts of being strapped down to some table and having electrodes stuck to his skull, maybe being injected with something to promote compliance and boost his cursed gift. He imagined all manner of horrors of flesh and ectoplasm being held behind those doors, a monster army waiting to drag him in there with them to join their legion of Bernie Wrightson knock-offs.

Chances are it was just another office.

'Well, let's get this over with,' Rose said, swinging herself out of the cart.

Kev had left his clothing behind at the cafeteria, embracing the freedom this place offered him, and trailed after her like a man-molded vapor. Clyde waited a moment, the worthless action of a stubborn man who knows he must do something but isn't yet ready to surrender his autonomy. He got out and followed them to the biometric lock beside the steel fortress doors, feeling the electric interest of the camera's eye tracking them. Rose went through the routine: fingerprint, retina, watching the red scanning panel flash green. The doors slid apart on well-oiled gears, and Clyde braced for maximum horror.

It was a library. Massive, but still just a library.

The short corridor was carpeted, with wainscoted walls of rich wood topped with a lightly patterned wallpaper, and antique kerosene lamps as wall sconces, the combined impression of which felt totally incongruous to the rest of the facility's cold, scientific, and military pragmatism. The corridor bled into a giant dome, at the center of which was a brass rail ringing the wide circumference of a hole in the ground. Warrens of ten-foot-high bookshelves were arranged in concentric circles, radiating out from that strange gap in the hardwood floor as though the whole library was built around it. There were even three upper levels to the library, each one arranged around the epicenter of that smooth aperture in the floor, as though some of the staff might suddenly feel the urge to toss a book or two over the stone balcony into that dark core below. Clyde imagined that only the Vatican or the elite of some secret society would ever possess a library like this, powerful types sitting before a giant hearth the size of a garage door and sipping brandy or virgin's blood. What would all this knowledge be worth? Could you place a value on it? Deep down, he somehow knew that many, many people had died in procuring such a wealth of information.

Plodding along like the curmudgeon he was trying not to be, he followed Rose and Kev. His eyes didn't know where to begin, but they hovered about that great pit for a few seconds too long.

Something moved in that pit. Something big.

Rose guided them around the outside of the bookcase maze, primly acknowledging a couple of middle-aged librarians in business-casual attire loading a trolley with books. She angled towards a more modern-looking wooden door with vertical glass inlay and aluminum pull bar.

'Hey,' Clyde called to Kev. Kev had been busy getting eyefuls of the various books, probably wanting to apply for a library card right there and then. Kev stopped and turned to Clyde, following his stare.

A spongy limb shifted just below the brass barrier of the hole. Whatever it was, it wasn't being coy, simply preoccupied with some other matter. Suddenly it rose up in all its towering, multi-tentacle-weaving majesty, a giant nematode with a tough, dry hide, rough as tree bark. The humongous creature lovingly held a number of volumes in its many appendages, each clutched to its metaphorical bosom, and set about returning them to their correct places on the shelves according to the Dewey Decimal System while passing other texts to staff members on the upper walkways.

Rose snapped her fingers to steal Clyde and Kev's attention away from such trivial matters. 'That's just Bookworm. You here to check a book out, or do you want to see Spector?'

Clyde and Kev followed her in silence but didn't lose sight of Bookworm until the door jamb blocked their view. She led them halfway down a corridor of offices, stopping outside a door with a simple black plastic plaque fixed beside it with white lettering: Philip Spector.

'I hope it's educational.' Without another word she marched back the way she'd come, leaving them here.

Clyde watched her turn the corner back into the library—the lair of the giant invertebrate horror—no longer sure if he wanted to knock on Mr. Spector's door. Kev gave him an eager look, abundant with fervent curiosity, ready to see what answers were stockpiled behind Spector's door. Clyde had promised his friend answers. Owed him answers. Hell, he still wanted some too. Together they would get to the bottom of their unorthodox place in this new, much stranger world. He rapped three times with his knuckles.

'Come in,' a muffled voice answered from within.

Kev was on the verge of waltzing right through the wooden door before Clyde was halfway to the handle. Mr. Spector sat behind his desk, a mess of folders, files, and books that could very well have been arranged by a madman, and all poised to collapse and crush his laptop. The rest of the office was pretty nondescript: a few old visitor armchairs facing the desk, some file cabinets, but what Clyde did find peculiar was the large display cabinet over to his left, loaded with bottles of all shapes and sizes: long and slender, squat jars, some with fancy twists, but all of clear glass and tightly capped. An odd item to collect, and definitely not from a beer or soda company. The room was pungent with the aroma of old coffee, and Clyde spotted the coffee pot in the corner.

Spector, perched over a few case files, eyeballed the two visitors over the rim of his thick-frame spectacles. He was somewhere in the murky fields of middle age but still handsome, with a full head of neatly combed graying hair. At least he wasn't another giant worm or some other weird shit, Clyde thought.

Spector's focus swept pendulously between Clyde and Kev—the man, the ghost, the man, the ghost—with an exasperated expression like they were Jehovah's Witnesses catching him at a bad time. Then something seemed to click into place for him, and his busy veneer dissolved.

'Forgive me,' he said, staying seated. 'Mr. Williams, Mr. Carpenter, please take a seat. I'll only be a minute.' Spector delved back into his reports, slapped one closed on top of the growing pile, making a few marks in blue highlighter pen in others, and rattling away on his laptop's keyboard.

Clyde and Kev settled into the pair of armchairs. They sat in silence for several minutes, looking about the office curiously. Clyde noticed three dreamcatchers twisting lazily from the ceiling fan sluggishly circulating the smell of burnt coffee. Then something about the glass bottles attracted Clyde's eye. Was it movement? He glanced at them again, finding nothing but a bunch of empty bottles. He was about to blame it on a loose eyelash or some sleep crust playing in his periphery, but then he was positive something shifted about inside one of them, or was it all of them? After several more double-takes he had convinced himself that there was something dwelling within those bottles. How? He wasn't sure since they were clearly empty. He nudged Kev and motioned towards the cabinet. Kev tried to share Clyde's fascination with the empty bottle collection, but after a minute of nothing, he shrugged at Clyde and continued to glance about the office for something better.

After a few more minutes, Spector closed his laptop with a slight sigh. 'Work never stops so long as people keep dying. I suppose I should be grateful for the job security,' he said without humor. 'You two must be the new recruits.'

'No.' Clyde threw a hand up instantly, his corrective tone harsher than intended. He leveled a hopeless glance at Kev, then back to Spector. 'Only Kev, here.'

Spector didn't look offended by Clyde's reaction; if anything, he appeared to be slightly amused. 'It's okay. At this stage I think I'm beyond being surprised by the behaviors of new candidates. I've seen skittishness, denial, bargaining, pissed-off, closed-off, and one guy even came close to having palpitations right there where you're sitting.' His easy grin was warm and inviting. 'Almost like the seven stages of grief.' His hands drummed lightly on his desk, a go-getting guidance counselor vibe. 'I know your heads are swimming with questions right now, so let's just roll our sleeves up and get right in there and work this out.'

Clyde went to talk first but found himself blabbering over Kev. Kev stopped, offering Clyde a wry grin and a go-right-ahead gesture. Clyde took a breath, beginning to feel dismayed at what he might now learn in this room. 'What's happening with us? With me?' His hand twitched in reference to Kev. 'How's this work?'

Spector laced his hands together. 'Due to your swift discovery and collection, our current records of you are pretty basic. Standard government details. Are you aware of any mediums or supernatural phenomena in your family history? Nothing is too remote or outlandish at this juncture, mind you.'

'No, nothing.'

'Are you aware of any past or recent encounters with practitioners of the dark arts?'

'Only my landlord.'

Spector paused, awaiting further details.

'No, nothing that I'm aware of.' Clyde could feel his pulse racing, a damp heat slowly pooling under his arms and the small of his back. In the back of his mind he was trying to decide if a camera was recording this little interview. *Of course it's being recorded. You probably can't take a shit in this place without a camera being up in your business.*

Spector raised his entwined hands, both index fingers resting against his lips. 'Well, you're a young man, but to develop your tether with Kevin—'

'Just Kev,' Kev politely interjected.

'—thank you; with Kev at your age, without any outside assistance, is quite late. Not completely unheard of, but uncommon. Many people first experience spiritual interaction as children, an innate but temporary ability that weakens progressively through their development, much in the way that collagen and bone tissue continue to degrade in older people. You unexpectedly flaring up in your mid-twenties isn't a complete freak occurrence; sometimes the potential was always there, waiting for the right stimulus.' His eyes were sharp behind his thick glasses, and Clyde imagined he was filing away the interesting points of the discussion without need of jotting them down onto paper. 'And is it correct that you're only in contact with Kev, no additional PLEs?'

Kev quietly bemoaned that label. Probably baffled as to what was so wrong with just calling a ghost a ghost. 'That's right, only Kev.'

'It provides a tremendous sense of entitlement,' Kev said with a smirk, then chuckling a bit more when he saw Clyde finally loosen up a little.

'Then that places you in the Level 1 category.'

'And is that like a lifetime guarantee, or can Level 1s get stronger?' Clyde felt as though he was slowly shrinking into his chair before the looming answer. He felt too small, too weak, and astonishingly, too ambivalent to understand his own wants and needs.

'I can't definitively answer that without testing, which we'll get around to shortly.' Spector's eyebrows rode up like black rainbows above his glasses. 'Getting stronger. Is that a goal of yours?'

The question sounded loaded. Clyde tried not to think of his mom crying late at night at the kitchen table; of flag-draped coffins slowly sinking into the freshly dug earth of Cypress Hills National Cemetery, two separate funerals bonded by a black, oily thread of repressed anguish.

Clyde saw Kev's look and knew his pal was astutely aware of the nature of his morbid interest.

Spector, too, for that matter, showed a gleam of wise comprehension; after all, Clyde knew Spector had likely read whatever file they had on him, which would undoubtedly include the facts about his KIA brother and dad. But to Spector's credit, he didn't put on any awkward airs of glib sincerity, maintaining his polite but almost clinical sterility. 'If it turns out you're a late bloomer and are indeed in need of future reclassification, or that you have the potential to push your abilities to those of a higher level through strict training, then I must inform you that you might wish to reconsider your decision to pass us up. It remains your god-given right to still say no to us, but the more powerful the civilian, the closer scrutiny we have to apply to them. I'm sure you can understand it's strictly for the safety of the public. I am at liberty to loosely disclose that there have been incidents in this department's past where lax oversight of certain extraordinary citizens led to some unfortunate outcomes. No matter the gifts some people have, they are still people, and life can twist some of them up pretty badly.'

Clyde's recalcitrant stare pushed into Spector. 'Are you the top dog around here?'

The question sidelined Spector. 'No, that would be Director Trujillo.'

'Then it would probably be quicker if I just told him my reasons for not wanting to sign up and let the news trickle down to any who care to listen.'

Spector leaned back a few inches as if to appraise Clyde, making a show of reading him like a cheap street magician. 'My former career was a bit checkered. I used to be a lot of things—a con man, a thief, a liar—but one thing I definitely wasn't was a company man. I could chew your ear off about the shamanistic teachings from over a dozen cultures or offer a laundry list of creatures whose diet consists entirely of freshly squeezed souls, but I didn't care very much for using my knowledge to help anyone other than myself. I made money, and connections, I found myself on some bad lists, and I watched my associate—my friend—get ripped to pieces because I got greedy. In those days I might have liked to try and portray myself as some dashing rogue hopping about the globe, and I would have turned my nose up at a place like this.' Both of his closed hands bloomed open like flowers, indicating the office space, the twirling dreamcatchers and the strange cabinet full of bottles. 'Some shady covert department hunting ghosts and monsters to earn a 401K? I'd have laughed my ass off. Until I found myself in a tough spot, and it was only when Trujillo offered me a place here that I realized how misguided I had been. The moral of the story is, sometimes the thing you need most is the very thing you're afraid of.'

'All the same, I'll choose to live under the microscope if that's my only alternative.'

Spector's lips curved into a quick, innocent smile as he prepared to drop the issue. 'Okay, I'm just making sure you're happy with your decision.'

Kev saw the look on Clyde's face and intervened on his behalf. 'He's not going to become a supervillain behind your back. Since I'm staying on, though, I guess we'll need to know if there's any kind of geographical range limit to our separation. Up until now the furthest we've been apart is about sixteen miles.'

'There are factors that can impact this on a case-by-case basis, but sixteen miles, you say? In my experience, if you can part ways up to a range of that magnitude, then I think you're probably good to go as far as you like.' Kev nodded with quiet relief. 'In some respects, I'd say that makes you lucky.' Spector shifted in his chair as though he was about to reach down and pick something out of a bottom drawer. 'So, are you ready to see what we can see?'

Clyde nodded without too much enthusiasm, feeling his doubts and his wants pressing up against him.

'I'm pretty sick of looking around hoaxy websites to learn about ghosts. Let's do...whatever this is,' Kev answered.

'Good, let's begin. Start counting sheep.'

'What?' Clyde asked.

Spector bent down and removed a strange contraption from the depths of his desk drawer. A kind of ornate box, metallic and a little scratched and worn, composed of three rotatable tiers engraved with strange pictograms, a Hadean Rubik's Cube. He slid it beside his laptop and clicked a button on the top tile of the winding box. As wind-up toys went, Clyde thought it looked a bit overindulgent. Spector remained where he was for a moment, watching them, the box ticking peacefully with the three tiers now rotating: the top and bottom clicking along in one-second intervals in a clockwise fashion, the middle tier running counter. Clyde was about to ask Spector to get on with it, to hit him with whatever useful information he had so that he could hurry this along and hop a ride back to the airfield, when he was forced to take a hard blink. A series of blinks then followed, each heavier than the last. When the attack of the drowsy blinks finished, Clyde continued to stare at Spector, who remained seated quietly behind his desk and the ticking contraption.

Something felt off.

Clyde was about to ask Kev if he felt okay when he saw Spector's visage begin to shift, almost imperceptibly at first, like an eye straining to discern a magic eye picture only to make up its own erroneous conclusion. Spector's face seemed to elongate slowly, just slowly enough for Clyde to cast doubt on his vision: the neat hair at his crown slowly rose up into two mounds, small hillocks growing and growing, until thick, robust bone was sprouting out into two curving horns on either side of his head; the healthy, desert tan of his face bristled with a thousand tiny black spots, growing and spreading until a hide of black fur covered his prognathous jaws, housing two white rows of flat gnashing teeth; the nose flattening widely into that of a grass-fed mammal. Spector's body didn't appear to alter, though, except for his hands, which began to morph, the fingers merging together to become tough cloven hooves like polished onyx.

And the box kept ticking.

Spector stood up, tall and proud, no longer a man but an infernal hybrid of man and ram. The eyes behind his glasses darkened but retained the curious human intellect. Before Clyde could so much as mutter a blue litany under his breath, the wall behind Spector pulled away into a vanishing point with the speed of a runaway train, during which time the other three walls, the ceiling, the desk and their chairs, the file cabinets and the display case of glass bottles, all dropped out of the world as the floor fell open like a trap door.

Clyde felt a dizzying head rush and might have screamed if he hadn't been so transfixed by the clothed ram creature in loafers, walking across the empty black void towards him with one cloven hoof out in what Clyde felt was a sign of peace. Clyde saw that Kev was no longer next to him, but he had sort of felt his absence beforehand. It was just him and Spector, adrift in a featureless ebon sea.

'Where am I?' he all but yelped, his voice carrying far and wide across the near endless negative space. The stark emptiness of this pitch dark undermined his equilibrium, almost unbalancing him. When did he stand up? What was he even standing on? Afraid to move, he braced his knees slightly and focused on the ram creature dressed in Spector's clothing.

'The boundary of your deepest internalized self.' The horned one spoke in Spector's chummy tone, smoothing his curly ram goatee between his cloven hooves.

Clyde stroked his arms out before him, thinking he had to swim in this midnight ocean, only to find that his thrashing didn't shift his buoyancy. Getting his panic under control, he realized he was breathing—of course, for he had just asked a question—and, feeling the firmness under his feet, he focused on that. 'Spector?' he gasped in fright. 'That you? Am I dead? This the astral plane or something?'

'In this form I am Ramaliak, a traveler of dreams.'

'This is a dream?' Clyde felt a little light-headed. 'This is freaking me out.'

'This is the pathway to the Median. Your own tiny tile in the infinite mosaic of the dream plane. Your quiet desires given voice. What do you dream, Clyde Williams?'

Clyde waited for a sea of crashing thoughts and desires, bruised hopes and imperious fears to wash in and fill this black abyss. 'It's empty,' he said, confounded.

The only sound was the continued disquieting tick from that box, counting down the seconds from somewhere outside of this oblivion. To Clyde's surprise, the abyss, its dimensions unfathomable, suddenly began to take form, the unseen vanishing point firing out a rapid series of comic-book panels on an unfelt wind, each one fluttering into a chaotic collage of Clyde's own heroes and villains battling it out in shades of pencil. The pages swept by like paper birds, close enough to give a hundred paper cuts. Clyde bled slowly, each minuscule slice drawing a ruby bead upon his arms and face, all of which quickly dried and blew away in brown flakes, leaving his skin unmarked. The endless flocks of pages had wallpapered the entirety of the black void, many of the edges still lightly stained with Clyde's blood.

Wrapped up in this vast room of Clyde's work, Spector perused the walls of information like a doctor reading a patient's chart, nodding sagely. 'It doesn't take a great mind to see how impassioned you are in your pursuit to become a successful artist.' He took a leisurely stroll along one wall, following a hundred spliced storylines existing out of sequence. 'Even when you close your eyes, your passion is imprinted behind your eyelids. That's good. Artists can show us the best and worst of ourselves, steal our breath and break our hearts. The complicated part for you is . . . ' Spector's hoof pointed towards something on Clyde's head.

Clyde touched his forehead tentatively, his hand exploring. Then he found it: a thread, smooth as silk and pulsing like a steady heartbeat. Carefully, he threaded it through his fingers. It glowed a pale blue. It was unspooling from a tiny hole in his forehead. 'What is this?'

'Our dreams and souls are connected as one. Dreams lead the dreamer to the heights of Olympus or the burning Stygian waters of Hades. Those who don't dream are truly dead, their souls malnourished. Those without souls can't create works of wonder or despair.' The box continued to tick away, almost in sync with Clyde's slowly relaxing heart rate. 'That right there in your hand is your soul thread. Your soul is knotted, as you well know, intertwined with another. That of your friend Kevin Carpenter.'

Clyde crossed the art installation of his bared soul, feeling naked before this violator. 'Where is Kev?'

'He's safe, of course. It may come as a surprise to hear that ghosts can dream too.'

Clyde pictured Kev in his private moments in their apartment, during the early hours when Kev thought Clyde was sleeping. Kev staring into space, thoughts besieging him. Kev, trying to act normal, the way he thought he was supposed to, but wrestling with his new immortal nature. Was Kev avoiding sleep out of fear? Scared to close his eyes again should he lose consciousness and this time never wake? 'What's Kev dreaming of?'

Spector had his hooves in his pants pockets, standing casually as if waiting for a bus. He ignored the question. 'I see your desires, but your troubles aren't far behind.'

The calm was shattered, the rhythmic tick-tick-tick of that box almost overwhelmed by the sounds of yelled orders, grinding tank treads, eardrum-rattling ordnance, screams and jarring rifle fire. The din could have been taken from a dozen war movies, recycled and regurgitated through the prism of Clyde's memory or imagination. The comic pages scattered away in a hurricane gust, leaving him and Spector standing in a pristine, blank white infinity. It was quickly bisected by a dark, wavering line to create a horizon for Clyde's eyes to focus on. With rapid motion, more lines appeared, too many to follow, producing a pencil-animated desert battleground: soldiers fighting and dying, planes splitting the distant sky, machines of death rumbling forth to perform acts of disturbing violence that, once witnessed, couldn't be forgotten. An explosion of scribbled fury went off a few feet near him and Ramaliak.

'Fuck! Is this safe?' Clyde dropped into a crouch, hands over his head. He knew this theater well and didn't appreciate the goat chewing over his problems like intellectual cud. Clyde had no concrete, factual information on the last minutes of his brother's or dad's final missions, but his imagination had worked overtime over the years to skillfully wound him with upsetting possibilities. All he knew was they died in combat. And he suspected their individual assignments were of the redacted variety. In any case, their wet work got them dead.

'You are safe with me,' Ramaliak said over the machine-gun fire. 'And understand that you have a degree of control in here. This is your lucid dream state, but it takes time to master that control. To swim against the emotional tides of your subconscious. I can teach you how. And when you have the strength, I can take you much deeper, to the depths of the Median. That's where you will discover if your soul thread can knot with others besides your friend.' Ramaliak waved his hoof, almost as a dismissal, and Clyde watched how his soul thread vanished from his fingers, becoming invisible once more.

The war continued all about this comic-book horror, leaving him an intangible observer to the psychic mayhem. Caption boxes came and went, coalescing from the dust to offer key information before disintegrating again on the hot wind. The caption box information had always been prone to change from angry episode to angry episode: his dad fighting against the Iraqi forces in the burning Kuwaiti oil fields; his brother working his way through some ISIS desert bunker in Afghanistan; all interchangeable, all unconfirmed, all the product of grief, speculation, and rage. This particular scenario was now a shell-blasted town square in a choking sandstorm, the poor long-suffering locals running through the rubble, away from the chaos they had no part in, trapped in the middle of another's war. A soldier fell dead at Clyde's feet, his helmet nowhere in sight and half his head blown away, a crosshatched shadow along the fragmented skull. The pencil work was his own but performed by an invisible god's hand. Clyde turned on the spot, scanning his impression of the ruined town until he found Ramaliak walking unscathed through a roaring rifle exchange, passing dead combatants, villagers, and donkeys.

'You chase your dreams, but your nightmares chase you. They're inseparable, your every want and deepest dread staining your soul like spilled ink.' His voice carried easily across the havoc of this imagined war zone. 'It's the soul threads of your father and brother you're curious about. You want to repair your broken family.'

Clyde nodded once, setting his jaw firmly. This may have been his dreamscape, but these dreams were buried deep, suppressed and snuffed by the morning light, for Clyde couldn't accurately recall many nightmares such as this. His waking soul, though? That was a different matter, for he had explored hateful places such as this too many times to count. Clyde could practically feel his surplus anima writhing about like a yoked primal beast.

The goat, bizarre in Spector's glasses, allowed the unavoidable truth of this statement to settle on Clyde. 'It's of little surprise, having read your file. Everyone with a glimmer of necromantic ability is curious about tuning in to the lost people they once held dear.' Clyde turned, a vacant quality about him now, watching black-and-white explosions and blood spatters continue to shade the landscape in graphite. Ramaliak gazed down at the quickly sketched faces staring up at him in frozen death. 'Are any of these your family?'

Clyde's brow furrowed, his attention hopping from corpse to corpse. He shook his head, recognizing none of the faces; they were all just interchangeable stock characters, people he'd draw for a warm-up exercise before erasing them from page and memory. 'No. Without their photos, I find it difficult to picture them clearly. It's more a feeling; even if their faces were blurry, I'd know it was meant to be them. Like strangers in a dream, right?'

'This is the first of the Median's three tiers: it's driven by the chaos of emotion, the dreamer's imagination, an untamed beast. As such, feelings carry tremendous influence here. The next tier down is the memory catalogues. And at the bottom, the innermost workings of the collective dreamscape, stitched together entirely of souls. That's where we must get to.' The ram watched an airstrike level a nearby block of buildings that were already missing their stone facades, the dust and smoke blinding the world in harshly scribbled dimness. When the hot veil of grit passed from Clyde's eyes, he saw the smoky silhouette of Ramaliak standing before him, living detail and color returning to him.

Clyde glanced down at his empty hand, remembering the feel of his own threaded soul. He clenched his fist, watching as it, and his arm, all became illustrated too. At that moment, he realized he, too, was only a dreaming representation of himself in here, ephemeral and weightless in an awful world. It was only Ramaliak, né Spector, who had retained his material form. His fingers gingerly caressed the point on his forehead, wanting to grasp the soul thread again, but they couldn't. It was like the pore was gone, sealed over. 'What if I can't bring them back?' Clyde's voice was shaky, his words weak with shame.

Ramaliak placed his hoofs behind his back. 'That's a possibility you'll have to prepare for. The number of knots a person can make depends on the amount of slack in their soul threads. But there's no sense in putting the cart before the horse. You'll have to acclimatize to the layers of the Median before I take you deep enough to find out. But if you're prepared to give me some time, we can find out together.'

A tear blurred Clyde's left eye: shed in a dream, but its touch felt a million miles away by his physical self. He was crying in his sleep. The teardrop fell and soaked the page he was standing on. 'If I can't tie any other knots, are there other ways I can communicate with them? Ouija boards or something?'

The ram-man walked across penciled scorch marks and passed clean through a pair of bodies, a teacher with a class hanging on the tenets of an explanation. 'There are other ways to invoke spirits, of course. Unfortunately, I am not permitted to do so, for that way lies ruin. It's a deadly undertaking with disastrous consequences, only fit for those of an iniquitous nature.'

Clyde wanted to challenge him on this, his eyes hot and wet, his cheeks burning. He was too tired to argue, his gaze a dry and scratchy tumbleweed skittering across the stark-faced troops lying dead in the sand.

'Until we know for sure how flexible you are, there's no sense in rushing to more reckless alternatives.' Clyde had been so riveted to the gory details of his own art that he had not seen Ramaliak until he was right on top of him, placing a supportive hoof upon his shoulder. 'If it turns out you can't anchor your brother and dad, remember you still have a responsibility to Kev.'

'Can you wake me up?' Clyde's voice sounded empty.

The desert scene erased away, marooning them once more in white abstraction. The darkness came back like a speeding tunnel, and the office rapidly bolted back together like a demolition played in reverse. Spector was a man again, sitting at his desk comfortably. He reached out and ceased the endless tick-tick-tick of that box of stolen sleep and secrets. Clyde felt his body molded to the chair and sat up straight, feeling flushed and a little warm, woken from a brief nod. He wiped away the telltale tear.

Kev was beside him in his chair, blinking away the nap that had blindsided him too. 'That was ... unexpected.' He caught sight of the clock on the wall. 'Was that several hours fast when we got here?'

Spector stared at the stilled metronomic box as though it was a necessary evil, something problematic he had learned to accept. 'The clock is right, I assure you. I'm sorry if either of you found that unethical. You wanted answers? That's how you get them.'

Kev looked surprisingly well rested after his reprieve from this physical plane, not having felt any desire to slumber since his death. He rubbed at his eyes, dislodging his glasses to really dig in there. 'What is that thing anyway?'

'Short answer? I'd guess you could call it a contract.' He rested his hand on the top tier of the metronome. 'This is my penance.'

Kev clearly wanted to know more, his appetite for the unknown growing hungrier with each bite. 'Would it be intrusive if I asked what the hell that means?'

'Are you still interested in sticking around?'

Kev seemed to be gathering his thoughts. 'More than ever.'

'Then I don't see much point in hiding away from my mistakes,' Spector answered nonchalantly. 'Okay, so, I told you I was less than altruistic in my previous life. This,' he tapped the box again, 'is the Sleeping Shepherd. The totem of Ramaliak, an ancient ram god who our records indicate arrived here, ooh, around about 11,000 BC in Mesopotamia. Ramaliak feeds off the dream energy of mortal souls, or free spirits too if need be.' He quickly made a slight calming gesture towards them both. 'Don't worry, it's harmless. I'm in control. The whole counting sheep bit originated from this. Some superstitious farmers believed Ramaliak to be a type of bogeyman and, fearing him and what their dreams would bring, would try to stave off sleep by counting their flock. Somewhere down the line this got muddled up and became a cute strategy to try and get some kip instead of avoiding it. Skip ahead thousands of years, and this staggering piece found its way into the collection of the British Museum. Not content to let some stuffy assholes stick it in a glass display case for tourists to gawp at, I decided to steal it. Which I did, successfully.' He smiled roguishly, and Clyde saw the grifter disguised in a college tutor's wardrobe.

'But then things got a little complicated for me,' he gestured at the Sleeping Shepherd, 'which is me putting it mildly. But then somewhere along that heady period Director Trujillo found me. Naturally, I wasn't happy to play ball at first. But that man's persistent. And he made a damn good argument to change my perspective on some things. Now, apart from little errands such as this, I only dream-walk to collate intel on red-flagged agency targets, steal the occasional dream, idea, or any important pieces of information; but it's not something I do lightly.'

Clyde realized Spector must have seen his blatant interest in the bottle cabinet earlier, for the man now indicated the cabinet full of assorted glass containers with one hand.

Clyde's interest was once again piqued. 'There are people's dreams in those?'

'Eh, well, one demon's dream is another man's nightmare.'

Kev phased through his chair for a closer look at the bottles, tentatively peering at them through the glass cabinet. One of the larger bottles, a big robust jug with an ornate stopper on top, almost seemed to shudder. Clyde joined Kev at the cabinet, his grim interest running counter to Kev's genuine sense of marvel. A barely visible movement swept around the inside of the bottle, looking a bit like a heat shimmer warping the horizon.

'Jesus... these are from demons?' Kev asked over his shoulder.

'Mostly. Either from an actual demonic species, or from a person with a troubling lack of humanity.'

'It must take some real nerve to wander about the heads of some people, some things.' Clyde sounded suspicious, but he wasn't sure of what precisely. Spector, the former criminal's motives? Hourglass itself? Or was he worried that he'd been stupid enough to allow the man to enter his dreams?

Spector didn't act bashful, instead answering with sobering honesty. 'It can be very dangerous to a novice and shouldn't be taken lightly. Even for me, some of the jobs I've taken for this company have been high risk. The Median is the layer between life and death.' Clyde looked at the three tiers of the Sleeping Shepherd. 'There are doors in there that can lead the sleeper back into wakefulness, and then there are some hidden in the far reaches that are essentially back doors into Erebus.'

'Erebus?' Clyde asked.

'The miserable hereafter,' Spector answered. 'Some of those doors, you open one, fall in or are dragged in, and you'll never wake up again. The trick is learning what these doors look like and how to avoid them.'

A grim silence settled over them. Clyde's eyes were lured to the dreamcatchers twirling peacefully from the ceiling fan and various corners of the room. He'd come here to learn about ghosts, which was more than enough, and now he knew there were demons, people who could wander about dreams—stealing them, no less—and a big, burly ex-hockey player who could create ice with his hands. His cramped apartment and his drawing board and iPad, his passion and his dishearteningly empty email inbox had never felt so attractive.

Spector got up, cracked his stiff neck, and walked a few paces to the coffee pot on top of the small unit in the corner. Refilling his cup, he offered Clyde one, which Clyde declined.

'Do you guys have any ghost blends? Or I'd settle for ghost beer if you have it.' Kev kept it light-hearted, but it was obvious his request was at least quasi-sincere.

Spector put the pot back and reclaimed his chair. 'One drawback about being me, my sleep pattern is perpetually fucked. You know of circadian rhythms?' He didn't wait for a response. 'Well, my circadia lost whatever rhythm they had a long time ago.' He paused for thought. 'On the subject of Erebus,' he fixed Kev with a gaze, 'I assume you have no recollection of your brief time there?'

Kev shook his head. 'Only darkness. Like being trapped inside the eye of a hurricane.'

Spector looked as though this was not newsworthy. 'In a way it's like being born again. Lots of noise and confusion and thrashing about. If you had remained there a bit longer, you would have developed a conscious existence and memories. It's probably for the best that you didn't,' he said, his voice sounding grave. 'Erebus is a terrible place.' He watched the black pool in his cup, gathering the reserves for the encroaching conversation. 'However, your lack of memory of that place also brings me to the toughest part of my job. For the purpose of transparency, I have to disclose this next part, and you have my apology in advance.' Clyde and Kev had the shared look of oncology patients awaiting test results. Spector sipped his coffee and took a sighing breath. 'After death, there are no pearly gates, no heavenly kingdom of clouds, no seventy-two virgins. There is only Erebus, or the Null, which the agency head-breakers prefer to call it. A counter-universe piled high with the dead. Our souls: good, bad, it doesn't matter, they all get dropped into that place to be picked over by the powers-that-be.'

Clyde blinked as if staring into a harsh sun. He threw a look at Kev as if expecting him to recall some repressed memory, or at the very least, show some solidarity in the wake of such gut-wrenching news. But he was left wanting.

'What the fuck!' Clyde said, his voice weak. 'That a sick joke, some more agency hazing?' Spector only stared at him silently. 'You're serious?' More silence. 'I don't know why you told us that. Why did you tell us that? You trying to get us hooked on antidepressants or something? Got a little prescription pad in your drawer there?'

'I've had to deliver that fact to one too many necromancers and their ghosts. And I had to tell you because, same as all those others, you both share a rare insight into an integral part of the living condition that ninety-plus percent of the population will never learn of until sometime after they take their last breath.'

'It does make a kind of sense.' Kev brushed his sandpapery stubble. 'I think I knew it the moment I got back. Even with the emptiness, and not knowing where I'd been, when I came back, I felt this awful weight on me, a chill in my bones, so to speak.'

Clyde could now see how Kev, having piece-by-piece overcome his sense of universal displacement since Rose had knocked on their door, had grown stout, and even in the face of such unbearable news, he appeared calm and accepting.

But Clyde himself was still reeling. He couldn't decide if this was an "ignorance is bliss" situation or if this harrowing revelation would help to ease him into a state of glum acceptance given time. Did it really matter? If everybody was confined to the same hell-bound epilogue regardless of their actions or beliefs, then they would all have the whole of eternity to get used to the idea. Still, his agnosticism had been sorely tested of late.

Kev's eyes carried a depth of acceptance and understanding that he had seldom allowed Clyde to see during their previous talks of this nature.

Morbidly transfixed, Clyde almost went bleary-eyed staring at some insignificant chip in one of the table legs. He swallowed a dry lump. 'So that's it, there's nothing better? Just fucking... *Hell*? Actual Hell? I mean, how come? Was there ever anything better?' Clyde was babbling, and knew he had to stop if he expected any sort of answer.

Spector's expression didn't offer any comfort; it was hardly ebullient. 'There's so much more to all of this than either of you can possibly know. And believe me, I know this isn't what you want to hear right now, but all I can say is, you'll have to learn to embrace the chaos.'

'Whatever, man. I could have learned about these damn powers without being told about the futility of everything else.' Clyde was still surging with a volatile mix of shock and anger, the first two stages of grief butting heads like competing bison. A queasy feeling started to turn over in Clyde's stomach, and he couldn't stop thinking about his brother and dad rotting away in some dead place. The same place that his mom would one day end up. And him, and Kev again, and old dependable Brian, his friend and manager at the comic-book store, and every other person he'd ever known and cared for.

Spector allowed Clyde to compose himself and sipped his coffee. 'You can't shine a light on an issue such as your condition and then be upset when you see some shadows, Clyde. You didn't ask for your ability, but you got it anyway, and now you no longer have the luxury of walking around in ignorance. It's a harsh roll of the dice, but there it is.'

Everything felt weightless and inconsequential. Clyde stuttered for some word or action to bleed off his mounting unease. 'Fuck! Then what's the point of all this? Why expend the effort and the resources to fight all this paranormal stuff only to end up in hell anyway?' He caught the equanimity in Kev's eyes, envious of his secret coping mechanism, which had granted him his oasis of calm acceptance.

'Did you believe in Heaven before Kev died? Or Stephen or your pop?' Spector asked.

Honesty was a tasteless lump in Clyde's mouth. 'No.'

'And did you sit around all day, every day, scared of dying?'

'No,' Clyde answered begrudgingly.

'Then, honestly, I don't understand your question.' Spector kept his voice relaxed and rational. 'You asked why we do this, why do we fight. Everyone will have to face the hardships of the other side in due course, but in the meantime, we protect them from forces that intend to bring that darkness sooner. We make sure this world remains a little brighter for the living while we can. Because the dark night is long enough.'

Clyde turned to Kev. His friend's expression told him that Kev's sense of purpose remained steadfast. It made Clyde wonder whether doing this, being here, was the one thing that acted as a salve against their shared inexorable oblivion. Some people threw themselves into their work to blind themselves to their pain. Was that what Kev was doing? Was that what they all did to get by in this fucked-up line of work? Clyde thought again about pestering Rose for that ride back home, and his Brooklyn apartment, and the comic shop, and his whole life and passion, which all felt so despairingly hollow and meaningless now. He thought about how much he wanted to call his mom, just to see how she was doing. His fingers went to the worry creases above his brow, as if feeling for the soul thread wagging about like an unearthed worm.

'Do you still want to see if you can hitch any more souls to your thread?' Spector asked, a flicker of empathy in his gaze.

Clyde pondered this seriously, trying to think through his anger. The silence in the room went unbroken. Clyde wondered how long it would take him to weather the Median. More than a day, that was for certain. A week? Two? A month? Shit, he thought.

'If Stephen and my dad are in some hell, then of course I do. I can't leave them there. Even if all I can offer them is a few more years away from that place, it's got to be worth something.' His stormy gaze drifted back to the Sleeping Shepherd. 'Shit, man. All I wanted to do was draw comics.'

'I know, man,' Kev consoled. 'I know.'

9

'**How could he just drop** that on us?' Clyde asked. He said "us," but the "me" was unmistakable.

Clyde and Rose sat in a parked jeep atop Indigo Mesa, with Kev waiting outside, sitting cross-legged on the hood and staring off peacefully at the gun turrets along the walls and the organized activities of the passing agents and staff. Rose had driven them up the too-many-ramps-to-count of the Mesa's interior parking structure until the fiery afternoon light poured through the windshield like a blast furnace. The surface of this huge tabletop reminded Clyde more of a retail park than what he imagined a military base to be: smooth, paved blacktop between the spaced-out hangars and buildings; corporate-type water features arranged in long concrete pools kept behind metal railings; wedges and strips of neat green lawn dotted about the place; light posts and barbed chain-link fencing around the distant perimeter. If not for the armed guards and concrete security towers, Clyde could pretend he was going to some desert mall. The north, south, and eastern surroundings of the mountain range were a colorful and interesting blend of grassland, woodland, and layers of dry rock.

Rose didn't express too much regret over Clyde's distress, just enough to make it seem like this was nothing more than a rite of passage. 'It wasn't any easier for me to hear. What you need to understand is that even if you still pass on us, you'll still be an unofficial member of the freak brigade.'

Up here, exposed beneath the vaulted ceiling of sparse white-cotton clouds and persistent sun, Clyde thought about the wise and the vindictive mighty beings that now, officially, didn't exist up in that foamy heaven. 'Yeah, well, it still just kind of sucked the joy out of living for me.'

Even in the interior shade of the jeep with the windows down, the warm breeze still felt like a dying man's breath attempting to circulate the muggy heat. Soft snatches of back-and-forth conversation rode the currents as agents and USAF pilots from Darnell crossed the flagstones from one building to another.

'That's one way to look at it,' Rose said, brushing a curl of silver hair behind her ear.

'And another would be?'

She shrugged, going for a glass-half-full approach. 'It makes you appreciate being alive.'

Clyde caught himself before he rolled his eyes at the sentiment. 'Awesome. Roughly seventy years of appreciation followed by endless misery. You know, I was cool with my thinking that the lights go out and then there's nothing. It wouldn't be my first choice, but...' He raised a hand and then dropped it redundantly. 'Maybe you think knowing the truth would make me appreciate life more, but honestly, I'm more scared now, because now I know what's really coming. It's like being stuck on a roller coaster you know is going to fly off the track at the next loop.'

The sun's rays filtered through Kev's back with a blue tint. It made Clyde think of the time he went on a family vacation to Miami. Sitting on the bottom of the pleasantly warm swimming pool, staring up through the shimmering surface at the probing Florida sunbeams.

'He's been very chill about all this.' He turned his head to Rose. 'It's freaking me out a little.'

Rose's slender, strong hands kneaded the steering wheel idly, as though navigating her through her own experience of Clyde's novel situation. 'When I came here from the hospital, I felt... Lucky is the wrong word. I don't know, enlightened? I lost three friends and found them again. It fucked me up thinking about the fact that they're dead, that their old lives, their families and dreams were all over, but knowing that there was something else after this gave all four of us a kind of hope. Like maybe life is only the beginning. So when Spector told me that I was right about that, but then ignorant of so much else, any comfort the afterlife gave me quickly turned to dog shit.' Clyde was rapt, waiting to hear how she came about her big secret to cope with the thought of burning eternally.

Instead, she compromised. 'Doing this job, you learn that the Null is hope. Things can get FUBAR for you over there,' she said, her head shaking with finality. 'But just like any war, souls can run, and fight, and survive. It's potluck, but that's all we get in life too, so what's the difference? In the Null there's a fighting chance, and that's enough for me to cling to.'

'Running forever? Fighting forever?' Clyde shook his head. He wasn't overjoyed at the prospect, but this talk of defiance in the face of death at least had him engaged. 'You guys must have something. Some strategy. What about those stones you mentioned on the plane? Or Spector and his creepy-ass bottle collection? Isn't there a way to create some better alternative?'

Rose almost seemed to pity his naïveté. 'Yeah, of course there is. We'll just stop death. Open a PLE rest home, stockpile billions of magic rocks and gizmos from now until forever, all for the recently departed to R and R in.'

Clyde deflected the ribbing with a hand, trying to bite down on the smile that was dragging up one corner of his mouth. He felt so profoundly superfluous. 'You can tease me all you like; I don't see how that sounds much crazier than any of the rest of this.'

Rose let her laugh trail off, sounding like she needed it. In truth they both did. She stared out of the driver's window and watched a black chopper take off from the helipad platform in the far west corner of the mesa, buzzing northwest across the blue-and-gold horizon like a fly. She cocked an eye at Kev, who could be meditating for all his lack of activity. 'Stones, bottles, books, any trinket you care to name, they can hold a soul, but they're all just holding patterns. I don't know about you, but if I had to choose between being dropped into enemy territory with a scrapper's chance, or being kept in some empty shell where I can do nothing but think about how much I miss everything I've lost, I'd take the former. Ten times out of ten.'

Clyde leaned his head back against the seat, heat-drained, feeling the sweat gum his Tshirt to his back. 'You're a soldier.'

'You can be too.' She let that sit with him for a moment. Clyde remained still, his eyes moving from the exit wound in Kev's back to the busy activity zigging and zagging across the compound. 'You're right, this is crazy. And you still don't know the half of it. I'm not sure if anybody does. There's a lot of mysteries out there. Maybe we'll still find our sunset to ride into one day.'

Clyde slowly turned to look at her, feeling the hook that had snagged his wayward attitude. He wasn't becoming no damn soldier, but maybe learning a bit more might alleviate his bellyful of tangled tension.

'You want to see something cool?'

'Will it make me more depressed or less depressed?'

She whacked him on the shoulder playfully, and Clyde could quite easily imagine her pulling his arm out of its socket with some playful wrestling. She swung herself out of the jeep, eager to change this scene of morbid reflection. Clyde watched her hip-check the door closed and march off towards one of the huge curvilinear buildings that could have fallen straight out of a Frank Lloyd Wright blueprint: lots of tall reflective glass walls and interesting geometric masonry.

Clyde stepped out of the jeep and paused, seeing Kev still sitting on the hood. What did Spector—or Ramaliak—see inside his friend's dream? Was it something troublesome? Is that why Kev was acting so strangely distant right now?

'You know, I wish you'd stop causing such a scene; you're embarrassing me.' Clyde leaned on the heat-absorbed hood of the white jeep. Kev smiled wistfully, making no judgement about his friend's hysterical reaction in Spector's office. 'Is it true what you said, about coming back and knowing that there was only Erebus and nothing else? You have no other memories?'

Kev uncrossed his legs and found himself waist-deep in the engine block. 'I didn't know anything, it was just this sensation, like a hangover. Like I was pulled from a bad dream instead of a good one.'

'And you still want to stick this out?'

Kev's eyes contained a hard-won peace. 'I didn't even know I could still dream. Been too scared to close my eyes again. When Ramaliak entered my dreams, you know what my nightmare was?' Clyde waited. 'That I'll waste my eternity in the same way I wasted my life.' A furrow scooped his brow. 'You still heading back to Brooklyn?'

"Brooklyn," Clyde noted, not home. Standing up here above Bosque Peak, surveying the 360-degree panoramic view of the distant sun-baked horizon and feeling like this whole place was a raised monument being offered up to the dead gods, he felt his obstinate need to fly back dulled slightly. 'Not just yet. I need to get my head right. And I want to see if Ramman can help me pull Stephen and my dad out of that place. That's a new one, huh?'

'As chores go, it tops running out of milk.' Unasked questions circulated behind Kev's eyes, and Clyde knew they were of a sensitive nature.

'I won't be replacing you. That's not what this is. You know that, right?'

'At this point I know very little.' Kev tried for a smile. 'But I'm interested in seeing where this goes.'

Clyde tilted his head towards the building where Rose was waiting. She was no longer alone. Sergeant Connors and Privates Darcy and Barros had entered the visible spectrum, returning from their base camp between worlds. The three of them looked at ease, discussing something trivial with Rose.

'You want to see something cool?' Clyde asked.

• • •

WATCHING ROSE BENCH-PRESS a Humvee actually was pretty cool.

The gym was a huge open space, littered with scrap iron—and a busted Humvee—in addition to the more conventional machines and barbells for regular agents. Clyde thought the surrounding huge glass walls would have turned the place into a boiling greenhouse, but the glass was tinted enough to absorb the blistering rays while still offering plenty of natural light.

As Rose knocked out the reps with ease, Clyde decided it was more than pretty cool, it was a much-needed distraction from the headache-load of what-ifs crashing about the insides of his head. Her sheer display of vitality, of life, helped push the gloom back for Clyde until he was grinning like an idiot. A quicksilver thought, like a distant seagull gliding over dark shores, seemed to tell him that this kind of impossibility was the very reason he adored comic-books and fantasy. Accomplishing what the dull rigidity of reality could not. And yet here it was in all its glory. Rose, a strong woman in life, now super-powered by her connection to death, curling and pressing almost four tons of crushing military hardware.

Rose lowered the machine with a joyous endorphin high. 'Okay, Casper, let's see what you can lift.'

Kev appeared a little daunted by the challenge, meeting her eye and then those of her fallen buddies. A giddy excitement seemed to rush through him as he picked up the gauntlet. Clyde thought back to the attempted mugging last night in the park, where Kev flung the thugs about like trash on the breeze. A Humvee, though? He had never attempted to push anything so high profile. He crossed his arms, captivated by this; now that they were away from the fear of being noticed and ostracized by the torchbearer-and-pitchfork crowd, he was curious as to what he and Kev might actually be able to accomplish together. Kev shook his arms out and slapped his palms together a few times, giving Clyde a look that seemed to say, I got this. He certainly tried his best. With a few constipated groans and juddering hand signals, the Humvee bounced on its shocks; it might have even squeaked a few inches across the stone floor.

'Impressive,' Rose chided, clapping her hands. Sergeant Connors and Privates Darcy and Barros added their own sarcastic motivation.

'Not bad, sweetheart,' said Connors.

Darcy wolf-whistled, swinging his guts about his head like a revolting crepe streamer. Kev took it all in stride. Clyde recognized the look on Kev's face; it was the look he always wore when he read something insightful, or when Clyde started to tell him about a cool job he'd been commissioned, or when he'd bought a bag of weed and a video game to fill up his weekend. It was the look of delightful preoccupation. Kev could be a paradox in that sense. For someone who struggled when faced with down time and his own thoughts, he sure enjoyed getting his head lost in the clouds. But now he had the simple, pure fulfillment of a physical task to fixate on.

'Yuck it up, assholes. I'll get there.' Kev grinned with exertion.

'That's why you're here, right?' Barros encouraged, floating legless like she was strung up on wires from the high ceiling.

Rose's competitive humor drained a little as she looked at Clyde. She told Connors and company to spot Kev for a minute and had a quiet aside with Clyde. 'Exercise is a great way to relieve stress, but I'm not trying to sell you a workout program here, so here's the catch. Since Kev wants to enlist, there might be a small complication. A compromise.'

Ah, fuck. Here we go. Clyde kept his lips sealed and listened.

'Remember your first day of high school?'

That was a curve ball. Clyde did remember it: the typical unease and resentment of institutionalized education. But Brooklyn High School of the Arts wasn't so bad, except it would have been a whole lot better if Stephen hadn't died a few years before, leaving Clyde in a numbing fog. Making matters somewhat worse was the fact that Kev had been in a different school.

'When I was in school,' Rose continued, 'I was a small girl. Frail, you know. Quiet too. And I was chum for all the big fishes. All those cheerleading cunts. They made my life hell for that first year, right up until I got sick of their shit. I got into weight training through a friend of my dad's, and although that didn't stop the name-calling, me kicking every shade of shit out of the lead bitch did. My point is, the Null is like the ultimate first day of high school. Loud, confusing, scary. They say when new souls first arrive, they're as helpless as kittens. But they can still sort their shit out when they touch down over there, clear their heads if given time. So it helps if you know how to survive and push back. Look at my guys.' Clyde shot them a glance, seeing them spur Kev on as he worked hard on that first aneurysm, trying to at least rock the Humvee's suspension.

'They may be dead, but they're still the same guys they were before they died. They're still trained soldiers who know how to fight. I'm not filling out your license-to-kill application here. You're still a civilian. But for your own sake, don't you at least want to be a hard, gristly meal for when you do wash up in the Null?'

Clyde stuffed his hands in his pockets, deeply unhappy with the sudden feeling of being conscripted.

Her tone changed, going from helpful advice to cardinal rule. 'Okay, how can I put this...? When you leave here and go back to your peaceful life of doodling and jacking-off to cosplay chicks, or whatever you geeky types do, and let's say Kev makes it to field agent status, he's going to make some enemies. Hourglass' enemies. If he becomes too much of a pain in the ass for some bad motherfucker, what'd be the easiest way to take him out of the game?'

Clyde was appalled at how he'd never considered this sooner. 'Oh, fuck!'

'"Oh, fuck" is right.'

'I'm going to be a walking target?' Clyde terrorized himself with queasy thoughts of not making it to the end of the year. 'But you said you offer protection for guys who don't join the team. Doesn't that include some enhanced measures for this sort of thing?'

Rose's honesty didn't lend much comfort. 'It does, if you want to spend the rest of your days in a safehouse or being routinely monitored. Never being able to walk down the street with ease. And then there's this.' Her weight sagged back onto one horse-muscled leg. 'The threats we face, sometimes a safehouse isn't going to cut it.'

Clyde felt as though his stomach was in a plummeting elevator. What if they went after loved ones too? He thought about his mom leaving the hospital and being dragged into a car or onto the back of a flying demon or whatever weird shit Hourglass agents had to face. He stared hard at the ground, wanting to burn this whole fucking place down. He'd been right all along; these assholes had had him by the balls ever since Rose knocked on his door.

'So what's your solution?'

'We train you to a capable standard, make you a hard target should the worst come knocking. Officially you'll remain a civilian, but really you'll be a reserve, with twenty-four/seven access to our services anywhere in the world. It's that or live your life as a damsel in distress, hoping that if the shit goes down, our surveillance team makes it to you in time.'

Irrational thoughts blared loudly in Clyde's head. He wanted to have strong words with Kev for wanting this, but it wasn't Kev's fault. It was his. His own messed-up genetics or magic blood or gypsy's curse; who the fuck knew? Point was, it was because of him that Kev was back here in the first place. But wasn't that an accidental blessing, and if so, did he really owe Kev anything else? Was it fair for Clyde to throw his own life away and become a reserve soldier against his will?

Rose must have seen the turmoil roiling across Clyde's face. 'If not for you, then do it for Kev's sake. We need all the reliable assets we can get our hands on, and knowing that Kev won't have some huge weak spot walking around out there, buying a latte with his ass in the wind, would help calm a lot of nerves.'

Clyde sighed, a long, draughty acceptance. Rose didn't rush him. Clyde thought of Stephen and his dad, dying in the dust on their own bullshit missions that accomplished nothing. But they were soldiers. Warriors, no matter how worthless their sacrifice. He thought about the possibility of knotting them to his soul thread. Seeing Stephen's face again, meeting his dad for the first time. What would they think if they learned he was too mulish and selfish to go through basic training to help out his best friend? A friend who could perhaps one day save some innocent lives. He imagined the shame of letting them both down.

'Okay,' Clyde finally chose. He hated how that answer rolled off his tongue. 'If I do this, how long will it take? A couple of months?'

Rose nodded vaguely. 'There and there about. You don't necessarily need to be fully combat-ready, just capable. But who knows, if you're anything like the rest of your family, you might breeze through it.'

'I want insurance that mine and Kev's families are protected.'

'Standard. No paper trails. You'll leave here a—' Rose almost blundered into a pun, 'excuse the expression, a ghost. You were never here, you return to your civilian life, and if Kev doesn't buckle in his training, we'll torch any and all documented connection he has to you.'

It quickly dawned on Clyde that such a monumental redaction of their history could well draw their friendship to a permanent close. He had to talk to Kev. He needed to know if he had thought this all the way through and hadn't been swept up in all the excitement.

'And would I be correct in guessing that my training starts now?'

Rose was about to answer when another voice beat her to it.

'Okay, rookie, let's go punch things till we feel better.' Ace stood at the entrance. He seemed a bit livelier in the air-conditioning.

For some indiscernible reason, Ace, the agent with no previous military background, seemed to put Clyde off the idea of training more than the formerly enlisted squad of four standing by. Something about the offer to get his ass beaten by a big, hairy Canadian with frosty mallets for hands worried Clyde. He had hesitated too long in answering, long enough for Ace to cross the gym floor, looking ready to completely bypass Clyde on his way to the adjoining room.

'Christ, kid, suit yourself.'

'Yo, hang on,' Clyde called, catching Ace before he could push through the glass doors into the boxing gym. The hell am I doing? Clyde cried out in his panicked mind. Rose's words rode over his own violated values, her opinion that a fighting chance in the Null was better than no chance at all. His legs had started carrying him before he had time to question how effective learning to brawl would actually be against monsters from the pit. But what about the monsters in this world? Shit, he could have been killed by a couple of muggers last night, so what if his association with Kev had him attacked by some real threats in the future? He threw a helpless look at Kev, who had briefly paused in his own struggles with the Humvee to watch Clyde and Ace's interaction play out, a pleased smirk on his face.

'This'll clear your head,' Rose called after Clyde.

Clyde glanced back at her but stayed quiet, carrying on towards the boxing gym. The proverb Iron Sharpens Iron was painted above the glass doors. He paused at the threshold, hearing Kev rattle the Humvee a few more inches across the floor, and Rose telling him to stop, directing him towards the weight racks instead. 'I was only busting your balls,' he overheard her say to Kev. 'Like building muscle, you need to start off small.'

Gathering himself, Clyde pushed through the doors. Inside the boxing ring, two sweat-soaked agents in 12-ounce gloves and shin guards were trading punches and kicks, their grunts and thudding shots audible over a steady electronic dance beat. A squad of agents were grappling on some of the open mats.

Clyde didn't want to be in here. Over the years he'd known a few nerds who could fight, including his brother, Stephen, but his own personal level of bullying had never reached the heights where it forced him to get good at it. Stephen had taught him some basics, which he himself had picked up from their dad, but Clyde only half-remembered them. Ace led him past the ring just as one of the combatants caught hold of an incoming round kick to the body and fired back a right cross with enough on it to drop his opponent like a bag of cement.

Ace led Clyde past a long row of punch bags and taller kick bags, only several agents were currently pounding away on them, towards the changing rooms, stopping to grab a pair of black shorts and a tank top from the stocked shelves. He tossed them to Clyde. 'They should fit.'

Clyde went into autopilot in the changing room. His thoughts and doubts and fears became nothing but a distant white noise as he changed into the training gear. After several minutes of steady breathing and staring into space, he walked out to meet Ace on an empty training mat.

'You ever had any fights before?' Ace asked.

'Some stupid high school shit,' Clyde mumbled, feeling ridiculous.

'It's a start. It doesn't need to be Madison Square Garden. Even if you get your ass kicked, you learn about yourself. Those high school fights, what did you learn about yourself?' Clyde caught the pair of MMA gloves Ace tossed at him. Ace gave off this formidable and ambiguous aura that seemed to declare an ability to be either protector or destroyer, depending on how you dealt with him. Clyde didn't want to make him the latter, especially in this proving ground.

'I . . . ' He faltered, fearing what he said next might soon be sought after in training. 'I don't quit easy. Even if I'm getting my ass kicked.'

Ace barely reacted, his countenance stone. 'That's the most important part. You can teach someone all the fighting technique in the world, but being a pussy? Some stuff doesn't wash out.'

Clyde heard the thuds and gasps of breath from the fighters in the ring, and the heavy punishment still being doled out upon a few of the heavy bags by the other agents. 'That's some nice wisdom, sensei, but I'm not Blade. Can't we start off with some basics, like jogging?'

'Kid!' Ace was already losing patience, his arms hanging limp in exasperation. 'I'm just trying to sweat out the booze.' He walked over to the sound system on a shelving unit near the boxing ring, iPod in hand. 'You guys mind if I shut this shit off?' he asked the sparring partners. Neither objected. He placed his iPod in the empty dock and hit play: "Limelight" by Rush started up. He slipped his large hands into a pair of well-used focus mitts, their leather split and peeling in parts, and walked back over to Clyde's mat.

'Okay. We'll go easy,' Ace said. 'This is just a warm-up. Now put the gloves on and let me see your stance.'

Clyde muttered a string of barely heard disapproval but slipped his hands into the MMA gloves. 'Okay,' he acquiesced. 'Fine, see?' He showed his gloved hands. 'But I told Titania out there that I'm only doing this to become a reserve, or whatever. I'm not signing up to get the official Hourglass T-shirt.'

'No fucks given.' Ace sounded sincere enough. 'Put your hands up.'

Clyde speared a quick glance through the glass wall into the weights room, seeing Kev. It was the happiest he had seen him in a while, twirling a 160-kilogram barbell through the air like an amateur baton twirler, with Rose and her squad cheering him on. Clyde was happy for him. Kev belonged here. As for himself, maybe learning some fundamentals might help keep the waiting hounds of Hell from sinking their teeth into his ass one day. He adopted the boxing stance Stephen had taught him long ago, orthodox, and showed Ace his basic jab, cross, hook.

It needed work.

10

HAVING SPENT AN HOUR DOING push-ups, crunches, and squats, and reacquainting himself with the fundamentals of boxing, Clyde had burned off his restless emotional energy, finding a new calm clarity to his thoughts. Following the impromptu workout, he still remained dubious of the efficacy of a pretty respectable jab-cross-hook combination against whatever creatures dwelt in hell, but who knows, maybe it'd leave him in good stead against any earthbound agents of Kev's future enemies. Moreover, he now found himself too tired to care much. Ace had said as much during the early steps of their boxing combinations. You hit something until you're too tired to give a shit. Works every time. Clyde thought it was a crude pearl of wisdom, likely prized from a busted and unwanted clam, but shit, it didn't make it any less true.

Sometimes all you could do was punch yourself silly until your troubles no longer seemed to matter.

He was hungry, though. Starving, in fact. Showered, dressed in his own clothes again, and with muscles stiff with pleasurable pain, he sat across from Ace in the mess hall, forking scrambled eggs and toast into his mouth like a man who hadn't eaten in days. Clyde still found his eyes repeatedly drifting off to the enormous glass wall and the cantilever that overlooked the depressed vehicle deck and the giant throat of the cavern curving off for what he imagined to be untold miles into watery darkness, the strip lights and power lines chasing the dark mystery.

Still choking down his much-needed protein, he swallowed and managed to squeeze out his curiosity before the next bite. 'That where Bookworm came from?' He remained surprised at his own casualness, broaching such a topic as though asking Ace if he'd watched any good TV shows lately. Outside of the grueling workout, Ace had shut down communication again. When he wasn't insulting Clyde about his technique or lack of strength and/or stamina, he seemed quite adept at losing himself in his own headspace. Clyde wasn't sure if Ace was thinking of paths not taken, maybe envisioning himself lifting the Stanley Cup in some an alternate life, or maybe just the joys of beating the snot out of hard-asses on the ice, but he found himself inexplicably comfortable in the company of the big knuckle-dragger. Even if he wasn't on board with the guy's penchant for 1980s rock and metal music.

Ace's eyes barely moved from the sports news website on his phone. 'No.'

That was it. Mystery solved then. Clyde almost choked on a bite of toast and did his best not to draw attention to himself. Ace paid no mind. The huge hall was only about a quarter full, maybe fifty or so agents coming or going. He made a conscious effort to chew slowly, concerned that he could choke to death and earn a quick pass to the Null—he quickly swapped out the Hourglass colloquialism for Erebus—shuttled in with all the other sad bastards who slipped on bars of soap or walked in front of buses while tweeting on their phones. The Embarrassing Death Economy Line. 'Where's that tunnel go?'

With weary disgust, Ace scrolled through the news articles reporting on the Rangers' trouncing of the Maple Leafs the previous night. He opened a new article regarding whatever else was new in the wide world of sports and answered with more tantalizing abstraction. 'What, back there? That's where the hoodoo live.'

Clyde allowed his food to digest; at least his body was being sustained, if not his curiosity. 'And they are . . . ?'

'Who, the hoodoo?'

'Jesus! Is this still part of the workout?' He squinted, wondering if all conversation with this guy was akin to bleeding a stone. 'Yeah, hoodoo. Who do they be?'

Ace grinned, slow as a glacier. 'They're the ones who started all this. Hourglass. Them and Director Trujillo.'

'And they live in a cave?'

'It's a nice cave. And it holds the Hourglass.'

'There's an actual Hourglass? I thought it was some symbolic thing, or an acronym or something.' Ace kept his nose to the sports news on his phone screen. Clyde almost sighed impatiently but caught himself. 'So, what is it?'

'A big pair of glass bulbs filled with sand.'

If Ace was happy to play the obstinate prick, then Clyde was happy to play the plucky enthusiast, if only to work on his nerves. 'Do I get to see these things? Are they people? What's a hoodoo?'

Ace calmly placed his palms down on the table. 'Only if you plan on becoming an agent. Even then, they're not some tourist trap you can snap a picture with before flying home. And they're people, of sorts. Higher beings is probably more accurate. They look like hoodoos. You know, those large, skinny rock columns—skinnier than you—that are scattered all over the place topside. Like them, but sort of human-shaped.'

'Humanoid.'

'Whatever.'

'And the Hourglass is what? Some way of tracking weirdos like us?' Clyde was sorely tempted to use the word "superheroes," but somewhere between his love of comic-books and his lingering indecisiveness about his own ability, he felt weirdo was more apt.

'Fucking hell, rook, I'm not the tour guide. Stick around and go pro, maybe you'll learn. Or ride the bench and don't.' Ace looked a little remorseful for his aggression. At least Clyde thought he did. If he did decide to stick around, maybe he'd discover a wide assortment of facial nuances to read him by.

'I kind of have to stick around for Kev's sake. At least for a little longer,' Clyde said. 'And until Spector gives me a full write-up of what I can do.' He crossed his knife and fork on his empty plate and leaned back in his chair, looking past Ace to the cavern outside.

Ace considered this without any real feeling. 'So what's it like in there? The dream space.'

Clyde gave him the shrug-off, not wanting to divulge his dreams to him. 'You've never been in?'

'I'm not carrying the dead around.' He frosted his fist until it looked like dense glass, a heavy mist orbiting it and cascading down in waves to the table and floor. 'Remember? That means there's no need for me to see the Median.'

'That's right. You're something different, aren't you?'

'Yeah, I'm Canadian.'

'Did Rose tell you about her time there?'

Ace rolled his eyes to the top of his skull, looking like he was haggling with a difficult car salesman. 'What is this? I'm not a card-carrying member of the sleepover club, so you can't share it with me? Stop being a dick tease and tell me what it's like in there.'

Clyde threw his hands up, not knowing what to say to him. 'It's a dream, man. You might be a walking beer cooler, but you still have dreams, don't you? Well, imagine having one about something you're too scared to admit you want to happen, except you got some strange goat dude sniffing about the place and trying to figure out how many dead people you can channel.'

'Goat dude?' Ace no longer seemed that interested. 'I'll stick with porn star threesomes.' He gave that some real thought. Probably swapping porn starlets around for his dream team, or maybe just adding more to the mix.

They sat in a companionable silence for a moment.

Something occurred to Clyde. A random thought, the germ of which had nestled in his headspace when Rose had recommended that he should train. 'I know you're only "Canadian," but do you know if there are guns in Erebus?'

Guns. Clyde hated them. But he knew that if some rotting beast was going to chomp his ass, he'd rather have one and not need it than need one and not have it.

'Only those you take over on the job. But I mainly kick ass for the home team, so I don't have much experience over there.' Ace's boisterous rough-guy side seemed to soften a little. 'Who knows, maybe after you get a face full of dirt you'll find a whole damn arsenal over there. Who's to say? Me, I'm just hoping that when my time finally comes, I get to stay cold as ice, you know what I mean?'

Clyde quietly picked up his knife, rotating its blade on the table, his thoughts trailing off. 'It makes me think about whether they both took their guns over there with them when they died. Ghost versions of them, or something like that. I don't even know if that sounds stupid anymore.'

'Your brother and your pa?'

'And if it helped them any when they got there.'

Ace didn't respond at first, the soft sounds of mingled chatter and cutlery on plates filling the space. 'Don't dwell on it, rook. The Null gets us all, but when you're there you can at least go down swinging. And I'll bet they did too ... if they had to.'

Clyde remembered his phone hadn't been returned to him yet. Security, confidentiality, et cetera. Surely he had earned some minor trust by now. He'd signed enough non-disclosure agreements, that was for sure. He wanted to check his email. And he still wanted to call his mom but decided a text might be best, not wanting to wake her up if she was on the night shift. Or maybe he should wait to see if he could make any progress with Spector first. Imagine that. He fantasized about pulling Stephen and his dad out of hell. Would he tell her if he could? Should he? Or would that only break her heart? Spitting in the face of dignity and the natural order. Maybe he'd be as good as dead to her if he conjured their embattled, war-torn selves from the other side.

'Can I get my phone back?'

Just like that, Ace reached into the pockets of his cargo pants and slid it across the table. He must have claimed it sometime before the gym session, when Clyde was snoozing in Spector's office. 'Knew I was forgetting something.' He closed the sports news on his phone. 'There are cell signal repeaters built within this slab of rock, even down here. You can talk and text, use the net, just don't be Instagramming your time in here. But you're not that stupid, are you?'

Clyde broached a question he was reluctant to ask. 'Will we be training with guns later today?'

'No. We'll get to guns tomorrow morning,' Ace explained. 'It's your first day. That's why we're being so nice to you.'

Was that relief Clyde felt? Trepidation? He didn't know, but what he did know was that he didn't like guns. In movies and games and stuff they were cool. In real life not so much. But what choice did he have but to learn at this juncture in his life? He imagined a rabbit fighting wolves. A rabbit who knew a few dirty fighting moves.

11

Mortis hadn't been lying about the scale of their fledgling operation. Konstantin rolled his neck, taking in the enormous warehouse. The Cairnwood Society had purchased this block in Red Hook purely for this detail, and soon it would be ground zero for harvesting from the original merchants of death. The ultimate authority. Konstantin almost admired the single-minded arrogance of such an endeavor, for only the deluded and the stupid stole from such beings. He would know.

Haulage trucks were parked nearby, awaiting the first of many potential cargos of untapped ore and alchemical matter, flanked by forklift trucks and uniformed labor preparing for the operation, and all overseen by a squad of hired gunslingers high up in the catwalks or walking the building's perimeter, ready to pull the trigger should anything go sideways. The shooters were all outfitted in sophisticated body armor, advancements that had superseded the tactical gear that existed when Konstantin was still a part of the military industry. Their rifles looked positively futuristic compared to the weaponry he was acquainted with from the 1980s up until '91. They certainly stood out from the various Kalashnikovs of the Union, Britain's NATO-approved SA80, or the Heckler & Koch models of West Germany. A dusty file flipped open in his memory, recalling key snippets of information from NATO's 1989 preliminary specs within their D/296 document: this ubiquitous model—assuming it was the same one these particular guards carried and not some tweaked variant—were FN P90s, a compact sub-machine gun with reflex sight and selective fire: semi, burst fire, or full auto. Manufactured by Fabrique Nationale Herstal, a Belgian manufacturer owned by the Herstal Group holding company. Described as personal defense weapons (PDWs), they were designed between the years of 1986 and 1990 and became a new service weapon in '91, right when Konstantin was on the run from a cyclopean Major Morozov.

NATO had requested a more compact cartridge than the then-current 9x19 mm Parabellum rounds to allow for a larger magazine capacity of at least twenty rounds. The manufacturers at Herstal obliged, creating a cartridge of 5.7x28 mm dimensions, with this reduced diameter actually allowing for the even larger magazine capacity of fifty rounds. The finished product now had reduced recoil while allowing for the penetration of up to a level 3A Kevlar vest.

Strange what information tended to stick, Konstantin thought glumly.

The patrolling heavies also had battery-operated CompM4 red-dot sights affixed to their rifles, a model of reflex sight with which Konstantin also had no familiarity, but he knew their type: they were simply another successor to an earlier model. Their sidearms looked to be a model of Glock, fitted with another technological feature he was unfamiliar with: EOTech holographic sights. He noticed that the guards also carried marked magazines on their belts. A specially developed cartridge. Talbot's earlier threat parted his gray matter like a bullet. Exorcist rounds. Filled with a special substance that could allegedly incapacitate or even kill spiritual entities. Developed by associates of Cairnwood, the good people at Aristov Ballistics. Konstantin knew of Aristov Ballistics, another defense contractor that raised a toast to hostile neighbors.

Konstantin followed Mortis past a huddle of workers in high-visibility jackets and hard hats, one of whom was helping a haulage truck back up into the empty loading dock in preparation. He had expected to draw a few amused looks from the passing faces, sneers of mockery at his necronaut armor, whispered blue-collar cackles about fancy dress parties or some such. Nobody, neither labor nor security, so much as batted an eyelid at him. It made him wonder if their polite behavior was paid for or if they were all accustomed to Cairnwood contracts and their eccentric associates.

Then he reminded himself of Mortis' hands, ten keys swinging casually at his sides, and the reason they were all here in this giant brick block that had until recently served as nothing more than a hotel for rats and pigeons.

Mortis led him to the rear of the building. A wide shoulder-high platform had been erected in the center of the floor, taking up much of the room's area. It was made of simple steel grating, with several sets of steel risers arranged at certain points along the flanks, and one wide ramp for the vehicles. Konstantin knew it was a staging platform without needing to be told.

Mortis took the risers to the top and did a quick realtor's presentation of the utilitarian platform. 'This is where I open the doorway,' he said, five keys waving at empty air. 'This platform creates a bottleneck with plenty of clear shots for our security, should anything unwholesome attempt to walk through. And the ramp makes easy access for our fleet of vehicles.'

'Talbot isn't here. Speak freely. Tell me you aren't as naïve, as stupid, as him?' Konstantin didn't bother to try and hide his severe criticism. 'You think we just walk into kingdom of dead and take whatever catches eye? And I thought your organization had been around long enough to develop brain.'

Mortis smiled, his cracked, pale lips resembling a reptile. 'Those few tattered maps you saw aren't the be-all and end-all of Cairnwood's knowledge. You best believe it. And I don't mind admitting that I'm not yet privy to the big picture of Erebus. But that day'll come.'

'I know slave when I see one.'

'Don't presume I'm a novice.' He inspected his keys as one might inspect for dirt under one's fingernails. 'We've already established a base camp over there, manned in rotating shifts by a dependable company of our private security. These armed guards,' his gray, boiled-egg eyes rolled about in his sockets at the present company of troops, 'are only here to protect against any local trespassers or external threats. Captain Agua, however, and his lieutenants offer us a more robust force, and they're currently stationed at the base camp to reconnoiter a defensible perimeter. They've successfully held the location, even fighting off a few skirmishes from the local riffraff. They're more than capable of handling the task they've been assigned. And we have you to help, of course; your map and your experience with the region.'

Konstantin could feel his passengers grow restless within his core. And the other one, that black, oily maggot sleeping dormant in his soul, attenuated within the housing of his blessed armor; but would it find new reserves of strength when they returned to its native world? He shook his head, so slightly as to be hardly noticeable.

'You have it all figured out, then. I'm sure Talbot and whoever signs checks will have nothing to worry about. But answer me: You really think Vor Dushi is all you need be concerned about? You're stealing resources from death lords. This won't go unnoticed by the Order's nine houses. You think their reach doesn't extend out to living world?'

A look of mild confusion lowered Mortis' eyebrows. 'That's rich, coming from you. Wasn't your whole sect founded on the theft of souls from a being you had the unfortunate irony of naming Vor Dushi? Soul Thief?'

Konstantin didn't share the wry amusement. 'Vor Dushi is just another prison warden. A serf for his House's lord, and I pledge no piety to the Order who merely rob humanity of light, casting their energy, their purity, into wind and darkness. But where your lot are thieves stealing from thieves for personal gain, the Rising Path strive to return the suffering souls to safe intermediary. There is a way to better place. I only need to find it. And when I do, I'll have the divine power to challenge the nine Houses of the Order of Terminus.'

'I've heard of your fairy tales. They sound just like a dozen others,' Mortis jeered. Konstantin allowed him his ignorance, knowing full well that he'd heard nothing of the Path's lore and the glory they knew of. For if Talbot himself was hazy on the finer details, his screeching pet monkey here was utterly oblivious. 'You know what's a good, proven way to scrape out a better future? Commerce. Wealth.'

'Temporary. Short-sighted solution for the benign. Where will your riches get you when your soul is thrown before their mercy? Because they won't barter in gold.'

'Don't you worry about my eternal soul, holy man. You worry about failing the Society.'

'Spare me your hollow threats. You can open the doors, but you're nothing but glorified concierge. A bondsman to watch over me. You have my map, but can you be sure of its accuracy? You need my knowledge of Eidolon Trench. And there's something else, something inside me, acts as early warning system in presence of Vor Dushi. It's a mark of great shame for me, but also something of a tactical relief. We're heading into enemy territory to raid a concentration camp. Make no mistake. Sooner or later, the warden will pay us a visit.'

Mortis harrumphed. 'Then I'd recommend you listen to your gut and be sure to inform me when it arrives. Don't forget what will happen if you refuse to comply. I give the word, and you and your whole gulag of holy rollers will be blasted beyond death.'

Konstantin briefly mused what lay beyond death, if anything. Was there a dimension behind Erebus, governed by powers to whom even the Order of Terminus were beholden? Or was it only an absolute infinity of nothingness? He felt the uprising of a score or more residents clamoring within him, eager to lash out and test Mortis' imposition. He silently quelled the insurrection. This was not the time to test whether the Exorcist rounds were a bluff or a genuine cause for concern. Mortis clacked his ten keys together, creating a sound like hollow bird bones scraping together, the keys forming a steeple in thought, his hands then falling back to his sides as he called over the foreman of the excavation crew. The foreman trotted over, decked out in scuffed work boots and the same type of gray uniform overall worn by his workers, a tablet in one hand and a thermos of coffee in the other. The foreman met them on the platform; the name Hammond was stitched into his overall above the name of the construction firm, Sharp Industries.

Mortis beckoned Konstantin over with a head tilt, the three of them forming a loose triangle around Hammond's tablet. Introductions were not offered by Mortis. That was fine with Konstantin. He took note of the almost grayish tint of Hammond's anxious face and wondered how much these workers were being paid. Jittery Hammond cleared his throat to quash his nerves, his finger sweeping through a few official documents on his tablet, landing on a stored photograph of Konstantin's neat, hand-drawn map. It looked to be a lengthy and daunting expedition. Konstantin knew they had also printed and laminated a few copies of his map, so at least these people had the foresight to anticipate dead batteries.

'I heard you're knowledgeable about this place.' Hammond's thick Brooklyn accent carried the faint echo of a lost child hoping for guidance. 'So, this is where the military scouts set up the base camp,' he explained, his tablet's stylus pointing to a red circle several miles up the shoreline, set in a clearing surrounded by a few shaded squares, each one a mile long according to the scale at the bottom of the page. 'We had some trouble with these shaded areas—'

'Sickle wheat fields,' Konstantin stated.

Hammond seemed to be envisioning the "trouble" he and his staff had run into within those quadrants. 'A few of my men wandered into them. They were... err—they died.'

Konstantin thought about the sickle wheat. Tall corn stalks with husks shaped like crescents, shining like mercury in the eternal dusk and capable of scarring steel plating. When they brushed against one another in the breeze, they sounded like knife blades clashing together.

'We managed to bring their pieces back, along with a few samples of the "sickle wheat" we carefully uprooted. We were calling it thresher grass, but—' Hammond blinked, as if putting his bad memories back in the box, '—but sickles, yeah, that's better. We were planning on pushing north of the outpost to search for a way around these fields, but now that we have your map,' his stylus trailed west from the outpost's red circle and curved around and then up past the several miles of shaded squares of sickle wheat, 'we see this is a clearing. That correct?'

Konstantin felt some pity for this man, another proletariat roped into dangerous work for the enrichment of others. 'That's correct, Mr. Hammond.' Hammond nodded, a bead of sweat on his upper lip, and the dismemberment of co-workers haunting his gaze.

'With Erebus lacking satellite and cellular communication, we have yet to forward the map to Captain Agua, but we'll cross over shortly and update him and his teams in person. Then we can up sticks and be on our way,' Mortis said, checking his watch. He then let his eyes slide over Hammond like filthy well water. He dug four of his keys into the man's fleshy shoulder, dismissing him. Hammond shuffled off, taking a drink from his thermos, which was likely spiked with something more than simple caffeine.

Mortis walked to the rail and rousted several drivers of the well-financed paramilitary security force. Hammond did the same to several of his own crew members, ordering them to hurry up and finish their coffees and late dinners by way of sandwiches; several of the men were loading up crates of bottled water, tinned foods, cellophane-wrapped sandwiches, protein bars, and hygiene products.

'It's kind of exciting,' Mortis said. 'This'll be the new gold rush. The true last frontier.'

Konstantin kept thinking about Talbot's agenda and what Hammond had said about having already ferried over some bushels of sickle wheat, a basic plant with the capability of kerfing steel. One thought led to another: souls for the energy sector; marvelous elements for some skunk-works weaponry or research and development. What else? Would they start slipping shackles onto some of the foul creatures who slunk about in that dead ecosystem, wallowing in the despair of weak and frightened souls? Beasts ready to burden.

This was truly Pandora's box, and Mortis held the key.

• • •

From a discreetly positioned spot on top of an adjacent derelict warehouse, a team of covert operatives had watched Acton Mortis and Konstantin Kozlov enter the heavily guarded building. The observers took notes, recordings, but it wasn't yet time to act.

12

HAVING SPENT MOST OF THE session going over the rudimental art of lifting with Rose and her bangin' and clangin' ghost squad—absorbing their collective advice about focusing his power, gauging how much strength was needed, and how best to apply it to the weight correctly—Kev was ready to call it a day, feeling wiped out.

But Rose surprised him. 'Lift the Humvee.'

Kev gave her a tired smirk, expecting it was just Rose razzing him.

'Seriously,' she insisted. 'Give it a shot, then we'll call it quits.'

Kev stared at the Humvee. Just looking at the thing tired him. 'Wasn't the 160kilogram bar enough?'

'It was a great start. But why not just see what's left in your tank before you call it quits?'

Kev stared at the Humvee again. He imagined his hands extending like liquid, malleable appendages, sliding beneath the center of the chassis, then turning as hard as iron. His lip trembled; his whole form in fact, was shaking like a leaf. The Humvee didn't budge.

But he kept staring at it, his focus laser sharp. He pushed with everything he had, and it was like trying to move a mountain. And then he heard a metallic creak. He thought he might somehow kill himself with the strain he was under, but then, with a moan of absolute torment, he raised the Humvee. Six inches. Then dropped it onto its suspension with a loud bang.

Kev fell to his knees. He had no reason to gasp for breath, but his whole being still felt as though it wanted to.

Rose and her ghost squad cheered and joked and gave him a short round of applause as he got back to his feet. He drifted over to the Humvee and sat atop it, tingling with a warm contentedness. It was impossible to keep the dumb smile from stretching across his entire face. It was comparable to those first delicious seconds of waking from a wonderfully lucid dream before reality failed you. He had never been so exhausted, but it felt amazing, euphoric even. Could all this be real? Or was he still dreaming in Spector's office? Jesus, imagine that. Strangely, it made him think about what he had once read about the Furies in Greek mythology, and their Norse counterparts the Norns, the fates scripting the lives of all. Well, thankfully, Kev knew for certain he was fully awake and not asleep in Spector's chair, for if this wasn't the case, it would mean the Norns, the Fates, or whoever was scripting this crazy, batshit world were a bunch of sophomoric hacks. Yes, he was awake, no mistaking that, and he'd never felt so alive in death. This was real: this place, these people, this purpose.

'Not bad for a first attempt.' Sergeant Connors cut in on Kev's pleasant reverie, his bullhorn voice softer now that the workout war was won. 'What d'ya think, Rosie?'

Rose, who only five minutes ago had been grunting and slamming a huge spare tire like a medicine ball, still had energy to spare from the looks of it. 'Not bad, little man. How you feel?' Using a towel to wipe off her face and neck, her silver ponytail shone in the sunlight, her face alight with pleasure from endorphins.

Despite his fatigue, Kev didn't want to lose this sensation.

'A little tired, but ... ready to go again.' His blue-glass vibrancy had dulled somewhat, the same as last night after the foiled mugging in the park.

Connors regarded him with a stern, guiding expression, an experienced soldier aiding a new private without becoming matronly, his hand cupping his chin, the fingers tapping some of the errant metal studding his jaw and cheek. He was a big and imposing man of strictly functional physicality, not the showy bulge of Rose's obsessive weight training. He may not have had Rose's pedigree in that particular discipline, but he was still her ranking officer, and more pertinently, unlike her, Connors was an actual PLE. A ghost who knew about the cost of exertion. 'Slow down, son. You'll get there. Getting a Humvee six inches off the ground is a hell of a first day.'

Kev felt a great swell of pride at their praise but knew he couldn't let it go to his head. For a moment there he had almost started to berate himself for being weak and soft, and not doing enough to impress them.

'He's not wrong.' Rose sipped something from a bottle. It didn't look like water, some protein shake, likely. 'You don't want to overload yourself. Isn't that right, Barros?'

Barros, who had been built more for speed than mass, back when she still had legs below the mid-thigh, smirked her cocky smile at the remark. 'Laugh it up, lady-balls. I used to do a mean calf raise.'

'Not with those ol' bird legs of yours you didn't,' Darcy countered. The big farm boy knocked Barros' helmet over her eyes. 'All her speed came from running away from fights.'

The pair became background noise, ribbing each other, giving their mouths a workout since they couldn't actually lift anything without the catalyst of Rose's body.

Kev pictured his big moment again, freeze-framing his triumph, the satisfaction almost ineffable. The Humvee, slowly but surely rising six inches off the ground. It made his exhaustion feel so inconsequential. Tired? Who cares! Mind over matter, he coached himself, and oddly enough his motivated thinking seemed to replenish some of his spent energy. And it came so easily when he tried.

Clyde sprang into his thoughts again, and this time he stayed. Kev pictured him sitting behind the wheel of the Humvee he had just levitated, and for a moment the brightness of his success dimmed a little, and the return of the guilt suddenly made imaginary Clyde ten times heavier, adding too much mass and crashing the Humvee and Kev's pride back to earth. He remembered why the guilt was back. He had been meaning to ask what Rose had said to Clyde before he shrugged an acceptance and followed Ace into that gladiatorial pit. It couldn't just be Spector, and the possibility of reeling in Stephen and his dad, that had lit a fire under Clyde's ass. Rose must have said something to him to have him volunteer into getting boxed around the head by the terror of the minor leagues.

Unless...

Kev was astute enough to know that Clyde was and always had been shorthanded in the male role model department, with a dad who was cold under the ground before Clyde was even crawling upon it, leaving him with an older brother who did the best he could to teach Clyde the ways of navigating this scary life: how to be a good person, caring, respectful, smart, and a reliable friend. Kev liked Stephen for the short years that he had known him, thrilled at the fact that he was a cool older kid— a proud nerd, no less—who could drop a guy with a punch and took zero shit from anyone. But Stephen dying when Clyde was reaching that crucial and awkward teenage minefield had definitely left him out in the cold. Had the cold now unexpectedly brought him a temporary substitute in Ace?

Either way, Kev was happy Clyde was doing something instead of sticking his head in the sand. And if Spector could help him, it would ease his own sense of guilt for wanting to stay here. Was that selfish?

'Stretch it off,' Rose told Kev. 'Or, you know, float a victory lap around the place. I'm going to crush one more set.'

Kev had meant to ask her what she had talked to Clyde about, but she moved as smoothly as a jacked-up leopard back towards the tire, and the moment seemed to have passed. Barros and Darcy fell in behind her, erased in a blink, returning to their HQ inside Rose's soul, or muscles, or wherever the hell they lived.

'Sarge,' Kev asked, 'you must have seen a lot of people react to the news about the Null. Fellow agents and such. You think Clyde will get his head around it?'

'You're his buddy, you tell me.' Connors read Kev's face and decided to add a dash of optimism. 'I've seen worse. Rose, she took it in her stride, but she always did lock up her worries so tight you'd need a goddamn wrench to loosen 'em.' Connors paused a minute and stared out through the tinted windows at the hot blue desert sky over the Mesa. 'Shit, I think I took it worse. It all happens so quickly. Being brought back from the darkness and the confusion, you fool yourself with ideals. Tell yourself that you'd actually been in Heaven or some such, and maybe the reason you can't remember is because it was too glorious to bring back to this dirty old place. Then you're told that the reason you can't remember is because you were actually too young in death to wake up and experience that place. The goddamn Null. And you're going right back there the moment the person carrying you gets deep-sixed.'

'That means dead, right?'

The ungodly slam of Rose's tire assault continued to test the acoustics of the giant glass-and-concrete box.

Kev thought about his last earthly moments. Moments he'd painstakingly gone over time and again, more so than the great moments of his living years: fuck-buddy hook-ups with Alicia and what's-her-name; going to Prague with Clyde for his graduation; that pretty-okay family holiday to Paris; and a whole lot more—most, really—involving Clyde, and none of which really celebrated anything he himself had actually done or achieved. But pushing its way to the top of the pile every time was lying there on the floor of Hamza's corner store, staring up at the thin rail light with those few dead flies lying in it like a fluorescent tomb, the ugly ceiling tile with the water stain, snacks crowding his periphery, hearing whatever chart-topping turd was playing over the speakers. He didn't know how much thought people really gave to their final moments, but he knew that those who did wanted something better than what he'd had.

Bleak as it was, it led to his epiphany, which, under the circumstances, was only a classier way of saying trouble. This was his second chance, his opportunity to right all his wasted years, but truthfully, it was another celebration of Clyde and his innate ability to circumvent life, however slightly. Once again, Kev was only along for a ride on Clyde's coattails.

And he still didn't begrudge his friend. Not a single petty resentment crossed his mind.

Clyde had a vision and a purpose, and he chased after it through setback and injustice. Kev knew he himself was just too free-flowing and indifferent to find his own path in life, but Clyde had helped him find it in death. 'It took dying for me to actually feel alive. I think I've been so giddy about having a second chance that I've hidden my emotions well, but honestly, I'm scared too. I've never been a soldier or any type of tough guy. I don't know anyone in my family who's done anything like this. At least Clyde will have raw potential based on his dad and brother. But I needed a purpose, and now I have one. I can't just wait around and watch Clyde age, waiting for him to turn gray and drop and wake up beside him in that place. And if my purpose can help even one person, even at my own expense, then at least it'll keep me from just sitting around waiting for my friend to die.'

Connors was placid, hearing Kev's sobering words. 'I understand that. I understand that too well. Every soldier I've ever met has felt the same from time to time. Nothing fucks you up more than too much thinking.'

'If you weren't entangled with Rose and the others, if you had a chance to live freely, as much as anyone like us can live, would you still choose to keep fighting?'

'Without a shadow of doubt,' he said enthusiastically. 'I've never much enjoyed thinking about my own mortality. The idea of amassing a lifetime's knowledge and reaching a physical peak only to watch it all slip away to nothingness. Bad joints, bad heart, memory like congealed pudding. That used to terrify me. Now I'll always have a war to fight. And when I'm back in the jaws of the Null, I'll fight some more until there's nothing left of my soul, until I'm faced with true death. And I know that's what everybody here at Hourglass will do. It's what you'll do too. And Clyde. Because we don't have any other choice.'

True death sat in Kev's mind like a heavy, black boulder. Heavier than any Humvee. Ideas, call them supposition, a hypothesis, about splitting a soul in half, breaking it down into its most basic constituent energies, until the personality was irretrievably lost, stayed with Kev. Was there a place beyond the Null? Above, below, next door, back entrances through the Median that Ramaliak traveled? He really wanted to peruse the archive of books in that humongous library. And seeing Bookworm again would probably remain a cool novelty for the foreseeable.

Kev posited a rational question. 'If there is a true death, complete nothingness, why are you still prepared to fight? You say you don't want to lose the talents you bled and sweated for, but if there's a void beyond the Null, then don't the stakes remain the same?'

It was evident that this wasn't a new idea to Connors, but he didn't seem to enjoy chasing answers and hypotheticals in the same vigorous manner Kev did, responding with a soft ah-well-what-can-you-do shrug. 'I'm too ugly to kill again.'

'That's one philosophy, I suppose.' Kev smirked and openly looked at the soldier's wounds. His own paltry bullet wound seemed insultingly quaint in comparison. 'Hey, maybe there's some paradise tucked away in a corner somewhere. At this point it seems stupid to play sceptic with the fantastic.'

The tire slammed again, loud enough to bust an eardrum.

Connors conceded the point, if only to change tack. 'What the hell were we saying?' He snatched after his thoughts like a bundle of banknotes stolen by the wind. He caught them. 'Point is, we're the lucky ones in a way. We're like session musicians, fucking great at our jobs, but we just need to turn up and do our thing. It's Rose and Clyde who're leading the bands; for them it's a responsibility. It's a lot to deal with, and I don't envy them.'

Rose had returned, barely out of breath. 'Skip the pity parade for me, and that goes triple for Clyde,' she stated calmly. 'He needs to get the entitled knocked out of him a little.'

'Entitled?' Kev didn't like how she said that. 'What's entitled about him? Just because he had a plan for his life that didn't involve military service?' She gave him a challenging look, and Kev realized he might have let a little too much bass into his voice. But he had wanted to ask what they'd spoken about. Seemed like this was his chance. 'Besides, I thought you two seemed cool after your talk.'

'We are,' Rose said, swigging back another mouthful of her shake.

To Kev's surprise, the senior ranking Connors was the one to play advocate to the civilian mentality. 'I can appreciate his perspective with all he's lost to the service. I've lost other young men and women, and let's just say the reactions from their families can vary. It's just Rose busting balls.'

Rose finished her bottle, and Kev expected her to do a disservice to her prowess by crushing the cheap plastic. She didn't. She would probably wait and crush an engine block later. 'Clyde seems like an okay guy, but he needed to get his balls busted, Sarge. You know that as well as I do.'

Connors didn't deny this, and Kev's confounded expression caused Rose to lay it out for him. 'If he sticks to his decision to pass all this up, that's his prerogative, but he has to be trained up to a particular standard before leaving here. It's company policy. Straight-up risk assessment.'

'What do you mean?' Kev asked.

'Ace, and the other departmental agents like him, they're known as Sparks. They have the luxury of independence and can choose to fight the good fight or stay hidden under a rock, teach kindergarten if they want to. But Clyde's a medium like me, and we both have to think of our partners as well as ourselves. Now, your circumstances are a bit more complicated. Unlike the situation with me and my guys, you can operate independently of Clyde. And that's cool, but let's say you stand with us and he doesn't. In that case, your biggest weakness—your Kryptonite, if you like, which is a reference I'm sure Clyde would appreciate—is walking around out there as a soft target. So we need to make sure he can take care of himself, because I for one don't want to be ass-deep in some high-risk operation with you covering me, only for you to get road-hauled back to the Null because Clyde got sniped.'

Oh, fuck! Kev hadn't given that a second thought. Well, he quickly rectified that, and a fresh surge of guilt followed. 'So if I chose to leave with him, we could leave without training?'

Rose shook her head in exasperation. 'Is that what you want? You've struggled to hold your water since the ride to the airport, and now you're ready to turn back?'

Of course he wasn't. He wanted this more than anything he'd ever wanted in his life. It was overwhelming how much this crazy place made perfect sense to him. But if he stayed, it also meant he'd be forcing Clyde to become, to at least some degree, the very thing he despised. A soldier. But this was different, wasn't it? This wasn't invading foreign lands and bombing non-combatants for corporate gain. This was fighting for the preservation of humanity as a whole. Where race, creed, class, and business had no stake.

Kev didn't know what to do. 'How did he take it? And don't bullshit me.'

Rose looked him square in the eye. 'He took it on the chin. With the way we teach, he'll be good to go back home in a month.'

The moment was quickly starting to strain when Connors said, 'Not bad work today, Curly. Rose, you got this. I'm going to make sure those other two idiots aren't sitting in my chair.' He atomized out of sight; apparently their little clubhouse war room had chairs.

'You should go talk to him, hug it out or whatever you do.' She glanced out at the lowering sun, grayish and dirty through the tinted glass of the western wall. 'Come on, I'll drive you back down. Don't want you getting lost inside the complex with no ID.'

Kev felt tense, hoping Clyde wasn't cursing him out right now. He felt that their upcoming conversation might be a doozy.

13

KONSTANTIN SAT IN THE BACK of an armored jeep and stared through the windshield at the giant keyhole-shaped doorway at the end of the bridge platform. The portal was singed around the edges with an energy of smoky infernal red, the color of an angry infected wound. He was about to enter Erebus, the realm of the dead.

Again.

Finally.

The soldiers of the private army had taken up positions around the warehouse's ramp and platform, the rafters too, their heavy-caliber rifles trained on the giant doorway should any uninvited guests begin sniffing around. Having made such jaunts in the past with nothing more than his runic armor and the tethering of his own soul and, of course, his own proven mettle, Konstantin found the imperiousness of the armed convoy distasteful and weak. Acton Mortis didn't seem to mind, sitting next to him in the jeep with his long, ungainly limbs folded up like those of a stick insect, expectation and the thrill of seeking out one's fortune quietly growing fat behind his eyes.

The engine growled to life, signaling the mechanical awakening of the convoy lined up behind them in the warehouse, ready to roll up the ramp and on into Erebus. Konstantin knew private armies. In his military career, he had come into contact with various militias and crazed foreign generals. But he had been out of that world of black budgets and privately spent wealth and state capital for a long time now. Surely the big players had changed some.

'The hardware belongs to Aristov, does same company supply all this security?' Konstantin asked.

Mortis played along like a good babysitter, treating Konstantin like fragile glass, or at least a potential threat. He seemed to weigh up the content of the question and the subsequent answer, found it relatively harmless, and divulged. 'The men belong to another private military contractor. Citadel Security Solutions.' Konstantin wasn't familiar with this particular outfit, but mercenaries were a dime a dozen, selling their services to the highest bidder for beer money. 'They're owned by an employee of ours, a local big shot here in New York.' Mortis made a soft tut-tut noise. 'And you shouldn't say Aristov like it's a dirty word. Nikhail Aristov is a good patron of Cairnwood.'

So, not simply the faceless company of Aristov Ballistics but the man himself: Nikhail Aristov, founder and CEO. It was a simple truism that men like him lacked any political identity of their own, content to work with whomever filled their wallet, but learning that somebody like him was a member of Cairnwood still troubled Konstantin.

'And it's because of him that you're here. Being a Russian national with some pull, it was he who had a word with the Kremlin and got you released from Peklo.'

And what a fool he was for having done so, Konstantin thought. Without the Arkhitektor, or a successful suicide on his own behalf, Konstantin would have had no way of making this pilgrimage so soon. He would have remained in Peklo, his mission suspended, trapped in that damned cell until he was nothing but dusty bones inside an empty suit of armor. But now here he was with a first-class ticket. 'Maybe I'll buy him drink one day.'

'Who's to say?' Mortis humored him. 'He drinks vodka. Shocking, I know.' Konstantin's smirk was more of a facial tic than any display of good humor.

The jeep purred up the ramp with a bump and shudder. Ahead of the convoy lay a sudden dichotomous change in environment, the brick and mortar of a Brooklyn warehouse becoming a familiar sight for Konstantin, the near-twilight permanence of burning stars and midnight-hued dunes of ash and splintered bone. The traction of the jeep changed sharply from the hard steel platform to the grainy desiccation of a vast coastline, the Shore of the Eternal Storm. Outside the window to his left, Konstantin watched the slow tide roll out interminable miles towards a distant roiling wall of electrical violence, a great and terrible barrier from which endless legions of the deceased spewed forth. Konstantin had often wondered if that stormy layer encircled the entirety of Erebus.

This crossing was invariably disconcerting for Konstantin. And for all of his hatred for this place, he had always entered it with reverence. It had been decades since he took that momentous step of his first journey, and decades since his last, that poisonous baptism at the hands of Vor Dushi. With the last of the convoy passing through the totemic keyhole, the locksmith had the driver pull over for a second, leaned out of the window to concentrate on the tall gateway, and sealed them in, the view of the Brooklyn warehouse blipping out of sight as the inter-dimensional tumblers slid back into place.

And the small caravan continued along the beach.

Mortis had made it all seem so effortless. In Konstantin's experience and knowledge, gleaned from hundreds of years' worth of archaic Rising Path wisdom, he'd never seen such a paltry waltz in or out of the dominion of the dead. It had always been a ritual with them, one of care and diligence, caution, and respect for Death's tyranny. He remembered his first time here, having graduated to the highest honor within the Rising Path, ascending to the rank of Mertvyy Dayver.

A Dead Diver.

'How you come to work for men such as these?' Konstantin asked, his eyes gliding curiously to Mortis' bony keys.

Mortis stared at his hands for a moment, a flux of emotions almost spilling across his drawn-out vulpine features: wistfulness, bitterness, pride. 'I'm older than I look,' came his reply. 'My father arrived here in the colonies in—' he whistled, amazed at the slippery passage of time, '—must have been 1848. He was a locksmith by trade, helping the English banks and nobility protect their vaults. And a few criminals here and there too, but you tell me the difference. When he arrived in the New World, he found easy work. His reputation preceded him, so his talents were sought after by the old and emerging seats of power. As was the tradition in those days, I apprenticed under him and took to the vocation like a duck to water. My father was a quiet man, very secretive, as adept at locking away his indiscretions as he was a client's valuables. And one day, when I was still a young man—I must have only been in my twenties—one of his secrets, a big one,' his eyes bulged like greasy marbles as he said this, 'sprung his careful lock. He'd been affiliating with some colorful types. Mystics, sorcerers, warlords, devils. You know the sort. Well, this menagerie had one commonality: they were all associated with the Cairnwood Society.'

Mortis seemed to revisit a distant place and time, pausing before picking up his thread. 'A skilled locksmith can make a skilled thief. As time went by, my father became desperately ill, contracting tuberculosis. It was some kind of miracle I never caught it, but by that time I'd proven that I could be left to my own devices. Knowing he was facing...' a long-knuckled key pointed out the window to this realm of rot and rancor, 'a place like this, he decided to try and pillage a Cairnwood Society holding, hoping to find some magic that could cure the incurable and wring out the filthy bacteria from his lungs. The Society caught him, and they executed him.'

'You're suspiciously loyal to group who slay your father. Have you heard of Stockholm Syndrome?'

Mortis' angular mouth curved into a sharp grin, genuine humor in his foam-speckled white eyes. 'My father got what he deserved. The Society had always been nothing but generous to us, but he went behind their backs and did the dirty on them. That's poor character. I was already performing jobs for their interests by then, and they tutored me in certain magic, which I combined with my knowledge of locks. It all seemed to happen so quickly. Before I knew it, I was the centerpiece of a ritual to turn me into the man I am today. King of the hidden vaults, master of security, and, more recently, a walker between the realms.'

Konstantin listened to how the penitence became bold and boastful. Mortis was clearly a mongrel in need of his master's acceptance. Thoughts of a young boy, scraping a servant's wage with his father, his large impressionable eyes going drunk and starry with the opulence of their employers, who lived such gilded lives so near and yet so far away. Now that boy was a centuries-old drudge at the beck and call of the Society, paying off a proxy's penance for his dad's treachery and still gullible enough, despite his labors, to believe he could attain a portion of their comfort and coin.

Mortis leaned forward, sharp elbows on skinny thighs. 'I know your little cult found a walkabout like this to be something profound and meaningful, but it really isn't. Death is all around us; you only need to find the right door.' Without breaking eye contact, Mortis' pronged thumb directed Konstantin to the windshield. The car slid to a stop on the sandbar. 'Here we are.'

The base camp was an orderly grid of large canvas tents, armored trailers, portable generators, and floodlights, sealed up with concrete abutments and chain link fencing topped with concertina wire. The tents served various functions: command post, med bay, munitions storage, and, of course, the barracks. Citadel Security Solutions had generous numbers. The Humvee cruised past a couple of parked Sharp Industries haulage trucks, the bed of one of which was loaded with what looked to be rock of an unknown mineral, a strange puce crystallization dotted about the strata. Konstantin didn't recognize that type of stone from his own visits, but he and his brethren had never gone about digging. And he certainly didn't recognize the unsettling trophy carcass propped up atop some scaffolding poles stuck deep into the ash dunes outside the camp's gate. In his studies at the temple, he had learned of many of the denizens that prowled this particular region: the ones that floated on the warm dead breeze like detritus in an updraft; the ones that sinuously soared the twilight skies with awful majesty; those that crawled, slithered, or sprinted with apex ease. His own experiences with the indigenous species had been varied, to the point on one occasion when he, Kuznetsov, and the Arkhitektor had lost their supplies of deer meat and had been forced to hunt and slay an almost mammalian brute, one of the lazier animals that grazed on soul residue like moss growing on rocks. Being forced to eat that creature had been one of the most frightening moments of his walks. Could a creature of the Erebian fields be fit for human consumption? He trusted the Arkhitektor's advice, of course, but the stomach had a mind of its own sometimes, stubborn and unwilling.

That thing impaled upon the poles outside the tent, though? Konstantin tried to make head or tail of it, his inspection only cracking the riddle as their Humvee passed by it, entering the base camp. It looked like a large, leathery bag, slightly bigger than a relatively tall man, with some type of vestigial wings, a sickly coloration of earthly browns and jaundiced yellow where this territory's alien light passed through its membranous skin. Konstantin also thought he might have spotted a blackish, withered hand and some long, ropy protuberances hanging from within the folds of the bag. For all his ghastly fascination with the thing, he was quick in his efforts to put it out of his mind. But the logical side of him, the thinking man with a well-honed skill set for survival, filed the horror away for later. Because, sooner or later, at the first sensible opportunity, his mission would see him breaking away from Mortis and the Society's hired guns. Physically, he would be alone in this wilderness, and he would very likely die in pursuit of his mission, but before he found what he was searching for, he would be at risk from an entire ecosystem, the likes of which the Rising Path had barely glimpsed.

The Humvee slowed to a stop outside the large command tent, where a pair of sentries stood, hard-eyed and equipped with the latest body armor and firepower to descend into Hell itself. Mortis was quick to jump out, keen to brandish the map in aid of the shameless pillaging of Death's homeland. Konstantin opened his door but remained seated, smelling that unique aroma of ash, dust, and something completely indescribable, an odor unlike anything on Earth, but sweet in its way; the Arkhitektor had once told him it was the spray of the tides. He still didn't understand how breathing was possible for mortals in this realm, for it was built for those who had breathed their last. But here he was, taking a lungful, the scents invoking memories of his last time here, the start of that harrowing encounter, following the Arkhitektor up that steep hill of silt and mineral, the immortal dusk a macabre beauty, burning in layers of orange and blue, like the last sunset of a dying star. The Arkhitektor growing bolder with each step, powering up the crest of the wide dune, hearing the plaintive beckoning of a sea of souls. The cylindrical channel of the nexus pulsing with a stormy glow, extending deep to feed fresh souls into the Eidolon Trench.

And from there...

Konstantin theorized that the fact that the living could breathe here was simply to bait foolish mortals to their doom. An absence of oxygen and atmosphere couldn't stop them from blasting themselves into outer space, so how bad could this place be? More souls for the eternal harvest.

He stepped out and closed the Humvee's door, glanced around the cold beach. His eyes fixed on something near the water's edge, something he had almost forgotten about. It was a long walking staff, tilted at an angle but still standing after all these years. He felt the internal nostalgia of Kuznetsov and the others of his sect. The Arkhitektor had once explained to Konstantin how the first priest, the founder of the Rising Path and thus the first to bear the mantle of Arkhitektor, had planted that staff on his first visit a great many years ago. At this distance and light one would never know, but the brass was deeply oxidized, a thick, flaky crust of blackish-green covering the length of it. Konstantin took a steadying breath and stared up into the sky, empty of all but stars.

It wasn't always this empty.

He remembered on some occasions what he had seen floating up in those starry violet skies. Several silvery skulls orbiting like grim moons, jagged teeth and horns. Sometimes they were so distant they seemed like small, shimmering coins at the edge of the cosmos; other times they were close enough, and large enough, to devour this whole desiccated terra. Where did they originate, and where did they go? After each of his walks, Konstantin was left with more questions than answers, for even the Arkhitektor and his generations of accrued knowledge and compiled tomes had only scratched the surface. In the end, as with everything, familiarity slowly bred contempt, and such spellbinding journeys became rote for Konstantin. He had suspicions about what the satellite skulls were—for what else could they be if not members of some dead pantheon with their scale and natural supremacy? Or perhaps they were curious members of the Order of Terminus, with one of them being the monarch of this territory, the ruler of the House of Fading Light. On occasions such as this, he found their absence unnerving. Were they plotting against the invaders, or simply indifferent to the tiny creatures sneaking into their home like woodlice?

He followed Mortis into the large tent, passing the silent guards. The tent was set up with a few collapsible tables, but instead of being dotted with maps and strategic plans, they were largely empty bar a few notes and some communication equipment. Konstantin noticed a few hard cases set aside, holding collapsible satellite dishes, and the two-way radios on the belts of the guards and the work crews. Operating in Erebus was like a trip back in time, before the skies were clogged with government and private satellites, before GPS and WiFi and cellular communication. A couple of techs were off to the side fiddling with radiocontrol transmitters, the type used for aerial drones, and first-person view goggles, troubleshooting about radio frequencies and antenna reception. Their jargon was of little interest to Konstantin; he was more focused on the important man in the room, the one with whom Mortis was standing. Konstantin took him to be the commanding officer of this outfit straight away. He had a hardened, humorless look, the type that grows over a person who has seen and participated in too much bloodshed. He was of average height, shorter than Konstantin, noticeably shorter than the pole-limbed Mortis, but looked structurally dense and lethal, thick neck and powerful shoulders, with dark-brown skin and short, black hair oiled back from his clinically dead eyes.

'This is Captain Agua,' Mortis curtly introduced. 'Agua, this is the celebrity adventurer I promised. I'm told he's also part guard-dog, and if he gets a sniff of old snake-necks Vor Dushi, he'll bark. Isn't that right?'

Konstantin heard the rhetorical nature of the question and felt their eyes testing him. He made a confirmatory noise, which sounded more like a throat clearing a particularly vile glob of phlegm, but they accepted it.

'Gulag, huh?' Captain Agua appraised Konstantin's necroarmor, his calculating eyes following the curves and points and loops of the foreign symbolism protecting Konstantin from any malignant spirits seeking shelter within his being. 'You really survived a run-in with the jefe of this place? But you don't seem too banged up. I would have expected a missing limb at the least.'

'I would have preferred missing limb.' Konstantin was acutely aware how focused he had become on the voices within himself. Somewhere beneath their ebb and flow of chatter, he sensed that greasy worm, lying still in his soul but tumescent with poison.

'I believe people learn from their scars. With yours we can learn to lock and load the moment it gets near. I'd say that's tactically useful.'

'You have much experience combating the things that populate this place?' Konstantin thought about the large, leathery bag displayed near the wire of the compound. It couldn't be a warning to other careless creatures, he decided, and only braggarts and idiots celebrated their kills in such a self-satisfied manner.

'Part of the job. Don't worry. If the big man returns before our operation is finished, we're more than capable of dealing with him.'

'"The big man"? Vor Dushi is but corporal lashings of a concentration camp guard. This land is subject of House of Fading Light. You don't know what we're walking into.'

Agua seemed unconcerned. A professional soldier through and through, even if he was now only serving his own fortune. The captain threw a skeptical glance at Mortis. 'If this guy's going to be this jumpy the whole time, I'll stick with good old-fashioned surveillance. I don't need him to ring the bell if snake-necks climbs out of his hole.'

Mortis leveled a stare at Konstantin, objectifying the Russian, making it clear that he was nothing but a tool, but he spoke to Agua. 'He's here for more than that. He's a walking ghost town, waiting to pick up more settlers. When it comes time, he's going to pull his weight, along with the soul cages we have set aside.'

Konstantin had already been informed of such items in this party's inventory, it being divulged during the last talk with Talbot. In past studies, he had read innumerable scrolls and texts on the various methods of confining the deceased to items: weapons, buildings, trinkets, vehicles, anything the engineer took a fancy to, really.

'Whatever you say. So, you got something for me?' Agua pushed, the niceties now over with. Mortis pulled out one of the laminated maps from his deep and dusty coat pocket. Agua placed it on a table, spinning it around the right way up. 'Good. I was starting to get a little fed up with our recon drones being plucked from the sky.'

'Out of the sky?' Mortis asked, craning to inspect the drone camera team fussing about with controllers and a small bank of computer monitors. 'Are you sure they're not just crashing like those two choppers did?'

'Positive.' Agua's eyes rolled up from the map to encompass Mortis briefly. 'The choppers went down from electromagnetic interference caused by those random soul winds. The drone cameras were functioning perfectly, right up until they were swallowed.'

Konstantin silently watched and listened.

'By what?' Mortis asked.

'Probably the bodybags.'

'Bodybags?' Mortis sounded eager, probably thinking about whether this was something Talbot and the inner circle might be interested in.

'You notice anything weird on the way in here?'

'That thing you've mounted out by the gate?' Agua gave a single dip of his head in confirmation. 'That thing could fly?'

'They don't look it, but bodybags drift about like leaves on a breeze. They're pretty fucking good at killing too. Taken out two of my men so far.'

'Have you managed to capture any alive?' Mortis asked.

'We're normally too busy trying not to die. Are they a priority now?' Agua looked annoyed, ready to challenge any last-minute complications that could jeopardize the completion of his job.

'No,' Mortis casually answered. 'I just thought they could be of some interest.'

'You can see how interesting they are up close if you like, but I wouldn't recommend it.'

Mortis tapped his long, pointed chin with a few keys. 'Have some of your men take it down, pass it to Hammond's guys. I'd like it secured in one of the containers before shipping out. Our people will likely get more out of it than one of your men hanging it over his fireplace.'

Although Konstantin had never run afoul of the hideous things, he was prepared to wager his skin that, for all their threat, they would pale before Vor Dushi. 'If simple wildlife of this land pose such threat to you and your men, why so confident about making stand against Vor Dushi?'

Agua didn't take well to people questioning his capabilities as a warrior and leader, and his cool tone demonstrated this. 'If you knew my background, you'd understand.'

'I only hope for your sake it isn't posturing.'

Agua straightened up, his jaw set, looking quite prepared to see whether Gulag's gauntlets were of any use in a fight.

Mortis intervened with a small gesture, his hand a barrier between them. Those two seemingly blind eyes oozed into Konstantin's. 'You're happy here? Excited in Hell's desolate heart, ready to manifest destiny and find your little gold ticket to a paradise that has eluded ... how many generations of your faith?' Konstantin held the sickly weight of Mortis' stare. Agua's rigid scowl smoothed out, and he shook his head in mild annoyance, returning to the drawn map. 'Now I'll gladly leave you to your delusion if you stop goading your travel companions. We don't have to put a few well-placed Exorcist rounds into you to rob you of your friends. Cairnwood could confect a more fitting punishment. How would you feel about immortality? Locked in a cell somewhere on Earth with endless days. Would that interrupt your holy mission?'

Konstantin allowed Mortis to feel powerful and listened to the voices inside of himself. He didn't know what Cairnwood was capable of, but his feeling was that there was enough magic and mystery woven throughout the universe for Mortis to make good on his threat.

Eternal life, a curse dressed as a blessing.

He'd play along for now. Maybe Agua and his platoon of marauders could be of some use when the time was right.

14

CLYDE WAS SEQUESTERED IN HIS quarters, a basic two racks and a table that offered no further plush comforts beyond what could be found in any regular military barracks. He didn't think Kev would have much use for the second bed, but there were no other new recruits to make use of it either. At least he had a window. That was a surprise. His room was built into the steep rocks of the mesa complex's northern side, so the window next to his cot afforded him some sense of comfort and liberty, a quite expansive view of the sinuous canyon trails slowly filling up with a dark tide of shadows. Being only several floors below the tabletop, he could hear the overhead drone of choppers coming and going into the evening's gloaming.

Right now, the sounds washed over him like a gentle surf. He had offered his autonomy to his pencil, allowing it to conduct his thoughts and feelings onto his sketchpad in free thought and expression. The nib was outlining a page of as-yet faceless shock troopers caught up in a scene of guns, ghosts, and fury. The layout lacked any deeper story and subtext, but it was one of those days. Leaning against the cement wall of his bunk, he could already feel his muscles whispering their discontent over the earlier training session, particularly his thighs. They would be screaming in protest this time tomorrow. His phone lay on the small bedside unit, temporarily forgotten now that he'd called his mom only to reach her voice mail. She'd be on shift, he knew, being run ragged trying to help reassemble the latest lot of chewed-up war vets. It was only after he ended the call that he realized how it was probably for the best that she didn't pick up. He had texted her this morning—Christ, this day was a shake-up of his usual routine—explaining how he might be unable to visit for a week or so, busy with a bit of this, a bit of that, completing a commission and chasing up potential jobs in the industry. He might now have to extend that line of vague nonsense for a few months. If she had answered when he called, he wouldn't have trusted his voice not to quaver into rambling delirium. Thoughts of home ran through his head, passing by so quickly that he barely recognized them: his apartment; his old home, which now only housed his mom. He waited for a pang of homesickness to lay him low, and it bothered him a little that it didn't. Despite his weary limbs and over-stimulated mind, he felt clear and focused.

His pencil scratched away. Out in the corridor he heard the footsteps and chatter of passing personnel but paid little attention. Then Kev walked in. He had reined in some of his earlier tap-dancing excitement and slowly crossed to the empty bed opposite Clyde. Clyde lowered his sketch pad and could feel the uncertainty radiating off of Kev in waves, a compass needle thrown into chaotic abandon from erratic and unpredictable fields. Clyde let his warm pencil rest and waited for Kev to spill what was bothering him. Kev clasped his hands together and let them dangle between his legs. Several times he tried to speak, and each time he stopped before the first syllable.

Clyde decided to help him out; his incomplete drawing of a world that mortified him would have to go unfinished for now. 'The last time you were like this, you had just dented my car.'

Kev smiled awkwardly. 'Actually, I think it was the time when I spilled beer over your drawings. Those ones you were going to submit to Vertigo.'

Clyde lightly drummed his pencil against his pad. 'Oh, yeah, that's right. I knew buying that car was a mistake anyway.'

'I heard about what Rose said to you, about the training.' Kev might have been sweating if it was still possible. 'I didn't even think of that as being a problem.'

'It's not.'

Kev looked like he had been slapped by an invisible hand. 'It isn't?'

They stared at each other for a long moment, and Clyde could swear Kev had never looked so guilty, or so entreating.

'Dude, have you given this some real consideration?'

Clyde went to continue drawing, if only to keep his hand busy, but found his muse had slipped out of the window, possibly taking to the sky and heading straight back to Brooklyn to accrue dust along with a future that seemed to have moved ever further beyond his reach.

'Yeah.'

'I don't know how to take this,' Kev admitted, fumbling about with his glasses. 'I know you'd sooner send some creatively worded hate mail to each and every comic-book editor you can think of than undergo any form of military training, but now you're saying you're cool with this? Really, honestly, cool with this?'

It was a necessary evil, Clyde knew, but he was swallowing a fairly substantial lump of regret. 'I'm far from cool with it. But this isn't just about me now. I'm doing this for you.'

Kev practically collapsed into himself like a punctured airbag, a forlorn expression molding his features. 'I'd say please don't put this on me, but...' There was no alternative, and Kev had the decency and the self-mindedness to understand this and left the ellipsis.

Clyde dropped his sketch pad and pencil on the bed for the final time, no longer inclined to draw a jazzed-up and explosive representation of the life he was advancing into with unsure baby steps. 'This whole thing, all of it, your death, my channeling you, it's bigger than both of us. I guess I just have to accept that our truth is stranger than my fiction. And I wouldn't be much of a friend if I asked you to spend the rest of my life hiding away. Plus I don't trust you to behave if you tried living somewhere alone.'

Clyde smiled, thinking about how much merry mayhem his bored friend would cause. The idle pranks he'd inflict on the general public until he went too far and became an urban legend. 'The Phantom Irritant, scourge of bus drivers.' Kev chuckled, a little speechless but relieved. 'This is my decision. You have every right to be here, with the specialists and all that. And since I want to see what Spector can show me, I'll do this booty-boot camp stuff just as a precaution to being horribly murdered in some future retaliation.' It sounded like a sick attempt at humor, but they both knew there was a nugget of possibility in there somewhere. 'But then I'm out.'

Kev nodded dumbly, obviously wanting to find the words that could adequately state the depth of his appreciation and his friend's sacrifice of ideals. He leaned forward off the empty bed and stretched out for a fist bump. 'Thanks, man.'

Clyde bumped knuckles and felt a strange charge flow up his arm and into his chest from the contact. He thought nothing of it; a minor sensation, like a static shock. 'Just promise me one thing.'

Kev's eyes were wide open and obedient behind his glasses. 'Name it.'

'When you're all official, try to keep your professional life out of my personal life. This isn't a Reese's Pieces thing.'

'Two steps ahead.'

Clyde watched Kev struggle to contain his smile, which was verging on cheek-splitting. Kev, a half-life with purpose. Clyde felt a flickering warmth for Kev's joy, one that was still too weak to thaw the chill of nervous anticipation. Tomorrow morning he'd be put through the meat grinder. He wondered if this was how Stephen and his old man had felt when they first joined the army. Loving family men, trained murderers. Then another somber thought crossed Clyde's mind. Once Kev got his badge or whatever, he'd probably see very little of him. It'd be like he was dead all over again. He knew Kev would have pondered this too, and yet it hadn't attenuated his eagerness to pursue this ambition. No sense in dwelling on what used to be, he supposed. Clyde had to focus on the future. Well, whatever happened between now and death, they would always have the Null.

15

THE BLUE SUN CONTINUED TO sizzle in the distant reaches of the doom-laden sky, its cold flame perpetually staring at Konstantin's back. He stood before another dark armored truck, parked near the perimeter fence of the encampment, watching Lieutenant Fenwick, one of Captain Agua's trio of top-ranking officers, issue a few orders to his Bravo squad before dismissing them. Fenwick looked like he'd tumbled out of some Norse myth, the bastard son of Thor, a blonde behemoth with a golden beard and ponytail.

Konstantin had carefully dispatched his immaterial spies while the Citadel troops and Sharp workforce bustled about, tasking them with some delicate information-gathering. Brother Kuznetsov and the others had returned unnoticed, like a dying breath on the wind, with facts and figures about Captain Agua's resident occupying force: three lieutenants, Briggs the Alpha squad leader, Fenwick the Bravo squad leader, and Castor the Charlie squad leader; with each squad currently consisting of two teams comprised of a sergeant, a corporal, and four soldiers; bringing the total manpower to twenty-four soldiers, six corporals, six sergeants, three lieutenants, and Captain Agua. Forty hardened ex-special forces operatives.

Konstantin didn't concern his eyes and ears with the civilian personnel. He didn't believe project manager Hammond and his contracted workforce would pose any threat to them once the time came for him to act. He had, however, reevaluated his original dismissal of Agua and his men; suspecting them of being just another bunch of maladjusted thugs had been too hasty. They were well-trained, sure, and highly lethal undoubtedly, but there had to be more to them than that. A typical cluster of violent apes who couldn't leave the war behind so long as there was profit to be had felt insufficient. Talbot and his paymasters wouldn't hand the reins of this lucrative and highly risky assignment to forty human guns, no matter how experienced they were. Their numbers would be double, triple, quadruple perhaps, if they were only the sum of their parts. After all, they were essentially walking down Death's front path to knock on his door. No, at least Agua, and most likely Lieutenants Briggs, Fenwick, and Castor, were hiding their own secrets. Konstantin knew he would have to play this carefully. Besides the unknown threat Agua and his lieutenants were masking, and not forgetting Mortis, he had to consider the weaponry the CSS were equipped with, both traditional and unique. He was now of two minds about his original plan to slip away at the earliest convenience, leaving the war party to the wilds. Agua could likely survive this place, he reasoned, and he had a map to the Trench on him. Konstantin was bound for the Trench and the enemies it held; he didn't need additional troubles following him in there to settle a score. It clicked into place for him: he wouldn't abandon this army. It was better to use them. And if they were to get themselves all killed, then that would scratch off one problem for him.

Lieutenant Fenwick flung open the truck's doors and clomped up the metal risers, expecting Konstantin to follow suit, as did Mortis, who loomed over his shoulder like a big scarecrow composed of too many joints. Konstantin obliged and climbed into the rear of the large, spacious truck. Even with all the equipment piled and bolted about the place, the interior had enough room to comfortably shift about in. Fenwick was unclasping the straps of the disassembled soul cages, and right then Konstantin knew exactly how Kuznetsov and the others felt, for he, too, felt the foreboding sentience of the trap components, a dull cognizance akin to that of any other ambush consumer; a Venus flytrap sprung to mind. From the outset, Konstantin couldn't wrap his head around how these cages would fit together or look when completed, but Fenwick flicked on a torch and rolled out a blueprint along the flat metal surface of a small worktop. The diagrammatic cages could be best described as industrial sarcophagi, the dimensions of height, length, and width being ten feet, four feet, and five feet, respectively. The iron coffins had a variety of soul traps welded deep into the metalwork, and wheels had been affixed to the rails along their backs for easy transport. The blueprints included a preeminent feature: each cage had a small cavity in the top crossbar to house a siren stone, a unique composite of fey minerals that performed a soothing song for wandering souls. His inspection leapt from the diagrams to any of the large number of hard cases piled around, any of which could contain the siren stones. His furtive scouring for the stones hadn't gone unnoticed.

'They'll create a lot of commotion once activated,' Mortis said. 'The spirits will have to be trapped quickly should Vor Dushi show up. The Trench will be the perfect spot; we'll bottle the spirits at the source and then hop back through the doorway.'

Konstantin scrutinized the cages for any structural weak points. If he couldn't find the means to circumvent their incantatory markings, or find the stones to dispose of, he was sure there was enough hardware and spite to make a dent in the frames, to crack the words into meaningless syllables.

'Each of the three cages is capable of storing up to two thousand souls,' Mortis said enthusiastically, like an old prospector preparing to ransack a gold mine. 'Your own wards only offer haven to the more virtuous of spirit, isn't that right?' A few key-fingers circled a gesture at Konstantin's necronaut armor. 'But not these contraptions. These aren't quite as strict. They'll allow any rabble-rouser in.' He smiled his decrepit grin. 'Cairnwood is a firm believer in rehabilitation.' The smile withered and blew away to join this landscape of dead things. 'Once the dinner bell is rung, you'll help mop up any eligible spooks who can't find a room at one of our own wonderful inns.' His palm and keys slapped against the framework like a bag of cat bones for emphasis. 'After you've reached maximum occupancy, I'll jump us out of there, and we all have a long weekend, basking in the knowledge that we are pioneers.'

Fenwick found his voice, deep and gruff. 'When we reach the Trench, I'll be overseeing the operation of one of the cages, with Lieutenants

Briggs and Castor overseeing the other two. We'll be taking up parallel positions along the cliff. You'll follow our instructions once we're up and running,' he told Konstantin. 'Taking a stand along our line, you can suck up your own spooks, and you'll have a flare gun if trouble shows up.'

Konstantin didn't like Fenwick's tone any more than Captain Agua's, but at least they were honest with their dislike, which was more than could be said for the phony attempt at friendship Mortis was flouting. It mattered little. Being former career military, it took more than snarls, sneers, and brusque attitudes to get to Konstantin. He was busy trying to find a sign, any sign, that would confirm his suspicions about Fenwick: that he shared some inhuman aspect like his commanding officer, Agua. His canines looked a little large in their quick exposure between words, like pointy white daggers, and his jaw looked robust enough to weather a kick from a mule, but none of these features meant he was more than man. Still, Konstantin wasn't about to rule out the possibility of Agua's lieutenants keeping a few nasty secrets.

'I'll do my part, don't worry about me. You should be worrying about yourselves.' Konstantin backed away roughly, forcing Mortis to step aside, and made to exit the truck. 'First we need to get there in one piece.'

16

CLYDE WAS WOKEN FROM AN awkward sleep by Kev. He had dreamed, but of what, he couldn't grasp; it was like steam dissipating in the morning light. Images of Spector and his bottle collection of stolen thoughts and lost, unconscious wanderings within the Median emblazoned themselves across the back of Clyde's eyelids. It was an uncomfortable thought, and it left him uncertain as to whether he should lament or rejoice his inability to revisit this most recent forgotten dream. It was likely just another muddle of disconnected troubles and desires, but since yesterday's meeting with the goat-man, he knew he couldn't dismiss any dream ever again. What if he had come close to blindly opening one of those doorways to Erebus Spector had mentioned, thereby unwittingly casting himself into death and leaving his sleeping body to grow cold and still in this very bed? Or what if he had perhaps accidentally communed with Stephen or his dad, or maybe called out to another lost soul? One thing he did know: as of yesterday, sleep would never again be a blessed refuge for his weary head. Rubbing his eyes, feeling the sun trying its damnedest to stifle the air-conditioned room, Clyde got up and was handed a glass of water by Kev. He accepted the water with a nod and drank away his thirst. Then, putting the glass down on the side table, Clyde asked, 'Did you sleep?'

'No.'

'No? What did you do last night?'

'Drifted. Tried to familiarize myself with this place.' Kev shook his head. 'But I still don't feel too familiar. Above ground and below, there must be thirty floors in this place, maybe more. A lot of it's restricted, different levels of clearance and stuff. And I couldn't move through some of the walls. I spoke to a few of the guards and staff on the night shift. They seem okay. You look like you didn't get much sleep either.'

Clyde's eyes were still droopy. His body ached from yesterday's training, legs stiff, arms too. 'I'm nervous.'

'Hey, we're in this together.'

Kev's fist came up, floating between them. Clyde gave a tired smirk and bumped it, feeling that slight charge tingle along his knuckles and wrist again, but nowhere near as potent as last night's. 'I just need to get some breakfast, then I'll be cool with getting my ass beat.'

Speaking of brutality, Ace crowded the doorway, a coffee mug in hand, his eyes bouncing between Clyde and Kev. 'Let's go, rook. Let's get your scrawny ass in shape.'

'What about breakfast?'

'You have to earn it. Let's move.'

Clyde looked bereaved. Kev looked guilty. Ace was already halfway down the corridor.

. . .

CLYDE COULDN'T REMEMBER the last time he had run so far. The chances were high that he never had because that's what public transport was for. He hurt, he was swallowing acid, and his lower back ached. So much for stretching. After crossing the first mile mark of the scorching trail, Clyde was given more water and a chance to cool himself in the shade of a hilly copse of fir trees. The hard, warm, and prickly carpet of shed fir needles was almost comfortable enough to sleep on. The break was all too brief, but Clyde was pleasantly surprised by the elk that wandered out of the tree line, grazing absentmindedly. It looked up, its large, peaceful eyes fixed on him. After a few seconds it looked away and vanished back into the woods.

Ace had also caught sight of the elk. He was emitting a gentle shroud of dry ice to keep himself cool, but the wisps never quite seemed to grace

Clyde's hot face or sweat-soaked shorts and T-shirt. 'We need to keep an eye out on these trails. There are bears.'

Clyde hated Ace right then. They carried on, the winding circuit exiting the cool, lush forest and becoming another tough jaunt through a barren valley, ending with Ace leading them both back up a rising gradient, the trail slowly circling all the way up to the tabletop, flattening out for a jog through a short tunnel of red rock before disgorging them about half a mile away from the huge glass-and-concrete box of the gym. The early morning sun caromed off the smoky glass roof and walls of the gym like alien death rays. Clyde wanted to drink water until he puked, maybe climb into a bathtub full of ice until he got pneumonia. His lower back continued to cry out, one of his running shoes had a stone in it, and his mouth was as dry as the dust and grit that made up this awful fucking land. Stumbling after Ace, trying to keep up with him if only to savor the cool vapors flowing from his slipstream, Clyde noticed the rugged personal outdoor gym over to their left, consisting of not much more than a duct-taped heavy bag hanging from an old chain and a few tires set up for footwork drills.

Clyde came to a graceless, lumbering stop outside the gym, watching Ace push the door open and head on in as though he had to perform an emergency workout. Clyde gave it a minute, scanning the other distant buildings of the tabletop, morbidly wondering what would happen to him if he threw himself off of the edge of this plateau to the canyons below. He'd probably survive the fall and get dragged off by a fucking bear, he thought miserably, dragged all the way back into the woodland for a fucking picnic. He wondered if he did die, did this funky place have any neat little charms that might allow him to stay here as a ghost, spare him any further exercise? Nah, he'd be jettisoned straight to that other place. He took a massive gulp of warm air and managed to keep his mood buoyant by thinking of his meeting with Spector later this evening.

Clyde spotted Kev through the gym's glass walls. He was with Rose and her team, with Rose throwing various weight plates at Kev, ordering him to catch the iron discuses and either toss them back or gently place them in various corners of the massive room in what might be a coordination exercise. Kev looked as flummoxed as Clyde did tired, accidentally dropping one weight plate he was supposed to return, and returning another weight plate he was supposed to stack; Clyde took some petty satisfaction at this. At least they were both miserable.

Ace led Clyde right back into the lion's den, where more agents were currently knocking the living hell out of each other in the boxing ring or sparring and grappling on the matted area, while others conditioned themselves on the heavy bags. It was the most physically grueling morning Clyde had ever experienced, but on a positive note, he managed a total of four pull-ups, a personal best, and just about wobbled his way to twenty push-ups on rubbery arms, all the while having Ace bark at him like an angry dog, and that was just the warm-up. It was only after Clyde felt like lying down and not getting back up ever again that Ace cleared the boxing ring for both of them and went over the basic drills he had shown Clyde yesterday.

Rehashing the basics, Clyde was relieved that most of what he had been taught previously had stuck, and only required a brief do-over to freshen up the practiced moves. He remembered that a punch was one big, chained movement, starting from the feet, up through the legs, twisting through the hips and along the shoulder, and he remembered that the knuckles didn't want to hit the target but rather, as Ace delicately reminded him, "smash the fuck out of what's behind the target." Clyde was feeling pretty good about himself after a few rounds, the exertion clearing his mind the same as yesterday, the task at hand his only concern, and even his lazy muscles were beginning to relish the fire. When Ace slapped a gum shield into Clyde's mouth and began to hit him back for several rounds of sparring, Clyde was so amped up with adrenaline, his hands were still palsied after his subsequent shower.

. . .

AFTER BREAKFAST, ROSE took Clyde to the gun range. He was unsure whether he would even be able to hold the gun steady long enough to line up his sight, but Rose was a solid tutor, breaking everything down for him into digestible chunks, everything from the basics of how to hold a gun, the components of a gun, the correct stance, the works. She drilled this with him for several hours until he was semi-proficient in loading his own pistol and at least hitting the general vicinity of the paper targets. Throughout the session, Clyde slowly relaxed and started to become comfortable with the Glock 19 and SIG P320, and he even thought but never voiced—he would never voice, for that would set a dangerous precedent—how much he admired the self-discipline it took to become a soldier, the mastery of skills such as this. He suspected he was more like Stephen and his dad than he cared to admit. But he was very cautious about how to view this revelation. He was enjoying the sense of being carved into an individual capable of handling himself, but he would forever and always refrain from encouraging any opinions that posit that military service is a grand and noble cause. He still had that bitter taste. The bile of being plucked from your dead-end life to go off and die for rich assholes who spent their careers pissing down the backs of the working class while telling them it was only a spot of rain. He kept squeezing the trigger the way Rose had shown him, his shots gradually improving with each spent magazine, and with each bullet he fantasized about those wealthy warmongers dying in their mansions from old age or old-age-related complications, and how much of a shock they'd all be in for when they found themselves in a battlefield of the damned. He clenched his jaw to keep from smirking and finished the clip.

'Check you out, Mr. Pacifist.' Rose unfolded her arms and stepped in close, taking the empty gun, hot and smoking, from his hand. She handed him a Colt M4 assault rifle next, and on the table lay a Benelli M4 semi-auto combat shotgun. This session could take a while.

. . .

THE REGIMENTED ROUTINE continued well into the evening, with the blue sky becoming an orange inferno. Ace took Clyde behind the gym to the sparse outdoor training area, throwing down a few old and discolored gym mats. He subjected Clyde to more of his physical abuse as well as his taste in music, hitting play on Journey's "It Could Have Been You," and as the sun slowly sank and the shadows grew long, Ace taught Clyde some self-defense drills the military had adopted from jiujitsu and kung fu; nothing flashy or foolish, but the practical stuff: escapes and applications of various holds and locks. Clyde was also taught some moves that didn't belong in any ring or sporting environment, ones that had strict field applications: nasty moves that all but ensured survival against any hostile. Clyde went through the moves slowly, the air cooling to a luxurious balm on his burning face and arms, chilling the trickles of sweat. He picked up one bruise after another, but each one felt like an important lesson, a mistake or mistiming that he wouldn't make again.

Until he did, of course, reinforcing the lesson.

Clyde was repeatedly hip-tossed and wrist-locked and choked until finally, having become familiar with the feeling of Ace's forearm sinking into his throat, Clyde was able to seize tight hold of the strangling limb and quickly drop down onto one knee, tipping Ace's bulk over his shoulder onto the red dust. Clyde tried to imagine being forced to perform these techniques in his civilian life should some assassin with a grudge against Kev decide to target him. He sorely hoped it would never come to that.

Kev was nearby, performing his own evening exercises, not focused on shifting tons of metal, as per Rose's specialty, but the more delicate act of plucking the various pebbles and rocks she was throwing about the place at random, forcing him to focus and clutch them from the air before they hit the ground, rotating several of them into a smooth cycle and then threading other stones through the circle. He dropped as many as he caught, accidentally crushing others into powder in an excited dash to catch them before they thumped the floor. But, like Clyde, he was supremely fixated on the task at hand, each passing hour of the day trimming away more of the fat.

Ace and Rose called it a day when the purple shadows turned navy and the lights of the floodlamps and buildings illuminated the tabletop base in a diamond sheen. And Clyde and Kev followed Ace and Rose to a quiet spot along the trail, away from the buildings and guards and scientists and jeeps, following the starry sky along an elevated ridge that bridged up and away from the mesa through a series of increasingly tall columns of rock, the terrain grown coarse with scrub brush and cacti. The winding road felt haunted, but by what Clyde couldn't tell; perhaps it was an atavistic sense, being in the presence of such ancient land. The very ground of this arid state seemed to hold some intrinsic truth, some magic that cast the mind back millennia to simpler, more savage times. Honest times. Clyde could understand why the Native Americans found such unrivalled beauty in such bad land. The steep road made a final shadowy twist, and they stopped upon a huge chimney of rock.

It was quiet up here apart from the wind, and the panoramic view was stunning. They were right at the western edge of the mountain range, with the north, east, and south forming a half-wheel of trees and valleys and bluffs, all bathed in moon and starlight. To the north was Mosca Peak, and to the south Capilla Peak. To the east, beyond the lights of Indigo Mesa and the crowded shadows of Bosque Peak, the Manzano Mountains drifted far away from the eyeline. The other half of the wheel was all laid out before them, the ground so far below that Clyde was hesitant to peek over the edge of the chimney. In the furthest reaches to the west, just before running into the royal blue infinity, was Darnell Air Force base, its large grid of blinking lights and ant-sized buildings set far back away from the nearest highway further off to the west, and only accessible from a guarded dirt road.

Clyde wondered how many people knew about this place, this chain of interconnected crows' nests. How many outsiders and hikers had spotted these columns from afar and curiously wondered about how they could get up here. It provided Clyde with a strange thrill.

'My parents were in the Air Force,' Rose said, staring wistfully at Darnell while taking a seat on a large, curved rock that nature and erosion had seemed to sculpt into a huge reclining chair.

Clyde stared at the air base. 'They're pilots?'

'They were,' Rose answered enigmatically. 'They didn't have much love for the ground. You'd swear they were part bird. They wanted to be astronauts, but even for decorated pilots the recruitment is tighter than a nun's sniz. So they settled for the clouds instead of the stars.'

Clyde took a breath; the air was pleasant, still a little heat baked but clean and pure. 'They retired?'

'Maybe. They disappeared during some mission. I knew I could never be a pilot. I prefer to keep my boots on the ground. So I joined the army, thought it might have made them proud.'

Clyde couldn't say this surprised him. He couldn't have guessed the specifics, but he suspected that Rose's attitude to serving this country ran a little deeper than simply having nothing better to do with her life. And hearing that her parents could have been, or likely were, killed in action made him feel a pang of remorse for some of his earlier outbursts. He wasn't the only one who'd had his family life torn apart by war. He knew that, of course—he wasn't delusional or that self-centered—but he wished he hadn't been so aggressively slanderous to the armed forces. 'Where was the mission they were flying?'

'Sealed away in some private document. Redacted up the wazoo.'

And, just like that, Clyde felt his old resentment for the military snag once more.

'They'd be proud of you,' he offered, feeling a little dumb for pretending he knew anything about how a couple of strangers might have felt about their daughter's career choices.

'Don't get all moist-eyed on me now,' she joked.

A good-natured laugh rang out from Sergeant Connors and Privates Darcy and Barros; it was the ribbing humor favored by people who knew the harsh ways of life. Clyde took it in stride. After the hell he'd been put through today, he was surprised at how quickly his bonds with them had formed.

Ace diverted Clyde and Kev's attention to their left, several miles southeast from Darnell, to what might have been a generic-looking roadside diner, lit up like a bug zapper amidst a sea of scattered boulders, prairie dog holes, and rutted land that seemed to go on for all of eternity.

'The Midnight Vulture,' Ace said.

From this lofty height, details were sparse, but Clyde was pretty sure there wasn't so much as a single vehicle parked in the lot. Upon further scrutiny, Clyde noticed that it was set even further back from the highway than the air base, as if to discourage the custom of even the most lost and turned-around drivers and truckers. So much for roadside diner.

'What?' Kev wasn't sure what they were supposed to be seeing except an ailing diner.

'The place looks deader than us, right?' Barros said, her thumbs jutting either side of her at Connors and Darcy, her tone suggesting that there was a "but" on the way.

'Everything isn't as it seems on the outside,' Ace said. 'What if I told you that grease trap is as crucial to our operations as any spiritualist or Spark, gunship or spy?'

Clyde and Kev exchanged a look; it was a reflex from their simpler times, always ready to mock or joke at something silly.

'Some things hide in plain sight,' Ace went on. 'Kev, you hid yourself away behind a ridiculous disguise.'

'Looked like the damn shoe bomber,' Barros cracked, sending a ripple of chuckles through Darcy and Rose, but the sarge remained square-jawed and tight-lipped.

'Clyde, I wish you the best of luck when we're done here,' Ace continued, 'but in the short space of a day, I don't recognize the kid with a chip on his shoulder.' Clyde didn't like being called "kid," especially considering he was in his mid-twenties, but he chose not to interrupt. 'You took some licks today, and believe me, there's a lot more to come over the following weeks, but you took them without being a little bitch.'

'I'm betting the apple didn't fall far from the tree,' Rose added.

'You and Kev have shown a lot of potential in a short space of time,' Ace continued. 'But you'd never know it to look at you both. Hiding in plain sight.'

'Is that why you brought us up here? For a trite analogy?' Kev asked, cocking a wry eyebrow.

'Fuck no.' Ace pulled a can of beer from somewhere deep in his cargo pants and pulled the tab. 'I just like the view.' He started guzzling the brew.

Rose leaned back on her elbow, staring at the stars piercing the ocean darkness of the sky.

'So, were you foolin' about that crusty diner?' Clyde asked.

Ace hunkered down on the couch slab of rock and shook his head. 'No bullshit. Director Trujillo is a regular there. Kind of his office. But only Kev will get to see how awesome the jukebox is in that place. Official agents only, you know. The coffee's good too.'

Puzzled, Clyde looked at the diner, glowing in the pool of darkness. 'You know, everything is so weird right now, I can't even tell if you really are fucking with me. I know it's a little off the beaten track for regular commuters, but answer me this: why would Mr. Super-shady director hang out in a diner, of all places? Isn't that kind of inviting? Inconvenient? What if someone pulled in just out of curiosity, maybe wanted some pancakes?'

'The diner exists on a ghost road,' Darcy explained cryptically. 'It exists in a sort of mirage. From down there, on the highway, it's invisible. You need to walk into its perimeter before you can see it. Invisible to satellite, infrared, UV, the works.'

'Then how come we're looking at it?' Kev queried.

Darcy continued, not verbally, but with an unhelpful and cryptic nod towards several of the tall, slender hoodoos arranged behind them on the chimney, some crooked, some mushroom-headed, but all with an almost secret sentience.

'Wait.' Clyde wagged a finger as though to pinpoint some escaped thought. He looked at Ace. 'This the hoodoo stuff you mentioned yesterday? They're magic or something?'

'Or something,' Barros said.

'This is the Land of Enchantment,' Sarge added.

Clyde's eyes seemed to absorb the giant crooked and colorful figures of uncertain mineral. From some angles they could be mistaken for skinny and crude rock impressions of humanity, like weathered-stone stick people with elongated limbs and heads. For a second he wasn't sure if they had ever so slightly altered their positions since he got up here, only a few inches, a few degrees.

Rose took the baton. 'They're not all plain old limestone. Some disseminate a rare form of energy, allowing for sight along the ghost roads. If needed, and with their help, we can travel those roads.'

'To the Null?' Clyde asked.

'When necessary.' Rose slapped the dust and grit from her palms. 'Like we don't have our hands full with threats on this side of the grave, there's usually one prick or two who like to stir shit up over there.'

Ace drank his beer. Clyde now realized that under this vast star-studded sky, there were a lot more hoodoos scattered around the area, some standing guard along some of the forking paths below them, others packed about the outer rim of the Mesa complex behind them, some only stunted structures no bigger than an average adult human, others soaring spires over a hundred feet tall. Were they all some strange form of ancient life, or only certain ones?

'A ghost road diner hiding in plain view by the power of hoodoo rocks.' Clyde had to say it out loud to hear it. 'Yesterday I might have told you to pull the other one. Is Trujillo a ghost too?'

'Nah, he's something else,' Rose answered vaguely and slowly got back up. She affectionately slapped the nearest hoodoo. 'Anyway, I'm going to get some rack time.' Connors, Darcy, and Barros all seemed to remember the hour, swept up in conversation, and bid Clyde, Kev, and even Ace good night before passing into Rose's corporeal form with a ripple.

Amidst this unsettling discovery of conscious rock, Clyde suddenly remembered he still had his appointment with Spector. He had been so busy with the rigors of training that he'd almost forgotten he was due to take his second plunge into guided sleep. He felt so worn out he doubted he would even need that Sleeping Shepherd contraption to put him under. Thinking about facing his dreams again, and what he might find in there this time with Spector, gave him butterflies. Such truth and raw power. Consequently, he then realized he hadn't checked his phone since before breakfast. Had his mom called him back, or texted him if she was still swamped in work? He felt that first weighty brick of homesickness settle on his soul, but he knew she was fine. His auntie was always there for her when he wasn't. His mom and aunt spent so much time together that he sometimes felt superfluous in his role of son. There was no underlying drama to this familial arrangement; it was a natural settlement that suited them all fine. He felt the ghostly presence of Stephen roam the corridors of his mind, joined by that of a father he had never known. He decided he wouldn't try calling his mom again until Spector provided him with an answer to his full soul-binding potential, an answer that he knew would only trouble him, no matter the outcome. For better or worse, he'd be returning home to Brooklyn soon enough, and he'd take his mom out for something to eat. Take his auntie and cousins too, if only to secretly celebrate his return to normality, as it were. Until then, he could send her the occasional text.

Rose nodded at Clyde with what might have been a bob of friendship, or maybe it was a simple look of approval for not dying or losing his mind on the first day. She was more vocal with Kev, though, her protégé. 'Rest up. You'll need to replenish your energy for tomorrow. I was taking it easy on you today.'

Kev's mouth curved into a proud smile, anticipating the challenge. He raised his hand towards Clyde, forming a fist. 'C'mon, man. Tomorrow's a whole new day.'

Clyde got up, dusted off the seat of his track pants, and bumped Kev's knuckles. A wisp of spectral light fluttered at their connection, and Clyde felt the tingling sense like never before. This was one such occasion he couldn't dismiss, his hand subsuming the temporary light, causing his phalanges and metacarpals to flash up like an X-ray, black bones under phosphorescent skin. Then, as quickly as it happened, it ended.

Rose looked pretty composed about the whole thing, as though it was a minor surprise. 'Wow... so how long has that been happening?'

Clyde and Kev seemed a little more perplexed, staring dumbly at their own closed fists. 'First time,' they both answered in unison. Clyde couldn't stop thinking about the flash fry of his skeletal fist. 'Did I just level up or get cancer?'

Ace didn't seem too interested. He finished his beer, crushed and pocketed the can, and slapped Clyde on the back before starting to slowly pick his way back down the path of rock arches towards the base.

'It looks like you just absorbed a little of Kev's power,' Rose said. 'You can siphon.'

Clyde held his hand out towards a small scattering of stones near the edge of the chimney, pulsing his arm in single bursts and expecting to discharge some type of super-cool blast. Nothing happened. 'Nah, I think it was definitely cancer.' He examined his defective hand by flexing his fingers and rotating his wrist.

Rose punched Clyde in the arm enthusiastically. 'Don't sweat it. We'll figure it out in the morning.'

'Right... cool.' Clyde was in quiet shock. 'I need to go see Spector anyway.'

Rose set off after Ace, leaving Clyde and Kev to mutely bring up the rear. The whole way down they continued to fist bump as though they were hoping to jumpstart a dead battery.

17

THE JOURNEY BEGAN AUSPICIOUSLY ENOUGH. Captain Agua's armored convoy left the encampment and set its course north along the shore, using the map to confidently bypass the acres of sickle wheat that clashed like metal teeth along the breezy dunes. Before setting off, Agua had expressed some healthy skepticism towards Konstantin regarding the map, not only because it had been produced from memory but because he didn't trust Konstantin, believing him to be a crazy old Russian monk with a questionable agenda and state of mind. As far as he was concerned, Konstantin was an acolyte of a demented fraternity. Of course, Mortis had reminded the captain of who paid their salaries around here, and that their tour guide shouldn't be trusted explicitly; however, their agendas were aligned for the time being. In the end, Captain Agua had ceded to Mortis' point, but still appeared to have little faith in Konstantin's map.

'These shithole boondocks of death's asshole might lack orbiting GPS satellites, but at least the drone cams operate via radio waves,' Agua said to the driver, loud enough to make sure Konstantin and Mortis could both hear in the back seat. He flicked the map disdainfully and angled his head to address Mortis and, Konstantin assumed, himself too. 'And I'm still going to be relying on Lieutenant Briggs' drones.'

'I would expect so. You brought them for a reason,' Mortis said. 'Let's hope no more of those bodybags, or anything else for that matter, gulp them out of the sky.'

Agua nodded, shared a look with his driver, then inspected the map again. A few minutes of blessed peace filled the vehicle before Agua piped up again. 'Cradle of Sorrows,' he said with mockery. It was the first stop on the itinerary. 'Sounds like a shit metal band.'

'It is apt title,' Konstantin said, patience already wearing thin. 'You'll see.'

Agua perused the map and his Lensatic compass for a spell, then stared out of the passenger window. His gaze became glued to the horizon. Konstantin knew what the captain was gawping at and imagined every soldier and civilian in this convoy was gawping too: undulating lazily across the endless dusk of the horizon, several miles to the east, were some more of the beasts Agua's men had recently called skeels. The skeels were a fearsome sight. Resembling commercial airliner-sized deep-sea eels and twice as ugly, they swam through the currents of the sky like, well... sky eels, hence their clever nickname. Konstantin knew the flying behemoths would be looking for an opportunistic meal: that of a soul searching for a way out, running, hiding, ultimately caught in the wrong place at the wrong time.

'Those skeels have kept a safe distance up to now, which suits me. They aggressive?' Agua asked.

'They're wild beasts,' Konstantin answered, wanting to remain cryptic, if only to get under Agua's skin.

'This company has plenty of firepower, some interesting little toys not fit for human consumption, and me and my LTs have our own talents, but I don't want this to turn into a big game hunt if we can avoid it.' Agua flicked a glance at Konstantin, seeming wary of taking his eyes off the skeels. 'All I want is to reach our destination hassle-free, if at all possible, complete our objective, and get back home before we incur the wrath of the local warlords. I know next to nothing of the nine Houses of the Order of Terminus, the ruling classes of this underworld—or fucking dead galaxy, or whatever the fuck this place is—but what I do know for a stone-cold fact is that I'm not in this to pick a fight or spit in the face of Death. Well, maybe spit and run. But Mortis, you and your posh friends are welcome to fuck with the Houses, so long as you do so after paying me and opening a door back to the world of cold beer and hot women.'

'You will be handsomely rewarded, Captain,' Mortis said. 'You have no reason to doubt that.'

Konstantin stayed quiet, staring at the skeels sailing over the dunes of a billion crumbled bones, most of which had been ground to a fine powder. Outside the passenger window, the distant terrain started to even out to a flat and cracked landscape.

The vehicle went up and over the first of a long series of bumps. The knobbed protrusions were the vertebrae of some giant subterranean beast, a titan of life brought low, or maybe a dealer of death that could no longer fulfill its obligation to survive in this environment. Up ahead, at least ten miles or so, a huge series of drunk-leaning towers dominated the featureless landscape, each one tiered with innumerable arches, and each arch lit from within by ghostly blue lights. Both sides of the road started to gradually rise up into a steep valley, going on to encompass the dead city like a bowl.

The Cradle of Sorrows.

He eyeballed the map again, and the long, winding line that separated this fucked-up locale from the next one in their grand tour of a dead world.

Complications notwithstanding, it was difficult to accurately predict how long the journey to the Trench would take. Konstantin had already explained—but Agua must have surely gathered from his own limited experience here—that time doesn't pass the same way in Erebus. In fact, it didn't pass at all. Time was suspended, with no calculable day and night cycles. They were a mortal concern, for clocks no longer ticked for the dead. Up until now, Agua and his men had been gauging time with their watches and the time stamps on their drone camera footage; their own circadian rhythms still functioning in accordance with their East Coast, USA body clocks. Agua neatly folded the map, looking ready to wage war on anything dumb enough that might crop up between here and the Eidolon Trench. And the convoy followed the blue suns in the starry, bleached sky.

Konstantin turned his eyes front, staring through the windshield at the avenue of bone, the vehicle shocks absorbing the vertebrae bumps becoming almost soothing. He let his eyes rest on the distant necropolis, then closed his eyelids. His reprieve was an island of tranquility, though it was an island of many, frequented by his fallen brethren who came and went. Unfortunately, his island of meditative calm always had one more occupant, his and his fraternity's own revered mentor, their Arkhitektor, the last in a now-cleaved line, blackened with the viscous sin of Vor Dushi. Being back in this cursed land, Konstantin was holding out hope he could help his mentor finally find absolution and peace.

The slow, intimidating march of time had done little to Konstantin's recollection of this place. This domain, this vast and uncharted continent under the aegis of the House of Fading Light, was woven into his psyche. Its landmarks were sometimes subtle, such as an outcrop of stone scratched with runes, but often severe, such as the ridge of a giant's rib cage jutting from the blowing dunes of mineral or the approaching cityscape of towering and nameless tombs climbing up to reach for the blue suns, for a heaven that was no longer there.

Keeping his eyes closed, he focused on the soft cadence of his brethren's chanting, the Rising Path bestowing a peace that could still a raging storm. He joined their circle in the temple of his mind, and he chanted to soothe their Arkhitektor, to relieve his marred soul of the maggot which slowly turned, writhing itself awake in increments and excitement at being home again. The past washed over Konstantin, memories carried on the gentle current of their prayers against the injustice of death.

・・・

IT HAD BEEN a painfully long and tense journey from Belgrade to Siberia, with a few close calls that had Konstantin choking on his own heart. But he'd managed it and now walked the frosty, inclement streets of Novosibirsk as a hunted man, seeing British Avalon agents or Major Morozov's men in every passing car, every phone box, every twitch of a curtain, and mentally building an inventory for the journey ahead. The Kuznetsk Alatau mountain range peaked at 7,146 feet; should his destination be at the apex of the mountain, he wouldn't require an oxygen tank, which saved some effort, but he knew this trip had the capacity to turn dire, fatal even, if he wasn't well prepared. He possessed his own knife and firearm, which were discreetly kept on his person, underneath his heavy coat, but he had a list of necessary provisions, including suitable clothing and a medical kit, a new compass, a map, and a large backpack to see him through. Konstantin had never been a man to blanch in the face of fear or be deterred out of action due to an uncertain outcome; he always had backbone, but even with the exciting thought of coming face-to-face with powers he had only observed and reviewed from afar, he wasn't too proud to admit that it would be total folly if this whole situation proved to be a catastrophic mistake on his part. What if his desperation to learn and to understand the thaumaturgical had overreached his reality? Fragmented thoughts of getting lost in the wilderness crashed into his rational mind: the cryptic breadcrumb trail of Jurgen Kross leading him in circles until thirst and starvation took him, or the hermetic monks' esoteric security leading him to a confused rambling in the mountains, falling prey to wolves or brown bears; he didn't think he would have to worry about Siberian tigers, but he still filed that away under potential threats. He discarded such worries, imposing his rigid need to uncover the secret truths behind the stale façade of humanity. Let confusion and wolves and bears descend upon him. It was still worth the chance. And what was the alternative? Defect to another nation's intelligence agency? Possible, sure. He could speak German and English. But he was too tired of serving men who were tied to flags.

He wanted more. He wanted knowledge that could raise him out of the mud. And so he headed to a hiking store, purchased the bare essentials, and with a head full of military knowledge and a heart full of true faith, fled east in search of the Propusk Mertvetsa.

Dead Man's Pass.

It was hard going. For several days he strode across sub-alpine veldts, hiked through dense forests of spruce and fir, and scrambled through waist-high snow drifts and glacial formations on his way up the uncharted trail. With the final, slipping dregs of his strength, he clambered beyond the lonely, formidable peaks and dragged himself atop those last steppes, his face raw and wind-chewed, his body pouring sweat beneath the warm insulation of his mountaineer clothing, almost convinced that his quiet doubts had been astute and that this had been a fool's errand, that he'd taken too many wrong turns, missed and missed again the vague route known only to those embittered travelers who were worthy of the destination. Crawling onto the icy stone plateau, he was hit with a sudden, exhilarating realization.

He had found it.

The Temple of the Undying Hope, home to the Rising Path. The excitement was so overpowering that it kept his heavy limbs moving that little bit further. The wide snow-powdered landing merged into an expansive courtyard, largely hidden by the protective shoulders of the neighboring craggy peaks, acres of trees, and a single flat, shielding outcrop of rock that practically protruded into a ceiling.

Konstantin scanned the area, his eyes delirious with joy, his eyelashes and brows dusted with snow. At first, a sudden despair attempted to clutch at his heart, a thought telling him this place had been abandoned. But then he caught sight of a figure standing, waiting expectantly in the torch-lit shadows of a large, jagged archway, dressed in warm, snow-matted bear hide; a trim, hardened figure, carved by harsh weather and asceticism, his skin pale and tough like wintery leather. The man was to be the greatest teacher Konstantin would ever know.

Arkhitektor Empirey. The Architect of the Empyrean.

Iskatel' Sveta. The Seeker of Light.

The elder had titles but, in true pagan fashion, lacked a "Christian" name or any other bestowed under Muslim, Jewish, or other regional faiths, for this was the bailiwick of the Arkhitektor, and here the Rising Path adhered stringently to their own rituals and offered tribute to no ancient pantheon. Konstantin never learned the great man's former name.

Konstantin approached the Arkhitektor on weary legs, mindful of the ice and rock, but he also moved respectfully, not wanting to intimidate the elder monk. But the Arkhitektor showed no fear, nor did he attempt to dissuade Konstantin's intrusion. And as Konstantin reached him at the threshold of the cave, the Arkhitektor didn't ask the trespasser his name or agenda, or offer aid; all he did was appraise the half-dead man.

And just when Konstantin was starting to think the monk might be mute, the Arkhitektor spoke up in a thick Russian dialect. 'You have just learned the first lesson: only those who harbor a natural capacity to peer into the mysterious frameworks operating beyond this mortal coil can find the Propusk Mertvetsa and the temple beyond.' Konstantin, as it turned out, was the mute, fearful of talking out of place. He waited intently. 'And few of this special sort ever stumble here by accident. The potentials who find this hidden place? They are seekers of something much greater than themselves. But it comes at a price. To prove their mettle for the tasks of the Path, the neophyte must first court death closely before the path becomes clear. They must catch a swift glimpse into the frigid heart of the void that consumes all life.' The Arkhitektor's wise gaze seemed to find satisfaction in Konstantin, as if he was deciding whether the trespasser was an anomaly or a "potential." 'And for those who lack such ability? They are set to wander these freezing, hungry mountains blindly, taking their chances with the wolves and the bears.'

Konstantin cut a glance at the bear fur swaddling the older man and wondered how well fortified and armed the sect were.

The hermetic priest led him inside, down deep into the bowels of the ice-scabbed mountain. Into the fold of the Rising Path. The scale of the inner sanctum struck Konstantin dumb. As they reached the bottom of the wide and winding declivity, he found an enormous chamber. The ceiling was too high to receive the firelight of the many bronze sconces, each one looking eons old and casting their fiery glow onto rows and alcoves of bronze statuary and ornamental works depicting what appeared to be portals, suns, moons, and sinister primordial faces. Konstantin considered it to be an anthropologist's dream. He followed behind the grand shaman, casting cautionary glances at the other monks dressed in animal furs and bones, standing protectively beside offshoot tunnels, their hands gripping large bronze spears embossed with more unidentifiable symbols. Conversely, the spear holders regarded Konstantin—the intruder—with a welcoming placidity. A bitter alkali tang became steadily more pervasive in Konstantin's lungs, and he found himself swimming through thick fabrics of the heady, pungent incense. Through watery eyes he noticed the source of the cloying odor: barrel-sized clay urns positioned around a mighty megalith, the stone arrangement rising out of the fog of burning, ground-up herbs. That was when Konstantin noticed the wall sconces were not actually lit by flame at all, but scintillating red plants, sprouting mesmerizing wreathes of light; and it wasn't confined only to the sconces, for Konstantin realized the glorious fauna—unlike any he'd ever seen—was winding its way between the flagging beneath his feet like weeds, and between the hairline cracks in the masonry and carpentry of the chamber like magma-borne feathers, growing all around in bushels of wildfire mimicry. He found it beautiful in its serenity. Konstantin thought such spectacularly luminous plant life only existed in the dark oceanic fathoms.

'Zar-ptica,' the Arkhitektor said, gesturing to the glowing plants. 'Named for Serbian folkloric firebird. It flew the skies of a mystical land, a benediction or a harbinger of doom. And it, too, was native to another world, one teeming with souls and foul creatures.'

This was the second thing Konstantin had learned, and he knew there would be much more learning to follow. More than he could have possibly hoped. For within the depths of that mountain temple, he discovered more about himself than the military had ever taught him. From that point on, his education was a school of profound enlightenment and gut-churning terror, of breaching the boundaries of his cramped knowledge and pushing himself to new limits. He was tested, and sometimes he failed, and sometimes he succeeded, but through it all he strived and, in doing so, discovered a deep well of untapped potential that elevated him above many of his contemporaries and predecessors in the Path; but theirs was a mission with no room for egos.

As time passed, the Arkhitektor came to view Konstantin as his greatest disciple, with a great swell of promise. Unfortunately, for all his merit, Konstantin also discovered his limitation, how he lacked the latent requirements to one day become Arkhitektor, the most noble and rewarding station within the clergy, for he did not hold within him the innate ability to open the great divide between worlds and would henceforth always depend on the guidance of an Arkhitektor to bridge the gap between life and death. However, he found another talent. While his brothers and sisters could all commune with the whispering dead to varying degrees, the Arkhitektor rejoiced in explaining how Konstantin was a vessel born to salvage the tormented. He could be a walking community of the blighted. A gift that could perhaps be of tremendous value to the Path's true purpose: to step into purgatory, what the Rising Path called Tsarstvo Proklyatykh, the Realm of the Damned, or as the Greeks and many other cultures called it—Erebus.

For it was in this great void that the Arkhitektors of past and present believed they would find the mythic Igla Nebosvoda, the Firmament Needle.

• • •

THE HUMVEE EASED to a slow halt. The parade of military and construction vehicles ground to a dead stop like a giant mechanical caterpillar. They'd reached the entrance to the city of mausoleums, each one so tall that they blocked out the azure ache of the cold suns, stranding the convoy in unsafe shade and the wavering light of a million eerie blue flames. The towering headstone columns were wreathed in thick ropes of vine, the unhealthy vegetation crisscrossing the stone flagging that demarcated the end of the desert road and the start of this mournful metropolis. Mortis, putting aside his novel, an old edition of Cormac McCarthy's *Blood Meridian* he had brought along with him, stared ahead at the wide, empty avenues between the circular towers. Agua and the driver were occupied, eyeballing the route ahead for any trap or ambush. After ten quiet seconds Mortis sought Konstantin's expertise.

'We look like hot meal sitting here,' was all Konstantin had to say.

'Onwards, driver.' Mortis left his literature closed, content to witness this peculiar place up close.

The raiding party passed along the gloomy intersections, featureless but for the dust-blasted marble, the numberless blue flames burning within each of the numberless archways of numberless towers, and the tangles of rotting greenery strung between them like washing lines and netting. Konstantin could tell the driver, Private Culshaw, was keen to put his foot down and get back onto the open road, leaving this troubled neighborhood behind. Konstantin didn't understand why. Hadn't the driver grasped the simple fact that nowhere was safe here, and that death in its myriad forms could spring from the ground, the sky, the shadow, the water, and the very air itself, its agents the bizarre beasts that populated this corner of damnation? Konstantin heard several of his brethren voice their portents. Konstantin didn't need reminding; he'd been present when one of them had fallen here, his skeleton most likely still eroding along one of these very avenues. After several dozen yards, he spotted the ornamental staff of the fallen apostle in question, bound tight by vines against one of the memorial towers, much like the one planted in the sands along the shoreline: bronze, with a helical twist at its head, and the shaft gouged with the usual script of the Path, though now ingrained with dirt. The dead cleric's name had been Baka.

As the vehicles pushed deeper, the chug of their engines seemed deafening, a challenge to any predators lurking in wait. Konstantin knew what entities waited in here, and it was much more difficult to sneak past with the clamor of diesel engines and hydraulics. At least these idiots were armed.

Mortis tilted his head, staring out of his window. 'I think I saw something.'

Agua tried to catch sight of the thing but was too late. 'What was it?'

Mortis didn't seem concerned, just curious. A gawker on safari. 'It was too far away to tell. Something walking from one tower to the next.'

Agua picked up his walkie-talkie and asked his lieutenants, the drone team, and even the work crew manager, Hammond, who was driving one of the huge trucks, if they'd noticed anything moving around. None of them had seen anything, but they all admitted that they could feel themselves being watched.

'Do you know anything about this place?' Mortis asked Konstantin, sounding very much like a tourist enjoying his holiday.

Konstantin could practically feel the restraint bursting out of the key maker, the full extent of his powers bridled by his own trepidation and superiors like Talbot. Still, Konstantin could sense that he was a little giddy to see what was waiting behind those other doors he was forbidden to open. It must be a terrible temptation.

'Each of these monuments,' his eyes tried to peer up to their peaks, but the roof of their ride prevented it, 'is waste bin for weak souls. Those who died prematurely. The House of Fading Light thrive on souls deemed unworthy by other Houses. Those deposited here have little value even to the Fading Light. The local landlords are content for Vor Dushi to cast them off here for scavengers.'

Mortis seemed piqued. Agua grew tense.

'What type of scavengers?' Mortis asked.

'The cradle eaters.'

A huge bang bellowed out behind their Humvee, one of the other vehicles taking some devastating hits, and Agua's radio crackled into life. It was Lieutenant Castor, urgently reporting that one of his Charlie Team cars had taken a hit. Hammond quickly joined in, shouting about one of the trucks hauling an earth mover having been rocked by a surge of blue light. Agua checked the wing mirrors and told his driver to floor it, relaying the message down the line to his lieutenants and their drivers. The command had only just left his mouth when, up ahead, several bizarre forms shambled into view, forming a line across the wide avenue. Varying in height anywhere between seven and twelve feet, the strange bipedal things moved with a crippled gait. Their skin like smooth, black marble, limbs too elongated to be practical, their heads like random clay sculptures of sphere, triangle, or some inelegant mash-up. But most striking were the hollowed-out cavities of their torsos, their ribs forming an empty cage filled with a blue flame, much like those burning in the omnipresent archways of the towers.

The weak, wailing light of demised infants.

It happened so fast: a group of small, ephemeral creatures, not much more than embryos in appearance, flopped out of the long, awkward creature standing in the path of the lead Humvee. The babies were monstrous, not all of them of human origin, some belonging to races that mankind had little to no knowledge of. They crawled and screamed about the floor, bound to the light of the carrier's chest cavity by their diaphanous umbilical cords. Following some unknown decree from the sculpture-man, the litter became feral, their mushy, unpleasant faces turning hateful. Private Culshaw stamped down on the gas, meaning to test their strength with several tons of speeding metal. Being spirits, the vestigial or unused limbs of the stillborn didn't hold them back. They launched through the air, passing through the Humvee's windshield, and latched onto Culshaw's soul. Agua watched in surprise and anger as Culshaw's body went limp in death, the school of horrors being pulled back by their umbilical leashes, dragging the soul of the driver with them. The Humvee's nose shifted right forty-five degrees, and Mortis braced for impact in the back seat, but Agua acted swiftly, reaching across the limp driver, opening his door and, with no other option, tossing his body out of the driver's seat. He took the wheel and course-corrected before the vehicle went into the corner of the approaching tower creche. The rest of the convoy had been boxed in, the sounds of gunfire rattling off the sides of the towering tombs.

Konstantin couldn't bear the thought of the infants being cut down by the Exorcist rounds of these terrible men. They were innocents in this. 'Agua!' he yelled out over the sounds of engines and gunfire. 'Target the carriers! The cradle eaters! Destroy them and the innocents return to their tombs.'

Agua threw him a dirty look before ordering his men to fire indiscriminately at all comers. Mortis seemed content to watch this all unfold dispassionately. Konstantin concentrated and filed down an order to his flock, finding Wagner, a German-born member of the brotherhood. Wagner rushed from his resting place, trying to wrestle the gun from Agua's hand. But Agua proved to be preternaturally strong, resisting Wagner.

Konstantin was about to swarm the captain too when the vehicle was rocked with a deafening bang. The sound of the gunshot left his ears ringing. The bullet had passed under Wagner's chin and exited the top of his head. Konstantin watched the ghost atomize into a blue smoky vapor.

'Try that again,' Agua challenged.

Konstantin wanted to choke the life out of him. Instead, he jumped out of the moving Humvee. Agua swore as he slammed on the brakes, bringing the vehicle to sharp stop. Konstantin watched the cradle eaters dragging their unfit forms along the foliated avenues, their scrawny necks struggling to support their oddly shaped, cumbersome heads. The rest of the convoy became a chain reaction of jammed brakes and squealing tires as gunfire roared from the windows of all the military vehicles.

Konstantin watched as random shots blasted apart some of the advancing cradle eaters, removing chunks of their large obsidian heads, but just as many bullets were dispatching their juvenile attackers instead, leaving the small forms of undeveloped beings to fade away into nothingness.

Konstantin was appalled, brimming with hot bile. He wouldn't stand for this, and neither would his brethren, who were fit to revolt within him.

The Rising Path had already fled out of him like a revolving door, alighting upon both the cradle eaters and the security forces: the former were beaten and robbed of their mewling stillborn before being torn apart by the righteous mob; a few members of the latter were dealt a harsh physical warning and told to focus their gunfire on the crudely constructed shambling things that continued to stagger towards them in clusters, their hordes of shrieking babies in tow. Konstantin felt a sharp stab of pain beneath his armor. Had the diseased tumor of Vor Dushi awoken within the Arkhitektor's soul? Down on one knee, his hand pressed to the breastplate of his necronaut armor, he decided that wasn't the case. And he quickly found out the source of his pain. Glancing up, he watched in despair as Artur, one of his comrades from the monastery, shuffled backwards a few steps, a crater in the side of his head. Artur's ghost dissipated into vapors. He felt several more twists of agony and scanned about the chaotic siege, seeing the Exorcist rounds put down more of his protectorate: Vadim,

Annika, Yefim, a score more. They all paid the ultimate price for their magnanimous acts while their executioners simply shifted their gun sights onto the stillborn that floated in the air from their cords like lost balloons, darting towards the vehicles in further attempts to snatch the souls from the living who had dared to pass through their dwelling.

Agua was out of the Humvee now, his trigger finger rapid and his aim true, his shots doing terrible physical damage to the snatching children that were dragging the corpse of his driver, Culshaw, into their ranks, his corporeal meat the dessert to his soul. It was no use; the driver was lost in a sea of greedy, red-glistening fingers and claws.

Konstantin stood up, trying to feel what connections he had left. It didn't feel like many. They had largely been eradicated forever. They deserved paradise, not this, and he had failed them. He knew none of Agua's men would dare fire upon him; should they dare, Mortis would likely leave them here for the remainder of their short, painful lives. And Konstantin had to remind himself that he was once a soldier. He marched towards the Humvee, noticing that Mortis continued to watch without lifting a finger to help, not wanting to demean himself with the labor. Konstantin found Culshaw's semi-automatic rifle lying along the wide avenue, removed the gauntlet on his right forearm, and raised the rifle, feeling the past flow back into him, muscle memories tweaked from a very long sleep. He assumed this weapon was also loaded with the Exorcist ammunition and trusted his aim enough to not slay the squealing children. They were frightened, he told himself, victims in all of this. With the selector set to burst-fire mode, he sprayed short but devastating groupings into the withered, triangular head of the nearest cradle eater. His aim quickly slipped from one target to the next, the caliber of the cartridges leaving gray, oozing masses atop the spindly necks, the corrupted youth quickly slipping their captors and soaring off in all directions, returning to the towering gravestones.

From the corner of his eye, Konstantin noticed that Agua had slipped his Glock back into its holster and marched towards the last line of sculptures barring their way. Konstantin had a few bursts left in his rifle and chose not to help him, though he did linger just long enough to watch what happened, and just as he had assumed, the captain had a secret hidden under that façade of humanity. Agua's hands began to glow from within, a barium hue that only grew stronger, radiating up his forearms like he was on the verge of becoming a radioactive disaster. A swarm of glowing green flies poured from his hands, speeding towards the remaining cradle eaters. The flies whistled and exploded on impact like emerald fireworks, reducing the carrion scavengers to multiple amputees.

Konstantin had seen enough to know what he was dealing with. For now, he had to find what remained of his brethren, feeling the first salty sting of tears in his eyes. He stamped towards the stalled line of trucks and Humvees, not paying attention to the drivers and passengers who continued to light up both the stillborn and their handlers. The three lieutenants had left their rides and joined the fray, ordering their men to hold their positions; if these three also had claim to any other spectacular skill set, then they were yet to express it, relying on their firepower to cut down the slowing ranks of attackers. The floating children darted towards random troops, small hands or claws or tentacles eager to pull back a large morsel of soulful sustenance for their keepers, only to be thwarted and flinch away at the last second by brutal, skillful shots to themselves or their owners. Without breaking stride, Konstantin used his last bullets to put down another cradle eater, its lumpy, imperfect hexagonal head shattering like a spoilt melon. Tossing the rifle away in disdain, he was on top of Lieutenant Castor before the officer could react and stole his sidearm from his holster. The hate in Castor's dark, smoky eyes almost made Konstantin react with violent intent, but within a split-second stare the mercenary read the Russian's motive and left him to it, returning to shoot and reload, shoot and reload. Subconsciously, Konstantin found it peculiar that the pall of gun smoke was beginning to adhere to Castor like a cloak, weaving itself before his very eyes as though by the hands of an invisible tailor. Konstantin plucked his eyes away and picked his shots as he walked, forcing himself not to casually put down the odd Citadel Security operative out of sheer judiciousness.

Finally, with some relief, he found Kuznetsov fighting alongside Alpha Team in protecting Hammond and his men. Even without his ceremonial bronze blade, the monk was dispatching the last of the forces with a release of repressed grief and fury, a storm of haunting wind flinging the cradle eaters against the nearest tombstone over and over, smashing their angular frames and hard heads into ruin, watching the blue flames die in their chest and their stillborn sail away. Before the final interlopers could be dispelled, the CSS suffered two more losses: Bravo Team's Corporal Parel, and Morris Lim, one of Hammond's digger operators, their fresh souls startled by the act of being pulled from their bodies, only managing to escape the clamps of the shrieking orphans when consecrated lead blew apart their respective controllers. Parel and Lim rushed back to try and reclaim their limp bodies, terror shaping their faces as they realized that for some illogical reason, they were locked out. Corporal Parel turned his attention to Konstantin in the hopes of finding an alternative shelter. He bolted towards the necromancer, only to be denied access, crashing off the armor like a bird flying into a pane of glass. The corporal, like his associates, was a black-hearted cutthroat, and unwelcome beyond the protective seals of the armor.

Konstantin ignored him and glanced towards Kuznetsov, who passed effortlessly through the armor, back into his honeycomb cell. Then Konstantin regarded Lim. He didn't know Lim's past. He might work construction, but that didn't mean he was a good man; far from it. But it was worth a try. Konstantin beckoned the scared Lim over, hearing Parel protest. Hammond was at Lim's body, his head bowed, forcing himself to contain his sorrow for his departed friend. Laying a hand briefly on the shoulder of Lim's body, Hammond stood up and watched the man's ghost pass into Konstantin and found a little solace.

'Sorry about your friend,' Konstantin told Hammond, seeing his ruddy, stubble-rough jaws fight to control their stoicism. 'Give him time to adjust, he'll come back to see you later.'

Hammond nodded despondently. 'I've known him fifteen years,' was all he said.

Konstantin turned on his heel, feeling empty now that his only company was Kuznetsov, Lim, and the disquieting presence of his disgraced Arkhitektor. Parel continued to spit foul language at Konstantin, asking what he was supposed to do now.

'You're stuck here,' Konstantin answered without the dignity of a passing glance, walking back down the line towards Agua, Mortis, and their Humvee. A single exclamatory gunshot broke the new quiet, and Konstantin spun around in time to see Corporal Parel's revenant vanish like smoke on a breeze, a gaping exit wound in his forehead. Lieutenant Castor, the sinewy, black-eyed commander of Charlie Team who Konstantin had recently glimpsed wielding a loose shroud of smoke, shoved his semi-automatic pistol back into his holster. Lieutenant Fenwick didn't object to the mercy killing of his man; he likely would have done it himself. And nobody else seemed to mind either. Konstantin liked Castor's face even less than the others. It spoke of cavorting amongst corpses. His attention snagged briefly on Castor's peculiar necklace of spent shell casings, and then, thinking nothing more of it, he turned back towards his Humvee.

Mortis was leaning against the Humvee, arms folded, with an expression that seemed to say, Are we done yet? Agua's expression was not so mild. But neither was Konstantin's, for so black was his spite and animosity for this man that he wanted to gouge his eyes out and leave him here, blind and lost, amongst the foul and the dead. He had put Wagner down for the crime of trying to spare innocent souls, causing his amoral thugs to escalate the senseless slaughter. And now all but two of Konstantin's entire sanctuary had been eradicated. Konstantin felt a great dearth of humanity at that moment. He didn't allow himself to mull on what he'd be willing to subject Captain Agua to. But now, more than ever before, he needed guns, and he needed men to help his journey. They needed each other, even if Agua and his curs didn't realize it.

The captain got right up in Konstantin's face, all spittle and venom. 'Let's get one thing straight, holy man, I don't give a goat fuck about your soft-hearted quest for picking flowers and finding enlightenment. I'll waste any soul I find in this dead asshole of a world if I have to,' he hammered home, a blocky pointer finger trying to crack Konstantin's armor. 'You endanger any more of my men, I'll skull-fuck you and leave you for dead along the side of the road. We got your map, and my employers will find someone else who can fit a bunch of men inside him.' Agua shot a confirmatory look at Mortis.

Mortis didn't confirm; in fact, he returned an empty-eyed, murderous expression that neatly clipped Agua's outburst, and then held up his right thumb. He sighed in resignation. The thumb key was cracked, though no physical pain appeared to register on Mortis' pallid face.

'What happened?' Agua asked, jaw clenching.

'One of those baby-snatcher things snuck up on me in the confusion. I must have cracked the key whilst fending him off.'

'Great.' Agua nodded, the news sinking in. 'That's fucking great. So we're stuck here?'

'Until I can cut a replacement key, we're stuck here,' Mortis corrected.

Nobody said anything. Konstantin was too bereft, trembling with the aftertaste of swallowed hate to take pleasure in Agua's misstep.

Mortis' face brightened a tad, and he pushed off from the ride and made to climb back inside. 'Might be a good idea to get back on the road. We're trying to keep a low profile here.' The crisp shutting of his door ended the scene, and all party members who had left their trucks and Humvees—either for survival or just to hear the vocal fallout between Agua and Konstantin—returned and got into gear.

Mortis fidgeted with the copy of his novel. 'Two losses is acceptable,' he said to the back of Agua's head, who was now the acting driver.

Agua silently steered them through the dark jungle of creeping vines, his eyes alert at all points, until the thoroughfare opened into another wide bend of dead dust and blue sunlight. The terrain slowly began to morph from the cracked stone of the Cradle to endless lumpy hills of damp black sod and poisonous weeds.

The captain finally broke his silence. 'What happens if we lose more men between here and the Trench?'

Mortis was opening his shirt, and his chest, the dark, light energy humming audibly. He checked with Konstantin as if to confirm that Agua's question was indeed that stupid. 'Well, Captain, I recommend that you endeavor not to lose any more men until, like I just succinctly explained, I can repair this key to open our only way home.'

Konstantin noticed how Mortis didn't sound too afraid of such an eventuality, though his attention inspected the sky quickly, searching for one of the awful sentient god heads watching from their seat amongst the soft burn of the stars. Konstantin had already checked and knew they were not being watched for the moment. The dead gods had little interest in their presence.

'Though I must say,' Mortis added, 'the way you handled those things back there, I'm wondering if we really need you at all.'

Agua remained silent.

Konstantin kept his peace and watched the toxic flora drift by.

18

CLYDE COULDN'T TELL HOW MANY ticks had tocked down here in the Median.

This was his fourth training day now at Indigo Mesa, and his fourth official session under the spell of the Sleeping Shepherd, or "Black Betty," as Spector/Ramaliak liked to call it. And it was still a hell of a trip. Another three-hour stint amidst his own hopes and fears. Thankfully, Spector had assured Clyde of his adherence to a strict confidentiality clause, preventing him from disclosing any of the nuttiness that might occur within the walls of Clyde's skull.

After the initial falling sensation, Clyde had been cast once more into a discombobulating array of emotional stimuli: the upper sleep crust of the Median. It wasn't a comic-book world like his taster session, but like the other previous occasions, it was dark and vague, the raw energy of his sleeping mind throwing out random environments and objects, unsure of what composition it was trying to make. The chaotic abstractions would find a form, only to dissolve and become something new, and each time Clyde would feel small and insignificant in the face of these thoughts and feelings. He watched as impressions of New York streets mashed into odd rooms he'd never set foot in; a bear charged out of the woods to slaughter an elk; and then he had a gun in his hand and was attempting to shoot a snowman in his own backyard, only for it to somehow keep dodging his bullets.

'What the hell does this one mean?'

'I can take you into your dreams,' Ramaliak said. 'But I can't read them. A lot of the time they don't mean anything. They're just thoughts plucked out of your head and blended together. But if I had to take a pop psychology swing at this particular one, I'd say you want to shoot Ace. Or at least what he represents.' Clyde turned to look at Ramaliak, a guilty look on his face. 'I'm not saying that's something you really want to do, just that a part of you isn't thrilled about what you're doing.'

Clyde silently pushed on, not wanting to confront Ramaliak's prognosis. Clyde knew he didn't want to shoot Ace. That was nonsense—incredibly, he was actually getting used to the guy—which meant it was likely that it was his muted anger and hostility towards his situation that was quietly festering and seeping out. In fact, it could be a type of survival response. His true self fighting back against his recent activities with Ace and Rose. But he didn't have time for this now. Ramaliak had brought him here for practice, to adjust to the demands of the Median, and that was what he intended to do.

Ramaliak continued to guide and shelter him through the noise and confusion of the shifting and formless narrative. 'How are you feeling?'

Clyde hadn't wanted to mention it, but he was feeling a little peculiar. A bit floaty. Had he been in here longer than the previous sessions? 'I'm okay. When will you take me down to the next layer?'

'The memory catalogues. I can take you down anytime, but I need to make sure you're stable enough. You heard of the bends? When scuba divers rush up from the depths too quickly? Well, if I rush you through the descent, it's kind of like that, but in reverse. Drop down too quick and you'll feel the pressure change between the dream layers.'

Clyde watched as a flying saucer hovered over what was supposed to be Darnell Air Force Base, though apart from the desert backdrop it didn't look much like the airbase. Rose was there, sitting in the cockpit of a jet fighter and getting ready to fly. To fight the UFO? To get eye-level so she could happily wave at a little big-headed gray guy at the saucer's controls? Clyde dismissed dreams as a load of nonsense. 'I said I'm fine,' he insisted. 'Can you take me down?'

Ramaliak stopped in his tracks and seemed to be examining Clyde's eyes. Whatever Clyde was feeling, this mental fatigue, he screwed it down tight and quietly begged for Ramaliak to overlook it. He looked over Ramaliak's tweed shoulder and saw himself sitting alone in a dark, empty room, drawing in his sketchpad by the glow of an unknown light source. A figure was there with him. He could feel that it was supposed to be Kev, but Kev was a charcoal smudge, faceless and quiet. A shadow with nothing to offer but imaginary company.

'I'll take you down,' Ramaliak relented. 'But I'm pulling you out at the first sign of trouble.' His words seemed to stir Clyde from a reverie, and he glanced over his own shoulder to see what Clyde had been staring at, but it was too late. The mirage had already changed again.

A hoof made contact with Clyde's hand, and the next thing he knew they were spiraling deeper, deeper into darkness. He could feel his stomach rolling, his body at the mercy of gravity, and his thoughts becoming drunk in their slurred speed. And as they fell, the Sleeping Shepherd continued to count down from on high.

With the jarring play of forces coming to a sudden halt, Clyde believed they had escaped the elusive twists and emotional blindsides of the outer layer of the Median and arrived at his archived memories. It was another dark void for the moment, but a light was gently powering up somewhere far away. He flirted with panic at having someone who was still essentially a stranger getting an eyeful of his history, most of it private, but the coyness felt a little foolish now. Ramaliak had already seen the inside of his head, an intimate experience that surely granted him some good faith. Besides, it wasn't as though Clyde feared any skeletons falling out of his closet. That soft light became a series of small squares, all connected in a lengthy chain, like a roll of film. One of the squares began to shine more brightly than the rest, drawing him and Ramaliak into it like moths to a flame. Clyde had to shut his eyes and felt himself buckling under the weight of this phenomenon. The blinding light softened again, and he slowly opened his eyes.

When the head rush cleared, he found himself standing in the kitchen of his old familial Brooklyn home. A warm and safe place.

His memory's depiction was accurate in some regards: the aged grease stains high over the stove, immune to scrubbing and any number of household cleaners, that one chipped wall tile at the base of the sink's windowsill, the haggard and worn linoleum of the floor, but it was a little blurred and uncertain in others, with the novelty fridge magnets and the windowsill plant being little more than a blurry impression. He realized his mom was standing immobile over the sink, her back to him, head low and shoulders shuddering. Crying. He felt like he'd been punched in the gut, knowing what was coming next, if memory served correctly. Sure enough, Clyde almost jumped when his younger self entered, a skinny thirteen-year-old in jeans and a Tshirt of The Tick. He remembered his younger self had been watching TV in the living room, quietly staring at the screen but not really seeing anything, knowing his mom was attempting to make him some dinner while she quietly wept over the news she'd just received.

He was afraid he would be seen by his younger counterpart, causing some sort of dilemma, but he was apparently an invisible presence to his memories. He tore his eyes away from his teen kid version and crying mom, and glanced around the doorway, knowing the living room would be empty, but unable to stop himself.

And it was.

Empty.

No Stephen.

His brother had always put on a brave face for his little brother and acted as the emotional bulwark between Clyde and their grieving mom, who had struggled quietly since the death of Richard. But Stephen wasn't there to help Clyde or their mom this time.

Stephen was dead.

This was the day Clyde and his mom had learned that their family had gotten even smaller. Cleaved in half. Just like his dad's death, Clyde heard that Stephen's was a brave and noble one. Serving his country.

It did nothing to alleviate his pain.

Thirteen-year-old Clyde could only silently watch his mom cry over the sink, looking unprepared to offer support of any kind. Clyde, not the little kid he was then, but the grown man he was now, stood mutely in this memory, recalling how he felt that day. That crater in his chest, in his very life, which he was somehow expected to live with. Trying to imagine his mom's pain too, and how she would have to continue moving forward for his own benefit, pretending everything was going to be okay. Clyde couldn't turn away from the depressing drama, his eyes flicking from the scared kid he used to be to his mom and waiting for her to turn from the sink. That didn't happen. Instead, she stopped moving; even her heart-wrenching sobs and shoulder hitching stopped. She had become a statue, a cipher of a mournful impression, as had the young man.

He didn't feel so good, and it wasn't just the miserable memory that had him out of sorts. It was becoming tough to stand up straight.

Was this what Ramaliak had warned him of?

Where was Ramaliak?

Clyde had to move before he collapsed. He wandered through this cold representation of his ruined childhood, built from feeling as much as memory, and found his way to a bedroom. Stephen's bedroom. It was just the way it was when he left to join the Marines. Clyde felt a hot ache in his chest, moving about the room, inundated with a million meaningless and yet invaluable conversations he had shared with his brother in this very room. Dumb jokes and confidences. He stared at the New York Knicks banner tacked to his wall, the PlayStation, and the posters of Outkast, Wu-Tang, and half-naked babes, the boxes of comic-books that had blown up Clyde's young imagination. He could feel his brother's presence in every square inch of this shrine.

The room began to unexpectedly bend and shift, details being rubbed out of existence by an unseen eraser. The interior quickly altered and became that of his parents' room. This was a more youthful memory of Clyde's, one he'd almost lost to the hazy mists of childhood. An eight-year-old Clyde stood before him, staring at his father's duffel bag, which Clyde had dug out and placed on his parents' bed. The boy he used to be had been obsessed with this duffel bag, the one his mom kept in the back of her wardrobe with a small gathering of Richard's cufflinks and ties and shirts, all of which had that heavy aroma of age and experience. Clyde went on to think of this fragrance as the smell of nostalgia. Watching this memory replay itself reminded him of how he used to rummage about in this duffel bag, carrying his toys around in it when his mom was out. And he'd wonder what faraway places this bag had seen. What adventures his dad had taken it on. All he knew back then was that his dad had been a soldier, and, having been spared the emotional trauma of losing him, Clyde was still too bright-eyed and naïve to think of soldiers as anything other than cool and exciting. Despite his mom's best efforts. And so young Clyde continued to think of his dad as some big war hero. One of the good guys, even though the man was nothing but an idea to him, a smiling face in some old photographs, or some words of wisdom and strength passed down through his mom by proxy.

Clyde looked at his younger self's furtive expression and recalled that familiar sense of intrusion that he used to feel as a child whenever he entered this room. It was a sense of the forbidden, that he was imposing himself upon his parents' private shared bond, one that reached back through their own youth as a smitten young couple, back before Clyde or even Stephen were anything but hypotheticals. Clyde turned away from the boy's meddling to the bureau, and his eyes found the old photographs of grandparents from both sides of the family, the frilly lampshades his mom had picked out, and Richard's passport and some other unknown documents his younger self had uncovered but was too young to fully understand.

He had to suddenly brace himself against the wall, feeling his balance tip drastically. There was a commotion in his head. A freight train of conversations all trying to talk over one another, and behind it all, the tick-tick-tick of the Sleeping Shepherd. Clyde's knees gave out, his vision blurring. With the pressure building steadily, he thought he could make out Ramaliak enter the bedroom, leaning in close to his watery vision.

'The hour grows late.' Spector's voice emanated from the black smear of the ram's head.

Clyde nodded like a jackhammer, wanting to be pulled out then and there, before his head imploded. The preliminary noise of the Shepherd's waking call echoed down from Spector's office to the Median, and right on cue, the Shepherd chimed, and Clyde felt the turbulent rush rocketing him back to reality. He blinked several times, his pupils dilating to the softly lit office.

He sat up in his chair, muscles aching from the training, seeing the clock over Spector's desk. One o'clock. During that first scheduled sleep session following his night atop the chimney stack with his team—was it strange how comfortable that word "team" sounded to him now?—he had asked Spector if he could just spend the night in the chair, or on the floor, and let the Shepherd guide him right on through until morning light and the fresh physical ordeals it would bring. But he'd known it to be a long shot, and that Spector would rather have a proper night's sleep devoid of babysitting him. And Clyde had been right, as Spector had politely turned down the idea, setting out a regular dream-diving timetable: 10 A.M. to 1 P.M. each day, right after Clyde's first training session and a much-needed breakfast.

Clyde had formed the habit of turning to the glasses of stolen dreams and malignant ideas occupying the large cabinet over on his left. It made him think about his own thoughts and dreams, fears and hopes, being bottled at the source and locked away. Could doing that change a person? Create a sort of Manchurian Candidate?

Spector stretched, the pop in his back loud and exquisite. Clyde envied such a great release of muscular stress. Each day had been a rigid routine of merciless body-breaking combat training, weapons drill after weapons drill, and basic tactics. In such a short space of time, he had become, though he was loathe to admit it, a version of himself that could probably kill his old self without too much hassle. Kev, too, had refined his coordination, increasing his sloppy long-range manipulation, while also increasing his strength; though he could still drain himself quickly if he wasn't economical with his exertions.

Clyde found it disconcerting how fast the military life had agreed with him, fitting like a glove. He still spent every evening drawing, though; he'd sooner die now and wallow in the Null than turn his back on his passion, and before long he knew he'd have to be making the ninety-mile trip north to Santa Fe to find a comic-book shop, unless he could talk to Ace and Rose about the safe use of the internet to buy any new issues online. They would give him shit for it, of course, but he knew it would be well-meaning shit.

Spector rolled his neck and walked over to the half-full coffee pot plugged in atop the desk near a row of filing cabinets, and poured two cups of the strong black stuff, passing the first one to Clyde. Clyde yawned and nodded gratefully. 'I knew it was too soon to take you that deep. Experiencing such lucidity is very demanding. So, are you going to ease off the gas now?'

Clyde nodded again in acquiescence, understanding he needed patience. There was a sense of relief, however, that the detrimental effects of the Median hadn't followed up into his wakefulness. 'I'll rein it back.'

He brought the cup to his lips, testing the heat. 'Not a bad job you have, though,' he said. 'Getting a government salary to sleep at your desk.'

Spector smiled and rubbed the bridge of his nose where his glasses had started to rub. 'Well, I wish I had more newbies like you. Truth is, I very rarely get to let Black Betty out of the pen these days. Maybe I should ask Trujillo about recruiting some more fresh faces with a talent for dead talk. I could get rid of the desk and bring in a couch instead.'

'The cookie crumbles.'

'It does.' That seemed to remind Spector, who quickly fell upon a packet of cookies he had lying on his desk. He didn't offer Clyde any, not wanting to interfere with his hard work with Agents Ace and Rose. 'The only sleep I get is in my office.' His smile was wry, but his eyes were baggy. 'I've spent so much time stealing secrets and helping mediums that my body clock is irreversibly out of whack; I think that's the technical term for it.' He raised his mug in a cheers gesture and poured coffee into his mouth the way people fill their car's gas tank.

'Sorry to hear that, Specs.' Clyde drank half his cup and got up, feeling a dozen aches and niggling pains poking across his body. 'I'll tell you one thing: I'll have no problem getting to sleep tonight.' He put his cup on the desk and made for the door.

'What is it now?' Spector asked, reclaiming his seat.

'Kev and I have training with something called the Djinn Lamp.'

Spector looked amused, his red-rimmed eyes full of humor and what might have been pity. 'Don't forget to stretch.'

Clyde gave him a curious look, then, 'Same time tomorrow?'

'If you can fit me in.'

'Better believe it.' Clyde left the office to see a djinn about a lamp.

• • •

CLYDE AND KEV stood in the middle of a large dome, fitted together by huge sections of hardened white polymer panels—capable of withstanding a grenade blast, they'd been told—and the floor was a series of concentric circles. Their furtive eyes stared at the recessed lights and panels of circuitry stationed about the higher reaches of the dome. He jangled his fingers a few times and flexed his fists to keep the blood moving, practicing a dry quick draw from his holster, staying loose for whatever was about to be thrown at him. His black tactical armor—a vest and joint pads—were military grade and a little snug, but not too restrictive in movement.

'Am I the only one who was expecting some ancient Arabic-looking lamp?' Kev asked.

'No. I was thinking more along the lines of Aladdin, not the X-Men's Danger Room,' Clyde retorted.

The Djinn Lamp was some conflation of techno-sorcery that Clyde didn't dare question or attempt to understand. Kev had asked about it, of course, and Ace answered with his patented flavor of vernacular and gruff, which wasn't particularly helpful. But what Clyde did parse was that the "Djinn" was literal, a reality-bending trickster turned mystical prisoner, and not just some marketer's brand name. His "Lamp," however, was a sophisticated computer, trapping him in coded bindings; it also stored a series of training programs and a seemingly endless reference list of known otherworldly entities and threats, the selected of which was then brought to life within the huge domed training room by the POW genie.

Clyde told himself that he shouldn't be scared about this as his hands stayed close to his dual-holstered pistols. He had to view this as a game. A bit of role play. He had spent the vast majority of his life breathing oxygen and comic-books, and now he was practically living one. On the other hand, the most physical damage a comic-book could offer was a paper cut. Kev was looking pumped and ready to get into it. Kev, who'd never been big on fighting in his living years, who'd sooner disappear into a book or a video game when things got tough, had become something of a barbarian over the last few days. But Clyde was the only one who'd been taking any physical punishment, and he hoped Kev wouldn't prove to be a kitten instead of a tiger should they ever encounter something that could smack ghosts back. Or maybe that was exactly what Kev wanted, Clyde thought. It might strip the allure of this life away from Kev, or at least make him consider a less physical and problematic role in the administration. Data entry should be pretty safe.

'Okay, rookies, just one week with the Djinn is like two weeks with the SAS,' Ace spoke over the intercom. He was observing them through the protective blast shield of the wide observation window. He had kept hold of the talk button, and Clyde heard him complaining to the Lamp technician about their chosen category of threat; something about switching it up from a level two-rated creature to a level three. Clyde hoped Ace didn't hold rank in this place.

'Time to put some peach fuzz on your nuts,' Ace bellowed over the speaker.

'Fuck,' Clyde muttered to himself.

Ace prowled about the control and observation room like a seasoned hockey coach. 'I'm hitting you with what we call a buzzkill. You'll see why in a minute.'

Clyde had no idea where the buzzkill would be coming from. Suddenly a huge man-fly hybrid lit up in mid-air, picking a random zig-zagging flight path around the dome on iridescent wings. It was somewhat faded at first, like a weak hologram projected onto a wall of mist, but the creature became more solid and detailed with each successive layering of light, the Djinn Lamp making it a reality.

Real enough to hit. And real enough to hit back.

Without warning, the buzzkill shot down from the apex of the dome, making a direct charge for Clyde. Clyde drew both his Glocks with a smooth flow. When he'd first tried this on the range with Rose he'd bungled it, almost dropping the piece. Not this time. He fired a torrent of bullets skywards, most of the shots going wide of the rapidly descending target, but a few hitting home into its tough, fibrous chest. He hopped out of the way as the thing landed on two powerful chitinous legs in the center of the chamber, its two compound eyes fixing him with an insect's impassionate regard. Before it could make a move, it was smeared into a wet burst of bile-colored ichor, some of which spattered Clyde's cheek. Clyde stared dumbly at the puddle of twitching veiny wings, then looked at Kev, who returned an off-hand shrug. The puddle erased itself in a single clean, digital wipe.

'A big fly? That's it?'

'Your arrogance will be the death of me,' Clyde said.

A swarm of buzzkills flitted about the dome, six-foot frames on large, powerful, translucent wings. Their collective buzz was like a drill in the ear. Clyde dropped into a squat, trying to find a clear target and not wanting to start randomly shooting the place up like an amateur; Rose would beat the shit out of him if she heard about such poor form after her repetitions. Kev lifted into the middle of the room, several of the fly-men passing through him in whining confusion. His hands shifted about like those of a crazed orchestral conductor, slamming one attacker, then another, into the walls or floor. Easy enough, but they just kept pouring in, and Kev couldn't do this all night without using up his energy.

One of the buzzing pests alighted next to Clyde, making to seize him with its powerful, thick-bristled arms. Clyde sidestepped the grab and placed two clean shots through one of its huge oil-and-water-sheened eyes, emptying its head in a gout of yellow fluid. Despite the swift dispatch, others in the party must have taken Clyde, the floor-bound, to be the weaker prey, with more and more of them beginning to circle and drop down in fleeting attempts at snatching him up. Clyde could feel his terror pushing and tugging him, keeping him on the balls of his feet, his guns constantly swinging about in short, tight arcs in his search for a clear shot. The previous days of endless drills with Rose and beatings from Ace hadn't prepared him for this.

Clyde replayed the conversation he'd had with Ace before coming here:

"Can the Djinn hurt me?"

"Pass me that six-pack."

Clyde knew that wasn't a good answer at the time. But he had still passed him that six-pack of beer from the rec room's fridge.

Two flies landed on either side of him, closing in with their hooked hands. Telling his panicked thoughts to shut the hell up, he went on autopilot and hoped it wouldn't get him dead. He smashed one of the dark hooks away with one gun butt and blasted a few rounds into its center mass with the other, stunning it, then used his parrying 9mm to blow apart the brain pan. With a fluid heel turn, he raised both guns towards the second insect, a bullet from each gun dropping it into a slump on the floor. All around the buzzing continued, fit to induce a headache. With a closed fist, Kev clutched one of the fly-men in place, holding it aloft by invisible forces, its powerful strength testing his endurance. Clenching his teeth, Kev's phantom grip ruptured the clasped insectoid, spattering its innards to the floor below. Clyde continued to be a moving target, running about the large arena, each new opponent in the armada meeting a quick demise from hot lead. But Clyde had missed as many targets as he'd hit, and when a buzzkill dropped squarely in front of his path, its hooks beginning to unexpectedly charge up a tracery of electrical energy, he brought his Glocks up in surprise.

He squeezed both triggers.

And nothing happened.

The buzzkill's bright-yellow and blue ball of electricity started to raise the long, spiky hairs studding its black arms. It unleashed the bolt, aiming to cook Clyde right through. Clyde leapt aside, performing a half-decent shoulder roll that didn't hurt him too much, and it certainly beat getting overloaded by a—that's when his brain finally connected the dots.

Buzzkill.

'Hilarious, Ace, you absolute prick,' Clyde wheezed, turning to face his attacker.

Out of ammo, he quickly fumbled for his combat knife and cast a betrayed look at Ace, slouching there in the control room, beer in hand, watching the stakes increase by the second without too much concern.

Ace leaned over the mic. 'You're out of ammo, but don't forget that little party trick we cooked up for you and Kev.'

'We only did it once!' Clyde yelled back, ducking and slipping the flies hovering in and out of his reach. He didn't even know if Ace heard him or cared.

Another wild bolt of electricity crackled and zapped the space in front of him, but he sidestepped all the same, expecting to get hit by another bolt any second. Another fly-guy dropped down, barring his path, its mandibles clacking together in what might have been fury. Clyde gripped its swinging hook arm and embedded the knife blade into the joint between fore and upper arm. The noise it made was almost as atrocious as its incessant buzzing. The knife scraped against lean muscle and cartilage like tough gristle. Removing the knife, he kept hold of the arm and slid closer, driving the serrated blade into one of the large bulbous eyes. That switched off its attack.

'Right, so ... party trick.' Clyde couldn't argue that it wasn't a better idea than trying to take on the rest of them with just his knife. 'Kev!' he called up, watching his partner whip his hand down onto a wounded fly, smashing it like it had been swatted by a giant rolled-up newspaper.

Kev had obviously heard Ace's big idea too because Clyde was suddenly being dragged up into the air, at first believing he was done for, that a massive fly monster had taken him and would soon frazzle him like a giant bug zapper, but it was only Kev pulling him close. They reached out and bumped knuckles.

Nothing happened.

'You feel anything?' Kev asked.

'Yeah, fucking stupid,' Clyde shouted over the incessant buzzing.

They tried it once more, and Clyde's arm lit up with a spooky Xray effect as a surge of cooling energy raced up his arm to his chest. Clyde flashed back on the gelatine ballistics dummies Rose had set up for him, the ones that resemble skinless jelly people, all artificial organ and bone. And how his hand had gone off like an RPG, the chest cavity of the first dummy bursting into a fountain of synthetic gore.

Kev held his position in the middle of the room, untouchable to the frenzied efforts of the diminishing fly armada as he glided Clyde about in a medium-fast loop. Clyde's expression had fused into one of manic concentration. He knew for certain that Kev was winging it with this little strategy, but he locked into the moment, using the siphoned power to thrust a violent discharge of telekinetic force into the oncoming swarm. He had tried to create a shield of sorts to smear the buzzkills like flies on a windshield, but he didn't know how, or if that was even possible, so he continued with the telekinetic shotgun blasts, and those he missed, he swiped at with his knife. The move was improvised and messy, with Clyde missing more than he hit, but those that were hit twirled to the ground, either pulverized or hacked.

He was about to start screaming at Kev in an undignified manner, shouting at him to put him back down before he sprayed the circumference of the room in projectile coffee, scrambled eggs, and toast, but he was spared the embarrassment, as Kev started to lower him amongst the corpses vanishing into pixelated light. Clyde's legs felt okay, his equilibrium too after a few seconds of light-headedness, but he made a note to tell Kev that next time they decided to perform a strategic move, then it had better be one he had some prior knowledge of.

The last three buzzkills hummed the atmosphere with their crackling charges, readying for a last-ditch attack. Clyde imagined their unknown voltage spearing him to the floor, turning his muscles rigid to the point of tearing, burning them from the inside out and overloading his neurons.

His mouth formed a tight line as he watched the flies dart about in agitation. In his periphery, Kev appeared a little winded. Adrenaline overload notwithstanding, Clyde, too, felt twitchy and nauseous, but he knew he could continue. He had a knife and no ammunition, but he could feel the last reserves of Kev's influence pulsing within his right arm. He didn't give himself time to assess the risk of his next move; he simply acted. Pointing his arm towards the nearest of the cycling flies, Clyde dragged the creature in on an invisible cable, and it arrived almost too quickly for him to finish his intent, but he managed to get his knife up in time, sticking the monstrosity through its tough abdomen and twisted the blade with the required force. The thing went dead, its buzz dropping in volume, the strands of electricity flashing out in an instant. Clyde allowed it to drop, feeling the vitiated ghostly energy dissipate within his fingers. Now all he had was a knife and two more flying threats.

Kev nudged his glasses up onto his nose and summoned a last gasp of effort, flinging the enemy duo into the observation windows with a couple of meaty thuds. Ace didn't flinch; he flashed his gap-tooth smile as if watching a hockey game, face-to-face with a player getting creamed into the stands. Kev continued to push, his arms and shoulders mimicking a man trying to push a broken-down car uphill. Their tough part-human/part-fly thoraxes finally collapsed under the pressure, their antennas twitching their last, and the paired bodies streaked down the window as though they had engaged in a collision course with a giant bus.

Clyde took a deep breath, his mile-a-minute thoughts trying to make sense of what he had just gone through. He knew he hadn't been in any genuine danger; the training wheels were still officially on, with the program set to pause or terminate should the simulation be about to deliver a killing blow; but still, he had just received his first taste of combat against a hostile threat trying to actively kill him. The memory of arriving here on his first day, that jeep ride through the scorching canyon, felt like a month ago, not the best part of a week.

Catching a breath, Clyde turned around, watching as Kev touched down on the ground.

'That was novel,' Kev said.

A burst of exhilaration spread across Clyde's face, a big goofy smile too much to stifle. He could feel the nervous sweat trickling down his back. 'That spinning thing...' he began, undecided if he wanted to warn Kev about doing it again in training or applaud his idea.

'The carousel?'

'Don't name it. Don't make it a thing, okay?'

The amusement in Kev's eyes told Clyde that his pal might have selective hearing on the matter. The blast doors whooshed open and in walked Ace. Clyde expected him to have cracked open his third beer by now, but the agent must be biding his time.

'Okay, ladies, that wasn't a total cluster fuck. The game didn't need to be cancelled, so congrats, you survived. But you moved about like a couple of quadriplegics on ketamine out there.' Ace stroked his handlebar mustache in thought, patting it like a small sleeping pet. He fished a few more clips of ammo out of his cargo pants for Clyde—he must keep them next to his pocket beer—watching as the trainee smoothly ejected the spent mags and reloaded. 'I'll call Rose in to get a second opinion. You're rerunning the program. Take five.'

Clyde and Kev passed a silent look between them.

Kev psyched himself.

Clyde quietly bobbed his head, gazing at the guns in his hands, and tried to convince himself that what he was feeling now wasn't contentment.

19

THE LAST FEW DAYS HAD passed without incident. In fact, they were mercifully dull: drivers sleeping in shifts; drinking bottled water, eating protein bars and military ready meals; washing themselves with cleaning wipes or when they encountered a clean water stream—the presence of clean water in this place still confounded Konstantin. It was the element of life, after all, so perhaps the very essence of this entire realm sustained itself on life.

The armored convoy passed through a diseased landscape. Worm-bloated mud banks and dark marshes of repulsive and bloated drowned corpses gave way to fields of macabre crops: headless spinal columns growing from the earth like crooked petrified trees, their ribs entwined and blooming with thorny lavender buds like strange fungal fruit. After consulting Konstantin's expertise on this darkly beautiful flora—which was, Konstantin admitted, limited in this instance—Mortis had made them pull over somewhere along the first acre of land, ordering Hammond to select a couple of his men to grab some tools and rustle up a few specimens of both seed and adult plant to stick in the truck's airtight storage units. The seeds resembled marble-sized skulls, as though the very root of the depressing plant was a withered corpse buried head-first. Hammond, acting against Mortis' censure, opted to get his hands dirty with his men. Konstantin couldn't help but admire the man for working shoulder-to-shoulder with his employees, a job that, for all any of them knew, could prove fatal.

The soul of Morris Lim had become a welcome addition to Konstantin over the miles and—according to their collective wristwatches and timekeepers—days. The man was trapped in a state of mourning over his fiancée and unprepared to delude himself with ideas of reversing his misfortune. Konstantin and Kuznetsov—Lim's new roommate—had tried to help him find some measure of peace, but being dead and in Hell, or whatever this place was, Lim was resistant to the monks' belief of finding a magic needle that could sew themselves a nice little paradise. Konstantin hadn't attempted to persuade Lim, but instead tried telling him that this was all a trial they would get through together. But Lim didn't want to hear it and had respectfully changed tack by telling Konstantin and Kuznetsov about what a good friend Hammond was, sharing barroom anecdotes and high praise for the man who had always been the type to roll up his sleeves and get in the thick of it with his crew. And Lim made special note to mention how Hammond had even saved his life once before, after he took a misstep and nearly went over the edge of a girder eight stories high in midtown Manhattan. Konstantin could see the truth in this testimony for himself as the foreman currently risked his own life by tangling with strange plants, all so he wouldn't have to bury another of his men. Konstantin had facilitated an open-door policy for Lim, allowing him to venture out of the honeycomb network and spend more time with Hammond and his other friends during their periods of rest. It had taken the other workers some getting used to, pretending that their old ways of banter and idle chat were still the same despite their friend now being an incorporeal wanderer whose body had been interred in a shallow grave a dozen miles from the place of his death.

Lim had watched his own service, for what it was. No last rites, only a few scared and lamentable words from Hammond, who had spoken with an apologetic wince on his wide, haggard face, his attention switching back and forth between the empty body and the ghost of the man standing nearby in numb confusion as the cold presence of the security teams impatiently waited with the vehicles, watching for any potential hidden threats lurking in the famished countryside.

Hammond rolled the skull seeds like dice in his gloved hand, allowing Mortis to scrutinize them curiously. Mortis told him to drop them in a temperature-controlled container alongside the other curious bits and pieces of this world: that foul bodybag creature chilling in a large glass vestibule, some labeled collections of unpleasant taxa, be they bug, bulb, or mineral. The printout of Konstantin's map was stuck to the wall of the mobile storage unit, pins and notations of potential interest keeping pace with their passage. With Mortis' interest satisfied, Hammond and his few handpicked laborers joined the rest of the work crew in the trucks, and the road trip continued.

On several occasions they had been forced to make detours from the mapped route, their cumbersome vehicles incapable of traversing the narrow rock passages, swampy canyon ledges, or dry corridors of iron-tough bone trees that Konstantin's foot-expeditions had managed in the past. On each occasion they had managed to circle back towards the charted route without too much trouble.

The large sibylline skulls still remained absent from the cosmos. They would usually have been glimpsed at some point by now, but Konstantin counted it as a small blessing that they hadn't, for he didn't need any further ill portents on this trip. Not until he reached the Eidolon Trench, at which point bad omens would be all he could hope for. Captain Agua had continued to exchange only the most pressing communication with him, asking for insights on the certain unavoidable detours along the predetermined route or for his knowledge and experience of known predators in particular vicinities. However, even with Konstantin's input, the captain had started to rely more and more on the aerial drones Lieutenant Briggs' team operated. Their range was limited to five miles, due to the transmitters and receivers operating on radio frequency waves, but five miles was plenty of area between the convoy and a potential abattoir. Of course, depending on the drones' current vicinity to the nearest soul channel, all it would take was for a screeching flight of escaped new souls to interfere with their reception or fry their electronics in the same manner that they did to the choppers. Or maybe some unknown raptor might develop a taste for plastic and circuitry.

Konstantin slipped into quiet reflection. Thinking about all the generations of Path members who had perished in this despicable pit, their souls torn from their flesh and devoured. Most of them were all faceless and nameless, they being before his time and his inauguration.

The burning temple flashed in his thoughts.

. . .

Konstantin remembered the scriptures of the Rising Path, written by the sect's earliest leaders during the 9th century. They told of the original Arkhitektor, the one who led select disciples into the vastness of the dead realm to map it and understand its mysteries. The story went that it was during one such investigation that the Arkhitektor encountered a glowing figure, wounded, half-drowned, and half-buried in the tidal waters of the Eidolon Trench, with the slender handle of the Firmament Needle just out of reach. The holy being of light beseeched the Arkhitektor, claiming weakness and infirmity, telling of the many eons he had been suffering there in obscurity at hell's doorstep. He regaled the human visitors about the nature of the Needle, which lay mockingly close to his hand, explaining how the wielder of this object could stitch together a heavenly paradise beyond this fossilized world and liberate the tormented, carrying them into a new eternal divinity and away from the injustices impressed upon every mortal being thrust into these hellish principalities. Putting his trust in the submerged crusader, the Arkhitektor and his small band of priests helped dig him out of the wet dirt and hoped that he was an angel and not a devil with a cruel sense of humor. But then tragedy struck when their now-great adversary, Vor Dushi the snake-man, was alerted to the activity along his waterways. The demon seized the embattled angel and the Needle for himself, and the Arkhitektor and his people were fortunate enough to escape with their lives.

Konstantin's own teacher had explained that during the incursions since those original journeys, many of the monks were not so fortunate as to return; in fact, they all went in prepared to make the ultimate sacrifice.

For Konstantin, the idea of going over to such a place, in search of the ultimate gift for humanity, and being able to preserve the souls of his fallen brethren should the worst happen was almost enough to choke him with emotion. Having been offered a role in such a monumental purpose, he decided he, too, would gladly surrender his life in helping to accomplish such an almighty task as finding the Firmament Needle.

That purpose dwarfed any trifling military skirmish of his former life, rendering his military career almost farcical. Those wars nothing more than small men picking fights with their reflections. Major Morozov and all the problems he presented had been reduced to those of an irritating gnat; how could he possibly be anything more when Konstantin was preparing to walk into the forbidden lands of the deceased?

The metalsmiths set to forging Konstantin his own suit of necronaut armor, just like the Arkhitektor's and the other Dead Divers before him, melting down the brass into liquid and creating an enchanted composite with handfuls of a special Erebian plant, Zar-ptica root, which, once cooled within the brass, created the impression of a rusty, blood-spotted sheen.

Konstantin would never forget the first time he entered Erebus. It was painted indelibly into his memory: the miles-long stretch of the Shore of Eternal Storms, which could have been picturesque if not for the mineral-heavy tides washing against the skeletal remnants of large, unidentifiable behemoths. And there were many other vistas that would stay with him right up until the day he became a permanent resident of that world of brutal beauty.

The Arkhitektor led the ritual as standard, standing before the congregation in his interdimensional armor, invested with protective seals and markings, Konstantin and the whole sect standing to attention before him and the looming menhirs. Through practiced methods the holy leader temporarily siphoned off a portion of Konstantin's soul, storing it in one of the multiple anchor points, crystal balls in brass fixtures built into the rock floor of the temple's altar. The grand priest then set about doing the same for the others in the small cabal of divers, the crystal spheres now golden with a peaceful lunar strobe. The Arkhitektor closed his eyes, lips moving softly, achieving a state of equanimity. It only took a moment for Konstantin to hear the low whistling, not much louder than the mournful wails of mountain wind spreading through the chamber's fissures. He saw a small hole piercing the space between the tall stones and watched in awe as the opening steadily increased its circumference, becoming an abscess, a dead mouth opening to swallow the living world. The edges of the portal stopped as they reached the designated bulwark of the holy stones. Erebus awaited them. Standing sturdy in his own prized and blessed armor, Konstantin steeled himself and followed the

Arkhitektor through the liquid portal, following as the mentor masterfully navigated the interstitial corridors between Earth and Erebus. Their loaned portions of souls trailed behind them like golden cables fixed to the globes, which shone like winter suns at their backs.

That first experience had been humbling for a mortal man, but ultimately it was a brief misfire, foiled by unexpected complications of hazardous terrain and injury. The subsequent journeys bore no richer fruit. His final journey, though... that was the one whose memory placed a cold hand over his heart.

For over a month, the Arkhitektor led Konstantin, Kuznetsov, Annika, and Iosif. They survived with the wit and guile of seasoned travelers, well-stocked with food rations and water. Traveling the familiar routes and locales, they followed that great alien-scaled structure—one of many—that resembled a sort of pipeline, suspended high in the air and glowing with sickly energy. This particular pipeline extended out from the rumbling vanishing point of the offshore Eternal Storm, leaving behind its shadowy and veiled installation point to traverse endless nautical miles before finally encroaching upon the land. These fey channels were an unknown network to the Rising Path. Another in a long line of mysteries. They branched above ground and below, but for how far and wide? The entirety of the kingdoms, as some scholars suspected? Possibly.

They followed the distant pulsing channel across the horizon, crossing the strange lands before reaching a steady rise of cliffs and winding tributaries pouring over the uneven land. With the soul channel disappearing behind a hill before reappearing in view, then obscured by further craggy up-thrusts of earth. The Arkhitektor began to move with renewed purpose, seeing the channel grow tantalizingly close, his gauntleted hand gripping his spear tightly. Would this be the day that the forgotten gods of life would bless them with victory?

Konstantin and the others kept pace, crossing the fjords and climbing the hills of river mud and sparse brown grass, their armor now a dull, aching burden, their food and water supplies half-consumed, but thankful that these last miles had been conspicuously devoid of prowling beasts.

That was when Konstantin heard the whispers.

The beckoning of unseen souls who had somehow escaped the great influx of the looming soul channel. Off to Konstantin's left, the land began to shear away, a giant estuary gradually submerging more and more of the landscape. The voices on the furnace wind continued to lull them in with solicitations and pleas for help. They pushed on up one final incline of damp silt, and Konstantin remembered seeing the Arkhitektor stop suddenly on the steep rise, silhouetted by the sapphire ghost fire of one of the blue suns, the red streaks of Zar-ptica glowing about his necronaut suit in thin volcanic fractures. Konstantin stopped beside him and tracked his line of sight. It was hard to miss after they had crested the gradient, for they all found themselves standing atop a massive cliff. Far below, the river flowed into a gigantic cove within the cliff face, and riding the air overhead was another river of sorts, this one not of water, but of the endless specters bobbing and flowing inexorably along that pulsing pipeline stretching all the way back from the jeweled dusk. Some forms were blurry, featureless caricatures of humans, others were of the unknown, for Death claims every world. The pulsing channel angled down, extending into a giant and bizarre apparatus built into the base of the cove, support beams of bone and wood, flesh and unknown, carrying the wailing new arrivals into the phosphorescent glow of the caverns. Konstantin was spellbound, and he had seen more than his share of amazing and paralyzing sights in this country so far. Allowing his mesmerized gaze to pull along the panorama, he had found himself wondering where the misplaced and sunken angel of scripture had lain and how he had come to be there.

And then it happened. Over the screeching wails of souls locked in inescapable commute, the wind began to pick up. Only eddies of sand at first, but before long a dust storm of biblical proportions was darkening the entire clifftop. The cliff had a rickety bridge of what might have been rope but could also have easily been tendons and skin, stretching over the entire width of the Eidolon Trench to the opposite cliff. It was from across this swaying bridge that a blood-chilling silhouette approached, a hive of writhing snake necks thrashing about atop a gangly body, every lumpy head focused on Konstantin, his mentor, and his brethren as though they were morsels to be devoured.

The Arkhitektor had wanted them to quietly sneak into the Trench's depths, hoping to find the Needle, and the angelic one if he was still alive, without creating pandemonium, after which they would settle on their next course of action.

But Vor Dushi had been prepared, perhaps waiting for these latest usurpers to challenge it.

The Dead Divers had made it this far, and their blood was up, thrumming with passion and zeal. Together, the five of them fought the demon bravely with bronze blades and sheer bloody-mindedness, but they were no match. Annika and Iosif fell in bloody heaps, and somehow, with a quiet calm, Konstantin managed to draw their dazed souls into himself, eliciting a furious response from Vor Dushi. During the struggle, several specters, either loyal minions of Vor Dushi's or perhaps driven by their own violent instincts, broke from out of nowhere and charged the priests, only to be rebuffed by their virtuous armor. This did not go unnoticed by Vor Dushi. One of its long, leathery throats began to work, hacking with a reptilian rasp, and its blood-smeared mouth spat up some dark, viscous fluid, clogging the Arkhitektor's sinuses like a fresh bubbling tar, leaking deep into his throat and taking him from within. Konstantin and Kuznetsov gripped their master's wan golden soul thread and hoisted it like a cable, dragging him away from the reaper's minion. Kuznetsov still had much fight in him and had wanted to charge the demon again, to fight until his last breath. And who knows, perhaps they might have got lucky. But Konstantin had shouted him down, referring to their afflicted Arkhitektor, not wanting to lose him due to their own needs of vengeance. If they were to attack again and fail, their leader would surely perish too, and the Rising Path within the temple didn't yet have a replacement candidate capable of opening the doorway between these worlds. Their purpose would be stilled until they found a new successor. A new Arkhitektor.

And so, exhausted and enraged at their futility, but with some fortune on their side, they both helped carry the Arkhitektor through the scouring dust storm, escaping the demon, the sullied light of their soul threads guiding them back down the sloping clifftop.

The return journey was tough going, their spirits diminished, sleeping rough in shifts, and the pallor of the Arkhitektor worsening over a time they couldn't measure, but somehow, over the course of what must have been weeks, they made the return trip back to the portal. A sharp tug on the grand necromancer's coil reopened their exit, and Konstantin and Kuznetsov carried the Arkhitektor through, seeing the shock and warrior aggression on their brethren on the opposite side of the breach. The portal sealed closed like a guillotine blade behind them, but safety was not secured. The vulgar spittle of the Soul Thief had already wrought its corruption deep within the Arkhitektor, slowly rotting him over the course of their return trip. The elder drew his bronze curved blade, and as his eyes rolled back to expose black capillaries, he suddenly set about butchering the younger, stronger monks with a vigor Konstantin had never witnessed before. Kuznetsov was the closest, and therefore the first to die. The sect fought back in confusion and reluctance, their surprise dulling their reactions, and by the time they subdued their grand priest, a number of their best men and women lay slain about the temple's central chamber. Remembering the shocked, dying expressions of Annika and Iosif, their armored bodies landing heavily in battle, Konstantin reacted on reflex, pulling these dying comrades into himself, sparing them the descent back into that hell and Vor Dushi's clutches.

Konstantin was scared, hearing the voices of the fallen rushing through his head, his body cramping and somehow changing. Clutching his blade firmly amidst this appalling chaos, he was teetering on the verge of raising it against his master and doing the unthinkable when he was suddenly hit in a pincer attack of his past and his present lives. He couldn't question how it happened or how they had found him, but several military soldiers had entered their house of worship, cutting the place apart with deafening rifle fire, and another was spraying jets of flame at the tapestries and fir tree benches. The accelerated fire oozed across every piece of wood paneling and altar, black smoke overcoming the usual fog of incense, the spilled blood mingling and flowing across the chamber. The flames roared voraciously. As the temple became a burning beacon, the Arkhitektor had turned his attention to Konstantin, the essence of Vor Dushi that now controlled him determined to add him to the growing pile of the dead, to spill him open and retrieve the souls he had stolen from him and his House masters in the Order. Konstantin didn't recognize any of his old mentor behind his oily black eyes; he had been reduced to an empty pawn. Over the sounds of screams and gunfire, Konstantin watched with some satisfaction as Major Morozov's retrieval team were shanked and skewered by his dying allies, falling on their spears. He would not be salvaging the souls of these intruders from the pull of Erebus. The Arkhitektor's mouth began to bubble with a black viscosity, preparing to spit Vor Dushi's infection into Konstantin's gritted teeth.

Left with no choice, Konstantin gripped his blade. And cut. He could still remember how performing that cut felt.

The Arkhitektor's neck was riven, scarlet flowing from the blade wound, and in his dying moments the arch monk clasped his pupil's jaw with a cracking strength and something, some hideous poison, not from his mouth but spreading from his cold palm like black tendrils, poured into Konstantin, slipping into his ear canal. The Arkhitektor's blighted soul had found a way to bypass Konstantin's armor. Konstantin should have shared his mentor's fate, becoming another extension of Vor Dushi's intent here amongst the living world, except something utterly unprecedented occurred. His constitution fought back, and somehow it overcame Vor Dushi's pestilence. There was a congealing sensation in his very core, the traces of the dark force clumping into a defeated lump, buried under meat and blessed armor. There had been little time to ruminate on this event; the temple was still in the throes of fiery death. Shifting the Arkhitektor's armored weight off himself, Konstantin got to his feet, watching in horror as his home burned down around him, seeing his fallen peers breathe their last. Enraged, he found himself hastily absorbing the life force of family, their pained energies caught partway between vanishing into the carbon-black ether and the unwitting vessel of his body. Underneath his armor he could feel his flesh continuing to change, a keen discomfort that became a chilly agony. It was one thing to know that he was capable of harboring the deceased, and something entirely different to experience it. Such loss and pain poured into him on a great scale. The Rising Path became chambered within him, their voices whispering amongst his own in a confused susurrus. Underneath his bronze gauntlets he could feel more of the geometric patterns begin to blister across his palms, forming rows of radiant hexagonal light under the flesh like a heat mat, and he could feel it happening across his body too. Such an ordeal. A great burden to bear.

Beginning to choke on the black fumes and withering under the heat, Konstantin ran. Without looking back, he fled that dead place, his eyes filled with smoky tears. He burst out into the glacial freshness of the frozen courtyard, embers skirting on the shearing winds in his wake, and collapsed halfway. There was a helicopter parked on the courtyard, its former occupants currently being consumed by the fire they had brought into the mountain with them. Konstantin lay there, watching the black rippling walls of smoke rear up to ravage the purity of the clouds above. Gulping in tarnished air, he could feel the cold, infected lump of his Arkhitektor—or was it now purely a part of Vor Dushi?—lying within his soul. He heard the thunderous approach of machinery splitting the skies.

Another chopper. Lying there on the icy steps in his armor, half-dead, feeling the souls of those he was able to salvage from the slaughter rushing through his body with a burning cold, Konstantin stared at the marble white of the sky and watched in detached confusion as a pair of black choppers, armed for more mass death if required, descended like mechanical dragonflies onto the plateau within the smoky, saw-toothed valley. Of all the cruel and humorous trickery of fate, Major Morozov had finally found him. It had taken six years, but the tenacious superior had brought him to heel, his one remaining eye having refused to blink in fear of missing the insubordinate who had cast him into a life of permanent half-darkness. They found him at the worst possible time. The old major, a fury distilled into his one remaining eye, entered the blizzard of the rotor wash with another small cadre of dark-uniformed mercenaries, dragging with him a beaten prisoner whom Konstantin still recognized through the prism of time and stinging eyes.

It was Jurgen Kross.

They had tracked down the occultist intelligence broker, using his knowledge and his innate power to locate the temple. Morozov put a bullet in the back of Kross' head, the shot going unheard within the roar of the engines. The major savored every step, moving towards Konstantin, looming over him as if he was delighting in all the ways he would hurt him. Six years was enough time for the bitterness to seep into every pore of his being, spoiling anything rational. He should have shot Konstantin dead there and then, but the vengeful man had decided it would be more fun to watch Konstantin rot away in a frozen pit, trapped with a bunch of other aberrations who didn't belong with humanity. The useful things discovered and imprisoned by the office of the Matryoshka.

Konstantin thought of Morozov's severed head staring up at him from a box. It should have brought him joy. It didn't. All it brought him was another dose of regret and senseless murder.

• • •

Konstantin broke from his reverie, and the first thing he saw was Captain Agua asleep in the passenger seat, and more senseless murder was immediately brought to mind with the massacre at the Cradle of Sorrows. He stared at the captain, trying not to indulge in wrathful fantasies, when he heard the quiet prayers of Kuznetsov coming from within his private cell. It was as though his brother had also lapsed into dark thoughts, perhaps sensing Konstantin's struggle.

But Konstantin's simmering hate became something else...doubt. It snagged on his thoughts. An insidious whisper telling him that his quest was foolish. That he would come up short again against Vor Dushi. That the scripture's account of a weakened heavenly warrior and his Firmament Needle were nothing more than a madman's delusion that had found favorable ears and minds over the centuries, like any worthy cult, like all the low-minded and unscrupulous doctrines pushed by an organized religion.

He gave a single violent shake of his head at the troubling rhetoric, forcing the doubts and thoughts of failure away. No. The Firmament Needle exists. He knew it did. He had faith. The shining angel had crashed into this darkness with a last hope, glowing like an ember in an ashen pit. And a devil had stolen that light. The same devil who was irrefutably talking to him now through the soiled and dormant soul of the Arkhitektor, that oily black grub stuck to the grand priest's soul like a cancer, surfacing from its long sleep and aware that it was on its journey back home to its cack-mouthed creator.

His hands settled on the breastplate of his armor, his fingers absently tracing some of the protective runes. They were the only things keeping Vor Dushi and Konstantin's afflicted master from seizing his free will and bending it to their own violent purpose.

Konstantin couldn't believe what things were coming to, but he actually wanted to talk to Mortis, if only to keep his mind occupied. But Mortis was befuddled with his own thoughts from the looks of it, staring out of the window at the fearsome land.

'Are you tempted to risk opening another door?' Konstantin asked him.

Mortis seemed surprised to hear him strike up a conversation. He had been picking up and putting down his book since the revelation about his damaged key, seemingly incapable of focusing on the bleak and pitiless novel, quietly fidgeting with the unholy machine under his coat, boxed into his chest. He glanced at Konstantin with those ghastly corpse eyes, then looked away to hide his nervousness. 'The thought does cross my mind. And we may have to if we get desperate enough.'

Konstantin had known for several days now that whatever dark magic ground the gears in Mortis' chest was acting up. Perhaps at one time Mortis had been able to remold his fingers to open any lock in any world, but if so, that versatility was somehow waning. And somehow, Konstantin found it hard to care.

'I know it's been a good few decades since you last did this,' Mortis said, 'and those bloody suns never set or seem to change, but how long do you think it'll take to reach the Trench?'

Konstantin took a deep breath and considered. The reclusive monks didn't have much in the way of concessions such as watches and the like; they'd been in the mountains too long. Without getting a copy of the map out, he recalled the weaving, twisting line of his charted route. 'With this transport, it might feel like a couple of weeks, but a wise man once said time is relative.'

Mortis snorted derisively. 'Maybe I'll hold off on throwing open any more doors then.' His left-hand keys carefully rolled back his right coat sleeve a few inches, and Konstantin expected moths to flutter out. Instead, he saw a branding burned into his bony wrist, and still pretty fresh from the looks of it.

Konstantin was going to leave it unremarked, but he didn't want to sit quietly with his thoughts right now. 'What is that?'

'When I first cut these particular keys,' Mortis said with another proud flourish of his bony fingers, 'my curiosity got the best of me. After a dry run of opening the door to this place, I opened a door to one of the other eight kingdoms. Security was a little more strict, shall we say. I was fortunate not to lose my hand.' He rolled his sleeve back, covering the indecipherable marking. 'I don't mind admitting I scarpered at the first chance I got. And I made the smart decision not to test any of the other doors after that.' He paused, not sure whether to continue. 'I was hesitant to even come back here. But Talbot treats me well. He could have killed me, or thrown me to the streets, or ... or worse, after what my father did.'

'He owns you. Don't get sentimental over it.'

A cadaverous smirk displayed Mortis' nubby teeth, but it wasn't humor; it was denial. 'I don't like that dead face watching us in the sky.'

Konstantin tried not to react, but he felt a sudden clench. He casually leaned across the back seat to snoop out of Mortis' window. One of the giant cosmic skulls had entered the starry velvet.

'You said you're familiar with a large skull peering down on you. Tell me, is it going to try and cook us like ants under a magnifying glass?'

Konstantin answered truthfully, finding no advantage in lying about this. 'They come and go.'

'They?'

'I've seen different ones. The Arkhitektors believed they could be one of two things: House monarchs ... '

'Or?'

'Or their gods.'

'Gods of the dead. It's nice to know that even rot and decay could have such structure and discipline.'

Konstantin could tell Mortis was beset by a quiver of doubt. And who wouldn't be when they were being stared at like lice by a planet of bone and cavernous eyes? He glanced up front, at Agua snoring lightly in the passenger seat, one of his Alpha Team sergeants at the wheel. 'It isn't too late to stop this. You don't know the repercussions this could have. Stealing from the Order—' he flicked his sincere eyes towards Mortis' window, 'from those.' He thought of the Order, of its kings and queens offering oblations of souls up to the skulls in the starry wastes.

'And what of you?' Mortis replied. 'Let's say you're correct about this Firmament Needle. You don't think stealing the means to craft a new heaven will upset a few powerful forces beyond your comprehension?'

'Of course I'm aware. Building a safe haven for deceased is acceptable reason to challenge status quo. Avarice isn't.'

'Ah, because making a martyr of yourself doesn't bring its own wealth? Sure, okay, you can't spend it, but knowing what we know, that death isn't the end, don't pretend you're not doing this out of your own vainglorious need to save everyone. That, too, is rooted in selfishness, and don't pretend otherwise. Hell, for all you know, I might use some of my wealth from this operation to open a few orphanages or give to charity.'

'And will you?'

'Not likely.' His grin was about as wholesome as a child-snatcher's. 'But people change over time. They can absolve themselves, just remember that. And if you should bump into this Needle after we leave you here, save a space in paradise for little old me. I need saving too, right?'

Konstantin held Mortis' mocking stare, then turned to watch the driver guide them past a couple more recognizable landmarks while throwing a fistful of beef jerky into his mouth. Konstantin was about to withdraw back into his thoughts when Mortis surprised him, clearly wanting to get something off his chest. What was more surprising was the crack in his haughty, carefully cultivated manner, which Konstantin had correctly assumed to be an act since their first meeting.

'You know what pisses me off?' Mortis asked, not allowing time for Konstantin to take a stab at the question. 'You fucking bible-thumping types. I don't give a shit if you're not a brand name like those Christian kiddie fuckers or Muslim desert savages, you all parade around with this air of accomplishment like you've uncovered some profound meaning that the hoi polloi are too stupid to grasp.' Konstantin sat and listened, hearing what his critic said but feeling complete apathy towards his argument. 'This brand-new Eden sham you're obsessed with? It's a hypothetical. Just like all the rest. What the Cairnwood Society is doing here is driven by commerce, sure. You don't have to like it. But in its own way, it offers an immediate salvation, unlike your endless promises and faith. Don't you think that all the poor bastards getting brushed off their mortal coils into this hovel would rather be dragged back out of here and given a job? Isn't that better than staying here and becoming food or long-term bargaining chips? And this is still only the early drawing-board stage. The private application of souls could be enormous, with a hundred and one uses. They'll find other things for them to do than to act as a mere battery or some such for Beelzebub. Before I die, I'm making sure to sign a contract with the Society's inner circle to suck my soul up like a vacuum the minute I croak, rather than leave me defenseless in this sewer for a single second.' Mortis wanted to say more, but his fire-

and-brimstone rant was a dog chasing its tail, full of boundless energy but incapable of going anywhere further.

Konstantin offered his rebuttal. 'It's good to see that behind your act you're as scared as anybody else. You don't belong in inner circle, Mortis. You're working-class monkey to Talbot. Him and his peers. A novelty with a use. You can pretend you're on their level, until you can no longer tell what is real and what isn't, but you, like your father, are nothing but conveniences to them. The fact that you've spent whole life around plutocratic filth like Talbot and Cairnwood and mistakenly believe that slavery is any type of betterment appalls me.'

Mortis was half-turned around in his seat, all knees and elbows, his second-hand arrogance ripped at the seams.

'Right now you have all the advantages with your thugs and your weapons,' Konstantin continued, 'and you've taken all but one of my brothers from me, but hear my words. Once our bargain is through, I'll spend now until eternity, my life and death, wandering every corner of Erebus until I find Needle. I'll rebuild heaven, and I'll recruit every noble soul I can to wage a tireless war against these injustices of death; and it'll be you and Cairnwood's flagrant rape of the dead that will be our first conquest.'

Konstantin took a shuddering breath, feeling the heat of his righteous anger warming his face, his passion beating inside his chest. He noticed that he was leaning halfway across the seat, but not so close to Mortis as to instigate a physical confrontation. Mortis' leaden gaze pushed back into Konstantin's for so long that he expected the key maker to react emotionally, lashing out or ordering the sergeant or the dozing captain to draw their weapon and put a bullet in his leg there and then. Konstantin had shown his cards and was deeply annoyed at his explosive tirade. He knew better than to act so tempestuously, and he could no longer go back to playing the obedient little serf. But his largest concern was the newly exposed cracks in Mortis' own conduct. Talbot had set him an important task, but Konstantin could tell from Mortis' eyes that he was truly afraid about that fractured key of his, worried that he might not be able to find another way back to the green grass and blue skies of home. And fear made people do stupid things. If Mortis became convinced that his abilities had inexplicably forsaken him, stranding him, and them, here, then what would stop him from turning on Konstantin or having him thrown before a firing squad of Citadel gunmen?

Off to his left, the landscape dropped away precipitously, placing their convoy on a high plateau. The gloomy fields running off to the horizon were marked by a distant series of giant stanchions, structures that, though scale-plated and connected by a pulsing beam of cloudy emerald light, might call to mind a series of bizarre telephone masts to the layman. Konstantin identified them as the relay towers of the nearest nexus channel, its pipeline guiding the new flocks of souls in from the stormy and tumultuous borders of purgatory and towards the inner domains of the dead.

Konstantin knew that, further down the line, this particular branch of egress connected to the Eidolon Trench.

20

KEV DRIFTED THROUGH THE LIBRARY, still feeling like a trespasser despite having the blessing of Spector and the academic staff. He had no idea what he was looking for in here. In all likelihood it was nothing specific, just a placation of his own curiosity. The Djinn training was a blast, and it felt incredible to be working alongside Clyde like that, not just with repetitive training drills but an actual combat exercise. And Clyde seemed to be having fun with it, which pleased Kev to no end. Now he was actually thinking of working up his nerve to broach a serious question to Clyde: why don't you stay on and become an active agent? Just thinking of asking him, that scared Kev shitless. It really would be pushing his luck, insulting really, like the guy wasn't doing enough for him right now, going through the grinder of military training on account of Kev's future occupation. Kev knew that if he started down this rabbit hole of argument and counter-argument, he would drive himself nuts, so he put a pin in the idea of asking his best friend to shake up his life any further and ventured deeper into the library archives.

He kept away from the intimidating presence of the Bookworm guarding those dizzying stacks of knowledge housed within the central chamber and wandered about the peripheral stacks. He chose these quiet aisles so as to not embarrass himself in front of such an ancient and mysterious organism, but this didn't keep him from wondering as to the importance of those texts that remained under the purview of the massive and imposing creature, big as an upended subway train and uncannily wise. Maybe one day he'd summon the nerve to ask the big worm about his collection, but that day wasn't today. Finding the outskirts of the library to be labyrinthine in scale, Kev decided that should he get lost in these winding stacks, he wouldn't bother calling for help but would simply phase headlong through rack, wall, or ceiling until he escaped the omnipresent leathery spines.

He tilted his head and examined a number of the books before him, backs broken and pages brittle. Many of them were not in English, but Greek, Latin, German, French, Chinese, Russian, Egyptian hieroglyphs, and others in no known human tongue. Among those that he could understand, he found that their subject matter was vast: works on the mischievous hobgoblin clans and their last known whereabouts; a centennial report of people believed to have been consumed by living paintings; appendices on otherworldly stones and their communicative abilities to gods; musings on beings who can communicate with the stars above. Then his attention was snagged by one particular work, an English translation of something called *Visions Through the Veil*. The author of the book was a 19th-century West Bengalese Jhakri priestess, and it was beyond a doubt one of a legion of other similar texts regarding the subject of the afterlife, many of which would inevitably be in this very library. Without lifting a finger, Kev softly removed it from the tight press of surrounding books and turned it over in the air. Wiping a thin coat of dust from the recessed lettering, he delicately opened it, mindful of the cracked spine. He skimmed it at first to gauge what material might be of interest to him. For a moment he wasn't sure of his motivation in choosing it and quickly grew troubled at the idea that maybe he was secretly looking for some awful revelation, some traumatizing vision of what a sentence in the heart of the Null really looked like. The wannabe academic part of him wanted to call it Erebus, but his time with Rose's crew and Ace had forever labeled it the Null. Thankfully, he found the despairing truth of the place easy to dismiss from his thoughts with only minor lingering harm done, reminding himself that there was little to be done to avoid it, so he might as well put his energy into the pursuit of knowledge rather than depression.

His eye caught on a large, two-page diagram that, according to the notation beneath, was illustrated by the priestess while actively under possession of a soul she was communicating with. The trapped soul, able to offer his thoughts but no earthly manifestation of his form, had charted the outer rims of Erebus, but much of the diagram seemed foggy and incomplete, like an artist's impression from an amnesiac. Kev cocked an eyebrow at the drawing, which was at once both quite helpful and completely useless. The dead realm was bordered by a wall of storms from which a number of what were labeled nexus points stemmed, tubular structures that channeled souls across the seas towards the patchy lands. These few diagrammatic pipelines also existed in obscurity, stopping at random points on the map, the cartographer unfamiliar with their full route. One of them ran at an angle, roughly forty degrees, Kev hazarded, towards a landmass that had several aliases but was most prominently labeled as the Shore of the Eternal Storm. Though, before long, this nexus point also stopped abruptly somewhere inland. Various other lines had been drawn across this continent, a terrain that was marked by dunes and bones, unintelligible structures that, if the diagrams and notes were accurate, could likely stand shoulder-to-shoulder with the Empire State Building.

Kev had read Dante Alighieri's *The Divine Comedy* after coming back from oblivion, sitting on the roof of his and Clyde's apartment, staring at that bastard liquor store between verses, and now found himself wondering if the man had had any genuine insight into Erebus or if it was just his own creative agency concocting his ideas of Hell, Purgatory, and Heaven. Kev had never been baptized and was proud of it, but now found himself wondering if Charon the Ferryman had previously sailed him across to the Inferno's Circle One, casting him out amidst the innumerable other souls who had been denied the light of a Christian upbringing. Kev looked at those nexus points, his mouth turning up in a weak smile. Maybe Charon was a skilled plumber and not a boatman. In any event, Kev also made the decision that when the time came—second time!—he'd use Rose's training to flip Charon's bony ass out of his rickety tub and beat him with his own oar. Assuming he was a real entity.

Kev closed the book. Well, he decided, whether it was accurate or not, Dante would sure know all about that place by now. So would Socrates,

Plato, Gandhi, Marie Curie, and John Bonham. He began to think of a few late celebrities he had liked and imagined them in the Null, and hoped they were doing all right. He was about to return the book and carry on searching for nothing else of note. It wasn't as though he had much else going on at this hour. Clyde would be sitting in his bunk or up on the rock chimney, ice pack on his latest bruises, and drawing until he passed out into sleep; Ace would probably be onto his fourth or fifth beer and watching the hockey in the rec area with some of the off-duty guys, or maybe in some bar in Santa Fe or the nearest town; and Rose was most likely still blasting targets on the shooting range or keeping herself to herself. She was tough to get a bead on. With the obvious exception of her love of lifting heavy weights, guns, and military service, he didn't know what she did for fun. Were those things all the fun she needed?

Kev picked up a few other tomes on the afterlife, went to turn around to head for one of the reading desks in the main area, and almost dropped the books in surprise when he found Rose standing a few inches behind his shoulder.

'Anything good?' she asked.

Kev laughed in embarrassment. 'Creep much?'

'Almost scared you to death.' She smiled, her eye catching the title of the book on top. 'I wondered when you'd get around to this.'

'This?'

'Research. You're a thinker.'

'Could you please not say that like you're some Southern farm hand?'

'Relax.' She laughed and took hold of the floating books. 'These are pretty limited.'

Kev watched her return them to their correct places and replace his stolen pile with a smaller but seemingly more informative collection. 'These are more fulfilling.'

Kev drummed his fingers across the top book, thinking about what to say. 'So, you read up on the Null too?'

She placed her hands on her hips and nodded. 'Stupid not to. Know your enemy.'

Kev rubbed the stubble on his chin, which would never grow again. 'Is that who our enemy is, Death itself? I thought this agency had its sights set a little lower. Evil wizards and stuff.'

She stifled a laugh. Kev found her beautiful when she smiled. 'Sure, there's always evil wizards and stuff tripping us up on this side, but on rare occasions agents might have to head over to the other side, so it's good to have some prior intel. Plus, we're not going to be here forever.'

Kev was bowled over by this blasé admittance. 'Hold up. Agents actually go into the Null, like on assignment?'

'Like I said, only on occasion: like if the agency has to play emissary on someone's behalf or drop off some criminal who has been fucking about with things he shouldn't have. It's not like our average Saturday night out.'

'How do you get there and back? Sleeping pill O.D. followed by shock paddles?'

Rose shook her head, amused. 'The hoodoo.'

'Again with the hoodoo,' Kev said. 'Those things must be like a geologist's wet dream. But you've been over there yourself?'

Rose tightened her lips. 'A few times. But agents follow their orders, and then they're pulled back out. We don't know the exact whereabouts of where we're sent to, or who we're dealing with. Even in death you can't escape politics. Matters of security.' Kev gave her a dubious look, at which she giggled. 'It's the truth, and even if it wasn't, it's the most I can give you right now, newbie. For now, you're stuck with the books.'

'Right, knowledge is power.' Kev felt a little jarred. Did the hoodoo have some type of international relations with the powers of the Null? Rose started moving along down the aisle, grabbed a book seemingly at random, and entered the vicinity of the Bookworm. Kev felt a little more at ease following her into the worm's domain. They sat at a large, empty table, in plain view of the worm's huge portal, though it had withdrawn into its depths for now. To read a book, Kev mused. Maybe it had a giant Kindle down there. Though Kev still felt it prudent not to talk above a whisper. Laying the books flat before him, he asked, 'On your trips over there, did you find anything that's not in any of these books?'

She gave him a strict glare, her eyes softening after a couple of seconds. 'Nothing of value.' She opened her own book, some light reading on the biomechanics and recorded feats of strength of various demonic species, and then paused. 'Is there anything specific you're looking for?'

It was a good question, and Kev didn't rightly know. 'The basics, I guess. I think mainly I'm trying to satisfy my morbid curiosity.'

Rose skimmed a page in her book without really glancing at it. 'That's what a lot of agents do when they can't sleep.' The soft light danced in her dark eyes and played along the smooth, tanned skin of her exposed arms. 'You want morbid, how's this? There are nine known lineages who sit all high and mighty in the Null, all with their own kingdom, and each one just itching to make you unhappy. They're called the Order of Terminus.'

Bringing the Bengalese princess' woefully incomplete map to mind, Kev tried to decide if nine lineages was a lot to fear in all that uncharted space or if it was a pretty paltry force. How big was a single kingdom's territory? Equivalent to Eurasia? Africa or the Americas combined? The size of a planet? Death was incalculable when one considered the unknown statistics of an unknown number of lifeforms struggling throughout the expanding universe.

The top book before him, *The Diminished Equinox*, had a badly worn leather cover depicting a crudely designed sun bowing almost deferentially to a moon. He flipped it open to the index to check whether a more complete map existed, or if there was at least a chapter focusing on these rulers of hell. 'Nine lineages?' he repeated, his finger sliding down the chapter headings. 'Is that a lot?'

Rose glanced up from her own reading and fixed her platinum hair into a ponytail. 'If you think of each lineage or House as a monarchy with a fully-equipped army at its disposal, then yeah, nine controlling armies kind of sucks.' She must have found what she was looking for in her book and jumped to the right page.

They sat and read in silence for ten minutes. Kev was filled with a deep sense of unease. The accounts he read of the Nine Crowns of Death were frustratingly brief and vague, though there was just enough to give him a sense of scale. After the brutal training and the advancements in his strength and dexterity, he had almost fallen into the trap of believing he was invincible. A real tough guy, but all it took was a few sparse paragraphs to make him feel inadequate. It was said that the Order was born in darkness, crawling in vestigial forms and growing with the prime universe. Even the most learned of necromancers didn't understand what came before these originators of death. The paradox of the Order's existence didn't escape Kev, for how can dead creatures such as they and their hordes function, build, organize, and rule, if truly dead? For them to operate in the way they do with their sorcery and might, would they not have to be living to some extent? Ancient philosophers drove themselves mad in pursuit of a concise answer to this riddle. Death, however, in all its forms, cannot exist without life, and so the shade was tied into an eternal fractious union with a great light. Kev tore through the following paragraphs in search of what this light might be, or at least had once been. Was it a heaven of sorts? And where was it now, since the Null was the only game in town? The book didn't tell.

'This whole thing still has me scratching my head,' he admitted.

'Ha! I can lift more than you, bro.' Rose didn't look up from the statistics until her smugness had abated. 'Which part?'

'What drives these things, these monarchs? Because they exist, therefore they must be living in some capacity, right?'

'This, coming from the ghost?'

Kev admittedly felt foolish but knew he couldn't let this one go. 'Go ahead and make fun, but I know you of all people have pondered this. My point is, Clyde is my power and my weakness. There must be something driving these guys. Some weakness to exploit.'

'See, I knew you were smart.' She kept the condescension playful. 'But before you start playing the noble revolutionary, you might want to consider that we here at Hourglass have a sort of truce with the Order. A live-and-let-live sort of deal. We don't fuck with them, they don't fuck with us. We are peacekeepers, after all.'

Kev quickly raised his hands in protest. 'Whoa, hey now, I wasn't saying revolution.' Or was he? He wasn't really sure what point he was trying to make. 'I'm not even an official agent yet. I'm just a curious guy. You're the one who handed me this book; I thought you were trying to get me on the same page as you to bounce some ideas off of.' He and Rose tried to read the truth in each other's gaze for a few moments. 'Look, for the foreseeable, I only want to graduate, then start small, beat on some of those evil wizards before I attempt to do anything as psychotic as slap some death god in the face.'

Rose was holding something back, cautious words held tight. And then: 'I'm aware of my insignificance in the big picture. Whatever Hourglass and the Order have going on is something I don't understand but I have to respect. There's a lot of moving parts in these kinds of arrangements. But when I die, I'll be a soldier with no agency but my own. And interests of peacekeeping go out of the window when you're about to be an hors d'oeuvre for some fucked-up rotting gods. You understand?'

Kev did. He understood very well, and the pair of them sat quietly with this, absorbing her declaration.

'But until that time when I put my boots on Null ground for the long haul, I'm an Hourglass peacekeeper.'

'Who knows, maybe before then we'll have all found a way to spend eternity in comfort.'

'Maybe we will.' Rose's answer was loaded with cynicism, and the mood called for a new topic.

'This is tangential, but speaking of the here and now, and slapping small-potato wizards, aren't you and Ace a little too capable to be stuck here training us every day? Don't you have any assignments or supernatural emergencies to deal with?'

'Always, but we got people on standby. And this has been my main post since I joined up, so I'd only be hanging around anyway.'

Kev nodded and glanced around at the soft lighting, his thoughts swiping back to another part of the *Equinox*'s obscure history of everything. 'You know anything about the "light"?'

'Forty-watt bulbs. Soothes the eyes.'

'Ha-fucking-ha.' His finger tapped the page, and Rose leaned forward a little, seeming to recognize the passage.

'I read around it, sure. Didn't learn much from the limited books, but legend has it that there was a big war between the light and the dark, and somewhere during the ass-end of it, a rain of stars lashed the earth. Stars... or Sparks.'

'Sparks? Like Ace?'

'Yup.'

'So Ace is some type of angel?'

Rose burst out laughing. 'You fucking kidding? You met the guy? No, Ace is no fucking angel. But whatever these lights were, let's say they got into the water supply during our early evolution.' She snickered again and sighed with satisfaction. 'Ace, an angel. You're funny, Kev. But that's all I could find on the subject.'

Kev's eyes roved across the paragraphs, but his mind was now too keyed up to retain anything. He would have to calm himself down and reset. He picked up where he'd left off, the passage briefly detailing what little was known about the Order of Terminus, collated from various apocryphal sources. Besides their House names, their biographies left a tremendous amount to be desired, lacking their roles of governance within the dead lands; the names and histories of the presiding monarchs and those of their own inner council members; their arrangement and politics; and even lacking any clear boundaries or occupations of their realms. Kev did find the names of the Houses, though, which was something, he supposed, though it was unclear which criteria, if any, ranked these ruling bodies:

The House of Fading Light
The House of Silent Screams
The House of Red Thorns
The House of the Blue Carapace
The House of Strange Fates
The House of Wise Stones
The House of the Glowing Reel
The House of the Celestial Spiral
The House of Cold Stars

'Well, that's a huge fucking help,' Kev said. 'And you picked this book because it was the most useful?'

Rose was still busy scanning her own page. 'You were looking for intel on the Null, and that is about as detailed as it gets from that selection. But if you want to educate yourself about earth spirits living in Irish hills, or which group of demons govern the Vatican, then you're in for a treat.'

Kev rolled his eyes and rubbed the bridge of his nose in frustration. 'I don't understand how in all of time and space, so little has been compiled about the Null. And you guys have access to both the place and the players. It's like some conspiracy to keep us from knowing. I mean, this is a state of ghosts and beings who can walk between worlds. Pick up a pen and jot down a few notes for us.'

'Hey, peacekeeper in training, you need to be careful with this investigative journalist kick you're on because you're only going to end up beating your head against the wall. But hey, if our vast selection of books isn't to your standards, you could always ask Bookworm,' Rose said flatly.

Kev leaned back in his chair, his shoulders phasing halfway through the wooden back, staring over to the huge empty pit, the ring of silver around the perimeter embossed with arcane symbols. He looked back at her, checking to see if she was messing with him. 'You serious?'

She shrugged her powerful shoulders. 'It is, to all intents and purposes, an employee.'

A nervous grin played at Kev's mouth, then faltered. 'Are they... are they like the limited editions he's protecting or something?'

'According to Agent Modi, the head of our paranormal intel department, they're the more specific works. You might find something useful there.'

Kev's unease quickly switched to suspicion. 'So why haven't you checked out any of those books?' His attention was pulled between her and the multi-tiered columns of shelves arranged around the worm's hiding hole, running up to the top of the domed library.

'Honestly, because I don't speak the languages that most of those books are in; many aren't even human. And, most importantly, some things are still above my paygrade.'

'But I'm not even getting paid.'

'Oh yeah.' She slapped her head, pretending to knock her brain into gear. 'Then I guess you'll have to make do with the other books. But you know, you should go over and introduce yourself to Bookworm. It looks big and scary, but it does have feelings.'

Kev sat with his indecision for a moment, eyeballing the big, deep hole and confused as to why he was scared of approaching it; he was dead in the living world and therefore kind of safe, plus he'd killed a bunch of man-fly mutants earlier, and then a horde of skeletal ice hockey players, which Ace had seemed to find amusing.

'I'll stick with these for now.'

'Pussy.' Rose returned to her book.

Kev was fine with that. He figured he had at least three decades of slapping evil wizards and nefarious earthbound cults before he had to really worry about rebelling against a necrotic pantheon.

21

For the last several hours, Mortis had sought privacy, opting to ride in the big, armored trailer of the specimen truck. He needed quiet to work on the damaged key, his thumb still crooked and the cut grooves wonky and twisted. He was trying hard not to panic now, which was another reason to separate himself from the rest of the men. If it got out that their way home was now void, there could be a mutiny. A riot. A senseless bloodshed that would leave the survivors fighting over the provisions and scattering amongst this harsh land. He just needed a bit more time. That was all. He'd fix this damn key. He, like his father before him, had spent his whole working life doing this very job, working with their machines and tools to create the little wondrous locks and keys for the miraculous and the mundane. It made no sense that he suddenly found himself lame of skill. The dark forge in his chest still glowed with its sinister black light. He could still feel its power rushing through him, same as ever. So why couldn't he remold this bastard bent key? Acton Mortis smashed a fist down onto the workbench, rattling a few tools hanging over it, and even one of the soul cage frames propped up against the wall.

Sitting back in the foldout metal chair, he stared at the horror suspended in the specimen tank. The bodybag, as those simpleton triggermen had nicknamed it. Christ, if he really had inexplicably forgotten how to perform his one skill, his pride and joy, would it be one of those things that would get him? Maybe more of those cradle eaters, should they stumble past another crèche of stillborn? A skeel? A god-sized death's head floating in the sky, reaching down to pluck him up, up there into space where it would gobble him down like a tangy ant? Leaning back in his chair, his breath whistling through his nostrils and his sternum folded open like some low-rent automaton, he stared anxiously at the brand burned into his forearm, poking out from his folded-up sleeve. A woeful reminder of what the other keys led to. A paralyzing thought gripped him, and he considered the possibility that perhaps one of those other realms might be his only hope of finding a way back home. Worse thoughts followed, prompting him, asking what he'd do if there was no way back for him. Nowhere in the whole of the nine kingdoms. His dusty white eyes lingered on the branding, which was the result of using the middle key of his right hand. Whose territory was that? The House of Red Thorns? He wasn't entirely sure, his thoughts distracted and feverish. He remembered those heated pincers, though, glowing like molten tips, and the smell of his own cooking arm. To this day, he didn't know if the things that had branded him had allowed him to escape, to live on as a message, a warning, or if his anguished thrashings had somehow sprung him loose, allowing him to literally thumb a ride back home like a hitchhiker in a dangerous land. He laughed skittishly. He may not be hitching a ride home any time soon at this rate. What was certain was that he had never dared to open that door again, or the seven forbidden others.

Mortis bit his lip in anger and saw Talbot's imperious smirk mock him inside his own head. Talbot, and the other kingmakers of the Society, all tossing crumbs down to the lackeys like his father, and now Mortis in his stead. This place was dangerous, sure, but those in the know practically regarded the House of Faded Light as a banana republic compared to the other eight houses. Mortis rolled his sleeve down to cover the branding. But even erratic republics produced their fair share of danger and opportunistic violence. Mortis was still risking his flesh and his eternal soul by skulking around this bastard landscape in search of wealth and power for the middle management like Talbot, and all so they might pat his head upon his return and say good dog, have a biscuit.

Konstantin's words had found him at his weakest. Perhaps he was no more valuable than the likes of Agua and his men. A tool for a job.

Nothing more. Shooting forward in his chair, not prepared to descend into self-pity, he attacked the problem of the bent key with a fresh fervor, trying to channel some of his unique energy into reshaping his crooked key.

To hell with Konstantin's words. He was a priest, after all, and that's what religion does, slips a comforting hand on your shoulder when you're beat, or as good as, fingers clutching possessively, its seductive lies tonguing your ear. This was the only life he'd ever known, and religious salvation was for the uncommitted. Mortis would earn his way into respectability. Time was on his side. And if it turned out that a failure here severed his prospects within the Society, then he'd succeed where his father failed and would use his knowledge of Society holdings and his expertise to crack every safe he could think of and flee with a king's ransom. But what if none of it did matter? Not legacy, accomplishments, or status, not when the future, no matter how distant, only brought him back here to this place or worse? Damn it, the monk's words again. Maybe he could look into some of that eternal life business…

Another plan slowly pieced itself together. One last hurrah should everything else fail and he decided to rip off the Society to get what he was finally owed. Nowhere on Earth could hide him from their reprisals forever, so why not try and barter with the devils themselves and buy a few hell-spawned acres from the Order? He thought of it as placing a deposit on a retirement home for when he died.

The black light softened, mixing and roiling into a brackish swampwater hue, then throbbing like an absinthe sky in his chest. His left-hand keys manipulated the bent and blunted key of his thumb like it was soft putty, not yet hardened to bone. The malformed structure slowly, so slowly, leveraged into its proper position, and finally it held, not bending back like rubber with a bad memory. But the cutting of the groove was the real tricky part. Mortis was becoming convinced it was this place. Somehow it was impairing his diabolical talents. Had the watchful skull god with its twisting horns sensed something it didn't like in him, working some form of magic to bar the thieves from making an easy escape?

The trailer rattled along with its peaceful rumblings, the sounds of diesel engines and hydraulics and shifting gears. No gunfire or screams, which was something, not that the peace aided him in his work. He couldn't cut the groove into the key. It felt like he was trying to flex a limb numbed with pins and needles.

'I might be able to help,' a voice offered, causing Mortis to jump up like he had sat on a spring. He looked up and found the Russian's last confederate, Kuznetsov, halfway through the trailer wall and the specimen tank, looking like he was climbing out of the tentacle-tied body-bag and pushing through the Perspex case.

'I don't need your help. This is what I do. Why don't you go and meditate or whatever it is you people do?' Kuznetsov didn't move. Mortis tapped the worktop in irritation. 'Why exactly would you want to help me? We're not allies in this.'

'I've been speaking to Konstantin, and we've agreed. There are a few good men here. Ones worth saving. Hammond and his workers.'

A second voice joined in shortly before the arrival of its owner. 'We shouldn't have taken this contract, but some of those men have families or debt. And the people they work for in New York, the same ones who own the construction firm and Citadel Security, you know they can't say no to them.' Lim stood there in his Sharp Construction uniform and hard hat. 'We'd like to ensure their safe return, for their families' sake.'

'But you and those mercenaries? Not so much,' Kuznetsov said, glowering at Mortis.

Mortis grimaced at the bad taste of this situation. He continued fiddling with his unfinished key, still finding it maddeningly intractable. The groove simply refused to be cut. He closed his sternum over like a bony trapdoor in what seemed like surrender, at least for the moment. 'What's your brilliant suggestion?'

'There's a plant that grows here. Zar-ptica root. Our original high priest brought some back with him, cultivated it, used its intrinsic properties to ease transitory state for non-Arkhitektors, helping them to pass over the threshold.'

'The same stuff that's suffused through your and Konstantin's armor?'

Kuznetsov made a soft throat-clearing noise in affirmation. 'Perhaps it could help with key? Provide a boost.'

Mortis was weary of this option, treating the information the way a mouse would a gleaming trap. He didn't like the idea of this Zar-ptica root, and why would he? It was a threat. A threat to his standing amongst the influential players of the Society. Despite his current shortcomings with his key-cutting, he still had value. A handyman capable of manufacturing fantastic magical locks and keys for most any purpose, and here he was, about to be upstaged by a plant, one capable of helping forge bridges between worlds. It made him think of free milk and unbought cows.

'It's not my ability to open doors that's the problem. It's that I can't even forge the key to begin with.' Mortis' voice went up in pitch, anger getting the best of him.

Lim gestured to Mortis' closed chest. 'Still, maybe this plant could kick-start your heart, so to speak. Could help with your cutting.'

Mortis stared at the wall in thought, his skeletal finger keys tapping a hollow bony rhythm on the metal workbench. He made them wait, if only to feel in control of the situation. A sad ruse, he knew. He leaned forward, his gangly frame like a giant marionette doll. 'Worth a shot. Where does this plant grow?'

'Large bushels grow along Zar-ptica's Trestle.' Kuznetsov nodded at Lim, and the workman quietly retreated from the trailer.

'Okay then.' Mortis grabbed his walkie. 'I'll have Agua pull over, and we'll consult the map and the drones.' Kuznetsov made to leave, but Mortis cleared his throat, and the ghost paused. He didn't want to say it. He really didn't. 'Thank Konstantin for me.'

Without a word, the last of Konstantin's ethereal acolytes vanished from sight.

22

IT WAS GETTING EASIER. STANDING with Kev in the proving ground, Clyde watched the Djinn's conjured forms disintegrate into golden particles, and he knew he was being pushed and tested. Ace would offer nothing but criticisms and find fault with everything he did, but Clyde knew he was succeeding in his curriculum far quicker than expected. He really was his father's son. In another life, in some comic-book parallel world, he knew he could well have been a US Marine. A third-generation hardened government drone, pointing his guns at whoever threatened North America's plans of world domination. *Fuck that*, Clyde thought, moodily racking the slide on one of his reloaded Glocks.

But he knew his progress couldn't be something as simple as being a born soldier; he suspected it was his connection to Kev. They complemented each other so well, and every time Clyde siphoned off some of Kev's telekinesis, it would temporarily leave him feeling... not necessarily *powerful* but *attuned*. Capable of rising to the challenge of each fresh new horror, no matter how much shit Ace gave him. And a realization had started to niggle away at Clyde, one that he felt too embarrassed to admit to: he found himself wanting to impress Ace. Standing in the plumes of gun smoke, he holstered the Glock and grabbed his shoulder-strapped H&K sub-machine gun, ejecting the spent magazine and grabbing a fresh one from the belt affixed to his combat armor.

A swirling nimbus of ghostly energy radiated up and down his hand and forearm.

Kev looked pretty steady too, the combined efforts of arduous combat and the parceling of some of his power to Clyde not having as much of a diminishing effect on him as in the previous sessions. They nodded to each other, the two-fold gesture declaring that they were both okay and that they were pleased with each other's performance.

Despite his leaps and bounds of natural potential, he still had to fight just as hard to shut out the conflicting thoughts and emotions about what he was doing. His mantra of *I'm not a soldier, I'm not a soldier, I'm not a soldier* was becoming increasingly difficult to believe. He had to remind himself that this was training, and training *only*, a program of extreme self-defense, and the moment Ace, or Director Trujillo, or whoever, signed off on the passing grade for persons of interest, he'd be on the first jet back home. And he knew that moment could be sooner than expected. His walks with Ramaliak were progressing, and Clyde was confident that he'd soon be mentally conditioned enough to reach down into the deepest layer of the Median. It was almost impossible to read a goat's face—even a goat-man's—but he could hear the subtle enthusiasm in Ramaliak's voice during the end of each successive episode. And yet it continued to instill that same trepidation within Clyde, the fear of what he'd learn about himself down there amongst the world of sleeping souls, and the possibility of coming face-to-face with the ghosts of more loved ones.

And he couldn't stop thinking about home, and how it seemed to beckon to him more loudly by the day. He had exchanged a few texts with his mom, just to check in. She was doing okay, and hoped that his art was doing well, and that he was eating enough because he's so skinny. At least he'd gained some muscle tone, he supposed. But he couldn't wait to get home to pick up where he had left off; his post-training nightly drawings—which sometimes took him well into the early hours—had begun to pile up, and he had decided to use this unconventional vacation of his as the source material for a new creator-owned intellectual property. A comic about soldiers fighting to get out of Hell, back to their families. It was still very much in the beta stage, with a ton of brainstorming and clarification to sort out, but he had some ideas for it and, most crucially, the hunger to work at it. He had checked his email two days ago, feeling the usual blow of disappointment from the lack of industry interest in his old art submissions. It was odd how that disappointment never seemed to lessen, no matter how used to it he got. It would always be that little puncture in his spirit that deflated him slowly over the course of the day, irritating him more and more as he tried not to think about it. But using this experience as loose source material was too good an opportunity to pass up. How many people in the comic-book industry had been given opportunities like this? Well, maybe Jack Kirby, if Ace was to be believed. But he felt more certain than ever that pursuing his own project was the future, and he would stop beating at the doors of the flagship comic-book companies.

'That slingshot move is getting pretty tight,' Kev said, self-indulging in his own proud bravura. 'And that jump-up shockwave thing you did was nice.'

Clyde, yanked from his brief autopilot musings about life after training, couldn't deny that they'd had a few moments back there that would probably have blown his mind if he wasn't still being so rigid about all of this agency box-ticking. 'It got the job done.'

Kev gave him a sneer. 'Oh, okay, slick. You play it cool, but I know you got something out of that. I saw it on your face. It's okay to admit to yourself that you're enjoying this a little. Because I know you are. Might as well have some fun here because it might be the last time we get to have any for a while.'

Clyde felt like a bit of an asshole. Too busy being critical about his improving soldier skills and feeling like a sell-out to his long-held ideals; thinking about going back to Brooklyn, possibly with Stephen and his estranged dad; and feeling trapped here, now, fighting the Djinn's constructs when he wanted to be putting all his energy into his as-yet-untitled new comic-book project to spite the industry that wouldn't give him the time of day. But how many days did he have left here to hang out with Kev? The weeks had sailed by with alarming speed. That's what happened when you were not allowed a moment to be bored. And when he was discharged and capable of killing to a satisfactory level—should the need arise—how often would he get to see Kev? Would Kev be allowed vacation time? Would he return to Brooklyn to catch up?

'I'm sorry, man. You're right. This is just some fun and exercise. A contact sport.' He smiled at Kev.

'Or, you know, a video game.' Kev offered a more palatable alternative.

'Sweet, cuckolded Joseph of Nazareth, ladies,' Ace called over the speaker. Ace sounded like he had gotten out of the wrong side of the bed this morning, like most mornings. 'Are you both scared of breaking a nail? I'm going to hit you with something big and nasty here.' Clyde could see him through the observation window, gesturing to the Lamp's technician to up the threat level. 'No more level-five playtime. Level seven. And I want to see you take their fucking faces off.'

Something started to generate in the ether, something big, powerful. A vanguard demon. A blubbery, navy-blue-skinned mammoth of an animal with as many teeth as there were rolls of fat beneath its chin, standing at six feet tall on two robust rhino-trunk legs. Two huge, inverted walrus tusks protruded from its bottom jaw up towards the dome of its rough-fleshed, earless scalp. To the vanguard's right, something else appeared, a slick, plasma-tinted gastropod that was roughly the size of a 4x4 off-road vehicle. The enormous slug belonged to a relatively newly discovered species, nicknamed blenders by the agency due to their very bodies being composed entirely of powerful digestive enzymes that could rapidly break down any organic matter they came into contact with, rendering even the sturdiest of physical specimens into instant puree.

Clyde allowed his sub-machine gun to dangle, pulling out his knife. He smirked at Kev. 'Just some fun, right? A video game.'

Kev took a second but returned the smirk. 'Or maybe a contact sport. You can still get fucked up in here.'

The vanguard roared loud enough to make a proud lion sound like a cuddly kitten and charged, flat feet pounding the ground like an earthquake. Clyde took a run at it, knife in hand, and briefly wondered if this would be the training session Ace would have to terminate in order to spare his life. If nothing else, it might make the surly asshole dole out some much-deserved respect. At full steam, the vanguard cocked a fist that would likely crumble a brick wall, but Clyde opened his right hand, palm towards the floor, and seeded out a little telekinetic boost, propelling himself up and onto its mountainous shoulders, its powerful swing hitting nothing but empty air. Clyde sank his combat knife deep into the steep sloping trapezius muscles of the vanguard and, gripping the knife tight, used his stored energy to acrobatically swing his legs high over the tusk-adorned head, planting his boots into the small of the vanguard's bulky back, pulling its cumbersome weight downwards. Before Clyde became trapped under its fat-wadded muscular mass, he rolled backwards and, using the last lingering dregs of his borrowed power, thrust out with both legs, launching the brutish thing directly over his head and into the hungry, slithering gelatinous mass of the blender. Wobbling through the rippling, jelly folds of the huge slug, the tusked combatant tried to swim and fight against its agonizing fate, but the muscle and protective blubber was quickly stripped from its body. The blender's watery environment transitioned from its straw-yellow hues to a cloudy blood red, the dissolving flesh forming gruesome turbid dregs of life. Suddenly the feasting bloat seemed content, idling as it digested its first meal of the fight.

The large-boned skeleton floated inside the blender like a mosquito in amber. Kev found his opening, lifting the huge slug into the air and watching as it instinctively started to curl up into a protective ball. It seemed to know what was coming. Kev wound up and hurled the slug like a fast ball towards the observation window, smearing Ace's view with a huge but disgusting coating of red and yellow chunks. It looked as if the windows had been targeted by an army equipped with strawberry gelato and custard. It was a move Kev had made his unofficial signature in these fights, but nobody seemed to mind. The messes always cleaned themselves up.

A high whine of static issued from the observation room, followed by a few stunned seconds of silence, and then an uproar of Ace's aggressive, profanity-riddled support, whoops and heavy-handed clapping. He probably even spilled his beer during his celebration.

Getting himself under control, Ace spoke into the mic. 'That was, like, fifteen seconds! Okay, ladies, I think your balls have finally dropped.'

23

THE CONVOY HAD PULLED OVER several miles from Mortis' new destination. A detour Captain Agua had been very unhappy to take, but seeing how increasingly pale—and somehow, ghastlier—Mortis had become over the past week, Agua had ceded to his somber instructions. Mortis had been spending a great deal of the time hiding away in the big rig, alone, barely using his radio, and leaving Agua to ride in tense silence with Konstantin; it was a good job Private O'Brien of Charlie Team was riding with them to provide some semblance of distraction for their tired hatred of each other. Agua had managed to figure out the reason for Mortis' shakiness without needing to be told, and it was just as well, what with Mortis acting in such a prevaricating manner.

And the reason was: they were stuck here. And what a creek without a paddle "here" was.

After a few quiet words with his three LTs, Agua had another quiet word with Mortis and made him confess about the situation, warts and all. Agua might not have been overjoyed to hear that this supposed miracle cure for Mortis' limp thumb had come from the mouth of Konstantin, but from Mortis' twitchiness, Agua knew that the situation really was as bad as he claimed. And Agua knew a lot of things: how to fight, how to survive; tactics to win a hundred battles; muscle cars; and beer. But he knew as much about magic and this rusty asshole of a world as he did about how to make a relationship last beyond the animal fucking phase, which was to say, fuck all. Hate it all he wanted, he and his men didn't have the upper hand here.

So here they were. Zar-ptica's Trestle.

Sounded great. Like everywhere else in this miserable shit hole, it was apparently named by some dick with a penchant for the dramatic. In fact, Miserable Shit Hole was probably a county somewhere further down the road, he suspected.

Agua had spent most of his life in the shit, so what was one more problem?

At least they had made the stop without incident, pulling in alongside a lumpy rise of hills. Lieutenant Briggs had reported sighting a few creatures skittering off after their arrival, but other than that, their presence seemed to go unnoticed. That didn't stop Agua from making sure everybody stayed focused, though; he didn't want any avoidable losses before they got to Eidolon Trench. There was no shortage of reinforcements he could call in from the warehouse, but that required Mortis, which meant this objective had now become top priority.

Agua got out from behind the wheel of the lead Humvee and stretched his lower back. Taking a sip of warm water from his bottle, he scratched at several weeks' worth of black beard. The air smelled oddly pleasant, reminding him of smoky wood on warm summer evenings. The captain chewed the last of a protein bar while he waited for Lieutenant Briggs' two-man drone team to assess the situation. The pair of drone operators sat on the hood of their Humvee, wearing their goggles and operating their remote controls, sending their RC drones east as the rest of Alpha Team defended them with hard, unflinching stares that swept the area for hostiles. Agua left the drone scouts to do their thing but stared off into the eastern gulf of shadowy twilight, the ocean of stars blinking in the mauve sky.

According to his watch, assuming it was still working correctly, they had been on this expedition for twenty-one days. For an outfit of battle-hardened ex-soldiers, it was a walk in the park logistically, especially compared to the tours of duty they had all individually completed in their various dirty and sanctioned wars, but what still continued to throw him off was the distinct lack of apparent order or logic to the day and night cycles, and being forced to measure time's passage from his wristwatch, beard growth, and the increasing confusion of his internal body clock. He turned a lazy look west and found the nearest of the two blue suns still lighting the landscape like dual midnight suns. Agua tried to put it out of his mind and turned back to the east, watching the tiny black specks of the drones vanishing against the gloom.

The two drones were getting close to Zar-ptica's Trestle now. Agua didn't know if this place actually had some type of bizarre train running about the place, but an elevated train track is just how Zar-ptica's Trestle looked, if not a little warped and aged, as was the ongoing theme with this place. It could have been constructed from iron—shit, it could have been constructed from gold for all he could tell at this distance—but it ramped up from the earth steadily and then leveled off, running off into the distance and out of view. What did catch his eye, however, even at this distance, was how certain sections of that giant frame appeared to be glowing red hot, like interconnecting lines of lava. He took a closer look with his binoculars and found no smoke, but it still looked like irregular spots of wildfire were clinging to sections of the frame like moss. He didn't like the idea of compromising his unit's safety by marching across a giant bridge that could be structurally compromised by heat, or whatever the hell that glowing shit was. And what was this? Were there symbols arranged into that great Trestle, sections of the effulgent beams twisted and wrought into unknown characters? He dropped the binoculars on the dashboard and walked over to where Konstantin was standing.

The cultist stood alone, a little way from the stationary troops and work force. Agua assumed he was having one of his private chats with the last of his sissy brothers, and maybe that dead worker too; Agua hadn't paid much attention to the laborer's name but knew he had continued to spend some time with Hammond and the rest of his crew. Lucky him, Agua supposed. Unlike Corporal Parel, who had been left behind at the Cradle with a nice new extra hole in the head. Agua stopped before Konstantin, his presence yanking the monk from his closed-eyed meditations. Konstantin regarded him silently, like a pest who kept sniffing around him.

'This best not be some trick you're pulling,' Agua warned. 'Having us change course for a fucking placebo.' Konstantin closed his eyes again. 'Is that the stuff that's going to take us home? A fucking disco plant?'

'Ask Mortis if he thinks it's worth your time,' Konstantin replied. 'He's the one holding your chain.'

'I'm talking to you. That gangly fuck is getting too jumpy for my liking. Now I admit I'm all out of better solutions right now, but if you are getting in his head and mixing him up to try and fuck us out here, I'll take you down with us.'

Konstantin opened his eyes again, and they shone within their dark pockets. His beard growth was more untamed than Agua's, coating his hollow cheeks and enhancing the overall effect of a mad unkempt monk with a calm zeal. 'If this is trick, you'll be first I kill.' He closed his wrinkled eyes again.

Agua didn't appreciate that. He never did respond well to bad attitude. It was this foible of his that had led to him ruining a distinguished military career by shooting his commanding officer dead before going AWOL. Which reminded him.

'It would be a shame if anything were to happen to Hammond and his boys. They already lost one. Tough break. So I'd be careful about making threats from this point on. Because this operation is starting to look kind of fucked from where I'm standing, and until I know we have a way of getting out of here, I might stop caring about the small details of this mission. You see, we're kind of alike, you and me. We'll follow up to a point, but if we get tired of eating shit, we have no problem becoming our own man.'

Konstantin remained blind and deaf to Agua; his brow furrowed in concentration.

Several miles away to the north, a sudden meteor shower of fresh virgin souls tore across the sky. Somehow, they must have managed to tear free from a nexus channel, though such a pipeline was nowhere to be seen from this vantage point. Was it over that ridgeline? Had the channel dipped underground as they sometimes did? Shit, Agua thought, maybe these particular spirits had been flying all across the sky, this way and that, for a hundred miles or more. He didn't understand the ins and outs of this place well enough to guess. These ghostly newcomers sailed through the ether in completely wild abandon, defying gravity for an indeterminate amount of time before slowly coming down into a depressed pan in the earth roughly 150 yards to the north; their rough landing made Agua think of the choppers he'd watched go down in this hellhole. He watched the diaphanous men and women scatter, terrified and confused. It reminded him of too many young men and women being dropped into combat zones for the first time. Something rolled out of a burrow in the grass and the dirt, something large, huge actually; it seemed like some type of insect that could only mobilize itself in forward rolls. It was swift, pursuing the souls across the nightly veldt. Agua didn't have to follow the hunt for very long.

'You kill for money,' Konstantin said. 'You murdered all but one of my sect. You fire on enslaved children when I gave you correct targets to eliminate. Don't ever draw comparisons between us. If I were you, I'd focus on getting Mortis what he needs. Then we can all get back to main concerns.' Agua had his sidearm jammed under Konstantin's jaw so fast it was almost imperceptible. Konstantin slowly opened his eyes. There was no fear there, only an exhaustion of his spirit. 'My map has been accurate so far. Can you be certain it is faithful rest of the way? Maybe I forgot location of next nexus point.'

'Maybe I'll just finish you anyway. I only took this gig because the money is good. The director of our firm has a few binding ties to Cairnwood, so I could put a slug through your head right now, wiping out you and your ghost, and not feel a moment's regret. I'll tell Mortis you became a wild buck, and I had no choice. I'll finish up here, return home, and get a paycheck and another gig. No sweat off my back.' He pressed the barrel deeper into Konstantin's jaw. The moment stretched, and Agua's finger continued to slowly apply pressure to the trigger. It was tempting. So very tempting. 'I'm in control here.'

A commotion sounded over by the drone team. Mortis was amongst the huddle, looking very proactive with the lieutenants.

Konstantin stared down Agua for several difficult seconds. The gun went back in Agua's holster. 'I'm in control here,' Agua repeated, moving quickly over to Briggs' team.

The operators stood around the live-feed screen, the radio wave transmissions of the drone cameras unimpeded by the recent scramble of spirits across the sky. Mortis watched the video feed pan over the Trestle. To Agua it still looked like sections of it were ablaze. The camera zoomed in a little more, granting a better view of the brush-fire plants burning away along the steep sides of the framework. Mortis, his hands buried in his coat pockets, straightened his stooped back, excitedly calling Konstantin over, but the Russian was already drawing close. Konstantin inspected the camera, the drone hovering in place above Zarptica's Trestle.

'Is that the stuff?' Mortis asked him.

'Zar-ptica root,' Konstantin confirmed.

Mortis looked closely at the two-man drone team. 'How far is it?'

One of the men removed his goggles. 'Four-point-two miles.'

'Threats?' Agua asked.

'It looks clear,' the drone operator responded, piloting his drones back to meet them halfway.

Mortis pulled his hands from his pockets and commenced clapping his hands to motivate the watchful soldiers. He had a new spring in his step. 'Let's move.' His hands were quick, pale blurs beating and clacking together.

Agua glimpsed the fractured thumb and hoped this stupid weed did exactly as advertised.

Engines firing up, the convoy raced to their new destination.

. . .

THEY REACHED THE base of the Trestle in swift time and, again, without incident. Konstantin was waiting for this place to turn on them. They had been far too fortunate so far, too safe and unfettered for such noisy travelers. He had only witnessed a handful of deaths personally during his walks with the Arkhitektor, but his master had divulged his own tales of loss, which was practically tradition amongst all precedent teachers and students. Mortis was seated next to him in the back seat again, still his usual sickly, pallid self, but animated by a little more hope. The damaged key of his right hand was folded at the knuckle and tapping against his chest. Konstantin had no idea how useful this idea was. It could be a complete waste of time, only for the sake of Hammond and his crew, he sincerely hoped it wasn't. He wanted them to have a way out of here, provided they survived the rest of the job. As for the rest of them, himself included, they could remain here forever for all he cared. They were all men of death in varying capacities; this was the perfect place for them.

The long, bumpy slope of the Trestle reached the plateau. The ambient light of the passing growths, teeming with wild abandon in parts, illuminated the interiors of the vehicles like majestic streetlights. Konstantin didn't know who or what had constructed this bridge, or why the Zar-ptica grew here. The original Arkhitektor had long ago warned his disciples to steer clear of this bridge but hadn't explained why. The point was, he had the providence of stumbling upon this unique plant, and that was good enough. But where did this bridge go? Konstantin used to ponder this. How far did it span? It took a little time, but in the end, he lost interest. These lands were one great mystery, and they could keep their abhorrent secrets. Unlike Cairnwood and their ilk, he only sought one thing, and when he got it, all these abstruse inner workings would be wiped away, for he would be a just and fair god.

They stopped at the nearest growths, the fronds of the cold-burning plants whipping and dancing like sleepy curves of flame along the edge of the bridge. Leaving the engines running, Mortis unfolded himself from the vehicle and waved Hammond out of his truck. Konstantin got out too, if only to breathe air that wasn't being shared with Captain Agua. Hammond and a select few of his men had gathered tools and were setting about positioning themselves carefully along the precipitous edges of the bridge, trying to find the best angles to come at the roots of the large Zar-ptica springing and bowing out from the crossbeams of the Trestle.

Despite Mortis' harried insistence that the plant was completely harmless, the workmen seemed keen not to touch it with bare skin, tucking the sleeves of their overalls into their thick work gloves.

The specter of Lim observed the work, advising where he could and getting annoyed that he couldn't lend a helping hand. Konstantin knew the poor man was desperate for anything that would keep him from dwelling on the fact that he was actually dead, and that if he were to pass back through Mortis' doorway, he would still be a ghost amongst the living, lost forever. What could Lim do then? Try and make it work with his wife and kids back in Queens? And when they finally got old and passed on, they wouldn't have access to a doorway between worlds the way he had. They'd fall into this place, unable to get out, and he'd be trapped on Earth, alone. Konstantin shoved the depressing reverie away as best he could, despising this natural order.

A shout of alarm traveled along the titanic bridge, the voice belonging to one of the security guards, who quickly followed it up with a burst of gunfire. Konstantin dashed out from between the line of vehicles, and what he saw chilled him. They were descending on them from the dusk like detritus on the breeze. A whole mass of them.

'Bodybags!' Lieutenant Fenwick boomed, almost as loud as his pump-action shotgun.

The fleshy bags glided through the air, descending ever closer with terrible speed. Bullets punched through them, spattering the sky with bursts of ichor. Konstantin was left wondering where they had come from. The sky had been clear only moments ago. Were they sheltering in the shadows of the Trestle below, hanging like bats, billowing up into the air when they sensed food nearby? The bodybags began to circle the train of vehicles, their man-sized mouths unzipping with an awful promise, tentacles spilling out like intestines, feeling their way through the air and dragging across the roofs of the large trucks. Soon they'd be lower, exploring the roofs of the Humvees, and then the heads and shoulders of the men.

Hammond and his hand-picked workers, Villanelli and Andrews, were preparing to race back to the dubious security of their trucks until security cleared the area when Mortis spat demands of them, shouting at them to commit to the task at hand and sever him a sample of the Zarptica root. Hammond gave him a queasy look but did as he was told, rallying his men to put their backs into hacking off the tough, fibrous fronds of volcanic light. Lim grabbed the shears from Villanelli, who was still trying to find a good angle from which he could attack the protruding plant without going over the edge, and told him to go back to join the others in the trucks. Villanelli looked to Hammond, who authorized this with a stiff nod, his attention fixed on the hard, straining work of his own busy hands.

Konstantin watched the bodybags float ever nearer, one of them looping a tentacle around the arms of one of Bravo Team's soldiers and hauling him up into the bullet-lashed sky, where he vanished into the black maw of the bag, right up to his waist, then his shoulders, and finally, his shrieking head. Konstantin's uses in a fight were beyond decimated, stripped down to Kuznetsov and Lim, but he wasn't going to simply stand here and watch Hammond and another of his civilian workers gamble their lives away, crouched down on the spine's ridge, waiting for a tentacle to whip down and pluck them up. He sent a thought, rousting Kuznetsov, and the pair of them raced over to Hammond to try and aid him in cleaving off part of the plant.

Mortis shouted, but his ordering of Konstantin to remain in the safety of the Humvee was ignored, or lost to the wind, the battle cries, and the gunfire. One of the bodybags hit the hard, chipped ground in front of Konstantin with a wet slap, sounding like a cow had tumbled from the sky. It lay still, shredded with heavy-caliber shells. Konstantin circled the thing and joined the workers urgently hacking at the undulating leaves with their shears. Panicked and careless, trying too hard to rip the plant away from the strange girders, Andrews lost his balance. He tried to put a hand out, but there was nothing to grab hold of. He stumbled off the side of the ridge with a surprised yelp that quickly turned into a short, terrible scream of shock. Konstantin didn't hear him hit the ground so far below. Hammond's eyes bulged in horror and, pausing in his labors, he leaned over the side and stared down at the base of the Trestle and the surrounding rocks, yelling Andrews' name.

Konstantin clambered up onto the side rail—the very spot from which Andrews had tumbled—and cast his gaze across the tenebrous crags below, finding no sign of the fallen man's body or spirit. With a silent command, he sent Kuznetsov down there to try and salvage whatever was left of the man.

Konstantin placed a firm but sympathetic hand on Hammond's shoulder, pulling him from his mourning and returning him to the importance of the job. 'We don't uproot this, we all die.' He saw the grief in Hammond's eyes, watching it quickly dry and harden into anger.

Hammond went at the Zar-ptica with renewed urgency, his burly muscles squeezing the handles of the hedge shearers so tight his arms shuddered with effort. Finally, the resistance gave, and the blades cut through the leaves and stems with a great release. They almost all twirled away to the gloomy rocks below, but Lim and the startled Villanelli managed to catch them just in time. Konstantin told Lim and Villanelli—a man whose name he hadn't learned—to run the plant to the specimen truck, his voice hoarse over the thunderous guns. Lim passed his drapery of leaves to the other man, reiterating Konstantin's message. Mortis, suddenly having a vested interest in the crewman's well-being, helped him carry the foliage down the line to the truck, sidestepping the soldiers' defensive positions.

'Andrews, he'll be down there, won't he?' Lim asked Konstantin, his voice meek and desperate for assurance. 'He died here, same as me, his ghost will be there, right?'

Konstantin could picture Lim flying down there into the unknown, heedless of the risk to his own eternal soul, needing to do what he could to aid a friend. Over Lim's shoulder, he watched Lieutenant Fenwick exhibit a trait that no ordinary man possessed, no matter how much time they put in at the gym: one of the tentacles had seized his blocky forearm, so he wrapped the rubbery limb about his muscular arm several more times for better purchase, then dragged it down from the sky with incredible strength, slamming it repeatedly into the ground until it stopped moving. Something slumped out of the bag, birthed amidst the slippery coils and ruptured fluids. The bodybags were not empty mouths, after all.

Not entirely.

Konstantin stared hard into Lim's eyes, needing to make sure that the man understood his words. 'My brother can handle this. If Andrews is down there, he'll find him. And I'll keep him safe, like you. Now, you and Hammond need to get to trucks. Go!'

Hammond was climbing down off the side rail when a whip seized his arm. With a cry of horror, he was hoisted into the air, the shears flying from his grip as his arm socket burned with the stress of hanging. He was dropped onto the roof of the nearest truck. The bodybag was on him in seconds. Somehow, it was able to stand upright, slouched but still vertical, before gracelessly collapsing its leathery weight onto Hammond's legs, the tentacles holding his arms apart. The bag's mouth unzipped further with slow certainty, something shifting about within the darkness of the large sack. Black, bony fingers dug at the opening impatiently, dragging it open further and revealing bone-thin mummified arms, a head, and shoulders. Hammond screamed in soul-chilling terror as the desiccated body lay atop his own, its eye sockets empty behind the moth-chewed wraps, its jaws opening with a tired groan to show its black, nubby teeth before they sank into the exposed flesh of his neck, right above his work collar.

Konstantin raced towards the truck, ready to clamber up the footholds and handles to the roof where he would impale the hideous creature with Hammond's dropped shears, but Lim had the advantage; stealing the tool from Konstantin's grip, he floated off like a jet of steam and alighted on the roof in seconds. Lim raised the shears, the twin points poised to drive down deep into the burnished flesh of the sack and its hungry occupant. The blades came down. The filthy bandaged corpse arched its back in violent protest, but its screams were a silent hiss. The scream of the dead. Hammond managed to buck the awkward weight of the monster off his thighs, then scrambled away and almost rolled right off the side of the truck before saving himself. Lim pulled the shears free, the impaled bodybag lying truly dead. More of the accursed things continued to ride the air currents, circling them like vultures, swooping in, then away when the gunfire proved too dangerous. Konstantin and Lim helped Hammond down, giving a cursory inspection of his bite wound before bustling him away to the interior of the Sharp Construction truck where the rest of the workers were waiting, armed with sledgehammers and shovels.

Mortis was quickly loping back down the line towards Konstantin, stooping lower than normal to spare his ears some of the savage roars of machine guns. He grabbed Konstantin's shoulder, the force suggesting that what he was about to say wasn't debatable. 'I need you with me.' He brandished the clump of glowing leaves as if in proof.

Konstantin noticed Agua and the lieutenants were ordering their own men back to the vehicles, their objective complete and not wanting to waste more combatants and ammunition. Agua wasn't even relying on his guns; his fists were supercharged beacons, unloading an artillery of emerald shrapnel at the incoming hostiles. Konstantin also noticed swirls of smoke and even some electrical discharges emanating from behind the blocky obstruction of the vehicle fleet. Right then he knew that it was the joint work of Lieutenants Castor and Briggs.

'Feed it into your chest!' Konstantin shouted back at Mortis.

Mortis wasn't about to take no for an answer, but Konstantin removed the freakishly proportioned fingers of Mortis and returned to the side of the Trestle. Lim was right back at Konstantin's side, his own wide eyes searching. Mortis glared at Konstantin's back for several seconds before striding away to the truck. The engines all growled to life, chugging and raring to go.

Relieved, Konstantin saw how Kuznetsov had recovered Andrews' spirit, arisen from his broken body and shifting about in a confused gait like one pulled from a deep dream. There was a change in the lighting, a sudden sweep of shadow blanketing the rocky ground. Konstantin lost sight of them. Seconds ticked by, each one everlasting, and he could almost feel something perish inside him, and for an unbearable moment he believed that he had just felt Kuznetsov vanish from all known planes of existence, his soul torn asunder by an unseen threat lurking in the amber shade of the Trestle's underpass like a hungry troll.

Something flickered down there, the amber light stripping back some of the heavier shade. Whatever was moving, it was rising up, coming into the full reach of the Zar-ptica's glowing aura. It was Kuznetsov, ascending from the rocks. Alone. Konstantin felt that dip deep in his chest, the optimism for finding the soul of Andrews quelled. Lim's shoulders seemed to sink in the face of the impending bad news.

Kuznetsov quietly shook his head. 'There was something waiting down below. It got him.' Lim shook his head and hurried over to Hammond's truck. 'Brother, you must get to safety,' Kuznetsov advised, watching the remaining bodybags continue to cluster about excitedly above them. 'I'll fight them off.'

Kuznetsov went to make good on his word when Konstantin stalled him. 'Nyet. We're done here.' Kuznetsov gave a final appraisal of the dangers drifting above them like warped jellyfish and instead returned to his chambers inside Konstantin.

An angry rhythm was pounded onto the roof of the lead Humvee. 'Hurry the fuck up or I'm leaving you here!' Agua bellowed.

Konstantin stared at him, not with anger, only disinterest. He turned his back on him and made for the specimen truck. Agua piled into his vehicle and the driver pulled a quick Uturn on the wide Trestle, the convoy quickly following suit as the dark, pulsating clouds of flesh descended. Konstantin exchanged a quick nod with the workman in the truck's cab and climbed into the back of the truck as it was starting to pull away. Mortis was already inside, ardently cleaving away at the strips of Zar-ptica.

24

NOISE FILTERED DOWN FROM MURKINESS above, the steady distortion of sounds. Though quieter at this depth, the half-remembered voices of people from Clyde's life echoed after him, growing fainter by the yard. Slowly, gently, he sank, deeper, deeper still, into the Median. The sights and sounds of unrestrained imagination and remembrance had slipped away in this woozy void, leaving him floating in a coma-like passivity with only the reassuring ticking of the Sleeping Shepherd to focus on, and even that sounded despairingly remote at this depth, similar to his own heartbeat in his ears. Ramaliak must be here somewhere, in a controlled fall with Clyde, acting in a sky-diving instructor capacity. Sure, he was here somewhere, but where? Clyde couldn't see him in this stygian spiral. And then, finally ... light. So much light it inspired a gasp within Clyde's heart with its indelible majesty. He found his body gliding high over a planetary mass of multi-colored neurons, the hemispheres of a brain knitted from rainbow LEDs. And then the vertigo claimed him once more, his eyes rolling back, a sigh of ecstasy passing his lips.

He managed to brave it, sensing Ramaliak at his side, hooves out and enjoying the free fall.

Clyde might be a step too wise to fall foul of his mind's emotive fantasies, and perhaps a session too experienced to retread the previously visited maps and dialogues of memory, but he was still a rank amateur down here in the Median, and without Ramaliak at his side he knew he could instantly stumble into the fathoms of his unconscious, lost and helpless, and only surface from these thrashing tides after sleep had had its fill, casting him back to the shores of reality like a shipwrecked sailor. Sleep was a tightrope walk between life and coma death, according to Ramaliak. And expiration was a very real threat to all sleepers, though only the exceptionally careless could manage to tilt themselves over that high wire into oblivion and Erebus: some might be cavalier and blunder down too deep into this glowing infinity of the Median and find that they couldn't get back to the surface; others might succumb to the nefarious wiles of the malevolent tricksters who danced and enticed down in this neon Atlantis.

Their soles softly touched down in the shining kingdom of color, the entirety of which pulsed with a measured synaptic rhythm. Clyde watched the innumerable wires beneath his Nikes thrum and surge like sleepy Christmas lights. The whole scene was pacifying, and Clyde's mesmerized gaze foolishly attempted to comprehend the scale of this place, the dense and layered world of luminescent yarn, colorfully crisscrossing in threads to form a dizzying landscape of hills and caverns, towers, and odd structures without rhyme or reason.

'Soul threads,' Ramaliak explained. 'Each and every one.'

Clyde involuntarily reached for his own invisible soul thread rooted in his mind, remembering that he couldn't see or feel it without Ramaliak's flourish. His hand fell away, but he felt weird, almost blasphemous, standing on the innumerable connections between mind and soul. He compared it to dragging his dirty shoes into somebody's home, only a couple of thousand times worse. He tried to imagine how many dreamers throughout history had participated in weaving this tapestry, this macrocosm of soul threads. How many trillions? And what about that first dreamer? Was their first walk a single glowing thread across infinite blackness?

'It's really something, isn't it?' Ramaliak still cherished the view, his large eyes drinking in the fields and outer boundaries of what resembled a vast and strange city.

Clyde knew his words wouldn't do it justice, so he stood back and allowed himself to enjoy the view for a spell. It felt rewarding to have finally made it down to this sleeping, alien world. 'What's the real deal with this place? The way you've described it, it sounds like a buffer between the living and the Null. How does that work? If our soul threads are fixed here in this psychedelic wonderland, how do they end up in the Null?'

'Try to think of the Median as a kind of womb. All these soul threads? Umbilical cords, attached now and forever here, in this ever-expanding womb. Upon death, the soul is clipped free and cast into Erebus, but the thread remains.' Ramaliak fell into the teacher's natural posture, short, neat steps motivated by thought and speech. 'And when those with talents such as yours come along, by intent or accident, they're able to call the loose spirit back through their severed thread. Things get a little wishy-washy there. Lingering energies trail between the severed end and the host. It might be easier to think of the phenomenon as an offshoot of phantom-limb syndrome.' Ramaliak made a wrapping motion with his hooves, tying his layman's lecture up in a bow. 'The necromancer summons the ghost back by tugging on the thread and binds it to their own. Voilà, ghost lodestone.'

'Okay ... cool. But this seems a little too neat and organized. Somebody must run it. Is it you, Ram-man? The rest of your kooky goat-man clan?' Clyde's easy smile melted away in the ensuing silence.

Ramaliak took his time in choosing his exact words. Then he abandoned his answer entirely. 'Let's save that question for another day. We're here for a reason, and as much as this place belongs on a postcard, we're here for business, not pleasure.'

Clyde didn't need psychic abilities to see Ramaliak's reticence. And he wasn't bigger than his boots, so he ceded to the expert. 'So how does this next part work? Stephen and my dad, are their soul threads here? I'm not standing on them, am I?' He shuffled his feet about, still feeling guilty about stepping on another's soul.

Ramaliak smiled at Clyde's awkwardness, his scruffy chin hanging ajar to expose a row of thick, blocky teeth. 'Don't worry, you're not mussing them up. You're a construct in a dream, and a weak one at that. No offense.'

'Whatever you say, man.'

'In answer to your question, their threads are just over there.' His hoof didn't point towards the glamorous magic of that palatial metropolis with its blazing electric avenues of otherworldly architecture but out towards a roving heath, wild and unkempt with oddly built trees, their warm soul lights radiating upwards in a placid attempt to paint the coal-black sky.

'I'm not going to ask how the hell you can find specific threads in this giant haystack.' Ramaliak shrugged modestly. Clyde stared at his destination and almost lost his nerve. 'Is it difficult to knot their souls to mine—if I can, I mean?'

The goat stuck his hooves in the pockets of Spector's blazer. 'The hard part was getting you down here. The binding is quite painless.'

They walked the short distance to the neon forest upon the hills. A pleasant dream walk that made Clyde's heart grow heavy at the endless beauty. Why couldn't the dead roam these visionary avenues and gardens forever? Cresting that gentle heath, gazing through the fever-dream confusion of yellow and green and red polyp trees, he felt the mildest of headaches gently tap against the inside of his skull. One that he attributed to his own soul thread, yearning for the coming bind. That was when he caught a slight movement deep in that shining forest. Or was it simply a trick of the hazy lights?

'Isn't there some type of security for this place?' Clyde tried squinting between the large, swollen polyps, seeking the half-seen creature in the malformed jungle, but the endless show-and-tell of pacifying light and soft shadow concealed the wood's secrets. 'Some authority to keep people like us from messing around with the souls of the entire universe?'

'Oh, there's security all right,' Spector replied earnestly. 'But as long as you're with me, they'll leave you alone. I'm kind of privileged in that way.'

Clyde was sharply attuned to Spector's casual gait and allowed himself to settle his excitement. Tangled amidst the softly beating lights, he started to notice that some of the soul threads had burned out like frazzled fiberoptic cables.

Ramaliak must have preempted the coming question. 'I must warn you, until I see them, I won't know if they're still lit or dark.'

'What do you mean?'

'A lit soul is still active, wherever they may be: Erebus, tethered to somebody else, et cetera.'

'And dark?' Clyde didn't know why he bothered asking.

'The soul has been completely destroyed. Nothing remains of them.'

As they went deeper, Clyde noticed whole sections of the bulbous lollipop trees had completely burned out, looking black and tumorous in comparison to the jolly and peaceful light of the other knitted soul bundles. He found his eyes eagerly bouncing from one clumpy tree colony to the next, then to the skein of the floor itself, as if he expected to find two threads labeled RICHARD WILLIAMS and STEPHEN WILLIAMS. They hadn't walked more than a few more yards before Ramaliak stopped between two lumpy leaning trees, and yes, they both had their share of dark and lifeless strands. Clyde's heart sank, but then suddenly lifted in relief as the Ram's hooves gently reached into the giant yellowish grape on his right and then the giant greenish one to his left, softly tugging at two long strands, still lit and vibrant. Without a word, he respectfully handed both soul threads over to a numbed Clyde, leaving him standing there speechless, one in each hand and his mouth half-agape as he inspected one, then the other, then the first one again. These sleeping wires, humming with a green and golden light, were the sum total of two of the most important people in his life.

Ramaliak stepped close. 'Depending on what happens next, you have to prepare yourself for the fact that—'

'I might not be able to bind them. I know.'

Clyde froze as something suddenly occurred to him: what if he could only manage to bind one of them? How the hell hadn't that possibility occurred to him before now? The decision was nothing short of ghastly. The choice of his father, the man who had given him life but, through no fault of his own, nothing more; or his elder brother, the one who had shaped and guided him in his absent father's stead. A gut-wrenching nostalgia, bloated with love and warm memories, told him in no uncharitable terms that he should choose Stephen if he had to. It seemed cold and uncaring in its insistence, but also so unflinchingly fair. And yet behind all that wounded logic, he still couldn't bear the idea of only rescuing Stephen and leaving his dad behind.

'Are you ready?' Ramaliak's ebony eyes were rich with sympathy and understanding.

Clyde overcame his pangs of doubt. There was no advantage in creating hypothetical problems. 'Do it.'

Ramaliak's cloven hoof passed before Clyde's face, deftly pecking at the ethereal line and gently unspooling a short length from Clyde's forehead. The thread regained its visibility under the manipulation of that surgically dexterous hoof. A funny sensation warmed Clyde's forehead as the thread was gently unraveled. He stared at the single soul knot within the middle of the line: the end of Kev's line, accidentally tugged free from its designated place here in the Median and looped about Clyde's own thread. Clyde held his breath, watching Ramaliak gingerly match up his thread to those of his brother and his dad, held lovingly in his hands. He imagined it must feel like watching a loved one lying on some forsaken hospital bed as a team of doctors rushed about like leaves in a hurricane, giving their all to save the patient.

Ramaliak tinkered, calmly and methodically trying to lash them together. First he tried one way, then another, but no matter how many times he tried, their soul lines simply wouldn't tie. The large ram's head finally looked up at Clyde, regret magnified behind those lenses. He didn't need to say anything. He just released the shining threads.

Clyde's hammering heart seemed to drop a few gears, and his thoughts went silent. He gently squeezed the soul threads of his brother and father as though they were their hands. A thought careened into his head. It was of some faceless stranger, their own slack strand knotted a hundred times over with the souls of family and friends and near acquaintants, picking and choosing whoever they wanted to spend time with. And all of a sudden, this whole idea felt violating. Maybe this was for the best. Would buying them a few more mortal years have been much of a comfort anyhow? They were both soldiers. They were tough, and he knew their souls were still vibrant for now, so he chose to imagine them both together in the Null, perhaps with others like them, surviving, maybe even prospering. Waging some great campaign against the darkness and the sharp teeth. And why not? He'd certainly seen much more outlandish things.

But he had come here because he wanted an answer, and now he had it. He might see Stephen again one day, when it was time. And he might one day meet the man who helped give him life, in that waiting world of death.

'I'm sorry if this isn't the answer you wanted.' Ramaliak took a step closer, and Clyde's slackened thread began to wind back up into his head, shifting sensuously like smoke. 'It is rare for a medium to be able to tether multiple spirits. The entire process is quite random, so this isn't on you.' The ram placed a consolatory hoof on his shoulder.

Clyde released his hold on Stephen's and Richard's threads, watching as they gently wafted their way back into the starry trees. 'It's okay.' He lightly touched the point on his forehead, a farewell of sorts. 'I'm lucky to have Kev. That's responsibility enough.'

The chimes of the Sleeping Shepherd rang from a million miles away, and Ramaliak gave a last look around. 'It's that time again.'

Clyde had thought he was ready to go, but he found himself staring hard at those two glowing memorial trees. He wanted to remember them exactly as they are, but he knew the vision would eventually fade like everything else. The incredible coral-reef world started to dissolve, the warm lights blurring into a watercolor mix.

With a blink, Clyde was back in Spector's office, stirring in the same old chair he had become so acquainted with. Spector rolled his neck about and got up to get his habitual coffee. Clyde sat quietly in the chair, alone with his thoughts.

Spector passed him a cup of coffee. 'So . . .' Spector blew on his coffee. 'What are you going to do now?'

Clyde stared at that big cabinet of stolen dreams and ideas, the musings of tyrant and terrorist. He'd had his fill of this place. Maybe there was something of a soldier in him. And maybe it would have made Stephen and his dad proud. But he wouldn't take that next step.

'I've done what I came here for. I guess I'm going home.'

25

CLYDE TOOK HIS TIME IN leaving Spector's office. It wasn't exactly what you'd call an emotional goodbye, even though Spector, or Ramaliak, or both, had inevitably gotten a little more intimate with Clyde's history and secret self than Clyde had originally expected. Spector had probably watched dozens of agents, in similar positions to Clyde, who had learned what they had to before vanishing back into public obscurity with nothing more than a few artificial sayonaras and a signed heap of NDAs. And so, with a few kind words, they shook hands. Spector's grip had been reassuringly strong.

Having taken a final parting glance at Bookworm—that thing was never not eye-catching—he passed by the blank faces of the resident research staff and climbed into the driver's seat of the electric cart he had left parked in the tunnel. For old times' sake he took the long route to the rec room, recognizing a bunch of the faces by now, adding a nod here and there. He thought about how chatty Kev was with some of these very same agents and staff. The guy had become like a whole new person in this environment. He really had found his place here. Clyde, on the other hand, had tried to feel that way, he really had, but even at the heights of his adrenaline-fueled stay, during the bloody and bruised camaraderie during sparring and weapons and tactics, he still felt like his geeky old self, cosplaying as a soldier, and was always quick to retreat to his sketch pad. He still felt like an outsider.

After driving around the complex to think things over, his route rigidly determined by his unofficial clearance level, he stopped by the living quarters, packed his few bits and pieces into his backpack, and then decided that he couldn't procrastinate for fear of changing his mind. He had to bite the bullet, and he had to do it now. He walked down to the rec room, finding Kev and Ace hunched over the air hockey table, and some off-duty agents throwing bills down on the proceedings. He knew these other agents loosely: Henley and Alban. He had managed to give Alban a pretty nice shiner during a sparring session last week. No hard feelings, though. Experience had indoctrinated Clyde in the unspoken primal bonds that often form between warriors, an earned respect that dowsed the flames of competition.

Ace ricocheted in a deciding shot and snatched up the wad of bills to a few cheers and some dissent. Clyde dropped his backpack on the empty couch by the TV and went over to join them.

'Turns out Ace isn't just a problem drinker, he's pretty good at air hockey too,' Kev said, sidling in, almost shoulder to shoulder with Clyde.

'At least I'm not allowed to hit you in this game.' Ace gave his approximation of a smile, gap-toothed and with a vague sense of imminent violence. Counting his winnings, he glanced at Clyde and somehow seemed to sense his protégé's displacement. 'What's going on, rook?' But before Clyde could begin to broach his awkward goodbye, Ace continued, 'I've been rewatching the footage of how you and Kev smashed through that vanguard and blender.' There was practically a twinkle in his eye. 'You know, whenever my team lost a game when I was a kid, my pa would drive us home in the bus, and he'd never put the heating on. I remember him driving us through Saskatchewan one night, all of us freezing our hairless nuts off—this was before my powers lit up—and we all sat there, teeth chattering, shivering. He did it to make us work harder in training, to play harder. Negative reinforcement. And I got to tell ya, there's no cold bus rides scheduled for either of you.'

Clyde had never been sincerely complimented by Ace before, if that's what this was. Or maybe he'd started drinking a little earlier today and felt like it was story time. Either way, Clyde already felt awkward enough and didn't want to shut him down mid-flow.

'After that performance, I ran it up the line to Trujillo, and he agreed with me.' Ace fished into his pants pocket and stepped in close to Clyde, surprising him with a commendation. It wasn't exactly a Purple Heart, but it seemed to mean something to Ace. The badge of honor was some hockey merch, a cartoonish hockey goon head, snarling and spoiling for a ruckus. 'I hereby announce you officially capable of handling yourself.'

Clyde didn't know what to say. He admired the pin sticking in his T-shirt and smiled, ashamed that it felt more forced than grateful. He hoped it didn't look that way to Ace. The big lug slapped Clyde on the arm, and even though Clyde had gotten pretty shredded with the weeks of grueling punishment, the heavy slap still managed to tilt his balance a few inches to the right.

'Guess who just got a contract?' Kev asked, manic as a lotto winner. 'I'm official. Trust me, if I could get an Hourglass tramp stamp, I would.'

Ace continued, 'His paperwork is being processed as we speak. Just say the word and we'll get to processing you too.' Ace didn't wait for Clyde's answer. He seemed too intent on filling up any subsequent silence with rousing enthusiasm. 'Just thinking about the damage you two unlikely gals could do is almost enough to get me hard.'

Clyde tried to smile at the typically crass locker-room talk, but he knew behind the macho language Ace genuinely seemed like he wanted Clyde to stay. It sucked to do this. It really did. He gave Kev a proud smile. 'Congrats, bro. You earned this. You killed it here.' Clyde would have pulled him in for a hearty hug, but he raised his fist instead, the pair of them bumping in celebration.

'We both did,' Kev corrected.

Clyde offered a small shake of his head. 'This couldn't have happened at a better time, really. I just had my last session with Spector. Turns out you're the only soul mate for me, dude.'

Kev muted his excitement, showing the proper respect for the moment. 'Ah, I'm sorry, man. Are you okay?'

'You know, I'm not really sure. Fuck, look where we are. I think we're all long past okay, but I'm living with it. It's all anyone can do.' Kev and Ace hung on his every word, needing to know which way Clyde was going to jump next. If Clyde didn't force out this next part, he feared he'd open himself up to compromise. 'Seems like your life starts now. Took you long enough,' Clyde tried to joke, but it sounded staged. 'I'm sorry, Kev, Ace. But it's time I get going. My bag's already packed.'

That answer didn't seem to thrill either of them.

. . .

THE RIDE BACK to Darnell Air Force Base was a bubble of awkward silences and strained goodwill. At least it was a short drive. Rose had called ahead to sort the flight and had decided to be the one to drive Clyde back. She had taken the news better than Ace, better than Kev too. But Ace's stony silence? That was weird. He wasn't mister cordial at the best of times, but Clyde had learned to read him a little. And he was positive Ace was disappointed, but he probably viewed this as nothing more than a hockey team losing a promising draft.

'So, I guess this is it.' Kev held himself firm, confident. Clyde knew his friend was a good match for this line of work, even if he wasn't at his side. They stood beside a strip of baking tarmac beneath a bright-blue sky, waiting for the small jet to taxi around into position.

Clyde tugged at the strap of his backpack, feeling antsy. 'You were hoping I'd get a taste for this, huh?'

'I kind of was, yeah. Admit you were enjoying it a bit.'

Clyde smiled. 'Maybe a little bit. If I ever get a comic published, I'll give you a shout-out.'

'Shout-out? You best be giving me royalties. Or at least free copies for life.'

'I'll keep an eye on your family, drop in now and then.'

'I appreciate that. Maybe if this ever starts to make sense, I'll stop by myself, try not to scare the piss out of them.'

'You probably should. I mean I got used to it, and I don't even like you that much.' Kev mimed a brief bellyaching laugh, then looked serious again. Clyde continued, 'You take care of yourself here. Shit's going to get real for you now. No more training sims.'

'You take care of yourself,' Kev corrected. 'I don't want you to choke on a hot dog and ruin the good thing I got going here.'

That responsibility. It still terrified Clyde. Holding both of their lives in his hands. But wasn't that the way it was for all soldiers? 'I'll make sure I chew.'

Clyde tapped the goon badge pinned to his shirt out of respect, feeling really shitty and a little sad about it, and waved over at Ace. Ace barely seemed to recognize him, and Clyde had to admit that it stung a little, and the unfriendly reaction made him wonder why Ace even bothered coming along for the farewell. It was surprising; Clyde hadn't realized how much Ace's approval had come to mean to him. Clyde didn't want to overegg their sparring partner/punch bag relationship, but he had the notion that a part of Ace had also been expecting Clyde to buckle and decide that he was a good fit here. Or maybe Clyde really was looking too deeply into it. Ace of all people. The ice-man personified.

Rose stood close, however, all professional courtesies for the send-off. 'You did pretty good for a nerd.' She gave him a half-hearted finger pistol and a crafty smirk. 'I think Kev carried you, though.'

'I think you're right,' Clyde agreed. He noticed that Sergeant Connors, Barros, and Darcy were standing about ten feet away, arms folded, nodding their farewells. 'Maybe I could send you guys a Christmas email.' Rose backed up towards the others, and Clyde turned his attention back to Kev. 'You'll get time off?'

'I'll make sure to haunt you quarterly.' They both leaned in and hugged, and for a moment Clyde was a breath away from changing his mind and staying. Who would he talk bullshit with back in Brooklyn when his best friend was out here in New Mexico, or wherever his new job may take him? Brian at the comic-book shop was cool, sure, and he had other friends circling various orbits of his old life, but Kev was Kev, and nobody had more mileage on their buddy clock than him. But Clyde had to make sure his mom was doing okay. He hadn't seen her in four weeks, and he knew his texts were beginning to sound a little dubious. Clyde patted Kev on the back, then waved farewell to Connors, Darcy, Barros, and Ace; the first three returned a respectful salute, but Ace just stood there, still looking unimpressed. Clyde walked towards the waiting jet.

'Maybe I'll see you in the Null one day, nerd,' Rose called over the engine noise.

'Who knows, maybe this nerd will save your ass.' Clyde boarded.

Inside, he waved to them from the window and watched the hot, dry clay of the desert tilt away and shrink. Then, for the duration of the flight, he wondered if his stubbornness had gotten the best of him. The plane raced east, away from day and into dusk.

26

THE OPENING PORTAL ALMOST DREW fire. The stationed guards, still pulling shifts in the Cairnwood-owned Brooklyn warehouse, had been killing time, with those on smoke or coffee breaks quietly talking about the likelihood of their commanding officers and colleagues now lying gutted and soulless somewhere in that unholy asshole of a dimension. The fact that an increasingly dismayed Edward Talbot had been showing up at the warehouse more and more these last days had only added authenticity to the staff's doubtfulness of their allies' safe return.

And so, it was understandable that when the giant keyhole cut a section into their reality, it caused a ruckus.

For a long, troubling moment, nothing more than a soft, eerie gale came through the open window to death's paradise, blowing in from the barren landscape.

There was movement. Silhouettes against a starry, brass-tinted sky. The warehouse guards kept their guns trained on the portal, awaiting orders from the stationed Captain Pike, or even Talbot himself. Like a slender-limbed spider, Mortis strolled onto the metal staging platform as if he expected a hero's welcome. Captain Pike and his men all lowered their rifles with an almost audible sigh of collective relief.

Konstantin followed, sandwiched amongst Captain Agua and his three teams, and feeling very much like the prisoner he knew he really was. Bringing up the rear were the workforce, a couple of whom carried Hammond in on a stretcher, his skin gray and clammy with sweat. Konstantin wanted to follow Hammond to make sure he was okay, but several soldiers took him from the workers without comment and carried him down the platform's stairs, loading him into the back of a dark van. Lim tried to pursue, to keep his friend company to wherever they were taking him, but one of the stormtroopers aimed a handgun, most likely loaded with an Exorcist round, at his chest. Lim stopped in his tracks. Konstantin watched the troops slam the van's doors shut, and the vehicle quickly drove out of the warehouse.

Konstantin spotted Talbot up on the second-floor gangway, his shirt sleeves rolled up, his executive-smart hair only slightly out of place. He was talking on his phone, looking harried. Talbot ended the call and descended the metal stairs without haste, creating the illusion that he was still very much calm and measured, but Konstantin assumed that really, he was angry about the significant delay in operational updates from Mortis. Konstantin became surplus for the moment, standing to one side of the platform, watching Talbot and Mortis fall into a quiet discussion near the stairs.

Agua's returned men joined their domestic allies, the two captains updating each other on the mission's status while the lieutenants and sergeants fired commands up and down the ranks: various soldiers guarding both sides of the portal while the Sharp Construction workers carefully backed the specimen truck onto the warehouse platform, with more soldiers watching as the workers readied dollies to fetch the containers of various minerals; a forklift truck was brought over for the bodybag. A group of the soldiers prepped for their imminent return across the border by rearming and nourishing themselves on energy bars, water, and caffeine.

Konstantin felt tired, all the way to his bones and deeper, a weariness to his very soul. He brooded, staring through the portal, feeling that almost hospitable warm breeze beckoning him back, the convoy of Humvees waiting for them along that trackless terrain. Vor Dushi wasn't too far away now, and each passing mile brought Konstantin closer to his inevitable reacquaintance with the region's slave master of the damned.

Konstantin ventured inwards, leaving the warehouse for the moment, to communicate with Kuznetsov, sharing a quiet space amongst the empty chambers of the honeycomb sanctuary. Unease spread its tendrils throughout Konstantin. He sensed the sleeping malignancy continuing to shift within the Arkhitektor's soul, causing the high priest to mutter and rave in his cell, suffering through troubled dreams.

'Don't let doubt undermine you now, brother. Don't fear the beast,' Kuznetsov soothed in his native tongue. 'We are so close. This is what we've strived for. This is our opportunity.'

Konstantin softly grumbled. He wasn't about to let Vor Dushi steal his will as he'd stolen so much else. No, Konstantin wasn't scared. He was growing impatient. He wanted to get back in there and get to the Trench as quickly as their vehicles would carry them.

'You misread me,' Konstantin replied. 'It is not doubt that you sense. I am restless. The closer we get to its stronghold, the farther away it feels. Still, I can all but taste our victory. We'll slay Vor Dushi this time. I'll fight it until my last breath, and then some. But before we deliver the finishing blow, we must learn what intelligence it possesses of the Needle's current whereabouts. Perhaps we'll even learn the outcome of the divine one who tumbled from the sky.'

'And if it refuses to talk?'

'Then we scour its den and see what we can find. Always moving forward. Never giving in.' Konstantin's blank, bearded face watched impassively at the drudges running about the warehouse, barking commands at the work crews busy loading the gathered samples of plant, mineral, and monster into the storage area next door. 'Soon enough we'll shake loose these animals.' A sudden splinter broke off his resolve; it was transient, there and gone in the blink of an eye, but it certainly didn't pass Kuznetsov unnoticed.

'What really bothers you, brother?' Kuznetsov solicited. Konstantin didn't answer right away, allowing silence to fill the numinous space. But the silence wasn't true; the Arkhitektor's troubled rantings carried throughout the honeycomb. 'You feel him reaching out, don't you? His rest isn't as peaceful or deep as it was before we returned to those chthonic lands.'

Not a day went by that Konstantin didn't feel the Arkhitektor lying in his poisonous coma, assailed by Vor Dushi's corruption. And if it was not for his own blessed armor...

Konstantin didn't want to think about it.

'He's responding to the proximity of Vor Dushi,' Kuznetsov continued. 'You have felt his presence grow with each passing mile, same as I have. There's nothing we can do but shut out the thoughts of our fallen father. Perhaps by ripping the diseased life from the many heads of Vor Dushi, we will grant him peace everlasting. It may even restore his soul to its rightful state. Ready for its ascension to glory.'

Konstantin hoped that was true. Their Arkhitektor had paid the ultimate price for his virtues and deserved peace. All previous title holders deserved rest and harmony, but for now their souls were unaccounted for.

'I want to bring Lim in,' Kuznetsov said. 'The man has bared his pain to us both, his anguish echoing through these empty cells. He can't return to his mortal life, so he might be willing to aid us in our quest.'

Konstantin briefly flitted back to the physical world, watching the man in question, a specter in overalls and a hard hat, milling about with his warm-blooded co-workers, doing anything he could to help and occupy his thoughts. He returned to the honeycomb. 'Once we reach the Trench, I'll be temporarily occupied manning the soul cages, but you could use assistance in searching the caverns inside the cove. Lim could be that man. Help cover more ground in seeking Vor Dushi's temple.'

They made a silent agreement.

'Would it help us if we warned the soldiers about the spies Vor Dushi employs along the Trench?' Kuznetsov asked.

'I have thought about this. We were unprepared for them last time. With the Exorcist rounds the soldiers have, I doubt those ghosts will pose much resistance. Personally, I think there'll be enough chaos one way or another that it won't hinder our plan.'

· · ·

'You took your bloody time,' Talbot said, somehow dwarfing Mortis by simple authority. His green eyes shone like dusty emeralds, watching the overall-clad monkeys unload the rock and seed and oil samples from the bed of the first truck. He had already turned his nose up at the bodybag specimen, dismissing it as something R&D might find a use for. Perhaps luggage for those with macabre tastes. 'You were supposed to keep me in the loop at regular intervals.' He listened to Mortis' excuses, the damaged key he had suffered early on, but how after some inexplicable difficulty he was able to repair it before using memory and some enigmatic trickery to recalibrate a corridor back here to base camp.

'That behind me,' Mortis said of the landscape waiting through the large, crackling keyhole, 'is only a day's trip from the Trench.' He stood tall as if to own the moment, proving that he was valuable, despite a botched timetable. 'I recommend you bring a deck chair and bottle of something expensive, sir, because this time tomorrow you'll have a front-row seat to watch as Konstantin and the soul cages suck up a huge supply of pending equity.'

Talbot rolled his sleeves back down and fiddled with his cufflinks, still flustered. 'I won't be here tomorrow. The headaches I have endured troubleshooting your continued absence have altered my to-do list.' He almost tutted and finished fixing his shirt cuffs. 'So, can I trust that you aren't going to bollocks this up any further? Can you punctually deliver three very full soul cages without a nanny present?'

'Without another hitch, sir. As we speak, Captain Agua is calling in additional in-house manpower. Ransacking the Trench's soul channel will undoubtedly be met with more stringent countermeasures than we have faced thus far.'

Talbot fired an irritable glance over at the captain in question, standing outside the warehouse, near the bay doors, talking on his phone. 'Do we require such indemnity? You already have Captain Pike waiting around here playing with himself. And when the operation is up and running, you'll already have the gate open for expedience. If things get hairy, he and his teams should be enough to help squash any problems that arise.' Talbot's eyes made a frank dismissal of Konstantin woolgathering near the portal, then found Mortis doing his best not to look doubtful. 'You're not scared of Vor Dushi, are you?' he teased. 'Because I'm confident Agua and his lieutenants alone have the right stuff to give some parasitic arsehole a good hiding.'

Mortis didn't dare question Talbot's opinion, not with the man already having his nose out of joint. 'Well...they have already proven that they can handle anything Erebus can throw at them; that artefact I discovered along Erebus' shoreline has paid dividends. Has Captain Pike been run through similar trials?'

Talbot checked his wristwatch in a practiced executive move; it was a very nice watch. 'No. I didn't get around to it. I've been busy, you know.

Surely you remember? That little gala at the Ivy Lounge I've been organizing for the energy crowd.' He tugged at the lapel of Mortis' old scratchy coat, not that such fussing could ever possibly improve its appearance. 'But hey, Pike and his boys can pull a trigger. And they have all that snazzy ammunition we paid for. Now don't disappoint me, Mortis. Not me. Not Cairnwood. There's a lot riding on this. You've already outshone your daddy. Now keep it up.'

Talbot skipped down the stairs, his Oxfords ringing out brightly on the metal, passing the soldiers and work crews without word. Out on the flood-lit yard, he hopped into his green Jaguar and peeled out for Midtown.

. . .

CAREFULLY POSITIONED ON the roof of an adjacent warehouse, several tactical-suited agents watched the high-profile target of Edward Talbot speed out of the cluster of warehouses. Their digital binoculars fired off the live footage to the surveillance team parked in a nearby van. The roof agents then resumed watching the patrol patterns of the Citadel Security squads occupying the site. It had been weeks since their intel department at the Madhouse—New York's branch of Hourglass—had flagged-up Talbot's last unsanctioned gateway into Erebus, but the agents knew how dirty this security firm was. They were guarding more than some old bricks and mortar in that place. The Madhouse staff had enough problems to contend with on any given day, many of them already concerning Talbot and his members' club, and what they didn't need right now was to be spreading themselves any thinner by dealing with a top-rank enemy playing around with the magic and death of Erebus.

The van's surveillance team, who'd been subsisting on bitter coffee and crap food, called it in. The local brass didn't specialize in inter-world affairs, so they immediately contacted the specialist branch that did. They called Director Trujillo at Indigo Mesa.

27

No emails. Clyde stared at the empty inbox on his screen. Some things never changed, it seemed. He was unsure of how he felt about this latest lack of opportunity. It used to be a shoulder-slumping sense of deflation, but not this time. Had it finally happened? Had he truly stopped caring about landing that great big life-altering opportunity to draw for Marvel or DC? Thinking about it... yeah, he had. Especially now, with all his new real-life source material to work with. It meant his other lukewarm project was going on the back burner, that of his undead-dabbling mobster quack Dr. Wertham. Logging out of his email, he supposed he could still make himself feel a little disappointed at the lack of responses—just a smidge even—if he forced it.

Why bother?

He had spent a month being tortuously molded from lie-about artist who could barely manage a jog around the block to a soldier who could take out a room full of octo-tongues—as gross as their name suggests—with only a knife and dogged determination, and yes, some notable enhancements from Kev. And through all this hardship, he'd still spent each sore and exhausted evening drawing. He would live and die an artist, and he didn't need the approval of some bigshot to work in the field. Any dreams of winning an Eisner Award, that Holy Grail of comic-book trophies, had been jettisoned several years back, a fact he could now actually confirm since no such award statue had taunted him or Ramaliak in the untamed outer layer of the Median. The creativity was the impetus, not the pursuit of plaudits. He could feel more and more ideas for his new project percolating away in his imagination by the day. And even if the big indie imprints wouldn't take it when the time came, he'd scrape the money together to print it himself. He'd find a writer to collaborate with, a professional colorist, and a letterer. Who knows, maybe he could talk to Brian at the comic shop again, twist his arm into getting involved in some capacity. Shit, he'd sell cheap copies from the counter at MC&C if he had to, stick his characters on some posters or on an old-school local newsletter for the store—such humble beginnings had put Ben Edlund on the map, and Clyde was a big fan of *The Tick*.

He sat back in his swivel chair and stared about his room. The orange glow of the streetlights sliced through the blinds over his window, casting a sheen across the collage of talented artists' depictions of heroics and their struggles across every febrile backdrop, against every type of lunatic and monster, and Clyde found himself quietly staring at the work of artists he worshipped, and for the first time in a long time, he understood why he loved these colorful, crazy little worlds.

They were eternal.

These heroes and villains, they all died, and they all returned. Always returned. Whether it be science, magic, or simply the industry editors who want to cash-in on a big marketable resurrection. Either way, their lives and adventures continued, decade after decade, generation after generation, and they always would. These beloved characters returned to restore the imbalance, bright and colorful, not a day older, while the lives of the readership petered on into obscurity and looming mortality.

Eternal.

Everybody quietly dreamed of immortality.

Kev entered his thoughts like a wisp of blue smoke, exhaled in on the frigid breath of the Null and all its unknown vastness. With everything Clyde had seen, anything seemed possible now. His truth had become more outrageous than art, more outlandish than these weird and wild comic-book adventures he clung to for thrills and excitement and, yes, comfort. He'd spent so much time struggling with the death of family that he'd unconsciously thrown himself deeper into the modern mythology of comic-books and their immortal characters. And after all this time, it turned out that forever had existed all along, or at the very least, an *extension* of existence. Unfortunately, it was hell.

Never mind, he had to focus on the here and now. The living world with its living problems. At least he had some temporary financial breathing room. The agency had deposited a small sum into his bank account for his time at Indigo Mesa. Hardly life-changing money, but enough to last until he found a more affordable, single apartment.

A single apartment.

Clyde suddenly realized how quiet the place now was. No sound. No atmosphere. A vacuum, and despondency slowly settled over him.

His phone vibrated on his desk, setting his athletic tone into excited tension, his muscles wanting to move and act, but unsure of where or how. It was his mom, asking if he was still coming around for dinner tomorrow. He texted her back immediately, looking forward to it. He hadn't seen her in weeks, and he felt guilty that their message traffic had been sparse, but he knew she had been just as busy as he had. Putting his phone down on the desk, he erased any lingering thoughts of life, death, Stephen and his dad, Hourglass and Kev.

It was his choice to come back here to pursue his art. And he knew it was the right choice. The fears of the fantastical would be with him night and day, right up until his death and then beyond. Right now, though, in this short time he had on Earth, he would use these fears to confect stories and joy, triumph and heartache. He would use them to create his own happiness and, if lucky, that of other readers.

Here we go!

Guns of Metronome.

A working title, sure, but it was something, and it was different enough from Hourglass that he didn't have to worry about legal ramifications or Ace knocking on his door one day, all hair of the dog and bad moods. He touched the goon pin—his medal of honor—still clinging to his T-shirt and slowly removed it, respectfully placing it on his desk amidst the line of comic-book bobble heads.

This felt good. A breath of fresh air, and a new start. He got up, paced about his room and the deafeningly quiet apartment for a little bit, then put the kettle on and picked up a pencil and his sketch pad.

28

KEV WAS IN THE LIBRARY, tired, hurting, and grateful to have a respite from Rose's training.

Just because he was in the middle of being processed by the department didn't mean she was going to take it easy on him. After Clyde had jetted off, she had proposed a celebration workout in honor of Kev's graduation. Personally, Kev would have liked a sit-down and some rip-roaring news about a ghost-friendly beer option. But this wasn't a holiday. Things would get serious for him from this point on, and he couldn't wait to throw himself into the work. The workout hadn't been too strenuous, mainly some fine motor tuning, but he could do with a day off. He had been tasked with creating small telekinetic microbursts, tiny but powerful blasts through any small target Rose and her crew could think of: pipes, radiator grilles, anything awkward, really.

As for ghost beer, Kev had made a mental note to have a word with Connors and company, or better yet, Ace; if it existed, Ace had probably drunk it.

For now, he was content to further satisfy his curiosity on what various cultures had documented on the Null. He was going through selected passages in a tome called *The Recherche Realms*, which he'd grabbed from the racks, still lacking the nerve to approach Bookworm. It wasn't even its physical presence that bothered him now; it was Rose's earlier comment about certain info being above her paygrade. If it was above hers, it was sure as shit above his.

The new guy.

He grinned wistfully, thinking about how Clyde would have viewed him taking pride in being an official company man, and the emerging sense of loneliness almost besieged him. Clyde was gone now. Not forever, Kev hoped, but this separation would be the longest of their lives. No more living in each other's pocket.

Kev tried to shut this attack of loneliness out and focus on his recent success. After a quick glance about the library, smiling chummily to a few of the library staff and academics whose eyes he caught, he stared down at his open book hard enough to make his eyes strain. This compilation of notes had been taken by a tenth-century French necromancer—and later translated—but as intriguing as it was, much of the information remained limited, and most of this was similar to what had been recorded by mages, knights, adventurers, ethically dubious alchemists, scientists, soldiers, and civilians, all of whom came from a diverse mixture of species and cultures.

He was turning a page when Sergeant Connors quietly appeared at his table. Kev was anticipating some good-natured chitchat and perhaps news of a celebration in his honor, but Connors remained tight-lipped and serious.

'Something's come up,' Sarge said.

Kev adjusted his glasses, holding the book half closed. From the look on Connors' metal-peppered face, Kev had an unhappy idea that there wasn't going to be a graduation party. Groundless worries of being turned down by Trujillo or some other ranking official took form in his mind.

'What is it?'

'Looks like you're going to be getting a taste of real combat a little sooner than expected.'

· · ·

KEV FOUND HIMSELF in a briefing room deeper in the complex. All glass and steel, lit like a dentist's office. Rose, Barros, Darcy, and Ace were already there when Kev entered; he stepped aside for Sarge to enter the room and rejoin his squad, then closed the door. Kev had expected more people to be present, like maybe a few of the scores of hand-selected agents milling about this complex.

'Time to slap an evil wizard?' Kev asked.

'Kinda,' Rose said. She had a tablet close to hand. 'The Madhouse, our New York department, has contacted us. They've gauged readings of some assholes opening portals into the Null. Said assholes are operating out of a warehouse in Brooklyn.'

Kev looked about. 'Well, isn't that some serendipitous shit?' He almost smiled, shaking his head at the wacky workings of the world. 'Who are they?'

'Widespread departmental hemorrhoids,' Ace answered. 'An old-money group called the Cairnwood Society. They're connected, powerful, but it's our New York friends who get the lion's share of the ass itch.'

Rose picked up the tablet and pushed a button, and the preloaded video footage blipped up on the wide wall-mounted TV. 'This footage was collated by a team of Madhouse spies.'

Kev watched various activities play out from multiple camera angles: well-funded guards patrolling the warehouse perimeter, civilian work crews moving things about, some fancy suit racing off in a plush, old-school car—Kev didn't know cars very well—and then a long-range zoom through a second-floor window; the angle of the long-range zoom wasn't ideal, but it was good enough to catch footage of a very odd-looking pair: a tall figure who looked like he belonged in a crypt, with horridly deformed fingers, and a scruff-bearded, ascetic man in a strange suit of armor. The footage fast-forwarded to the odd pair reentering the portal with a number of armed squads and several trucks, with the portal shrinking out of existence behind them.

'Don't the New York bunch have people who can handle this?' Kev asked.

'Usually,' Private Darcy grumbled.

'They had a strike team of heavy hitters, most of them Sparks. But they were recently taken off the board by Cairnwood,' Private Barros explained.

'Any incidents involving the Null get directed to us,' Sarge added. 'Trujillo and the stonies—that's my own parlance for the hoodoos—police all import and export between here and there.'

Kev recalled what Rose had said about her previous assignments in the Null, not that she had divulged a great deal.

Rose tapped the tablet, opening a few stored agency files on the couple who had vanished through the key-shaped portal. 'If it wasn't for the presence of these two—' she pointed to the tall, cadaverous man with the bizarre hands and the gaunt mystic in the armor, '—the Madhouse would have dealt with this themselves. The spindly guy who looks like a corpse warmed-up is Acton Mortis. He's long-term Cairnwood.' Surveillance shots showed Acton Mortis at private meetings throughout the city, his awkward form hanging over various people like a crooked tower with knife-blade fingers. Rose fired off the Cliff Notes regarding his knack for circumventing locks that shouldn't be tampered with. 'We believe he's still only a small fish in the organization, but if he's being used to sneak into the Null of all places, then he could start fucking up in a big way.'

A few additional surveillance shots appeared of the well-dressed man who had sped away in the car, pictures of him walking out of powerful buildings and sipping drinks outside expensive cafés and bars, a phone usually pressed to his ear. His compiled biography went no further than his name, Edward Talbot, and the fact that he was linked to Cairnwood.

'Our agency knows this guy is somewhere around the middle-management level, but other than that...' Rose shrugged. 'But he's a slippery little prick who pops up more than pimples on a teenager. We do know there's more to him than meets the eye, but any agent who has ever gotten close enough to find out wasn't in a very chatty mood afterwards.'

Even without Talbot's innate monetary smugness, Kev figured there must be something more to the suit and tie, something to garner such confidence. 'You can't spell puissant without pissant.'

'Puissant?' Ace asked.

Kev shook his head, not wanting to distract from the briefing.

Rose pressed the button one final time, opening the last file. 'This guy—' the prison profile of Konstantin "Gulag" Kozlov flashed up to fill the screen, his background covered in a bit more detail, though much of it still redacted, '—is a red flag and a quandary.'

Kev tried to absorb what he could from the scrolling pages, but they moved fast, and clearly the files were only there for a quick show-and-tell, a visual glance at who they were interested in. But he did catch the name Rising Path highlighted on one of the documents.

'Kozlov belonged to a Siberian cult whose whole M.O. was the pursuit of a mythological doodad called the Firmament Needle, which they believed could be used to create a new heaven,' Rose picked out the highlighted points. 'A great big fuck-you to the Null and its ruling classes.'

Kev couldn't keep the name Firmament Needle from threading itself through his every thought.

'There was some kind of incident in the Rising Path's temple, and he found his ass getting frosty in Peklo, a Russian military black site for quirky individuals, which is where our tech guys were able to get his file from. We don't know if Cairnwood sprung him through official or unofficial channels, and it doesn't matter: the result is the same. At this juncture, we don't know if Talbot and his bosses have bought into the heaven angle and maybe want to see what Kozlov knows about this needle.'

'Or?' Kev posed.

'Or he could be there under duress. The Peklo files we obtained document his ability to house an undetermined number of souls.'

'So... they could be using him to smuggle souls out of the Null?' Kev posited.

'That's a possibility, sure.' Ace's hands moved like a sculptor's, forming a blade of ice. 'Too early to say for definite.'

'According to Trujillo, the hoodoos have been experiencing a number of large tears opening and closing within the Null. Nothing special about that, but these weren't the usual effects of a bartered soul here, or a small migration there. They were large doorways.' Rose brought up the warehouse footage again. 'The first doorway Mortis opened was shoddy craftsmanship: the size fluctuating all over, opening, closing, like a screen door with a fucked hinge. Almost as though he was trying to gauge the size needed for the flow of transport, like that convoy of trucks and Humvees, for example. But then things went quiet for a while, until now. Whatever they've been doing over there, whatever they're bringing over here, it needs to be stomped on, and quick.'

'Why would they do something like this? Choosing to barge their way into there of all places?' Kev asked. The question was rhetorical, but often they were the only questions fit to be asked of such profoundly ignorant and stupid acts.

Ace completed his artisan blade and twirled it point-first on the table. 'With a guy like Gulag at their side, I'm saying they want to collect some souls for profit or war. That's all it ever comes down to, and both outcomes usually dovetail. To them it's worth the risk. They're equipped enough to take the chance of pissing down death's back.'

Kev felt a sudden need to move around, a restless energy begging him to act now. 'Okay then, so we go and trash this whole place.' Then the penny dropped. 'Hang on, how do we stop Mortis and Kozlov? Are Trujillo and the hoodoos sending us into the Null?' Excitement and dread formed an ill mixture in Kev's stomach.

'No need.' Rose leaned on the table, testing its structural integrity. Kev was sure he heard it creak a little under her flexed guns. 'The Madhouse guys were able to pick up snatches of conversation between Mortis and Talbot. Mortis said he'd be opening the rift again in approximately twenty-four hours, that's midnight East Coast time. We'll be waiting for them.'

Time became fluid for Kev. Twenty-four hours had never felt so long and yet so inadequate. This wouldn't be a training exercise. No more Djinn. He'd be going into real combat, against guys who walked the line between life and death.

'Those goons manning the warehouse, are they just goons?'

Ace gripped the frozen, translucent blue handle of the knife and disappeared it somewhere on his person. 'Unconfirmed. They're part of a private security firm called Citadel Security Solutions. All ex-military. All assholes. Sounds simple enough when we're rolling in there with our advantages, but they're owned by a local suspected crime kingpin who is himself a name in Cairnwood's little black book. There's a possibility some or all of them are juiced-up on something. So no cowboy shit when we get there. We treat these with a healthy dose of fear and respect. Then we fuck 'em all up.'

'And what about Kozlov?'

'It's difficult to say. My gut tells me he's there under duress. Judging from what the files have on the Rising Path, I think he'd sooner die than help a group like Cairnwood. They were a noble and righteous lot for a bunch of priests. But until we know exactly what his situation is, we need to exercise caution. In any eventuality, we need to extract him from his current handlers.'

'And the Firmament Needle?' Kev's thoughts practically glowed with the image of some haloed needle and a secret heaven.

Ace became a little sullen at this question. Rose, Sarge, Darcy, and Barros seemed a little more undecided. 'Don't piss like an excited puppy. There's as much hoaxy bullshit in death as there is in life. There's talk of it, some stories and what-ifs, but nothing confirming it. But if we pull this off, I promise to let you have a heart-to-heart with Kozlov.' Ace went to leave. 'Anyway, it's Miller time.'

Kev watched Ace exit the room, his eyes following him through the glass wall, marching past agents and staff and looking like he wanted nothing more than to throw himself headfirst into the enemy stronghold. But with a day's wait, Kev figured Ace would go and burn off a little energy on the punch bags or the Djinn, maybe use that new knife of his. Or maybe he would simply crack a few beers and watch the hockey. Kev felt a single tremor of doubt lance through him and wished he could feel as confident as Ace looked at that moment.

Kev noticed Rose's gaze weighing on him.

'You're ready,' she said.

Kev nodded a little too much, too quickly. Sergeant Connors, Barros, and Darcy all seemed to be silently approving of Rose's verdict. All Kev could think of was that Needle sewing a glorious afterlife.

And Clyde.

In Brooklyn.

On the doorstep of a looming battle.

29

CLYDE PUSHED HIS PLATE AWAY, stuffed.

'I don't think I've ever seen you eat that much before!' Corrine said. She had insisted on cooking them a nice piece of salmon and steaming some brown rice and vegetables for dinner, rather than relaxing as much as humanly possible during her day off. Her nursing job at Bay Ridge's veterans' hospital helped keep her trim, but also undoubtedly contributed to her eye bags and the ever-increasing gray hair weaving itself through her curly bob cut.

Clyde blamed his appetite on his additional muscle, which, while still trim and athletic, was operating at a metabolic efficiency he'd never known before. He pulled out the excuse of having missed breakfast and lunch; he was a starving artist, after all. Well, starving was probably pushing it, but he knew his mom was accustomed to him being a disorganized sort who would get so wrapped up with his drawing that he'd forget to breathe if someone wasn't on hand to remind him.

But he certainly hadn't missed his breakfast, having downed four egg whites and a bowl of cereal right after his morning run and push-ups.

Morning workouts. Egg whites for protein. Ace and Rose had a lot to answer for.

In fact, lying in bed that morning, following a late night of preliminary character designs and loose plot ideas, he had briefly considered backsliding into his civilian routine: hit the snooze button a few times, then lounge about until he was ready to get some more work done. But the military regime had stuck. He simply had to get out of bed and move around. And he knew it was for the best. The whole reason for his intensive training could be for nought if he was to allow himself to become a lazy and undisciplined potential target. He had his freedom, but he needed to stay sharp; something that he knew wouldn't be too much of a problem. Case in point: following his workout, he'd spent the morning at MC&C, hanging with Brian, catching up and lying about where he had been, and all the while finding himself on random flights of fancy where demon assassins would burst through the door, intent on clipping him to strike at Kev. It was tricky to act so normal again, and he had to remind himself that Kev had only just become official, so he might not even get sent on assignment for weeks yet.

'How's the comic-book store going?' Corrine enquired.

Clyde knew it was an innocent question, with her only wanting to get up to speed with his current affairs, but the fact that she blew right past his attempts at making it as an artist rankled him a little.

'It's cool. You know, nothing changes: serve a few customers, shoot the shit with Brian. It's cool.' He almost didn't say it, but then, 'I'm going to stop sending my work out there. Thinking about focusing on my own title. If I can get that off the ground and into print, I'll get to maintain all creative control and reap the royalties.' Corrine sipped her glass of red wine and tried to look supportive. Clyde thought she looked so tired. 'That's the plan, anyway. Something to focus on. I ran it by Brian earlier, and he's cool with me bouncing some ideas off him.'

Corrine looked like something heavy was on her mind. Clyde sipped his bottle of beer and was about to ask her to open up when she came right out with it.

'Can I say something, hon?' She didn't wait for permission. 'You've always been a very talented artist. You always will be, whether you make it or not. But I'm a little concerned about you spending every night alone in your apartment, trying to force this. When Kevin was living with you, at least you had a social life. And I miss that boy, he was good for you. But with him gone, I think it's time you try to . . . ' Reticence got the best of her, hobbling her sentence. 'You know, I don't even know what I'm getting at. I just worry that you're going to wake up one day when you're forty, fifty, sixty years old and realize that you're still in that apartment, your best friend gone, and still trying to catch your big break.'

Clyde could see the warmth and love in his mother's eyes and heard her own loneliness echoing from her past years. He could feel her projecting her own hushed fears onto him.

'I can't even afford to live there past thirty, so fear not.' His attempt at levity went down like the Hindenburg.

'I don't want you to miss out on your life, trying to chase something that might not happen.'

Clyde inhaled deeply, tried to gather his thoughts, and exhaled like a burst air bag, unsure of what to say. 'This is all I've ever wanted to do.' His admission sounded so embarrassingly adolescent, lacking the former oomph it had once carried in his strident thoughts. He still loved illustrating, he'd be dead before that ever changed—he quickly swatted aside any ideas of the Null—but now that he thought about it, it triggered an unwelcome insecurity deep within himself. It no longer felt so simple, so safe, to chase this down. And he hated the taste of this new doubt.

'Of course, and I'm not saying you should stop. But it worries me to see you so obsessive over trying to force this.' Corrine placed a hand to her brow, regretful of bringing the whole thing up. 'I'm sorry, hon, forget I said anything. If it makes you happy, then you do it and you don't ever stop. Who am I to say otherwise? It's all chance. Everything in this life. Chance and little more. And life doesn't give a damn about anybody's plans.' She held herself up, shoulders back and proud. 'If this makes you happy, then who can argue?'

Clyde reached over and placed his hand over hers. He didn't think and noticed the slight bruising and scraped skin on his knuckles. He almost jerked his hand away again, but that would only raise suspicion.

Too late.

'Have you been boxing?' Corrine examined his hand. 'Calluses and bruised knuckles?'

A defensive smile was quick to Clyde's lips. 'I got a few bumps moving boxes at the store, caught my knuckles on a shelf in the storeroom.' He was impressed with his deft ducking and dodging and settled his hand on hers again. 'I know what you mean. I know you're only looking out for me. But don't worry, I promise not to become a cat lady.' Corrine slapped his hand away, her motherly concerns evaporating in the glow of her smile and laughter. 'I miss Kev. Always will. But I have other friends at the comic-book store. Life goes on, right? Now, enough about my problems. How are you doing, really?'

She feigned absolute delight in discussing her latest adventures in the hospital's wards, but all playing aside, she had never denied that it was a tough but very rewarding job, helping the wounded troops get back on their feet wherever and however possible. Clyde had heard enough melancholic tales from her regarding the unfortunate servicemen and women whom she had struck up a bond with over the years, only for them to never leave the premises, taking an unfortunate turn while in surgery or struggling perpetually with the damning effects of substance abuse or psychological ailments. It was stories such as these that he always found hard to bear, their details only salting the wounds of his KIA brother and father. Even after his brief time at Indigo Mesa, he still didn't understand why anybody would choose to serve their country; rather, the fat-assed hoarders of wealth and power. His recent experiences may have softened him a little— just a little—to heeding the call of duty, but it had to be a righteous cause to bear arms. Hourglass filled the bracket, he thought (he hoped), then he killed the muse. He listened to her stories, wanting to ease her troubled mind. Corrine had close colleagues at the hospital to share quiet sympathies with, but Clyde had always taken it upon himself to lend an ear at home, not wanting her to carry around all that secondhand suffering.

'You remember Amanda, the helicopter pilot?' Clyde vaguely recalled. 'She's reupping, heading straight back into the army.'

'Good for her.' Clyde sold this sentiment but didn't invest in it. Better luck not getting shot down this time, he thought. By the way, the country remains the same.

He inspected his right fist, visualizing the metacarpals beneath the skin and idly imagining the power he shared with Kev. Kev and Rose and Ace all fought for room in his thoughts. Spector too, both his human and goat-headed versions. He wanted to swat away the evocations of Hourglass, which were fast becoming a swarm of flies.

'You seen Jas lately?' he asked, wanting to get away from further talk of armed service. Auntie Jasmine and Corrine were practically inseparable. Corrine seemed happy to have her memory jogged.

'Oh, I forgot to mention. We're going to visit Clara next week. She's got a new place in Queens. You should come with us.'

Clyde had never been too close to his cousin, a likely result of neither of them sharing a single interest, but over the years they had always managed to wing it for the sake of social etiquette. 'I don't know, I'll have to see if Brian needs help at the store first,' he lied.

'Well, let me know. It might do you some good.' Corrine got up to put the plates and utensils in the sink, but Clyde made her sit back down, telling her to finish her wine while he did the washing up. His dad had taught Stephen to do this from a young age, and Stephen had impressed the same lesson onto Clyde.

Filling the sink, he scrubbed the plates and thought about how he'd been so determined to get back here, so adamant to do only what was strictly necessary to help protect both himself and Kev before fleeing Indigo and all its harsh truths about life and death and relatives he couldn't help, things he couldn't ever change. But now that he was here, he felt like such an outlier. Where had his former life gone? The one where he didn't feel like a soldier waiting for a war. He looked about the apartment, conjuring the elusive ghosts of memories. Did reminiscences become ingrained in the walls and furniture, or were they his and his alone, sunken into the second tier of his own corner of the Median?

If he ever got the big break he wanted, the first thing he would use the money for would be to buy his mom a new apartment. Let her own ghosts of this place find the sleep they sorely needed. Sadly, he knew they wouldn't sleep. Her memories were bonded to her sleeping mind in the same way his were to him. He thought of Ramaliak gently unravelling the soul threads of Stephen and his dad from those glowing polyps, their souls still very much alive, just elsewhere. Lost somewhere in the Null.

The Null.

His imaginings of what that place must be like formed a farrago of darkness and fiery light, a moon-shimmering glisten of slime, teeth, growls, and heart-thudding terror. All the versions of Hell he'd encountered throughout his immersion in pop culture were closing in, crowding out his every thought. He couldn't bear the idea of his mom in that place. He had been tormented off-and-on by these nightmarish musings on the walk down to his mom's apartment. Pacing the streets, he'd seen nothing but people blissfully ignorant of what awaited them. Saw the rows of buildings grow teeth and scowls to chew up and swallow them; the buses and the subway trains were wagons filled with blood and soon-to-be-rotten meat, the screams of the bodies soon to be heard echoing throughout the pits and valleys of the Null.

Clyde stacked the dishes, unplugged the sink, dried his hands, then polished off his beer, wishing it was something much stronger and a lot bigger. He returned to the dinner table. Could he still do this? Pretend to live this "normal life" and bury himself in his work? See his mom and Brian and the guys at the store without wondering what horrors would befall them all in time? He wanted to scream and smash and break until he was too exhausted to care about what happened to him, or to anyone.

'You want to put a movie on?' he asked his mom. It was all he could do to take his mind off his troubles.

30

The Firmament Needle. A holy needle to weave a glorious ever-after adjunct to the Null. Or did it erase the Null? Kev hadn't a clue. Either way, it was an escape and an alternative to what was unequivocally known. He chided himself for latching on to this conjectural hope, feeling supremely gullible. Those Rising Path folk might have some magic beans to sell too. How about that? A giant beanstalk right up to St. Peter himself. Rose and the others had seemed to practically sneer at the idea during last night's briefing on the upcoming mission, relegating it to the kiddie pile of Santa Claus and the Easter Bunny.

But why? he quietly seethed. What was so ridiculous about this device? He, too, was always a cynic by nature, and yet here he was in the library, standing before the gargantuan Bookworm, which seemed to lean towards him with an almost comical air of expectation. He wouldn't have the clearance to ask for what he sought, yet here he stood, unshaken. Sure, he'd spent his life a cynic, but look at what his life had become. Why should this Needle be where the line was drawn?

'Hi,' he said to the worm. The worm remained stoic. 'You have any books on the Firmament Needle?' Without hesitation, the tremendous creature rose up in a column through the rotund tiers of bookcases, its many feelers hanging limp at its side, except for one slender appendage unfurling outwards to pluck a single, lonely text from a shelf. The worm returned promptly, the book absurdly tiny in its prehensile grip. Kev received the book, staring at it in bewilderment. The original title was in a language not of this world. Par for the course, really. But some later scribe had elegantly scrawled *Origins of the Dread Paradigm* upon the innermost leaf, and Kev had suspicions that this title might have been of the voluntary editor's own creation. One book. One single, lousy book with information regarding an object that could spare every living soul the epitome of despair. Yeah, he certainly felt like a bit of a tool for daring to hope for such things. Plus, it was beaten to hell and looked like it had been dumped in a river or two over the years. Millennia? And what was this thing made out of? It seemed like old leather, but from certain angles it shone with a strange light.

'Thanks,' he said to the worm.

The Bookworm returned to its affairs, and Kev found an empty table. He still had some time to kill. Ace had confirmed that they'd be flying out from Darnell at 8 P.M. to arrive in Brooklyn by 10. Time enough to get in position for a midnight raid, providing Mortis and Kozlov returned at all. Kev kept playing with the idea of calling Clyde. How could he not? A strange blend of excitement swirled in his torso. First of all, there was the obvious reason to call him. *Hey, dude. Has it been a single day already? Wow! Hey, guess what, you won't believe it. My first assignment just popped up. In Brooklyn! I know, right? Maybe fancy dropping what you're doing and getting involved? Because check this, I'm actually pretty fucking scared right now. Yeah, I know I wanted this, please don't throw it back in my face.* Then of course there was the whole Firmament Needle thing, but since he wasn't prepared to believe that himself just yet, he wasn't prepared to offer his friend any false hope.

Kev abandoned the idea of contacting Clyde. He had made his position perfectly clear, and Kev had to respect that. He opened the book to the index page to get an idea of what he was in for, only to be quickly dismayed. Many—no, most of the chapter headings were in a language not dissimilar to that of the face's title. Skimming randomly through the pages, he found that only some sections had been translated to English of the Ye Olde variety, while certain others had been translated into other human tongues that he could vaguely identify but couldn't read. Any thoughts of pay grades and security clearances flew out of the window.

He had been provided the tome only because the Bookworm obviously knew he'd get jack shit out of it. Kev briefly wondered if giant educated worms had a sense of humor. Undaunted, he decided to skip to the index at the back, just in case, and was amazed to find the English-translated Firmament Needle listed with its page number. Skimming to the page in question, Kev kept his optimism in check. And he was right to do so. While he found the name Firmament Needle, joined by what appeared to be its French counterpart, Aiguille de Firmament, and what he guessed to be Arabic, Greek, and some variants he didn't quite know, the references were buried deeply in dense chunks of alien symbolism.

One page.

There was, however, a brief sequence of pictograms that looked to be detailing a story. In terms of layout, it wasn't quite on the level of Clyde's comic-book pages, and the artwork made Kev appreciate Clyde's talent with the pencil all the more, but the imagery got the job done in a crude sort of fashion. The pictures showed what appeared to be figures projecting rays of light, some race of energy beings standing defiantly against darker, more intimidating entities. These light people were then shown as divided, but in what sense Kev couldn't say. Were they in disagreement? Parting on good terms? He moved on to the next pictures in the series. The big scary, things looked to be overpowering the light people, with droves of captives being led into giant circular constructs of some kind.

Not very helpful.

But then, before the war was lost and won—and according to the artist's vague diagram—rays of light beamed down, not just across one world, but numerous.

'That'll be the Sparks,' Kev uttered to himself.

But then what was this? It was too frail to be a spear...a needle? It, too, falling from the sky with one of the light beings. Too bad Kev couldn't read where they both might have landed: the associated pictogram looked like waves. A sea perhaps? Wind? What did it matter? His unfamiliarity with the language didn't mean much when even the best minds Hourglass had at their disposal couldn't parse anything useful from the text. In the concluding pictures, darkness reigned, followed by nine crowns with what were most likely their respective coats of arms below them. That didn't take a genius to crack, and Kev thought back on the few House names he could recall. He very much wanted to talk to Konstantin Kozlov. He so hoped he wasn't some whack-job. But first the monk had to return from the Null, and that freaked Kev out a little. He was game, despite his growing agitation at sitting around waiting, to tackle anybody whose business was slaughter and misery and devilish pacts, but he never thought he might have to get so close to a doorway back to that hazy memory of the place Clyde had rescued him from.

He glanced at the clock up on the wall between the stacks. Only a few hours to kill before the flight.

31

They had reached it. The Eidolon Trench.

And it was as imposing as Konstantin remembered.

Imbued with a deep and profound wrongness. A violation to human eyes hungering for hope.

The screen's time stamp of the advance drones had verified the hour as 9:32 P.M., Eastern Standard Time. That was before the drones had erred in their flight, drifting out over the vast bay and losing themselves in the ambient electromagnetic energy humming from the high apparatus of the nexus channel ferrying in the latest arrivals of souls, fresh from life. The drone cameras had broken up into washes of static, their radio waves scrambled by their proximity to the deceased.

Nevertheless, they were on Mortis' schedule. Before the screens went snow-blind, Konstantin had watched Lieutenant Castor's operators glide the drones high above a sprawling landmark that matched up with Konstantin's map, the natural signpost having left an imprint in his memory: a huge shanty town clinging to the uneven ground of the western cliffs, constructed from bone scaffolding and scrappy, patchwork flesh, all bound together tight by residual soul matter. The place looked as desolate as he remembered. Had anyone, or anything, ever occupied this disturbing little hamlet? He glanced around for any signs of those same spectral spies who had distracted him once before. Softening him,

Kuznetsov, and the Arkhitektor up for Vor Dushi's arrival. Apart from the dead breeze, nothing seemed to stir.

Far across the trench's mile-long divide, accessible only by that same old rickety bridge, were more of the poor accommodations of skin and bone. Konstantin hadn't noticed much of what lay beyond the bridge last time on account of the terrible sandstorm that had been set upon them. He felt a disquiet begin to occupy his thoughts, silencing them, owning them. All his wasted years had led him back to this, finally, and he couldn't abide the idea of another failure.

The convoy pulled to a stop along the cliffs with some trepidation, the soldiers piling out with weapons hot, searching sky, land, and even the metallic-colored sea off to their left. Running high above those heavy, alien waters lapping at the base of the cliffs, the nexus channel gradually dipped, its series of huge and scaly sea-bound masts guiding the soul pipeline into the gigantic cove nestled into the Trench's natural conclusion. From his high vantage point, Konstantin ignored the gently swaying bridge of long bones and tendons that traversed the chasm and stared beyond the skeletal shanty town, his gaze locked onto that massive dark cavern: a substation of souls housed within, awaiting collection for this land's House. The House of Fading Light. Bottom feeders of the Order, scrounging like starving mutts on the souls of the weak and the infirm, some diseased since the womb.

Vor Dushi would be in there somewhere. And the first of many answers, Konstantin hoped: the location of the Needle, and perhaps even the seraphic one who fell from the sky, unwittingly inspiring the creation of the Rising Path. At the very least, Konstantin hoped for some promising leads for him to chase down. Tasked with such a vital role for the House, he knew there was some wisdom and intelligence scattered amongst Vor Dushi's many heads; it wasn't a mindless beast. This damnable operation was sophisticated, organized, and too important for a thoughtless savage to oversee, and thus surely a trail to more knowledgeable authorities could be found within that cave. Even if it meant he had to bleed the information he sought straight out of the demon. Perhaps that was an inevitability. A cosmic rule set in motion during their first encounter. He'd know shortly. Konstantin could feel the tormented Arkhitektor continuing to budge and shift within him, his infection drawn to its owner's increasing presence.

'We won't need to go in there.' Mortis stopped beside Konstantin on the edge of the cliff, his greedy gaze gliding over the cove and Trench before stopping to size up the giant soul transmitter of the nexus. 'Size of that bloody thing.'

The souls continued to shriek past in a blurring train. Mortis had certainly regained his lost confidence since the Zar-ptica root had fired up the peculiar engine in his chest. He walked with more of his usual swagger, most likely copied from Talbot: project control and make it a reality. He wasn't fooling anybody, though, except for maybe himself.

Konstantin glanced down at Mortis' shoes, seeing how his toes were right on the edge of the cliff. A strong gust could likely help him over the precipice to the troubling waters below. He listened for Kuznetsov and Lim, knowing that they would be attuned to his consideration. If they opposed what he was thinking, then they were keeping their opinions to themselves. It would be so easy, a simple elbow to topple him over. He casually folded his hands together, tucking his elbows in like wings. All he had to do was let one fly. Then make his way down the treacherous, rocky outcrops to the lair of the beast. He thought of Agua and his men, and their bullets and their power chasing him the entire way down. Foiling his mission. The Arkhitektor was getting more restless by the second. Konstantin lowered his elbows. He would wait until the soul cages were up and running, when the men would be busy and the spectacle distracting. When Vor Dushi would leave its dwelling to unleash its wrath upon these trespassers.

Making to turn from the cliff edge, Konstantin caught an unpleasant smirk on Mortis' features.

'It would have been so easy,' the key maker said, evidently having sensed Konstantin's murderous motives. 'All it would have taken was a little push.'

Without comment, Konstantin headed over to where the workmen were unloading the disassembled cages from the trucks.

...

EVEN AT ITS narrowest point, the Trench must have been over half a mile across. The lieutenants had their orders, and Captain Agua watched them as they controlled their teams and the workers, setting the cages up 300 yards from each other, far enough away for the siren stones to bleed off large quantities from the nexus stream without causing an incomprehensible riot of souls, but also far enough apart to prevent becoming one large grouped target for Vor Dushi.

Konstantin was still watching for any sneaky specter who might launch out at them and bludgeon, and he could feel Kuznetsov's own prudence.

And still, nothing.

It was too calm for comfort. He had been expecting the Trench to have triggered its defenses by now. And yet there was no chaotic wind or excoriating grit. It was making him more anxious by the second, reliving the wild ferocity of the guardian's previous attack, clambering across the bridge, hidden like a terrible shadow within the eye of a storm, and then charging them. Had the House of Fading Light fallen into anarchy since their last visit, its territory and all its resources currently unclaimed for the moment? And there was still no ambiguous presence watching them from a perch amongst the stars, no curious death god watching them like game pieces. Could this place really have been abandoned? Or was Vor Dushi frightened by the much larger presence of intruders? No, Konstantin knew that was ridiculous. The Arkhitektor was practically spinning about in his chamber with dark joy. The Soul Thief was waiting for something, but it was certainly going to raise its many heads and drink deeply of blood and soul before they were through here.

Konstantin switched his attention from the hungry mouth of the cove to Fenwick, Castor, and Briggs overseeing the quick assembly line of metal tombs. Hammond—when he had been able-bodied—had overseen multiple dry runs of their assemblage back at the warehouse, and now the workers ran through the steps with ease. He felt bad for Hammond. Whatever that bite had sent ravaging through his system, he didn't expect the man to beat it. *That's enough wallowing*, he thought.

Time to get ready.

You both remember the plan?

Kuznetsov and Lim affirmed and quietly used the opportunity to drain out of Konstantin's body, slinking away down the scree and jag of the rocky ramps towards the cove, careful to avoid the inspections of the Citadel personnel. He watched them disappear down the narrow, precipitous slopes without incident, sending his prayers after them. He didn't know what they would find in that cavern besides a growing mass of fresh souls bawling in confusion and fear like adult newborn, what other dangers lurked in wait, but his faith beseeched that they find the divinity this universe sorely needed. Feeling his accursed all-father continuing to kick and rebel in his gut, Konstantin mentally prepared himself for the likelihood that he'd have to glean the useful intelligence from the keeper of the Trench itself. He placed a calming hand over his breastplate, lightly running his finger in an ouroboros benediction, confident in its ability to protect him from unclean spirits, external and internal.

'Konstantin!' Mortis called over from his grand position of standing idly about, twiddling his keys. Agua and Fenwick joined him to watch the hired hands of Sharp Construction slot together the final components of Alpha Team's cage.

With one last glance towards his departing brothers, Konstantin answered his summoning.

Mortis held one large hand out towards Konstantin. It looked like a large, pale, dead spider with its five remaining legs akimbo. In the palm lay the three siren stones, waiting to be embedded into the cages. 'What do you say, Gulag? Ready to smash the champagne bottle against these fine vessels?'

32

When Kev heard that they would be briefed by Director Trujillo, he expected a face-to-face with the agency's founder, either somewhere within the Mesa or maybe at that strange diner, the Midnight Vulture.

Instead, all he got was a voice over a speaker as he and the team loaded into the back of a troop transport truck headed for Darnell; it wasn't just Kev, Ace, Rose, and her ghost squad on board, but a team of agents, all equipped for heavy resistance: body armor, assault rifles, tactical helmets.

According to Rose, the as-yet elusive director was unavailable; stuck in communication with the hoodoo. The large rear compartment of the transport truck was covered in canvas, lacking windows, and Kev was tempted to pop his head through the canvas to see the barren stretch of desert concealing the diner.

'From what I have gathered, Acton Mortis' expedition started at the shores on the outskirts of Fading Light territory.' Trujillo's voice was easy, calming, but also had a slight and unidentifiable scraping quality that Kev attributed to the tablet's speakers. 'Ordinarily it would be welcome news that Mortis' keys are incapable of bypassing all of Erebus' checkpoints, but his significant head start means he's likely already closing in on his destination. That's partly on me, mea culpa; even the hoodoo can sometimes struggle with monitoring every little blip that opens between the living worlds and Erebus, but thankfully our agents in New York were able to record Mortis' conversation. The recon team is headed by Agent Higgins. You'll rendezvous with him on-site, and Rose, you'll assume command of the operation.'

The director paused, and Kev heard more of that scraping sound in the background. 'Providing Mortis and his forces don't get themselves killed in the interim, I'll need you to come down hard on him and every one of his men the moment they step foot in that warehouse. No half-measures. I don't care about tossing him to Erebus' authorities. Kill Acton Mortis.'

This was all starting to feel terribly real for Kev. Legitimate life-and-death stakes. Kill or be killed. But could he be killed? A bunch of guys with guns didn't scare him. But what about Mortis? Could that freak hurt him? He tried to wall off his anxieties, staying in the moment.

'What about Kozlov, sir?' Rose enquired.

A soft breath came over the speaker as Trujillo considered the question.

'I believe his heart's in the right place, but his faith is part of a lunatic fringe, and potentially problematic. But I see no need to kill him. Bring him in if possible. If not, well, I think you know.'

'Yes, sir,' Rose replied, no hesitation.

'I understand we have a new agent,' Trujillo said.

Kev tried to find his voice, but it croaked. 'Er-sir!'

'Agent Carpenter, I've heard excellent things about you from Rose. Remember your training, and I trust you'll do fine.'

'Thank you, sir.'

'Good luck.' Trujillo ended the transmission, leaving Kev and the others to travel the rest of the way to the air base in silence.

. . .

THE JET LEFT the strip at Darnell Air Force Base at 8 P.M. sharp. A sensation of utter displacement had hollowed Kev out. At once he was almost overcome by excitement and yet felt utterly trapped and victim to what was racing towards him. The jet speeded high across the desert plains of New Mexico, losing him in a muddle of clouds and barely glimpsed earth.

He was heading back to the home he once knew. Ace sat in the opposite aisle, wearing his old hockey jersey over his military attire. Kev assumed it was a lucky totem at first, but the fact that Ace also had an old-school goalie mask resting on his thigh made Kev ponder Ace's state of mind: Did he view all this like it was some brawling sport? Kev briefly thought about talking to him about the whole heap of nothing he had learned a few hours ago from *The Dread Paradigm*. The light people warring against the others, like photons piercing the dark, only to lose. And light, or Sparks, cascading across the worlds. And the Needle. But what would be the point? Ace was a Spark, but he probably didn't know anything further about the Sparks' unique ancestry than Kev knew about his own. Plus, Ace looked really intense right now, and it wasn't like he was Mr. Chatty at the best of times.

Rose sat across from Kev. She looked occupied, her own thoughts probably locked onto the dangers that lay only a couple of hours away in the Big Apple. Her muscular bulk was dressed protectively in tactical armor. Sarge sat pensively beside her, but Darcy and Barros had opted to reside within the collective quiet space of their command center, fixed somewhere between her muscle and reality. Kev wondered what it was like in there.

He stared out of the window at the wisps of cloud vapor below and thought about calling Clyde for the fifteenth time or so. He was speeding east towards home; why wouldn't he drop Clyde a notice about their imminent arrival? He hadn't mentioned it to his present company for fear of appearing distracted and unfocused, but he felt like he should tell Clyde about the Firmament Needle. Because what if it wasn't bullshit? What if it was a true thing, capable of saving Stephen and Clyde's dad, and everyone else, for that matter? Imagine saving the entirety of life from the despair of the Null.

But that wasn't the only reason he wanted to call Clyde.

He was afraid of fighting alone.

Sure, Rose and Ace were with him, and further down in the jet's fuselage were the squad of highly capable agents decked out for war—plus another team from the Madhouse were waiting for them at the rendezvous site—but still, Kev imagined a storm of fiery death shredding everybody of flesh and bone. This would be real combat he was engaged in, and no matter how much bravado Ace and Rose had poured into him in training, he was utterly terrified. Thoughts of fucking up were like flies around shit. And even though he didn't want Clyde to be dragged into this should it go sideways, he was beset by memories of their shared training, the successful trials of the Djinn Lamp, which had gained him a seat on this very flight. And still, he felt as though he'd somehow cheated in his victories. As though Clyde, in their pairing, had spared him from the danger of facing the Djinn's hordes alone.

Clyde was right, Kev realized. If this was it, should he somehow be destroyed, he should have taken the time to visit his mom and dad and sis. Even if it shocked them, or gave them heart attacks, he should have seen them one last time in case he never had the opportunity to find them in the Null.

'You okay there?' Rose was watching Kev fidget in his seat.

Kev glanced from the window, pulled from his swirling thoughts. This was everything he had sought since coming back. A reason. A purpose. A dedication. Holding her stare, he tried like hell to look cool, calm, and focused. He was certain that he was fooling nobody.

'Never better.'

The plane was making its descent into New York before he knew it, and just as quickly, the oppressive dread settled in.

33

It was happening. Konstantin could feel it in the air. The three siren stones lured the souls with their mysterious frequency, pulling them from the nexus stream. Only a few at first, but more and more as the soul cages established themselves as interesting draws. He himself stood on the bluff before the middle cage, a lightning rod tempting the chaotic swirl of the building soul storm. All about, the soldiers tensed, watching the souls one second and then quickly scanning the terrain for any approaching threat. But Mortis was ignoring the larger scene, only watching Konstantin stand there, a small silhouette commanding the masses, his body trembling as refugee after refugee slammed into him, vanishing into the strange safety of his magic.

Konstantin could feel each new occupant careening about the hives of his torso, seeking a cell to call home, and there was plenty to choose from. It started to feel uncomfortable, like the hot, dull throb of lightly strained muscles. He hoped there would be a natural occupancy that would bar further ingress before they burst him from within.

Through all the clamor and spectacle, he felt the Arkhitektor going berserk.

With his eyes squinting against the wailing tempest, Konstantin kept a close eye on that tattered bridge of ragged flesh and giant bones. He was waiting for his adversary to show upon the opposite cliff, a small and terrible figure from a distance, and ready to make its swift crossing. It was then that some part of him suggested he turn his head askance to check on the long, perilous slope angling down into the foreboding cavern.

And he was glad he did.

Something moved in the stormy light, making its ascent, serpentine necks rippling and agitated at the affront being set against their domain.

Vor Dushi was upon them.

Light, distance, and the hurricane gusts of souls clouded finer details, but Konstantin could swear that there was a hint of recognition in the slitted eyes of those seven heads. He didn't know if Kuznetsov and Lim had managed to bypass this approaching terror, but right now he couldn't wait for them to return.

Several souls of unscrupulous nature tried to charge into Konstantin, only to be soundly rebuffed by his armor, distracting him from the stealthy approach of Vor Dushi steadily climbing the slope. The unwelcome souls found shelter in the cages instead.

Konstantin made fists of his gauntlets and faced the approach of his adversary, but as the Soul Thief topped the rocky ramp, Konstantin heard barked commands and the bite of gunfire, all of it directed on the many-headed being. Vor Dushi greeted the attack with a septuplet chorus of roars, high-frequency screeches really, like those a bat might make. Vor Dushi's two long arms raised their claws to the sky, and what followed was an army of hell, scaling the cliff face with the ease of spiders, a rabble of contemptible revenants, and stabbing down from the sky like giant carrion birds came the—

'SKEELS!' a soldier yelled into the wind.

The two great creatures swam down with terrifying speed and grace. Vor Dushi had upgraded its gate security since last time. And something else occurred to Konstantin in that tense moment: Vor Dushi had been waiting for his arrival. The skeels had probably been watching them like hunting falcons from high amongst the stars. And maybe that's why the watchful god heads hadn't returned for further inspections. The trap had already been set.

34

THE SOLDIERS COMMENCED FIRING UPON the attacking dead, their ammo tearing the violent mob apart and casting them into a state of fear and doubt. Agua pulled out the big guns, his hands powering up with jade effulgence, and a swarm of warhead fireflies launched upwards like emerald darts to meet the first skeel head-on. Lieutenant Briggs shouted commands at his men in Alpha Team, ordering them to break out the missile launchers, which they did with precision and haste. For his own part, Briggs needed no conventional weapons. His skin began to glow like thin paper stretched over an electric torchlight. His vascularity crackled like live wires beneath his skin and muscle as all around him rockets roared upwards towards the attacking skeel. The RPGs and Agua's assault made a hot, smoky ruin of the first creature's giant head, raining foul gore and giant needle teeth all along the cliffs and the Trench, its body plummeting down in an uncoordinated mess to smash and rumble the cliff.

Briggs didn't lose focus, not even when one of the huge teeth thrust down like a javelin into the ground a foot from his position. He watched the second skeel close the gap, eclipsing him in its hunter's shadow. His flesh continued to sing with an electrical hum as a dozen or more garrote-thin cables whipped out of his arms, shoulders, and back, each one locking onto the enormous flying threat like harpoons carrying a crackling surge of high voltage. The skeel became wracked with spasms, its coordination marred and its course suddenly indiscernible. The electricity cooked it until its huge eyes popped and oozed, dripping from their sockets. The giant eel hit the cliff edge like a flopping blue whale, mighty and terrible, its stinking, smoky scales enough to make Briggs' eyes water.

Konstantin held his position, loosely following the plight of the soldiers fighting off the two proud sky titans but mainly keeping vigil on Vor Dushi as it made its way towards them all with little to no fear of their offensive capabilities. The cages were still rattling like barn doors in a twister, filling up and showing no sign of maximum occupancy. The Sharp Construction workers were making a beeline for Mortis, surplus to this fight and calling for him to open the portal. Konstantin didn't want to see any more of them perish in this madness. Something else caught his eye, some momentary movement within the smoking and flayed flank of the electrocuted skeel. Behind those smoking and oozing scales, he saw a grouping of souls trying to squeeze out of the dead thing. That's what those things are, he then realized: giant flying prison barges scarfing down any wandering souls. The spirits poured out of the giant mouth like a wall of dry ice, heeding the call of the siren stones and seeking refuge amongst the three cages. One prison to another. The last of the swallowed unfortunates slipped out between the prison bar teeth just in time, with gravity pulling the skeel's lengthy tail down over the cliff's edge, where it crashed into the foamy depths of the Trench.

Vor Dushi continued its march, untroubled by the automatic firepower being brought against it. Even the might of the Exorcist rounds could offer no worthwhile assistance. Konstantin gave a cautious glance towards Mortis, the key maker's dirty old coat flapping in the hobbling gusts of wind, his right thumb vanishing into mid-air as he flung open the door to the warehouse, a huge keyhole shape tearing a chunk out of reality. Konstantin saw the stationed warehouse troops all jump to attention, racing forth to monitor the gateway from their side with their rifle barrels up. To Konstantin's surprise, something exploded behind them at the distant rear of the warehouse; he couldn't discern its teeth-rattling boom from the havoc raging all around him, but he did witness a number of Citadel personnel draw away from the gateway to face the unexpected intruders.

Who could that be? Konstantin thought.

Such musings were a luxury he couldn't afford as he watched the Soul Thief commence its slaughter of the guards.

35

THE BANK OF MONITORS WENT dead inside the guards' pillbox security hub. It provoked a practiced and efficient response from the trio of guns waiting within. Captain Pike, a deathly pale, broad-shouldered bruiser with a goatee, shaved head, and an old habit of wearing stylish sunglasses—one must look cool, even at night—jumped out of his chair. The back-up generator would kick in any second, but he was paid well to keep an eye on the premises.

'Check it.'

The other two obeyed, fluidly filing out into the gloomy warehouse grounds, their Heckler & Koch CQBR carbines raised. They would not be alone: Pike spoke into his radio channel, alerting his perimeter security team and setting them to scour every shadowy corner, nook, and cranny of the site's large, open space, including all utility buildings and under every parked truck and car. Pike exited the small pillbox as the generator came on, the dozens of yellow and green perimeter lights flashing up in the cold, dark night. He checked the wide, grime-coated second- and third-floor windows of the main building, now lit up in a deep glacial blue. He moved quietly for a big, heavy man, his eyes keen behind his shades.

. . .

KEV WAITED IN the sparse banks of shadow, staring about the neighboring warehouses from his cover behind a crumbling brick wall. They were all quiet at this hour, standing empty behind chain link fences. Ace and Rose had coordinated with Higgins and the rest of his waiting Madhouse team upon arrival, listening to the rundown on everything they had scoped out. The local agents still had men posted on the rooftop of the adjoining building with night-vision scopes on their rifles, though they wouldn't be much good with all of the building's dazzling floodlights illuminating the grounds. Everybody had a job and was ready to do it. First, a team from the local branch would disable the warehouse's main power supply; they had diesel back-up generators, but the brief blackout would distract the security forces long enough for the second part of the plan. For his part, Kev was to run a frontal assault with Rose and Ace while the snipers positioned on the southern building's roof covered them. The team of agents from the plane would be split in two, attacking the main building from the western and eastern positions in a pincer move.

Kev stared across at the huge, three-story brick fortress. *Fuck me, it's bigger than Costco*, he thought. It had four wide vehicle bay doors evenly situated across the length, each one shuttered tight, and a line of large, dirty windows running end-to-end across the upper floors. The open ground was set with cameras mounted up on walls and poles, most likely linked to the back-up generators. Black military vehicles with the security team's CSS brand were parked around the massive open lot like sleeping animals, and near a couple of abandoned, rusty shipping containers in the northern corner was the guard house, built as sturdy as a pillbox.

This was it, Kev thought. It surprised him how a dead guy could still be so nervous. It wasn't like he could get shot or stabbed or blown up. With a little concentration, he had affixed an ear piece in place, making it float within his immaterial ear, allowing him to stay in contact on the communication channels with the others. It only dawned on him in doing this that he didn't understand how ghosts could even hear, since they were not physical and therefore not subject to sonic vibrations; but after everything else, it didn't seem very important.

An update from one of Agent Higgins' spotters on the roof reported the portal gateway opening up inside the warehouse. Mortis was punctual, Kev had to hand it to the creep.

Ace's attention settled on Kev like a powerful weight. 'Game face, rookie.'

Over the comms, the blackout agent gave a three count. All cameras, floodlights, and the warehouse's internal lights—shining through spots in the dirty brown windows—went dark. There was no excited commotion from Citadel; they were pros. With the power knocked out, the perimeter guards quietly assessed the situation over their own communication frequencies and took defensive positions. Before the generator could shed any new light, Kev focused on the distant cameras that would observe their approach and popped them into twisted glass and plastic.

The former harsh glare of the floodlights was replaced by a number of yellow and green LED lights strategically placed to lay open the darkness, attached to poles and fixed to walls and sections of the cracked macadam. Kev nodded to Rose and Ace. The three of them moved quickly, cutting across the open ground, staying low. Kev cut a short route through parapet walls, parked vehicles, and random pallets and barrels, with Ace and Rose racing to keep up.

The biggest guard manning the pillbox had stepped out, briefly checked on the main building and started to move, his voice whispering a curt command into his throat mic. Pike received his reply a split second before Ace stepped out of the gloom and inserted a skewer of ice into the base of his skull.

Rose dragged another guard behind a truck like he was made entirely out of straw and twisted his neck around just as easily.

No shots fired.

Kev reached the side of the warehouse just in time to watch the pair of sentries out front get silently dispatched by the snipers at his back. All the bay doors were sealed tight, but Kev could slip through like water through a crack. Ace and Rose drew to a stop at the opposite corners of the building. Kev watched them carefully slip into their planned service entrances: Rose wrenching her locked door open with a brief metallic squeal; Ace freezing the handle on his and then shattering it and its lock housing. Kev walked through the sealed cargo door, finding himself in the midst of a very well-guarded operation. The blue light of the LEDs might actually go some way to camouflaging him, at least for a crucial moment. Still, there must have been scores of men, all prepped for harsh combat in armor and weaponry. He slipped behind a concrete support column and took in the scene. The space was huge, with a few forklifts and stationed Humvees near some of the other shuttered bays, and manned walkways crossing the upper floors to bridge the work and offices areas of floors two and three. At the far end of the warehouse was a large metal framework, a ramp running up and into the huge portal window looking out into a dry and barren war zone. Men in uniforms were charging out from the Null. Not soldiers. They looked like construction workers, overalls and hard hats, barging through the several squads keeping a fierce vigil on the portal and readying themselves to make the plunge and assist in that otherworldly fray. The other guard teams were more spooked by the blackout—and also the radio silence from the dead guards outside—and were beginning to search the premises.

Now that he was in motion, Kev was relieved to find his actions were distracting him from his overthinking. He knew he had to be a shark, always moving forward. Leaning out from his cover behind the pillar, he found a guard watching the portal from his stairway landing. The guard had a few grenades on his belt. Well, Kev thought, Ace and Rose wanted a distraction. He focused his energy, reaching out towards the guard. It took delicacy and concentration. Kev pulled the pin on one of the grenades without the hired gun being any the wiser, and then hurled him upwards to the gunners fanned out across the third-floor walkway. The human grenade might have issued a cry of alarm if he wasn't so shocked as to his newfound ability to fly. Before the confused cluster of troops could react, they were reduced to wet matter and fragged armor, the grenade's shrapnel tearing through a number of the snipers and toppling another over the railing to become a broken heap below. And so, with one move, the entirety of the local force became divided, training their considerable numbers and firepower on three skirmishes: west, towards Ace and his small back-up team; east, towards Rose and hers; and lastly, staying put to watch over the portal activity. Kev would close in straight up the middle and take care of the latter.

The stark realization that he had just killed several people was too potent for Kev to ignore, but between the aggressive torrents of bullets and the knowledge of the larger situation, he knew that he could accept it for now. Compartmentalize it. He would have to. These were not good people. And more killing would be necessary. From somewhere up above, Kev watched a human ice sculpture plummet and shatter into several large pieces, looking like red slush on the inside. Ace skated into view, gliding across the walkway on a sheet of frost, one hand holding a regenerating shield of ice, absorbing shotgun slugs, and in the other a frozen broadsword. With both he bludgeoned and skewered his way through a grouping of guards like a balletic Viking. Elsewhere, a parked jeep was kicked with enough force to render the handbrake moot, the vehicle skidding across the concrete with a shriek of locked tires until it crushed a couple of guards positioned by a low buttress. After booting the jeep like a kid kicking a can, Rose popped into eyesight for a brief moment, just long enough to crush another enemy's rifle barrel before picking him up and swinging him helmet-first into the corner of a concrete pillar. Kev looked away before the impact, not needing the visual and grateful he couldn't hear the connection over the din of multidirectional gunfire.

Over his earpiece, Kev heard several of their guys go down, declaring dead team members or their own critical wounds. He couldn't help but run a visual of the mounting dead being whisked into that giant gateway to the Null. Despite his orders and his training, he found himself wanting to shadow Rose and Ace, absolutely focused on covering them despite them not needing his assistance. He decided that they would be better served if he continued to put down more of his own attackers instead of worrying about theirs.

Moving out from behind the pillar, he felt a sharp tug at his shoulder. A moment of confusion. What was that? What just happened? Then the pain registered. Searing and pronounced. Staring dumbfounded at his shoulder, Kev realized he'd been shot. How? He didn't understand, but somehow he had, and now he had to deal with the fact that he wasn't untouchable.

The sharpshooter slowly made his way around the gangway, ignoring the pitched battle below and the icy wild man smashing through defenses on the other side of the building. The rifleman kept his eye trained on the pillar and the wounded ghost it concealed.

Knowing the shooter was moving along the rafters for a clean shot, Kev tried to seal off the pain. He phased through the pillar to compose himself, only allowing a fraction of his brow to protrude through the concrete, a chameleon keeping watch on a hunter. With deep focus, channeling his abilities into such a small target, he fixated on the sniper's gnat's-eye-sized rifle barrel. Within the grooved cylinder, a small pea of blue light was born, growing steadily until it bloated the whole barrel. His face twitched, shuddering with the effort and the pain of his shoulder, maintaining his control over such a small and precise field. He hoped this worked.

The marksman exhaled slowly as he beaded in on the face jutting out from the column. And squeezed the trigger.

Kev saw the distant rifle buck with a violent bang. The backfire shredded the sniper's face with bits of metal, tumbling him backwards over the railing and onto a column of wooden crates. It provided a petulant, angry satisfaction.

Fuck you.

Payback didn't fix his shoulder, though. He couldn't believe he'd just been shot. The pain was immense. The shoulder was going to slow him down, but he couldn't allow it to stop him. Not after everything he'd been through to get here. But more than that: he needed to find Konstantin. He couldn't allow someone with his knowledge to get caught in the crossfire.

Still, his shoulder really fucking hurt. He made a note to ask Rose about PLE-specific pain relief if he got out of here in one piece.

A tingling sensation ran through Kev. At first he thought it was his final moments, the feel of his immaterial form readying to dissipate from this world. But that wasn't it. The light quiver became a strong tug, sending ripples along the invisible binding between himself and Clyde. Its meaning was unmistakable.

Help!

36

CLYDE ALMOST SPASMED HARD ENOUGH to wake his mom. She'd fallen asleep on her end of the couch watching some crappy, dull movie, and Clyde hadn't been far from doing the same. But the yank he just felt, like his brain was being lightly whisked.

What the hell was that?

It went again. A deep tug in his skull. Not pain, but more like a head rush.

All he could think was Kev. Or a tumor. *Please be Kev.* Was he in trouble?

Again. The pull. Again, and again. It was, he realized, an urge. A calling. A compulsion.

He couldn't understand how he knew, but he felt as though the pull was some strange force trying to drag him to Kev's location. Good luck with that. What was he meant to do, book a flight to Albuquerque? He checked his mom; she was out for the night but not snoring yet. She needed her rest, spending so many of her hours helping the damaged bodies and minds of others. He hoped he'd never have to burden her with his own damage, but the tugging sensation continued. He struggled to think of what to do. Kev didn't have a cell phone—an issue that might have to be addressed if this were to become a thing. Now what? Call up Indigo and ask for advice, hope he didn't have to hold the line as he was directed to an advisor?

Tug.

Over and over in its slow rhythm. It didn't cost him his equilibrium, which he was pleased about. He didn't need to be clattering about and falling over chairs right now.

He put a blanket over his mom and left a note for her. With a passing glance at Stephen's old room, and then that of his parents, he quietly opened the apartment's front door and paused. He gave the living room doorway one final look, thinking about his mom lying in there, asleep. He tried not to think that it might be the last time he saw her. Stuffing his feelings away in some dark closet of his mind, he quietly closed the door behind him and hurried out of the building.

The tug in his mind continued its fervent activity. With more of that useful yet confusing ambiguity, he had the notion that Kev wasn't too far away, certainly not in New Mexico at least. He didn't know how or why, and with the thudding of his soul he didn't care about the nitty-gritty, he only knew that he had to find Kev. Had to respond somehow. First, he had to flag a taxi. That, too, could be difficult in practice, not so much with the flagging but the directing. What would he tell the driver? *Bear with me, I'm being guided by occult forces.*

What the hell, he was certain cabbies had heard stranger things. Racing north to the end of Clermont Avenue, he felt his heart gallop alongside the frantic tug in his mind, wanting to lead him ... where? West. *Kev, is this you? What the hell is happening?* He didn't know what he wanted more: to hear Kev's voice pipe up in his thoughts, explaining exactly what the hell was going on, or to remain insulated from him but also confused. Waving a taxi down at the intersection, he jumped into the back of the hack and told the tired-eyed driver where to go on a street-by-street basis, the tugging becoming more urgent as they gradually closed in on the location. It was like the weirdest game of Marco Polo he had ever played, and he hoped he had enough cash to cover the expense. Fortunately, the put-upon driver went along with it without too much trouble or suspicion.

Twenty minutes later, Clyde found himself and the cab in Red Hook, steering clear of the plush and trendy rehabilitated sections of the waterfront and sticking to the dark, industrial streets. Over the sounds of the radio station, he and the driver both heard what sounded like pitched battle. The cabbie stopped at the corner of Wolcott and Ferris, refusing to go any closer to what was quite clearly a gun battle being waged in the isolated region of dockland. Clyde couldn't blame him and threw the fare plus tip through the partition and bounded out of the ride. Running down the wide, dark stretch of cracked cement, surrounded by imposing tenebrous buildings set far back behind desolate parking lots, he tried to think what his plan was here, lacking even the most basic idea about the situation he was charging into. He was also alone, unarmed, and without any form of protective clothing, clad only in jeans, Nikes, and a red hoodie, and with nothing but a set of keys, a phone, and some spare change in his pockets.

And this wasn't training.

Could he find a gun in there? Certainly, from the sounds of it. But could he put his training into practice during such high stakes? He thought of Stephen and his dad, US Marines killed in the line of duty. Then he thought of Kev, in trouble and perhaps facing a swift deportation back to the Null. He thought about how much he didn't want to lose his friend. The tug pulled him towards the huge building at the far end of the street, near the edge of the Upper Bay. The cacophony of gunfire was terrifying.

37

AT THE EIDOLON TRENCH, THE shroud of dust descended. A storm of eye-stinging grit scrubbing out the blue suns and distant stars, stirring further chaos into the proceedings. Vor Dushi, Konstantin realized, had somehow managed to command this destructive, impeding element, this unknown power a means of thwarting the pillaging mob. Konstantin had stopped paying attention to the teams of soldiers desperately trying to defend their soul cages, emptying clip after clip into the inexorable advancement of the House of Fading Light's regent. With eyes tight against the scouring winds, he stared past Vor Dushi's bloody passage through the gunners, hoping to find, perhaps to willfully call Kuznetsov or Lim back to him with some good information. It wasn't to be. The top of the ramp remained dark and empty in Vor Dushi's wake, beset only by great gusts of sandpapery grit.

Konstantin wasn't going to stand here and wait for the Soul Thief to slaughter his way through the lot of them. Not with the Arkhitektor matching the inhospitable weather with his own turbulent activity from deep within. Even over the parade of new and confused voices orienting themselves within his ark of flesh, Konstantin heard his old mentor rebelling against the protective suppression of the armor. It was beginning to hurt. A cold, flat pressure in his chest.

This was what he had anticipated. His moment was fast approaching. The moment to utilize this chaos, and the deaths of these amoral men, to slip his leash, abandoning his employers to their own folly, and enter the caverns on faith. Should his own faith prove to be as hollow as the bravado of Mortis and Agua and Talbot, then Konstantin would fall back on his Plan B. He'd fall on his sword; but ideally, he'd find a way to make Vor Dushi fall on it first.

Lieutenant Briggs and his cage team were now directly in the path of Vor Dushi, the creature's seven heads flailing like agitated snakes, each head bearing two eyes that burned like hot embers in the dark-sepia winds. Konstantin slowly started to back away from the line of soul cages, and over the fury of the screeching gales and ceaseless pops and bursts of gunfire, he heard a deep, pulsing hum of electricity. Briggs was lighting up like a dynamo. He aimed his unique network of living wires at the attacker like neuronal whips, charging up to zap Vor Dushi into a quivering mess of limbs and heads. Electrical jolts arced through the air, igniting dust particles into brief flecks of fire, and surged through Vor Dushi's body. It might have stunned him, maybe even incapacitated him, if Briggs had time to put more juice into his wires, but the many heads and mouths were too ravenous to allow Briggs the opportunity. They all bit down in sequence, picking a chosen portion of Briggs' body to sink their hooked teeth into: crown of his head, neck, both arms, both legs, and one clamped down onto the meat of his lean right flank. With a little wriggling to secure a good bite, each reptilian head pulled away in a different direction, a practiced move that tore Briggs into multiple pieces, his glowing nerves quickly turning dark under his bloody skin. Alpha Team lay scattered about in wet, red odds and ends, their freed souls joining Briggs in drunkenly taking flight for the very soul cage they had been ordered to protect.

The gunfire continued to pepper Vor Dushi's advance. A rocket whined like a banshee through the tremulous air, almost blown off course by one particularly strong gust, but Vor Dushi, perhaps sensing the greater threat the explosive warhead posed, slid out of the way with the swiftness of a matador eluding the horns of a charging bull. The missile struck upon the edge of the cliff, blooming like an orange-and-black rose in the sandstorm. Vor Dushi's fourteen blazing red eyes glared at the late Alpha Team's now unprotected soul cage, its seven sets of jaws clacking like castanets. The hydra's heads and arms set upon the near-full receptacle and rapidly twisted, bent, and bit through the large sepulcher. The siren stone became dislodged and fell to the hard, lumpy ground and was crushed like cheap glass under the stomping soul collector's heel. The abundance of souls, still largely disoriented and confused from the birthing of their death, dissipated quickly, the constituents of this glowing assembly scattering about; some were dragged back by infernal attraction to the nexus stream and pulsed towards the caverns, but many others scrabbled and fought their way towards the two remaining soul cages, the last ports in this ungodly storm. And a smaller wave stumbled and lurched towards Konstantin, only to be batted aside by another unknown force. It seemed so cruel and random, but anyone who had read of their mortal histories would know why this last bunch were rebuffed by the monk's seals.

. . .

MORTIS LOOMED OUT of the swirling walls of sand to clamp Captain Agua's arm. He had to scream over the wind for Agua to hear him. With the one shattered cage's occupants now added to the other two tombs, they would surely be at full capacity. He ordered the captain to have his remaining lieutenants retreat through the portal behind them, to drag the cages over before it was too late, even though the warehouse cavalry looked overwhelmed by some additional, unknown force. Agua hid his fear well, but even his bland expression couldn't quite hide the fact that he agreed this was the wisest course of action. For all the critical and harsh words he'd directed at the dumb Russian cave-dweller, he'd been wrong about the lethality of Vor Dushi. Briggs... he had been dismembered like a flimsy plastic doll. Agua had fought alongside Briggs through more hellholes than he cared to remember, many of them after they dropped out of the army, discarding their Green Berets: taking down jungle-savage dictators in Sudan; drug lords in Argentina; crooked Roman Catholic militias in Eastern Europe; it didn't matter who, so long as the pay was right. And Briggs was always there with him—as were Fenwick and Castor—ready to throw down his life for his warrior brothers. Agua shook off the hard-digging fingers of Mortis and hurried over to Lieutenant Castor, shouting over the keening winds and ordering him and his men to jump into their vehicles and put their foot down until they passed through the rippling doorway. Castor and his men did so double-time, exchanging one hot zone for another, seeing the battleground that had inexplicably broken out inside the warehouse.

. . .

Konstantin had almost become a ghost himself amidst the panic. Crouching low, one gauntlet-heavy hand warding off the eye-watering silt, he watched Castor's ride drag the trailer-bound cage through the keyhole and fought his way around Vor Dushi's rampage towards the cove's slope, each step a straining effort.

38

CLYDE FOUND HIMSELF IN A block of disused warehouses, but standing out amongst the dark, ailing block was a brick fortress lit up like a landing pad for an airplane. Strips of green and yellow LEDs clung to walls and even ran along the ground itself. The sounds of all-out war raging from within the building had Clyde in a cold sweat, and the several dead bodies littering the ground didn't help ease his tension. He stuck to the shadows where possible, running swiftly and light-footed towards the outside of the building. The tugging sensation in his head slowly abated. If this was, in fact, the work of Kev, then he was somewhere inside. Clyde felt the nervous sweat begin to warm and prickle him beneath his T-shirt and hoodie, dampness on his lower back. His mouth dry.

Making it to the side of the building, he found a few more dead sentries in body armor. Their uniform had an insignia over the breast that he didn't know: Citadel Security Solutions. He sincerely hoped that they were the enemy in all of this. After a quick inspection, he found their armor to be intact—their heads not so much, which was why Clyde didn't allow his gaze to linger on the damage—so he quickly and respectfully started to confiscate the weapons and armor of the nearest, securing it over his own person. How long would it be before the local cops arrived? He wasn't an official Hourglass agent, but would he be protected by them should he end up in police or federal custody? Sure, the agency needed him to an extent. Still, he had to survive this first.

With his sidearm holstered to his belt, he checked the rifle's magazine. Full. These guys had been killed without getting a shot off. Keeping his barrel low, he was about to begin searching for an unlocked door when he thought he saw a shadow move across the roof of the warehouse across the way. Snipers? Fuck! Whose side are they on? A bullet splintered a brick an inch from his head and would have likely decapitated him had he not jerked his head around to gawp at the snipers.

Not wanting to wave at them in the hope that they were Hourglass, he hugged the wall and hurriedly made for a metal door at the end of a small concrete ramp near the corner of the building. The door had been wrenched off its hinges. An iron door. Please, be the work of Kev or Rose.

The unabated clamor of war was terrifying, rattling his eardrums and scraping his nerves raw. The deafening volume was practically vibrating the bricks. The invisible thread teasing at his forehead suddenly renewed its frenzy, its demands almost harder than his own heartbeat. He took a steadying breath, didn't feel much steadier, and tried to imagine this was all an elaborate exercise of the Djinn's. The gun in his hand promised to protect him, and he swept into the carnage, hunched slightly, his rifle and his focused gaze moving as one, scanning for information on the scene, friendlies and hostiles. The blue light from the dozens of LEDs made him feel like a tiny lizard in a giant terrarium. The gun smoke in the air was sharp and acrid. The conflict seemed to be moving through the warehouse, heading away from him beat by beat, bullet by bullet. He moved down from concrete pillar to wall to pillar, passing more scattered bodies, all rag-dolled and broken. Some of them looked like Rose had used them to beat down doors. He pushed on.

A distracted guard rushed out from a concealed alcove to Clyde's right, spinning in surprise and swinging his rifle up to kill the latecomer sneaking into the fight. Clyde used the guard's surprise, his fresh muscle memory taking over, and quickly put a short burst into the CSS shooter, two shots center mass. The two combined shots punctured the toughened fibers of the body armor, the second round embedding itself in the man's chest. The man went down, struggling to breathe. The struggle was brief, his eyes going dark and empty, leaving only a surface sheen of artificial blue light.

The body didn't disintegrate into a million mystical pixels like in training. Of course it didn't. This was real.

Clyde had just killed a man.

His hand trembled, but savagery reigned all around, indifferent to his troubles. There was no time to think on it. Kev needed him. He blotted out his act and moved, controlling his breathing, depending on his newly tested killer instinct to get him through this. The soul thread continued to wind him in. Please, Kev, he thought, don't be dead. Don't be deader!

Clyde was moving from a pillar to a parked forklift truck when his attention was arrested by the huge portal at the far end of the building. All about it was open warfare, with multiple shooters lined up on a raised metal platform, on the verge of either entering or exiting through that giant keyhole in reality. A sound above him, a rustle, weight shifting on metal. A rifleman was about to bear down on him. With the shooter having the higher ground, Clyde knew it wouldn't end well for him. The bullets chased him from the spot, ringing and clanging off the forklift and forcing Clyde to dive behind the nearest bullet-pocked pillar. The cover was quickly chewed into chalk dust before the shooting stopped. Risking a glance, Clyde found to his dismay that it wasn't because of the elevated shooter's compromised sight; it was because there was another CSS soldier on the ground, angling around to get a jump on him, his approach masked by the skull-pounding noise and confusion. The ground soldier was out of ammunition, but he had a wicked combat knife and the belief that surprise was on his side. And the running guard was fast. Before Clyde was able to bring his rifle up to aim, the guard was upon him, knife racing down for the exposed area of Clyde's neck. In such close quarters, aiming was out of the question. Clyde brought the rifle up, barring the stab and, by putting some torque into his hips, twisted both his rifle and the knife away, quickly returning the rifle stock back and up into his opponent's face. The guard went down, eyes closed, and his nose burst into a crushed rosebud. Knowing that the sniper would still be waiting for him above, waiting for him to make a run for it, Clyde stared down at the unconscious guard, an idea forming.

The sniper waited patiently, shutting off all distractions, his sharp, calculating stare waiting for his target to pop out from behind the pillar. He watched the upper half of the knocked-out guard's torso get dragged behind the column. Seconds later, Clyde strafed out from behind his cover, his neck tucked into his shoulders, and hiding as much of his body as he could behind the shield of the comatose mercenary. Damn, the guy was heavy. It was much worse than when Ace had forced him to sprint up and down the canyon trails with the heavy bag over his shoulder.

The sniper seemed to care little for team spirit and commenced firing, several shots punching into Clyde's improvised roof, the impacts heavy, wobbling him, but he was able to make it out of the open combat theater, finding better shelter in a long brick corridor running along the perimeter of the building. Clyde dropped the dead man, scanning the immediate narrow area. Pissed at himself, he now realized that large sections of the left-hand wall were installed with windows. Perfect for any killers out in the thick of it. But he was safe for the moment. He tried to orient himself, feeling which way the soul thread was trying to pull him. Down the corridor. Past the large windows that he doubted were ballistic proof. Staying crouched, he hurried towards the end of the corridor, when—call it instinct or random chance—he peeped through the glass at the right time and spotted something curious. At first it was a jumble of confusing blue shapes. Then his mind found structure and form within the farrago of blue on blue. It was Kev, coincidentally blending into the blue atmosphere of the generator lights, leaning partially in and out of a concrete column. But what was wrong with him? Was he hurt? On the other side of Kev's cover—to Clyde's right; was that north?—the violence showed no signs of letting up. That other half of the warehouse was a kill zone fixed around the crackling gateway.

With a pounding heart, palms now slick on the rifle and a fine layer of sweat on his upper lip, Clyde shuffled out of the corridor and bolted towards his friend.

'Kev!' His shout was barely heard over the blasts and cracks of gunfire.

Kev couldn't disguise his shock and delight at seeing Clyde sliding in to share the cover. Clyde saw the twisted expression on Kev's face and knew it wasn't fear holding him here; it was pain. His attention hooked onto Kev's hand, staunching a wound that hurt but couldn't bleed.

'What happened?' Clyde shouted, his body tucked tight against the column, shoulder-to-shoulder with Kev.

Kev seemed confused and a little humiliated, not sure how to admit that he was a ghost who had somehow managed to get himself shot on his first outing. 'Sniper. Hit me with something. I'll figure out what later.'

'What? *Fuck*!' Clyde's rigid gaze swept the catwalks above them, then dropped down to the main floor to sweep for any circling threats. 'What's happening?'

'Long story short, these psychos are opening doorways into the Null, trying to drag souls back here for slavery. Turns out that's our jurisdiction.'

'I turn my back for five minutes,' Clyde said. Kev tried to smile, but it quickly dissolved into an ill curling of his lip. 'Ace and Rose?'

'The gang's all here,' Kev tapped the ear bud floating beside his ear, 'and still alive for now.' He relayed the news of Clyde's unexpected arrival to Ace and Rose and received their current sit-reps. 'Rose is over there somewhere.' He pointed to where Clyde had just come from. 'Ace is to the west. They're both halfway to the portal.'

'So what's the play?' Clyde asked.

Kev tipped his head in reference to the portal, teeth grinding against the pain. 'Our targets are on the other side. The Null. We need to bring them back over here. One of them... this Russian monk—' Kev clipped it off. He seemed to have more to say but had chosen not to. Clyde knew it was something important, but he also knew that if it was crucial to this very moment, he would have spilled it already. 'We can kill 'em all, but the monk's not with them. We need to bring him back alive. Guy's wearing some ceremonial armor covered in glyphs.' Kev's eyes drilled deep into Clyde's. 'We need to bring him back. *Alive*.'

Clyde nodded without question. 'Can you move?'

Kev groaned but still looked vital enough. 'I'm not sitting this out.'

'Can't believe you got shot. Can you lend me some, before we move?'

Kev raised his fist. 'Only a little. I did just get shot, you know.' He grinned sickly. Clyde raised his fist. They bumped their fists together briefly, vapors of blue light transmitting from the ghost to the mortal.

Clyde shuddered as if somebody had just walked across his grave. 'Okay, that's enough. Rose is east, Ace is west, we're going straight down the middle?'

Kev agreed, gratitude pouring from his eyes. 'Thanks for coming, brother.'

Clyde gave him a look of compassion, one built on two young lifetimes of memories. Then he shook his head incredulously. 'First day on the job, and we're going into the Null. Well, if we don't pull this off, at least we don't have too far to travel.'

'You watch your ass and stick close.' Without another word, the spirit of Kev melded back through the column and out the other side. Together they moved straight down the center of the warehouse.

A pair of guards was up ahead, holding their defensive position, their guns searching for any intruder. They must have sensed Clyde and Kev coming in on their periphery, and with a smooth, practiced motion honed from years of service and wet work, the CSS duo raised their rifles and fired. At least they tried to. But no matter how hard they strained, they couldn't squeeze their triggers. It was as though their fingers had suffered some form of paralysis, some unseen force halting their intentions. With the telekinesis of a pissed-off and wounded poltergeist, Kev ripped their guns right out of their grips with savage force, simultaneously disassembling both rifles into their constituent parts. Before the surprise faded from their faces, Clyde was moving in close, not wanting to waste his bullets. He blotted out thoughts of decency, of human life extinguished. He, like Kev before him, had compartmentalized. These were soul slavers, and they had shot his friend.

Kev dragged the first unarmed unfortunate as though he were attached to an invisible wire, pulling him right into Clyde's path. Clyde stepped right through him with a stiff right-armed clothesline, crushing the guard's trachea and flipping the choking man in a graceless somersault. The second guard was reaching for his sidearm, but Clyde was too quick, his hand darting out and pinning the guard's hand to his holster, then using his free hand to deliver a stiff right uppercut that lit sparks behind the patrolman's eyes. The punch momentarily stalled the guard's ambition to draw and shoot, allowing Clyde to grip the back of his opponent's head with his left hand and land two more stiff shots with his right before ragging his enemy's neck into a vise-tight guillotine choke. Clyde felt the body go limp in his arms and dropped him, leaving him unconscious in an unflattering sprawl. Kev stared at the sleeping guard and, after a moment's consideration, made a small twisty hand motion, breaking the guard's neck. Clyde looked at him.

'He's a hired killer. Put them all down.'

Clyde couldn't argue. They covered a lot of ground, the CSS forces now a disorganized shamble. Up ahead, the long metal ramp sloped up towards the huge portal, showcasing a different chaotic scene, lost within lashing grains of ashen dirt. A large clustered fire team remained in a semicircle round the ramp and the portal's threshold: part of the squad were at the top of the ramp, waving something through from the Null's side; other shooters angled defensively around the wide flights of stairs on either side of the slope, spraying bullets at what Clyde gathered must be the closing-in of Rose and Ace, tying an offensive knot and tearing through the last of the perimeter defenses on either side of the building.

Before any of the remaining ramp guards could track the danger slicing up the middle of the warehouse, Clyde leaped higher than humanly possible, catlike and graceful, landing on the second-floor walkway. From this perch he quickly spied another dispirited squad falling back, retreating away from the blizzard of cold blood and impaling icicles blowing in from the west, its conjuror a terrifying maniac in Kevlar and an '80s serial-killer hockey mask. Clyde followed the path of this retreating party, wanting to cut them down before they could regroup with the larger force creating the rampart near the portal.

Clyde checked on Kev, seeing that he, too, had spotted this enemy force moving down the aisle of crates towards Clyde's position. With tight, precise movements, inspecting every corner with their rifles, the nearing mercenaries didn't think to glance upwards at the overhead catwalk, passing right beneath it to enter the main body of the warehouse.

Unholstering his pistol, Clyde dropped down into the middle of them, and Kev's timing worked in perfect synchronicity. The moment Clyde's boots hit the ground, so did the magazine clips of the whole squad. Each of the guards stared down at their lost ammo like they had all dropped a fat wad of hundred-dollar bills down a drain. Clyde rose up from his landing, unloading barks of lead, pulping the heads of the first two. A third rushed Clyde from behind, attempting to club the back of his head with the empty rifle. With a smooth single motion, Clyde ducked and stepped backwards in a forty-five-degree angle, the rifle stock grazing the hair on his neck, and reared up right behind the clubber, placing a round straight through his brain stem. The arcing slice of another empty rifle curved towards his jaw, but Clyde got his hands up and parried it away with a soft vibrational push of his empty left hand, then squeezed the trigger in his right, piercing a hole through the assailant's throat. The guard fell to his knees in gurgling shock. A part of Clyde knew he had gone cold inside, the rational civilian part of him hiding from the natural killer that sleeps in everyone. Deeper in some than in others.

He sensed more movement at his back. The last of the empty-rifle team, disregarding any futile attempt at a swift, skull-crushing bludgeoning, took a smooth step backwards to create some space and chose to drop his rifle and grab for his semi-automatic handgun. With an agile shuffle step, Clyde closed the short distance and kicked out like a mule, the impact knocking the wind out of the guard, who was still in the middle of bringing up his pistol's iron sight. Clyde spun and fired a shot straight through the crown of the winded, doubled-over soldier. The visual was ghastly, threatening to repeat itself over and over again in Clyde's quiet moments. But again, Clyde swiped it away, refusing to allow himself to think about what he had just done. Kev was right. These were amoral killers, and this wasn't the time to go soft. Looking right, he found Kev slamming the heads of three guards together, their bodies collapsing into a muddle of tangled limbs.

Then something large and dark growled through the portal gate with frightening speed, flying down the ramp and narrowly missing the troops stationed at the threshold. It was a Humvee, hauling behind it an attached trailer bed chained up with some bulky metal contraption. Either through chance or intention, the Humvee was on course with Clyde. Kev reacted instinctively, sending a wave of air up underneath the roaring chassis and flipping the vehicle into a fatal spin, the engine still revving and the tires trying to find traction in mid-air. The armored machine crashed through one of the concrete supports in an explosion of dust and stone chips, landing on its roof and sliding on a bed of sparks into a stack of old crates, toppling them all about the vehicle.

Standing at the humming edge of life and death, the soldiers abandoned their post and charged over into the Null, having received some signal for assistance, or perhaps believing that hell itself might be temporarily safer. Clyde and Kev were watching their retreat when Rose burst into view from their right. She was unmarked and carrying a forklift truck over her head. With incredible power, she hurled the tons of metal towards the fleeing personnel on the platform, which made an unsightly mess of the slowest of them before crashing through the rail, bumping and banging onto the concrete floor on the other side. There was scant time for Clyde and Rose's quick reunion.

'There he is!' Kev exclaimed, pointing somewhere into the Null.

Rose didn't need her comm channel to hear his words; she was close enough to the portal and Kev to see who he was referring to. Konstantin Kozlov. The pair of them took off with a burst of speed, straight up the ramp and over into Death's domain.

Clyde wanted to shout after him, to tell Kev to wait, to not go in there. It was far too late. He ran after them, his gaze bouncing between the looming portal and the west side of the warehouse to check if Ace was inbound. The portal was fast becoming incoherent, becoming just another giant dirty window in this terrible place, the world beyond losing all focus and clarity within the dark, lashing sandstorm. After another couple of seconds, the gate constricted into nonexistence, like an eye into a darker universe blinking closed.

Clyde dropped into a slow jog, then stopped, and was left staring at a sandy ramp that now led to nowhere except the brick wall at the rear of this smoky building. He could feel the throb in his head starting up again, the binding thread to Kev stirring about like a snagged fishing line. He had pulled him back once, somehow. Could he do it again? How? How did he do it last time? It was automatic.

He quickly checked that none of the weakening exchanges of battle were being directed at him and squeezed his eyes shut, trying to imagine dragging Kev back here through the folds of that dead realm's membrane. His fists clenched, his mouth uttering a primitive language of struggle and want.

Kev wasn't coming. He was fighting the beckoning, turning it into a tug of war.

Whoever that guy in the funky armor was, Kev and Rose had deemed him important enough to throw themselves into that gullet of doom and despair. Clyde unclenched his eyes, feeling the first blurry sting of a tear welling in his eye. Whether he could communicate along the wire or not, he sent out a plea to Kev, simple, obvious, but no less powerful. *Please be careful.* Clyde couldn't lose him over there; there would be no return for Kev should that place destroy his soul. He thought of Ramaliak walking him through the deepest tier of the Median and tried not to think about Kev's soul thread blackening into lifeless string, a singed fiber in a great, vibrant blanket.

A bullet whizzed past Clyde's nose. He crouched, looking around. He found the shooter over by some crates to his left, busy holding down cover fire in two directions. It was Hourglass, not CSS; one of the agents fighting alongside Ace. Clyde remembered whose armor he was wearing and considered removing it. Both options were terrible. He kept the armor and gave the Hourglass agent a not-too-friendly push, just enough telekinetic oomph to put him on his ass while he slipped away.

A metallic bang shuddered the airwaves behind Clyde. He spun around to face it quickly, readying himself, sliding behind the cover of a column and checking how many rounds were left in his magazine. The bang came again, harder, more insistent this time. It was coming from the Humvee that had torn through the warehouse like a multi-ton missile, demolishing a column like a toothpick. But the vehicle was on its roof now, going nowhere. Clyde quickly allowed his eye to shoot over to his right, to the west side of the building, where he hoped Ace and a few Hourglass agents were mopping up the last of the resistance. The passenger door of the Humvee blasted from its hinges like it was spring-loaded, flying across half of the warehouse before crashing into the large, thick tire of an empty armored truck. Clyde had flicked a switch internally, focusing on the perceived threat ahead of him and not the problem of his missing friend. He stared down the iron sights, spying the ripped-open side of the Humvee, his steady finger resting on the trigger. Something small was thrown from the vehicle. A spent shell casing. The spent full-metal-jacket casing unexpectedly burst into a noisy emission of gas, quickly enveloping the immediate area in a cloak of obfuscation. Beneath the blue lights the gas resembled frigid air pouring down from a snow-capped mountain. Clyde threw his left arm over his nose and mouth, his right hand keeping the gun ready. He had anticipated the vapors to be acrid, incapacitating, perhaps even deadly, the thrower prepared to go out in a blaze of toxic glory. But apart from the limiting effects on vision, the swirling weight of gas delivered no other harm. Then the screams of pain and soul-wrenching grief started up, a deafening cacophony of gunfire and world-rattling heavy artillery, the atmosphere-shearing whoosh of jets carving up the sky overhead, and more of the weeping and shrieks of innocents caught in a bloodshed they didn't ask for and were too powerless to prevent. Weeping children, pleading mothers, and death grunts of fathers. The sounds of rape and murder.

Clyde went cold inside, soul-sick and needing to put an end to the audible horrors. None of these appalling sound effects were from the current climax of this battle. This he knew, but he had no definitive answers as to where they were emanating from. Was it part of the smoke? That empty shell lying on the cracked cement like a conqueror's token of victory?

Clyde took his face from the crook of his left arm and crouched low. The Humvee was a shadowy mass in the rolling plumes. A dark figure bolted from the vehicle in a sprinter's crouch, a black leopard robed in the circulating mass of smoke. A chill ran down Clyde's spine, his stricken gaze sweeping about him in a full circle. The cries of victims made him want to drop to his knees and bury his head.

The obscured figure sprung out from Clyde's right, and a shock of white light flashed through his brain as something heavy hit him above his right ear. With his knees buckling and his balance gone, it was like being backed over by a van. He went sprawling, his pistol scattering across the hard ground, tendrils of bluish smoke seeming to claw it away from his eager hands. Scrabbling to face his ambusher, he watched the hidden soldier materialize from the wailing smoke, entering their small circle of clarity, the gas trapping them both in a lazy but robust cyclone.

The soldier raised a closed fist, shaking it, the sound of more used shell casings jangling together, each one housing another of his battle-ravaged memories, of black-ops slaughter from different corners of the globe. Lieutenant Castor listened to the music of his warfare and took a deep breath, savoring the lungful. He dropped another shell, letting it bounce once and roll over to Clyde. Clyde sprang to his feet with a push, stepping away from it as if it were radioactive. He hadn't noticed it before, for it had occurred so fast, but before the next wave of screams and pleas and brain-rattling explosions burdened him, there was a split-second flash of a figure rising up from the brass jacket; it was a memory of the animal standing before him, a memory of his younger self, muddied and bloodied from killing. The memory-man was gone in a blink; he had led his awful sensory assault onto his target, and his tour of duty was over.

Clyde snarled, trying to force out the audible atrocities, and gave the real Castor a look of total disgust and hatred. They were ten feet apart, but that didn't matter for Clyde. Summoning his reserved telekinetic energy, Clyde spun on the spot with a head-high round kick, the trauma-bombs whipping from Castor's hand as the ghostly extension of Clyde's strike covered the distance to hit him. Castor looked mildly amused at the trick, his eyes becoming black and his grin contemptible. He pulled a hooked blade from his belt, good for gutting, and wove it through the air as if orchestrating the symphony of remembered terror and pain.

Clyde waved him on. Castor charged. Clyde shadow-boxed, a fluid flurry of fists batting the air, but nevertheless, they each impacted upon Castor, knocking dents into his ribs and torso. Staggered, grunting, and winded, the sadist still hustled forth, intending to glide his half-moon blade into Clyde's femoral artery. Waiting for the lieutenant to get within physical striking distance, Clyde sidestepped and pushed out with both palms, the pulse of energy blasting into the flank and shoulder of Castor, launching him fifteen feet away, where he carved a man-shaped corridor through the swirling smoke screen, bouncing and rolling into a heap. Castor was quickly on all fours, his gray eyes like storm fronts, shaking the fireworks from his head.

Tensing his palm and pushing outwards, Clyde's eyes narrowed, surprised by the physical durability of this butcher's resistance. A great pressure was bearing down on Lieutenant Castor's neck, forcing it sideways into a rotation that threatened to break his cervical column. With a grunt, spittle dripping from his bottom lip, he proved to be capable of further considerable strength, fighting against the torque, the vertebral grinding sensation ceasing by slow degrees.

Clyde used the soundtrack of sobs and begs of non-combatants to push him on. He moved closer; even in the poor light he watched the vessels and tendons bulge in Castor's tough, wiry neck. Too much resistance, and Clyde felt his own strength waning. Gasping with the effort, his arm shaking, he quit the battle of physical and ethereal strength, spotting his sidearm lying unattended within the smoky gloom. With his outstretched hand he pulled the pistol out from the screaming smoke, feeling it slap into his palm. Nice and solid. Castor made it back to his feet just in time to have his head snapped back by a single neat round of hot lead. As he fell to his knees, limp, the smoky walls of unsanctioned fascist slaughter dissipated into nothingness. Clyde couldn't control his anger. It shook him to his core. He stomped over to the prone Castor and put another round in the back of his head. Better safe than sorry.

He was still trying to get a hold on his hate for this piece of murderous amoral shit when he felt a cold breeze prickle his skin. Then a voice at his back made him flinch. 'Good of you to stop by, rook.' Clyde turned to see the big guy, face obscured by his hockey mask, his number 9 hockey jersey over his tactical uniform, and a chilled cosmos of icy particles encompassing his right fist. Behind Ace, two Hourglass agents were scanning the immediate area and calling in to HQ. 'But wrong dress code.' Ace poked him in the chest, and Clyde was reminded again of the enemy armor he was sporting. 'Agent Higgins almost blew your head off.'

'Kev and Rose, they jumped in.' Clyde couldn't hide the panic from his voice.

Ace slid his mask up and huffed out his chest. He looked like he was taking a breather after a rigorous third period. 'Then I guess we should go in there and get them.' Clyde was going to ask how, or just unload a deluge of other questions, but Ace was too good at playing the guiding coach. 'The local boys will have this place on lockdown in ten minutes.' Ace nodded at the surviving agents standing ten feet away, confirming the kills of the nearby enemy combatants. 'They'll chopper us back to the jet.'

The jet? Clyde wanted to take a swing at something. There was no time for a two-hour flight back to Indigo Mesa. They had to get over to the Null, and now!

'Come on, I think it's time you meet Trujillo.'

39

KONSTANTIN STOPPED MID-STRIDE, CLUTCHING AT his chest, his face red and sweaty above his sand-blasted beard. The rocky slope was right there. So near, so far. He was wracked with pain, his master tearing him up from within, a sharp carving sensation in his chest, sending his new settlers fluttering about the honeycomb like a hundred startled birds at the dark presence waking up amongst them. The armor's suppression of the afflicted Arkhitektor was lessening in the close proximity to his poisoner, giving him strength to challenge its bonds. Konstantin dug at the grit in the wrinkles around his eyes and forced himself to keep moving, pushing on towards the slope while maintaining the distance between himself and Vor Dushi. He kept his head on a swivel, making sure none of the CSS, or Mortis, were watching him.

Wait... where was Mortis? The visibility was appalling.

Agua's shouts were stolen by the gale, his arms waving in the back-up teams from the warehouse's jump point. Lieutenant Fenwick was securing the chains on the last soul cage and readying to beat a hasty retreat under the captain's orders, the driver already grumbling the Humvee's engine like a hunting dog eager with the scent of its quarry. Lieutenant Castor had already managed to escape this place with a cargo full of souls soon to be forced into wearing chains in service of another. Konstantin wouldn't allow Fenwick to take out another cageful. He bent down and stole a combat shotgun from the severed arm of the nearest dead soldier and helped himself to the man's last grenade while he was at it. None of the living mercenaries seemed to notice or care; their attentions were still on the seven-headed terror chewing them up one by one. Konstantin was thinking on how best to take out Fenwick's Humvee. Try to time it correctly and lob the grenade towards the keyhole, where it might erupt underneath the passing chassis? He had hoped Vor Dushi and its minions would have made shorter work of the cages, but the CSS were efficient in their roles.

A shape started to rise up not fifteen feet from Konstantin's position. It was Kuznetsov's head and shoulders, sprouting up from the uneven ground, his face full of promise. And that was all Konstantin needed, finding a resurgence in his will to hold on against the Arkhitektor's revolt. He had to get down there.

A brilliant sheen of emerald light briefly turned the walls of spiraling dust into dirty jade, like green lightning charging through the belly of a cloud. Konstantin ducked as a precaution. It was Agua, letting loose another flurry of his energy-cluster bombs, but where was it coming from? Konstantin believed himself to be the target until he tracked their jeweled trajectory towards the silhouette of Vor Dushi, its red eyes piercing the dark veils. The emerald hornets hit like a miniature carpet bomb, a series of violent concussions kicking up shockwaves and gouts of rock and earth. The assault continued, Agua stepping closer, face angled down from the storm but still managing to sharpen his aim, moving towards the demon, his jaws locked in anger. The relentless blasts had Vor Dushi staggering backwards, almost falling but catching itself, yet still stumbling closer to the edge of the cliff. Konstantin paused to watch, transfixed by Agua's attack.

The Humvee's headlights lit up, its driver trying to make sense of the brown-out, aiming for the hellish red outline of the giant keyhole. Konstantin watched it speed and bounce towards the portal and pulled the pin on the grenade. The winds were furious, and Konstantin clinically wondered if the gusts would spoil his throw, maybe even accidentally destroying his human form. He watched the Humvee and its soul cage race from right to left and found his moment, lobbing the grenade underhand to try and minimize the wind's effects. The element was on his side, stealing the grenade from his hand and carrying it towards the keyhole. It landed in a small depression of sand, right under Fenwick's passing Humvee. The lieutenant saw all this, diving out of the vehicle and bouncing painfully across the ground. He was spared the rip of heat and shrapnel, but the blast destroyed the trailer and the soul cage, its residents robbed of their false asylum and scattered once more to the four winds.

Mortis seemed to rise up out of nowhere, hidden by the storm one minute, there the next. Rendered mute by the storm, Konstantin watched his furious pantomime, arms flailing at the loss of a second soul cage. Konstantin was desperate to hurry down the slope towards the cove, to find Kuznetsov and Lim and the answers they had found.

But Mortis wasn't far away. And he was distracted by his tantrum. But with Agua and Fenwick still breathing, Konstantin knew he would have to make this quick. Without time to debate, he hurried over to the rage-frothing Mortis, drawing the combat knife he had retrieved from the dead soldier. He could have shot-gunned the man in the back of the head, but he had a better punishment in mind. Appearing like a sand wraith beside Mortis, Konstantin seized his pale, bony wrist, twisted the taller, wiry-framed man around, and swiftly sliced off the tip of the key for his wide-open doorway. Over the howling wind, Konstantin could barely hear Mortis' scream. He saw the portal begin to flicker a few times like a scrambled TV reception, but before the warehouse blipped out of sight, he noticed two unknowns enter; a short but powerfully built female soldier, and a male ghost. Konstantin didn't stick around to find out who they were; he smacked the base of the knife handle into Mortis' head and watched him drop to his knees.

'You can die here,' Konstantin shouted to him over the storm.

Then he ran, ignoring the painful stop-start crush working its way about his torso like a living stone seeking an exit.

A trail of earth kicked up all about him. He now had the full attention of Fenwick and the reinforcements. He ran for the slope down to the caverns, the armor not aiding in his flight. As he ran, he stared off to the left, just in time to see Captain Agua do what Konstantin and none of the Rising Path had managed; he sent Vor Dushi teetering over the cliff, down far, far below into the waters of the Eidolon Trench. The fall of his great nemesis filled Konstantin with doubt. If it were dead, he wouldn't be able to get answers from it.

Assuming it had any. Assuming he even could.

He didn't dwell on it. Kuznetsov must have found something worthwhile down there. Still, he was disappointed it wasn't he who had avenged his sect. The pain subsided in his chest, the infection boiling within, the Arkhitektor congealing into a stagnant surrender.

He stopped at the crest of the slope, knowing that Agua would turn and spot him before he made it down. Pumping the shotgun, Konstantin blasted a slug at Agua but narrowly missed, more grit compromising his aim. He racked another round and fired. A bubble of green light was encompassing Agua's arms, the explosive payload charging up. But Konstantin's second lead slug stole a cry of pain from him, becoming muffled by the storm. The green glow went out, but grunts of anger still carried through the gusts. Konstantin had hit him, but how severe the damage was, he couldn't tell.

The war started up again in his wake, but he wasn't the target this time. It seemed like that unknown pair of newcomers were. He may not know their purpose, but Konstantin wished them both luck, and quickly but carefully made his way down the rocky slopes. Agua and Mortis would be out for blood if they survived this unexpected fresh attack.

The giant's mouth of a cavern lay not too far ahead.

The last of the Dead Divers made his sure-footed descent.

40

KEV KEPT HIS HEAD ABOUT him as he passed over the threshold into the Null, trying not to become overwhelmed by the weird, the wonderful, and the terrible tableau unfolding before him. The scathing dust storm covered most of it, with only pockets of clearer vision opening and then closing in manic rhythm: the dismembered bodies of soldiers dead or dying; a giant shadowy serpentine form undulating high in the sky, its tenebrous form bobbing its way towards the skirmish playing out around the cliff; and the mysterious beam of light passing along a series of strange relay tower structures rising up from the horizon and the distant sea. Nexus channels, Kev recalled from the *Equinox*'s diagram. Soul pipelines. The angle of that pulsing light beam reached across the water and closed in near the cliff, where it slowly declined from Kev's current vantage point, ducking down behind the cliff edge. That was the direction in which Konstantin had hurried off. Kev barely managed to make out the tall, carnival-barker form of Mortis, clutching a hand to his chest and chasing after Konstantin, who, if Kev wasn't mistaken or fooled by the compromised vision, had been briefly surrounded by a swath of small green lights. It was a lot to take in so quickly, especially with a bullet wound chewing away at his focus.

He sailed down the ramp to the rocky ground, shoulder-to-shoulder with Rose, the pair of them catching the attention of the troops they had chased over here. The squad turned on them in surprise, but Rose was too close for them to have much of a shot. She dragged one soldier close to her as if he weighed no more than a stuffed animal and launched him into the others with such force that multiple broken bones and concussions would be the least of their problems. The one or two who were still conscious and able to get up from under the heap of armored bodies should have played dead. Kev willed their necks to break, and they twisted around as easily as those of chickens. Leaving the fresh pile of raiders in their wake, Kev and Rose hurried through a confused jumble of hulking trucks and Humvees, seeking a path towards their targets and hoping not to get turned around in this blizzard of dead skin. Breaking out from the small huddle of vehicles into a clearing, a giant shadow passed over them as though from some passing aerial titan. Kev stared up at what looked like an old, haunted locomotive with a piranha's head, undulating and scuttling through the air a hundred feet above them, concealed mostly in the dust.

'The dust storm, it's letting up,' Rose said.

'How can you tell?' Kev asked.

She held a hand up, the hard scrubbing grit starting to ease. 'I can feel it.'

Unknown to either of them, Vor Dushi had stirred up the dunes of corpse ash into a fury of blinding confusion, but the creator had taken a long fall.

'Ignore it,' Rose said of the sky eel, pouring her stamina into her huge quads, running as fast as a cheetah across the uneven plain. Kev whipped through the dead air beside her, eyes locked on the winding, rocky path fifty yards ahead and not the curious horror gliding above them.

A shadowy human bulldozer charged out of the falling curtain of dust, hitting Rose with a dropped shoulder and sending her sprawling like a tumbleweed down a dirt road. Fenwick. His blonde ponytail was dark with dust, same as his beard, shades.

Two more CSS triggermen appeared, flanking their lieutenant. They looked normal enough, but the raising of their rifles made Kev think of further holes being torn into his spirit form. Shit, he was tired. With a mental command, he took control of their hands, forcing them to turn their rifles on each other. Pressing their trigger fingers down, he unloaded a three-shot burst into each of them, aiming high. Floating the rifles from their limp hands, he held them out before him, scanning the open area for Rose and the meathead. Even with the storm diminishing, he couldn't see where they had gone. But he heard them just fine. The jackhammer slamming of incredible punches and kicks ripping dents into trucks—they had both wound up amidst the vehicles, trading blows powerful enough to make impressions in steel.

Kev watched a truck rock on its suspension so much it almost tipped over. The flying eel thing was continuing its territorial pass of the area, not straying too far from the nexus channel. He ignored it for now and flew over to Rose to give assistance. Alighting between two of the rocking trucks, he found Rose slamming knees into the bigger guy before grabbing him by the throat and bouncing him off the high armored sides of both vehicles. Fenwick grabbed the crushing hand on his throat and twisted her wrist, locking her arm out and forcing her down onto one knee. Kev aimed both rifles at the lieutenant, lining his sights so as not to risk hitting Rose, afraid that a misfire would not only hurt her but might kill Sarge, Barros, or Darcy. He squeezed the triggers. Both rifles clicked empty.

Rose snarled up at Kev. 'I don't need air support. I got this.' Planting her free hand on the coarse, dry ground, she hopped up and used her legs to scissor-sweep Fenwick's own legs out from under him, stealing his dominant position and regaining her trapped hand. 'Get after Mortis and Kozlov,' she ordered. 'I'll catch up.'

Kev wasn't about to argue, but he did say one thing before flying off towards the cliff's declivity. 'Heads up.'

Rose looked up from her narrowed letterbox vantage between the two tall trucks, but there was nothing to see except for a strip of empty sky. But her nod assured Kev that she knew of what he warned.

Kev reached the perilous path, spying a giant cove in the Trench's bay. The nexus channel surging forth into the cavern.

Terror gripped his still heart. He had never felt so alive.

. . .

FENWICK LIFTED ROSE over his head with all the showmanship of a pro wrestler and bounced her off the truck's armor. Rose hit the ground with a thud, coughing a cloud of dust. Fenwick didn't stop, his malice matching his demigod strength, and he wound his leg back and kicked Rose in her ribs. The sharp pain was awful. Grunting breathlessly, she protected her side as she mentally assessed the damage. Nothing was broken. Yet. A large hand, built for hard labor and cruelty, gripped Rose's throat and hauled her to her feet, her back rattling the side of the truck.

'You're a damn fine piece, lady. I like my bitches strong. We could have been good together.' Her ribs may not have been broken, but they sure as hell hobbled her. Fenwick sniffed her like a dog. 'But you got the stink of crotch-sniffing betas about you.'

She was struggling to breathe through the thug's squeeze. Fenwick pivoted his hips and threw her like a shot put, her body's arc going for height, not distance, and she impacted only several feet outside the alley of trucks. She got back to her feet, preferring to die that way than on her knees. She could hear the shouts of anger and encouragement from within the command center, the voices of Sarge, Barros, and Darcy becoming a mingled partisan union, pouring more and more of their bitterness into her muscles. She wouldn't let them down. They needed her. She needed them. And only she had the means of giving their strength purpose.

Darcy spoke up again, telling her to watch their six. She knew what he meant; she could practically feel it moving in slowly behind her, gliding through the last of the dust storm: the skeel, readying itself for a bite.

If Fenwick had spotted its presence, he didn't react to it. He was too busy eyeballing Rose. 'What do you say? You think we could make it work, honey?' His lascivious smile showed a larger-than-average canine tooth.

Rose played up her injuries, thinking how much time she had before the eel was upon her. Barros told her it was low to the ground, maybe only four or five feet in the air, as though grazing for sustenance. It had the scent of Rose's three souls.

Fenwick leered over her like a statue of a conqueror. Rose was swift. She released her sore ribs and jumped up to drive the point of her head into his nose. Something definitely broke, and she felt a warm wetness dribble down her forehead. Before the white lights could clear from his vision, she drove a satisfying knee straight into his balls.

The eel was closing in fast.

She gripped Fenwick by his uniform and hauled him in close, whispering into his ear, 'I get bored playing with little boys.' Keeping two good handfuls of his jacket, she dropped down onto her back, pulling him down on top of her but bracing a boot into his stomach for leverage. Rolling onto her shoulders, she flipped him over her, straight into the open tunnel mouth of the skeel.

The huge thing passed over her by only a few feet, blotting out the light of the returning blue sun. It was like lying under a passing convoy of buses. Denied its intended meal, the skeel crashed through the parked trucks like they were empty soup cans and soared upwards into the sky, circling back for another pass. But Rose was already up and running towards the jagged slope.

'Come on,' she called into Sarge's command center with an adrenaline junkie's smirk. 'Let's finish this.'

41

Ace was heavy on the pedal, speeding them both down the darkening desert road. Clyde's eyes were gelled onto the welcoming lights of the Midnight Vulture Diner, coming up on their right. The place looked typically deserted, the L-shaped parking lot an unnecessary concession. There was a hollowness in Clyde, making him feel like an empty bottle. It wasn't the sickness of being forced to kill anymore—that had ceased, which was troubling in itself. No, the unmistakable vacancy in his gut was fear.

A chopper from the New York division—the Madhouse, as Ace had referred to them—had expediently dropped them off at a private air strip, where both he and Ace were jetted west back to Darnell. It had taken less than three hours, but that short, never-ending period had been crammed with sharp, erratic thoughts of Kev and Rose, none of them nice. Kev was already wounded.

Shot! Explain that!

Ace had debriefed Clyde in a bit more detail about the operation during the plane ride. The Russian guy, Konstantin "Gulag" Kozlov, and his cult intrigued him a little, but it was Kev's sudden fascination with the monk that intrigued him most. Obviously, anybody with a hint of sanity would choose heaven over hell, but even with all they'd been through together, Clyde knew Kev to be cynical to a fault. But then, Clyde once more referred to his previous point: after all they'd been through ...

But still, Kev's sudden need to get in front of this crazy monk once more proved to Clyde that Kev was still the master of guarding his deepest thoughts and fears. Clyde had been scared shitless, and confused, and angry at this entire shift in his world since Rose had knocked on their apartment door, but Kev was the one who had stayed loose and casual with his own existential terror, finding curiosity where Clyde only found impositions and threat, and all along Kev had been keeping a tight lid on all his true feelings of terror and the great ever after.

Treating it all glossy and casual, just his call of duty. A need to be needed. Nothing more. No biggie.

'You did good, rook.' Ace's voice went almost undetected in Clyde's reverie. 'That was some stand-up shit you pulled back there. Entering that place with no back-up.'

'Didn't seem to do much good.' They were heading east from Darnell, straight from plane to borrowed jeep with a duffel bag full of supplies borrowed from their own go-stash kept on site. Skidding out from the air base, they drove along an empty restricted road, and it wasn't until Ace took a barely glimpsed fork in the road that the neon box of the diner appeared out of thin air. The Haunted Road, Clyde remembered. He stared out at the passing desert, seeing a few tall and skinny rock formations—approximations of humanity if you looked hard enough—posed along the horizon, a thin layer of purple bleeding along the low, bumpy mountain ridge, the last blood from the dying day.

Hoodoos and their Haunted Road. Director Trujillo and his nowhere diner. 'Quit that mopey shit. Rose and Kev will be fine. This game ain't over yet.'

Sitting there in stolen body armor over his street clothes, damp from battle sweat and nerves, Clyde still felt like he was part of a cavalry about to charge in just in time to see the blood dry in the soil. He had pulled Kev back once without even trying, without knowing how. Why couldn't he do it now? Learning how to perform such an act had never come up with Spector, so just wishing it to happen apparently wasn't the trick. Was Kev somehow resisting him?

'Have you ever lost anybody?' Clyde asked, his voice low.

Ace kept his eyes on the private road, and after a few seconds he nodded. 'My mom.'

'How do you deal with it, knowing where she is?' Silence. Clyde thought he had crossed a line in asking. It wasn't like they ever talked about anything other than training and superficial stuff.

After almost thirty seconds of nothing but the engine drone and the occasional bump in the road, Ace surprised him. His tone was softer and more patient than Clyde had heard before. 'When I still played hockey, I used to lose sleep before any big game. No messin'. I'd watch all the tapes I could find of the kid I'd be expected to throw down with. Often there was no tape. It wasn't like I was in the majors. But those tapes I could find, I'd watch them over and over, then I'd lie in bed staring at my ceiling. But the next night, I'd go out there and do what I had to do. In the moment, I felt great. It's the waiting that fucks you. Because when it was game time, I'd remember that, no matter how it turned out, I was a fighter. We all are. Everybody. I don't give a shit what your background is, where you're from, or how long you've been a vegan. Everybody has fight in them. We're all apes. Some of us just fight in different ways. My mom never had a bad word to say about anybody. You could call her a doormat and,' saying this, Ace looked from the road to Clyde, shrugging a little, 'you wouldn't be wrong.' Eyes back on the road. 'And she was still the toughest person I've ever known. It was cancer that did it, that and a battery-load of related conditions, and yet she remained cheery and hopeful and strong right up until the day she died. Her being over there, if she's still in one piece or not... I know she would have taken it with a "fuck you" and a smile.' A calm silence filled the jeep. The diner was only 300 yards away now. 'I wish I was as tough as she was.'

The jeep nosed off onto another dirt road, heading straight for the Midnight Vulture's lot. 'So Trujillo and these hoodoos send us over there. I can track Kev, but what if we land a thousand miles away from them?'

'Won't be a problem. The hoodoos are amongst the best travel agents this side of the Null.' Ace turned the wheel, taking them off the dusty trail and into the empty lot, parking under a halogen orb. 'Before we go in, I want to say I'm proud of you. And I'm sure your brother and dad would be too.' Clyde felt a confusing mixture of pride and sorrow stirring in his chest. 'But before we start turning into a couple of little pussies, let's get in there and over there.' Ace climbed out of the car and started walking to the diner's entrance. Clyde grabbed the duffel bag full of weaponry and ammo from the footwell and followed.

. . .

THE DINER'S INTERIOR committed to its strange ruse, with red leather booths, chrome stools and matching countertop, jukebox against a cream-colored wall, even the wall recess behind the counter providing a glimpse into the kitchen beyond.

And yet not a single customer, staff member, or fellow Hourglass agent with a cup of coffee or a plate of pancakes.

The jukebox was playing softly, though, some old-timey tune Clyde didn't know. R. Dean Taylor singing about there being a ghost in his house, adding an almost humorous quality to the scene. Clyde couldn't decide if it was an ironic circumstance or an amusing choice selected by a sentient or perhaps haunted jukebox.

He glanced around, the weight of the duffel bag digging the strap into his palm. 'Is Trujillo here?'

Time was almost audible in Clyde's head, each second ticking away with the sound of chopping wood. Ace told him to take a seat at the counter, so Clyde did, hauling his bag up onto the countertop with a heavy clatter of iron and steel. Curious but impatient, he watched Ace and the empty diner, then unzipped the bag and went about loading the semi-automatic handguns and the sub-machine gun; checking the blade, and the few grenades, and the extra clips; fastening it all about his person. Ace hadn't checked anything out of the armory for his own personal use.

When Clyde felt prepared to take on an army, he dropped the empty bag on the floor beside him and noticed that Ace had vanished without a trace. It was only him and the jukebox now. 'Ace?'

No answer.

There was nowhere for Ace to go. He couldn't have slipped behind the bar and entered the kitchen because he would have walked right past Clyde, and he hadn't walked off to the restroom at the far end because Clyde would have caught him in his periphery. 'Ace?' he called again, spinning around, only hearing the music and the soft squeak of his metal stool. Their car, the only car, remained parked outside, right in front of one of the large windows. Empty. The quiet, spotless diner was fast becoming unnerving for Clyde, and he was just about to climb off his stool when—

'Coffee?' The voice was rich and deep. A man in a nicely tailored dark suit was standing behind the bar as though he'd been there all along, fiddling with the coffee maker. His skin was naturally tanned and weathered, his hair short and neat and black as raven feathers, with a sharp nose and eyes like coal. A man whose heritage harked back to the natives of this vast and ancient land. Clyde gently lowered himself back onto his stool, giving another persistent glance about the diner for Ace. The man, dressed like any other government official with a decent salary, was swirling the coffee pot about, the black liquid sloshing around thick and strong. He began pouring some into a white ceramic mug for Clyde.

'Director Trujillo?' Clyde assumed.

The man smiled congenially, but it seemed to state that this wasn't a social visit, despite the hospitality of his coffee. He finished pouring the cup and placed it before Clyde. The scent of it was strong and enticing, but also a little peculiar.

'Mr. Williams.'

'Where's Ace?'

'He's here.'

Clyde was about to glance about again like a lost dog but stopped himself. He didn't want to appear rude to the man who was supposedly capable of helping him, but every passing minute was a twitch of his insides. It had already been a couple of hours, and he couldn't stand wasting time while Kev and Rose were dealing with who-knew-what over in the Null. 'Director Trujillo, sir, with all respect, Ace said he'd called ahead to explain the situation, and I really need to—'

'The situation.' Trujillo nodded, as though considering a small, tricky puzzle. 'You're not an official agent. You're a civilian who, while having received some first-rate training from my best agents, took it upon himself to perform an unsanctioned rescue mission on behalf of your friend.'

Clyde wanted to be polite, but this pointless review of his actions felt counterproductive. 'Look, if you need to take some type of disciplinary action, can you do it later? If you can get me over there—'

'Don't interrupt.' Trujillo's dark eyes hardened, their wisdom and experience immured within stony shells. 'Drink your coffee. Trust me.'

Clyde wanted to object but knew he'd only be creating further stalling actions. He carefully sipped the hot brew, trying not to burn himself. It wasn't a brand he'd pay for; it tasted bitter, with an almost soapy tang. It left a residue on his tongue like a film of moss. 'I admire your tenacity, young man. Ace wasn't wrong. You walked into an unknown situation against unknown odds to help a friend, and here you are, prepared to race in and do it all again.'

Clyde scraped his carpeted tongue along his upper teeth. 'Kev's my best friend. I lost him once.' Clyde forced down another swallow.

'I'm aware,' Trujillo answered, returning the pot to the hot plate. 'And his reason for throwing himself headlong into Erebus is also admirable.'

'The Firmament Needle, and some monk. Konstantin Kozlov, a.k.a. Gulag.'

Trujillo slipped his hands into his pants pockets, appraising the diner about them. 'This is sacred ground. It's been in my family for many generations. My ancestors were part of the Coyotero tribe, Western Apaches. It was they who first encountered the hoodoo while trekking around the rocky tracks of Bosque Peak one dusky evening. The Coyoteros revered the land and the sky, and respected all the creatures that shared them with man. The hoodoo were no exception to this rule, despite their fearsome outward appearance. It took a little time, but my ancestors' reverence emboldened them to approach the hoodoo, who became most active when the sun was bowing out and the moon was supreme. They discovered that the hoodoo could communicate with them, only after they had earned their trust. The hoodoo are timeless guardians, tasked with keeping watch between the barriers separating the living and the dead. To earn their trust is a great honor. Such secrets were closely kept for a long time, passing quietly amongst our tribe from generation to generation, but only to those deemed wise enough, and noble enough, to keep this knowledge private.'

'And together you created some sneaky hole in reality to hide from outsiders. But why a diner?'

Trujillo smiled a little. 'I'm of a generation that grew up around diners such as this. Since I was a boy, I've always enjoyed their atmosphere. People passing through, coming and going, stopping for a brief respite before continuing on their journeys. It seemed quite adventurous. So it felt almost poetic to design this bubble in such a style. Perhaps I'm a little sentimental in that way.'

'So how did the government find you?' Clyde's heart was tripping along, its rhythm slowly increasing tempo like a drum. He took a breath and held it, not wanting to pay too much attention to it should it exacerbate further. Was it the coffee? He was beginning to feel himself slip into a soft trance, loosening his tension. Had he been drugged?

'Because I *am* the government. Ex-military and CIA. I communed with the hoodoo, suggesting ways that my unique position could use government funding and discretion to produce an outfit that could assist in the ongoing surveillance and protection of the barriers. They agreed. There were already others functioning in such capacities throughout the world. Forming Hourglass made sense for the security of this nation. We've come a long way from teepees. Just doing our part to police the threats whose actions could create an imbalance between the sides. Let's just say that the power players of Erebus are not something you would want to antagonize. Things could get... unmanageable. But that's as much as I can divulge without breaching classified information.'

Clyde was feeling like he needed to move about but was scared he'd fall down. His eyes felt unfocused for a few seconds, his breathing heavy, but the spell quickly began to wear off. 'Where's Ace?'

'Right here, rook.' Ace seemed to pop into existence, slouching on a stool next to him, his goalie mask pushed up onto the top of his head, one big arm leaning on the counter.

Clyde blinked away the drowsiness and gazed suspiciously at Ace and Trujillo. 'What was in that coffee?'

'You want to pull your friends out of Erebus, don't you?' Trujillo asked. Clyde couldn't tell if his eyes were playing a final lingering trick, but Trujillo seemed to be slowly fading away. Clyde nodded firmly, the small arsenal he was equipped with taking up space in his thoughts again. 'Then that coffee is what you need to help you travel through the hourglass. I'll see you downstairs.' Trujillo had completely erased himself from the diner. Clyde looked at Ace in confusion.

'Okay, rook.' Ace punched him in the shoulder. 'You were curious about the hoodoos. Let's go see them.'

· · ·

THERE WAS A lift in the kitchen. A large chrome disk that would have looked at home on a 1950s flying saucer. There was some other form of dimensional trickery going on to make such a large platform fit within the confines of the Midnight Vulture. The long descent was cool, the air invigorating Clyde, prickling his cheeks and arms, the soft white footlights only adding to his impression that he was some Martian arrival descending onto an unsuspecting planet. The elevator came out into a huge chamber, a secret government vault of steel built into the smoothly hewn red rock. In the center of the chamber stood a gigantic hourglass, at least three stories tall and surrounded by bipedal hoodoo, moving their stone limbs with stone joints. They all lacked faces, only possessing smooth, blank slabs resting atop pebbled necks and rocky shoulders, but they seemed to quietly watch as Clyde and Ace stepped off the elevator platform. Clyde could not help gawking at the stilt-limbed stone sentinels ringing the giant glass timer. The white lights recessed in the chamber's metal floor streaked them in angular shadow and hot, glaring definition. As Clyde got nearer, he noticed that he had to reassess his last observation, for one of them did have a face, a crudely chiseled countenance. This one was much smaller than the others, human-sized. It also had a suit, streaked here and there with reddish chalk dust. Trujillo, in the hardened flesh.

Ace stepped up and greeted the rock giants with a respectful nod, then did his own impression of a quiet and disciplined statue. Clyde snapped out of his boyish wonder routine; he was a soldier now, somehow. How had that happened? A soldier who had spent the best part of a month dealing with crazier things than stone people. And he had killed people a few hours ago. A bunch of them. He stopped before Trujillo, his eyes taking in the sculpted details. The director pretty much looked as he had upstairs in the diner, only this version of him was more like a rough, unfinished effigy. Only the eyes remained human.

'How do you feel, Agent Williams?' Trujillo's voice was the same, a detail that Clyde was pondering when he realized abruptly that he'd been addressed as "Agent." His surprise must have shown on his face, for Trujillo went on to explain. 'Ace informed me that you handled yourself impeccably well at that warehouse. Trial by fire. If that doesn't qualify as agent material, then I don't know what does. I'd say it's at least cause for probationary status.' His mouth remained quite flexible, but there was definitely some slight rigidity about Trujillo's jaws and tongue. 'I'd say the apple doesn't fall far from the tree.'

'You know my dad... or-or my brother, sir?'

The director glanced at the hoodoo for a brief moment, then gently shook his head at Clyde, his neck and shoulders scraping together like flint shards. 'I'm afraid not, but I've seen their records. They both served with distinction. Good, brave soldiers.' All Clyde knew was redacted information and vague platitudes. Did Trujillo know the full stories regarding their deaths? 'It came as little surprise to find you have such potential. You could be a great addition to this agency if you wish to be.'

Clyde didn't move, he barely even blinked, but thoughts of struggling away endlessly to create art that nobody would likely ever see filled him with a tired resignation. He loved his art, and he always would, but now was not the time for any long-term career decisions. 'If I get back in one piece, I'll make my decision, sir.'

Trujillo seemed happy enough with that answer. Some of the hoodoos at the back began to silently shift about, performing an unintelligible ritual around the giant hourglass, looking like pious worshippers parading around a giant totem. The hourglass began to turn over in the air, a system of hydraulics smoothly rotating it, the gentle movement throwing a giant shadow across the chamber and stirring the air with a strong whoosh. Clyde guessed there must be half of Brighton Beach in the giant glass timer. Its shape made him think of the infinity symbol, life into death into life. *Is there a true end? Maybe the spirits who perish in the Null just end up somewhere else, their ghostly vessels taxed by some other powers-that-be.*

'The sand in here,' Trujillo commented, 'is ground down from the original settler hoodoos. Even the glass itself is formed from their superheated rock. The minerals are unique and allow for passage into Erebus. The coffee you drank contained a small amount of it, not to grant you passage per se, but to help the hoodoo and me keep track of you when you're over there. Think of it as a type of nanite GPS. When the time's up, we will know how to find you so we can exfiltrate.' Clyde glanced over at Ace, a question forming on his lips. 'Agent Tremblay drank his coffee long ago. It's a one-stop fix. Agent Hadfield had hers with two sugars.' Trujillo's rigid mouth didn't move much, but humor was evident in his dark eyes. 'Diplomacy is a delicate business, but our agents do have roles to play over in Erebus from time to time. Our role is largely supervisory, a two-way customs and immigration, but for any issues of trans-existence crime such as this, the situation demands a more hands-on approach. With the minerals in your blood, we'll be able to guide you and Ace straight to Agent Hadfield's position.'

Clyde was very relieved to hear this, having spent the last few hours quietly stressing about having to rely on grasping along his and Kev's soul thread in a hostile world where everything would view him like a meal on legs. 'Do we only have until the sand runs out? An hour?'

The hoodoos had gathered closer, their footsteps surprisingly gentle for their size, but still providing booms like distant thunder on the natural stone ground. They raised their hands up, arms flexed at their elbows, imitating a meditative pose. Their large, rough stone fingers began to grind together. The sound created a soft, warm buoyancy in Clyde's head, almost like a soothing itch.

'For safety reasons, we operate in hourly intervals. If you need more time, and we deem it necessary, we'll spin the hourglass again,' Trujillo explained. That entrancing sound continued, reminding Clyde of two marbles scraping together in his boyish hand, only on a much louder scale.

Clyde was beginning to feel like he was losing mass, becoming insubstantial in this physical world. Ace had snuck up on him and slapped him on the back. 'Okay, rook. This is it. Sudden death.' He pulled his mask down, getting into character.

The hoodoos continued to rub their blocky fingers and thumbs together hypnotically, almost creating sparks.

'Good luck, agents.' Trujillo watched Clyde and Ace as they dimmed from this realm like dying lights, cast into the space between differing states of existence, and were guided straight through from the stormy shores of the Fading Light's outer reaches to the deep caverns of the Eidolon Trench.

42

For several hours, Konstantin had walked through the cavern in a state of awe and revulsion, wishing he shared his escorts' ability to drift through wall, floor, and rocky obstruction. With the patience of saints, they guided his slow, human progress. The size of the watery cavern was staggering, its ceiling hidden high above in shadow, with only the multitudes of glistening stalactite points to prove that there actually was a ceiling somewhere up there; and stalagmites jutted upwards like wet, calcified teeth from the cave's bottom jaw. Such characteristics were unremarkable, only mineral deposits, but the great heaping mounds of souls that crowded the place warped any semblance of normality the cavern might have otherwise presented. Every soul was pitiful in its confused mewling, bound in slick membranes like phosphorescent grubs. Their feeble song of sorrow made Konstantin want to retch, and the persistent draft of air carrying its unpleasant aroma redolent of old, dry mucous only exacerbated his unease.

But even the horrors of this cold, damp lair couldn't slow him down, not with Mortis and Agua close behind. Because where else could they go? What else could they do but follow him down here?

He was led by Kuznetsov and Lim, the ambient light of the soul sludge helping to guide his footing across the uneven ground. The plumbing of the soul nexus had dipped deep into the water at the cave's threshold, moving down into the subterranean bedrock of the cavern; where it ended, he could only guess. Konstantin couldn't fend off the grim thoughts of how these embryonic hills had formed. Had these souls somehow leaked out of the underground pipe, rising up through the rock like damp and coagulating in these tunnels? It could be that Vor Dushi had manually bled them from the pipe and left them lying around for sustenance.

Konstantin rounded the widest bend in the tunnel yet, and what he found at the end stunned him. There it was, in all of its majestic and macabre splendor: Vor Dushi's sanctum.

The residence of the House's lackey was a strange structure, the unorthodox geometry of it making it more resemble a huge cube—no, an oblong, one that had been heated during construction and then twisted slightly, molded by careless, inexperienced hands into a warped tower. The exterior walls of the building were entirely plated with filigreed metal panels, a bas-relief of prehistoric hieroglyphs catching the light of the luminescent water that had carved a huge moat around this chthonic dwelling. Konstantin couldn't see a way across the moat. He peered over the edge of the tunnel floor into the pool, seeing it as a tributary from the trench outside, running deep into this spiteful cave. All these engulfed souls and the blighted waters, were these the namesake of the local powers? The source of the Fading Light?

With his refugee cargo continuing to turn restlessly within him, surging about like passengers on a storm-tossed freighter, he found it hard to focus on performing a risk analysis for what lay ahead and the actions he was about to take. This was a good thing, he decided; after all this, he couldn't allow fear of failure to stall him. Kuznetsov floated over to him, explaining that there was a high ridge of black stone that formed a cloistered bridge over the water around the other side of the building.

'Did you enter?' Konstantin asked Kuznetsov, his stamina fading but his old, weary eyes shining with a cautious optimism.

Kuznetsov challenged the infernal building with a stare. 'I thought it best to get you down here first. Before blood was spilt.'

Without further delay, they started round the edge of the moat.

Reaching the bridge, Konstantin was almost impressed by the sophistication of its architecture, the enormous arcades below it further reminding him that the Soul Thief and its masters were not mindless animals.

It wasn't until he was halfway across the bridge's black paving stones that the pain skewered his chest again. The Arkhitektor, awoken once more. Was Vor Dushi still alive?

An accidental scattering of stones caught his ear, the scrape and clatter cutting through the endless mourning of trapped souls. The careless footstep had come from behind him, beyond the bridge. Mortis and Captain Agua. Even if Vor Dushi had somehow swum back to its abode, about to cut off Konstantin's entry, Konstantin knew he couldn't stay here, pinned between enemies. He had to take a chance, one way or another.

Turning away from the direction of his pursuers, he caught Kuznetsov and Lim's attention and wearily continued on towards the looming sinister structure.

Leaving the bridge behind, he saw the large entrance into the structure, not a door exactly but an aperture within the off-kilter façade. No door? No clear way of preventing intrusion? Konstantin felt a knife-twist of uncertainty. This was too easy. Was this a result of arrogance on behalf of the Soul Thief? A rationalization grounded in the fact that few beings, few humans, had ever made it this far in, and therefore security was not crucial in such an unforgiving place? Or maybe Vor Dushi had not sealed this construction in its desire to force an engagement with the intruders.

Behind him, surging beneath the long bridge, the lap and gurgle of the ill-colored river continued its flowing music within the damp cavern, but it wasn't enough to drown out the interminable wailing of the multitudes piled high and shrink-wrapped in that unholy goo, and stuck all about the chamber and its ridges. The dire scene gave Konstantin the impetus to stride through the high and wide aperture in the necropolis' wall. With his knife held tight, and Kuznetsov and Lim flanking him, he entered the baffling architecture.

Only a creature such as Vor Dushi could call such a place as this home. The huge chamber was lit by four white-hearted blue flames, each burning away atop a ten-foot-tall pillar of clumpy mineral and arranged in the room's four listing corners. The whole structure was significantly taller than the view from the bridge had led Konstantin to believe. It was a spiraling tower with no visible ceiling, drilling upwards into the cove. How far underground had he traveled? The stone slabbing of the chamber floor was quartered by four lanes of metal gridding, the half-moon shapes cut into the metal panels providing a glimpse into the shining, rushing waters far below his feet. All four lanes met at a central point in the chamber, a huge circular well ringed by several metal tiers arranged into a short series of steps leading up to the circular hole and the whirlpool below. Konstantin didn't know how to process this scene, or what he felt.

Was this all that was here?

The story of the original Arkhitektor, finding the wounded being of clean and nourishing light half-submerged in the tides of the Trench, cursed to hold the blissful Needle yet too weak and impoverished to utilize it. He knew he was naïve to expect such a grand and paradigm-shifting device to still be here, in the clutches of a mere brutish knight of the Order's weakest House, but a gentle voice had held out a little hope for such an outcome. But that wasn't to be. His was the hard road. The Rising Path... perhaps they were only destined to descend deeper. Into the bowels of hell, and obsession, and despair. Only there would their noble quest end. At those reaches he'd find the Firmament Needle.

This was all a test, he decided. Another trial.

Nothing good came easy.

Pushing back his tears of exhaustion and trauma, he locked down his tempestuous emotions. He would walk on as far as his legs would carry him, he would cross lands and seas no human eye had ever beheld, face down any and all infernal entities as he trespassed from the contiguous borderlands of one House's kingdom to the next. And whenever death should befall him, he would face it with steel in his eyes and stare down the true death, the death of his soul, before he allowed it to become a commodity for the dead monarchs to barter with.

Konstantin could sense a cold mockery chuckling away deep inside himself. Not his humor: the Arkhitektor's. He turned to his companions, seeing their own doubt and confusion, and issued them commands that he could not himself execute. 'Kuznetsov, go high. Go all the way to top of tower. See if you find something: a switch, another floor, a clue, anything at all.' He turned to Lim. 'Head down the well and do the same. But be careful. Stay away from water.'

Konstantin stared about the vast chamber again, resolving to find a hidden passage or anything of note along the four walls, the four large flames coloring the whole scene in burning sapphires. Konstantin tried not to listen to the worried murmurings of his new wards within his body, still confused by their death and their new state of existence. And he tried not to hear the dark parasite existing inside the Arkhitektor, laughing with his voice, a cruel joviality at Konstantin's disappointment. Konstantin made it three paces across the chamber when he heard a howl of pain. It came from down in that well, the shriek blending with the white noise of the swirling waters. Konstantin froze and stared over the lip into the huge, dark mouth in the floor, the flickering blue flames throwing steady shadow animals about the room, their lives violent and short-lived.

Something was moving down there. Steadily climbing up out of the well. It wasn't Lim.

A lance of hot pain shot through his insides again, twisting him up, the laughter losing the cadence and pitch of the Arkhitektor and becoming something deeper, distorted, and wholly malevolent. A large talon clattered onto the lip of the well, followed by its companion. Konstantin could see the hideous round heads and their snaking necks making frenzied figure eights as Vor Dushi climbed out of the subterranean waters below, its long shawl of flesh dripping water like a waterlogged raincoat.

Kuznetsov had descended again, taking a position next to Konstantin.

The reverberating laughter became a voice inside Konstantin's head, echoing down the hallways of his every thought and private space. 'I remember you, interloper. I stole your master from you, and from himself. I still feel him,' Vor Dushi tapped a large, scything claw against its sternum as it spoke, 'in you. All these years, such misery for him. Misery for you. And still you come back, to a place you have no claim to.' Konstantin tried to block out the confusion of voices speaking in unison inside the cramped confines of his head, shaking them loose, but it was as useless as trying to fight off the urge to breathe. None of Vor Dushi's seven mouths moved their lips; they enunciated every word directly to his mind in his native tongue. 'You don't understand the importance of this place and these waters. They're the residue of life's fruit, nourishing these lands, feeding its creatures. This place ... it is the entropy of all living things. The lymph node of all realities, collecting the detritus of life. I am the bitter sweetness of death, the flowers on a grave. And your tribe has spent so much time trying to find a way to destroy us all. Us, the inevitable conclusion to everything.'

Konstantin had been focusing his eyes on the crack between two stone flags to ease his imbalance. He forced himself to look at the horror standing proud before him. 'The living deserve a choice. And they had a choice long ago. I know legend of fallen holy warrior, washed up and forgotten along this very Trench for many years. Half-drowned and sick from these waters.'

Several of the necks entwined slowly, sensually, the eyes of these heads staring venomous thoughts into Konstantin. 'The world eats the world. Everything falls under teeth. It has always been this way. Death always wins.'

Konstantin fought the lie. A hand to his aching temple, he pursued the guardian's fallacy. 'It was our grandmaster who found holy warrior. But the angelic one was too weak to save us, to use tool of our salvation. It was you who took Needle away. You and your corrupt kin, you stole our chance at paradise, set damnation against all of living. You all prey on us.'

'As does your kind with your livestock. Your kind have even been known to prey on each other. The living aren't victims for death, worthy of sympathy. They're another piece of the large, hungry machine. Nothing more.'

'I'll never stop searching. I'll travel these lands until I find Firmament Needle. No wall or weapon will hold me back. Next, I'll pay visit to your liege, the monarch holding your leash. And if his keep fails to offer any worthwhile intelligence, he might at least like to know how I got by his gatekeeper.' Konstantin's attitude drew seven snarls from Vor Dushi.

'You'll never leave here, monk. Your whole line has failure in their blood. I'll drown you in the waters that ailed the holy warrior of your scripture. Your body will wash away, and who knows where it will end up?'

Konstantin caught the slight signal from Kuznetsov. 'Then you might want to be quick. You have more uninvited guests at your gate.'

Vor Dushi became aggravated, several of the heads baring their hooked teeth, the necks bustling together in a rustling bunch. 'Then I have a better idea how to deal with you.'

Konstantin almost doubled over, caught himself with a wince, then fell to his knees, a foam of saliva bubbling between his clenched teeth, his eyes jammed shut in convulsive pain. The Arkhitektor roared with long-awaited triumph throughout the soul haven of Konstantin's body. The necronaut armor couldn't hold him back anymore. The brewing power of the black soul worm dug deeper and deeper into the Arkhitektor, driving him to perform Vor Dushi's bidding.

Kuznetsov stared helplessly as his brother was racked with agonies. Without word, without hope, he charged Vor Dushi, if only to buy Konstantin a few precious seconds to get to his feet and escape and fight another day. He flew halfway across the chamber when he hit an invisible wall. Looking about in inert confusion, he stared at the fourteen hateful eyes of the hydra. Something pulled him backwards, some force, back towards Konstantin.

Konstantin was tearing at the straps and buckles of his breastplate as though they burned red hot, ripping his gauntlets off and dropping them to the floor. His eyes swirling into two black holes, tongue unable to squeeze through his rigid jaws, he tore his tunic open, exposing the glowing framework of his hive.

. . .

Kuznetsov was reeled back into Konstantin's body, gasping at the cold, unmistakable change that had darkened the tunnels in such a short space of time. The sanctuary had become a wild growth of ugly, oozing vines. An ominous laugh vibrated through the tunnels. Kuznetsov was about to attempt a desperate communication with Konstantin when a movement caught his eye. It was the vines. They had their own agency, moving like an orgy of black adders.

This was a safe haven no more. Before Kuznetsov could react, they reached out, circling his wrists and ankles, crushing, tearing at him. His screams echoed throughout the honeycomb, but they were brief. In moments the tangled growths were stretching his mouth wide until his jaws split, crawling down his throat, clogging his chest and abdomen. They tore his soul to tatters.

Vor Dushi had made a new home, deep in the heart of Konstantin.

. . .

Mortis stepped off the bridge, the burning nub of his severed key now a distant but perpetual tingle of weeping nerves. According to his wristwatch, which he had checked in the glow from one of the many phosphorescent mounds of pleading, he'd been wandering down in these rocky bowels for a little over three hours. Captain Agua seemed quiet but unfazed by the inhospitable environment and the long, challenging walk across craggy clefts, steep horns, and valleys, but his quiet demeanor told Mortis that he was far from content. Mortis knew that he wanted Konstantin dead. They'd had issues since day one, and now, not only was the entire operation burned—not entirely the Russian's fault, mind—but many of Agua's soldiers were dead, or as good as. Mortis took a weary breath, out of practice for such physical labor, his thighs complaining about the uncharitable slopes in these caverns. He no longer cared if Konstantin died or not, as long as he could retrieve his thumb first and repair any possible damage to its design. He refused to think about the Zar-ptica leaves wrapped and stored in their Humvee, and whether they were still in one piece. Who would have thought he'd suffer a second key-related misfortune, and so quickly? It almost made him want to laugh ruefully. If he did, though, he wasn't sure if he'd be able to stop.

Mortis' need to prioritize finding his thumb over killing Gulag had already caused one argument with Agua. Agua seemed to think all Mortis had to do was wave his hands and say Abracadabra and a new, perfectly crafted key would grow from his stump. If only it were that simple. First, he needed a bastard finger to reattach and manipulate. Second, he was quietly confident of, and mortified about, the high likelihood that some unknown force in this land was nullifying his forgery talents. Who knew? Maybe when that cradle-eater creature had first damaged the key, it had afflicted him with some foul local ailment, messing up his ability. Agua, in all his ignorant glory, had even suggested that Mortis simply use one of the other eight keys and got in a huff when Mortis explained that walking into any of the eight other worlds wouldn't bring them any closer to home. Konstantin was their best and only option for the moment.

Now here they were, standing on a tall, rocky island, the frothy waters creating a huge moat below them, staring up at a strangely twisted, metal-plated building that looked like it was growing into the darkness high above them. The washed-out emerald light from the bawling hills of souls had vanished on this side of the bridge, replaced by large, crackling flames of a bluish hue that reminded Mortis of giant Bunsen burners. Mortis paused for a moment to survey all this and prayed that Konstantin hadn't given them the slip inside this devilish structure. Agua didn't pause to consider what possible dangers lay in that blocky tower, and Mortis found himself being pulled along in the military man's wake. Crossing the threshold of the doorway, Mortis felt his future rot away like so much garbage.

Konstantin stood before Vor Dushi, breathing heavily, face flushed with hot pounding blood, and his armor scattered about him. The hexagonal layers that scored his whole torso and palms were blazing with dull red light. The last acolyte of the Rising Path didn't seem to be standing defiantly before his great nemesis but rather in a state of patient subservience. Slowly, Konstantin turned his head, his black marble eyes staring through the meat and bone of Acton Mortis, right into the succulent soul, like an oyster in a shell.

Agua, ever the pragmatist, didn't stand there and wait for the enemy to strike first. Up to his forearms he was already radiant with the green armada of imminent destruction. The super-hot tracers would tear the place apart better than any heavy-caliber machine gun. The mystic would be a cloud of pink particulate, and this time he wouldn't stop firing until Vor Dushi was a large pile of mincemeat. He brought his forearms up, ready to unload like supernatural mini guns.

And then he choked wetly, his body seizing up, iron rods replacing his bones.

Konstantin was watching Agua like a starving man staring at a hot meal. With a gentle curve of his finger, his hands dangling at his sides, Konstantin beckoned Agua's soul from his body, the trauma wiping away the mercenary's consciousness. The body fell down, empty. Konstantin held Agua's soul there, watching it with dull interest. Bringing his hands close together, he mimed tearing a piece of paper in half and, accordingly, Agua's soul reciprocated, splitting right down the middle from crown to groin. The two halves would not be salvaged. Neither sustenance nor currency, they were merely waste.

Mortis had almost let his bladder go in witnessing this and was about to turn tail and sprint out of there, back across the bridge, possibly taking his chances on one of the other domains of Erebus. The branding on his arm be damned.

But a voice locked him in place, though no vocals disturbed the air. The voice, a chorus of seven, was inside his head. 'Bridge maker,' they called him. 'I have a proposition for you.'

43

Rose blocked out the pain in her ribs, and after several hours of second-guessing her twisting route through this pit, it was her hunger that was taking precedence over the pain. Her ribs would heal, but the fight with Fenwick had taken a toll. Titanic feats of strength and fortitude tended to do that to a person. She was a professional, however, and her constitution would never allow her to quit. Blanking out the hunger and the pain, she soldiered on in search of Kev. Being on this side of the Null, the digital comm link between her and Kev was as dead as everything else. With a bit of luck he would have located their targets by now.

After several more minutes she found herself before a long, skinny walkway of stone, reaching over a great chasm. It wasn't much better than a balance beam in gym class, and the wavering stone even looked a little slick from the pervasive dampness. She tiptoed towards it, seeing no better route across the gap. The ambient glow from the heaping mounds of gelatinous souls was far too dim to offer much insight into the depths of the massive ravine, but the sound of gurgling water provided her an answer. Another tributary from the Trench's main channel. With delicate steps she crossed to the other side and arrived not a second too soon, for what sprung out of the ill-lit saturnine might very well have caused her to slip off the bridge.

It was a portal of light, spilling into existence like a translucent tropical plant, diaphanous petals blooming open like windows to the aurora borealis. Rose took a breath, dropping her raised fists and feeling some of the tension leave her body. Clyde and Ace were fired out of the interdimensional tunnel of the plant's bud, landing in a crouch several feet from Rose. Ace looked okay following the journey, but Rose could see the dizziness and nausea shaking Clyde's balance.

'Fuck...' Clyde breathed, staggering like a drunk as he stood up.

'That first time's a trip, huh?' Rose smiled, her white teeth shining behind her dusty face. 'Good to see you again, nerd.' She admired his armor and guns. 'First the warehouse and now here. You must have got real bored, real quick, of that civilian life.'

'Not exactly.' Clyde closed his eyes for a few seconds to compose himself.

Rose nodded her head at Ace as if his appearance here was a foregone conclusion.

'Mortis is up ahead somewhere, chasing down Kozlov. I got held up, but Kev went ahead.'

Clyde snapped into focus. 'He's already wounded. C'mon, we need to get to him before he does anything stupid.' Clyde took the lead, his proactive energy raising no resistance from his teammates.

'You know where you're going, rook?' Ace asked, frosty swirls beginning to fall and writhe from his hands.

'I do now. I can sense him. It's how I found you guys at the warehouse.'

'Like getting your dog chipped, huh? Then let's not waste any time. We have an hour.'

It wasn't long before the three of them found the huge, cloistered bridge crossing the water, fit for any castle keep, but the castle was too alien and unconventional to meet with their expectations.

'There.' Clyde pointed, appearing to struggle in detecting Kev at first; his friend's color palette was causing him to blend in with the bluish pyres burning atop the columns organized about the island.

They hurried across the bridge and reconvened with Kev. He had been performing some light reconnaissance, and his expression eloquently told them how much deep shit they were in. He still seemed weak from the gunshot wound. 'It's good to see you guys, but I think we're a little late.'

44

CLYDE WAS ARMED WITH A sub-machine gun, two handguns, a knife, and the last remnants of Kev's borrowed power, and he still felt completely insignificant standing watch over the scene playing out before him. Something born of nightmares was standing imposingly at the center of the palatial but empty chamber. Seven heads on seven long necks undulating euphorically towards the dark heights of the room, a long cloak of skin hanging from its outstretched arms, the patchwork flesh damp and glistening in the blue shadows of the burning fires.

Clyde recognized the two other men from the files Ace had shown him on the flight back to New Mexico. The ex-KGB agent turned necromancer stood pacified before the frightful demon, his armor shed and his aged, sweat-oiled torso wrapped in binding crisscrossing razor slashes of light, like staring at a honeycomb burning from within. It looked painful, but the shaman seemed to be completely at peace.

Then there was the target of this mission, Acton Mortis. Clyde had been given Cliff Notes on his abilities and background, but seeing his chest opened up like a pair of bony saloon doors into a cosmic void threw him for a second. The key maker had an air of malleability about him, a fresh convert eager to ingratiate upon a new messiah. Then, as Mortis' voice echoed across the large space, rising over the crackle of flames and the turbulent eddies of the pool far below their feet, Clyde understood the sudden propitiation of the Cairnwood Society underling.

'Yes, YES! My lord, forgive my trespassing, please, and I'll do whatever you ask.'

'You can start by providing me an offering,' Konstantin replied, his voice vaguely monotonous. 'You owe me souls. A lot of them for what you did here.'

'With your help, I'll throw open a doorway back to Earth. I'll rip the locks right off, open a rift to anywhere you wish to go.' He held his hand up to Konstantin and the entranced sky-gazing snake-demon, but Clyde couldn't see why from this distance.

Were the monk and the demon together in this?

'I only need you to return my key and lower the negating forces of this realm.'

Kozlov obliged with a papal hand raise. A light ripple coursed through the chamber, but it was so indistinct that a single blink would have had those present miss it entirely. Mortis' missing key was not returned; instead, he stared in wonder at the new nub sprouting swiftly from his stump, one knuckle, two knuckles, three; the ghastly elongated appendage was shiny and new, and ready to be cut like fresh clay. The power within his chest fired up like a cosmic furnace, and Mortis seemed to realize he was losing part of himself, but the thought was distant, like a voice on a faraway radio.

A series of loud cracks and pops broke the moment, and several unseen projectiles ripped into Mortis, with several more entering the gaping star field of his chest. Clyde was done waiting to see how much worse things could get, his finger still on the trigger, the barrel smoking. If the bullets had hurt Mortis in any way, he kept a brave face.

'Shit,' Clyde muttered. He moved forward, his team at his side, and recommenced firing at Mortis until his clip was done. The gangly intruder of realms took each shot in his stride. 'Is he fucking bulletproof?'

Nobody answered. Nobody knew.

Still crossing the large chamber, Clyde grabbed a grenade from his belt, pulled the pin, and lobbed it.

'No!' Kev shouted. But before he had a chance to reach out and swat the grenade away, a portal opened like a trapdoor in the air and swallowed it.

Passing through the bloodstream of the universe, the grenade's timer ticked, ticked, until it was expelled through another portal, arriving directly behind the unaware forms of Clyde, Kev, Rose, and Ace. The clink and rattle of the explosive clinking against the stone floor spun the four of them around. The grenade went off with a deafening, frightful bang and a maelstrom of shrapnel, whipping up a cloud of obliterated stone and scorched air.

Clyde thought it was the last thing he'd ever see and wondered why he was still standing, when he realized through his shock that Kev had pushed back against the grenade's explosion with a counter-force, a protective concavity that absorbed the ripping metal fragments and shockwave of heated air. Clyde was about to apologize, or thank him for saving all of their skins, but Kev's eyes told him not to worry about it.

'We need Kozlov alive,' Kev said.

'Mortis, a doorway,' Konstantin ordered, one slave to another.

'To where?'

'Anyplace with a feast of uncollected souls.'

Mortis watched the speedy approach of his enemies and reacted. Feeling enhanced by the innate power of Vor Dushi swelling though his veins, Mortis was no longer required to stand close to a door he wished to open. He simply reached out, pointing towards the air beside Konstantin, and watched as a portal opened into a crowded and extravagant gala of old money and wealthy benefactors.

■ ■ ■

KONSTANTIN—GULAG STEPPED through the doorway to a stifling hush of conversation and music. Amidst this sea of high society, crystal chandeliers, champagne flutes, silverware, and rich wood-paneled walls, Konstantin pushed and shoved his way through the crowd until he found himself in the middle of the dining room. Scores of drunken eyes stared at him as though he was some derelict who had somehow found a way to sneak into their private conclave. However, the collective disgust of the elite strata failed to segue into horror or shock at the monk's unnatural, inhuman condition, as one might expect. Gulag's black eyes found a worthy morsel.

Edward Talbot stood near the podium on the stage, champagne in hand, his conversation with a small gathering of international diplomats and industrious energy titans now put on hold. Talbot stared at the intruder stinking up the Cairnwood Society dinner and, upon recognition—and perhaps the realization of the great big mistake that was about to bite a chunk out of his arse—he calmly, leisurely, walked away towards the arched glass doors to the balcony of the Ivy Lounge. The other members of the Cairnwood Society's inner circle were not far behind him, each of them carefully backing away, not wanting to stir a dangerous stampede that could prevent them from making it to their helicopter stationed on the roof of the opulent hotel.

The heavies in suits, shades, and earpieces guarding the doors around the room jumped into action, quickly and professionally approaching the oddity who had entered through a doorway in the ether. Gulag heard Vor Dushi in his head, whispering to him through the voice of the Arkhitektor. Some of these leeches in tuxedos and ball gowns were not strictly human, not anymore, but they were still alive. What would they taste like? A part of Konstantin wanted to pursue Talbot and his ilk out onto the balcony, to take and take from him until his smarmy expression was nothing more than a withered skull. But Gulag felt his puppeteer calling him to action, and quickly, before those tainted ones amongst him proved their danger.

Gulag shuddered, a sucking sensation quavering his center, and a barbaric horde of violent intent flew from him, a shadowy mob seizing the wrists and throats of the decadent human parasites, flaying their unwholesome souls from their saggy and soft torsos, and dragging them unwillingly back towards the dark pit of Gulag's body. The outmatched security detail, unprepared for such a threat, shared this same fate. The struggles tipped over tables and chairs, brought forth a discordant wail of grief and shock, and sparked wholesale panic as people rushed to escape. They were too slow. Gulag trembled, a hurricane in his bones, and with Vor Dushi at the reins, he ripped the souls away from every last one of them. Their bodies lay where they fell, sprawled over chairs and tumbled half under tables.

45

SEVERAL ACCURATE BULLETS AND SLIVERS of hurled ice took Mortis in the chest and abdomen, keeping him occupied and unable to shut the doorway to the soul harvest.

'Keep him busy,' Kev called. 'I'll get the armor and follow Kozlov.'

'I'm with you,' Rose declared.

There was no time for debate or options. Clyde could only hope that Kev wouldn't do anything too reckless. He was still moving awkwardly, clearly in pain, but he dragged the breastplate and gauntlets over to him as he sailed like the wind, making a beeline for the doorway, Rose charging along at his side. Clyde stared down the barrel of his rifle and finished emptying his second clip into the tall freak yanking icicles out of his torso. Kev and Rose made it through just as the doorway sealed shut.

'Any ideas?' Clyde slapped his third and final magazine into place.

Ace didn't get to answer. He skated along beside Clyde on a sheet of ice only to have a keyhole suddenly open up directly in front of him. With no time to skid to a halt, he passed through the portal. Clyde faltered in his stride and realized with a flash of panic that he was now alone with Mortis in a demon's realm. How much time was left in the hourglass? With no better ideas, he raised his rifle again and squeezed the trigger. The rounds ripped right out of this reality, entering through another portal. Two wormholes opened opposite each other simultaneously: the first one brought Ace speeding in from out of nowhere, the second spat out Clyde's last volley of bullets. It happened so fast that Clyde barely had time to register what had happened; all he saw was Ace lose his footing on the ice and bounce along the ground in a heap.

. . .

THE IVY LOUNGE was a mass of fresh corpses, with the last of the holdouts still struggling vainly to hold onto their souls from the grunting, laughing, shadowy thieves. Kev saw one of the shaded killers straddling a woman over a long dining table, her sparkling cocktail dress dazzling under the gentle lights of the chandeliers. The dark cloud of a man had his hand inside her head, and with a playful grunt he dragged her screeching soul out of her person, not spilling a drop of blood. With his growing torpidity and the numb agony of his shoulder, Kev wasn't keen on picking an unnecessary fight. Instead, he found Konstantin in the middle of the room, the final souls drawn towards him like water circling a drain.

Kev was about to voice his concern, but Rose was way ahead of him. 'I can't get this armor near him. And he's going to put up a fight.'

Kev's reply left his mouth before he could decide if his idea was good or bad. 'Maybe I can keep him busy from within.' Rose's wide-eyed expression made Kev think it was a bad idea. 'If you get the armor on him, I should be able to pass back out. That's what the files said. Only malevolent spirits are restricted from passing the armor's sigils.'

'You're not in too good a shape here. What if there's more of these shadow guys in there?'

'If you have a better idea, I'm listening.' It wouldn't be long before Konstantin's attention, or that of his minions, found them huddled low in the corner of the room.

'We'll go with him,' a third voice said. Sergeant Connors had materialized, his eyes cold like steel. Rose recognized that look and knew she would have no chance of talking him out of it. Darcy and Barros appeared beside him.

'If we're going to do this, though, then we need to do it now,' Barros added, turning to look at the drag of final souls slowing down. The room would be quiet soon.

Rose turned the armor over in her hands. 'Then get your asses in there. Just make sure you make it back out.'

Kev raced across the dining room, across a carpet of bodies, with Sarge, Darcy, and Barros at his side. Halfway across the room, several of the blighted souls turned from their fresh kills, their smudged smirks and angry appetites falling on the four ghosts speeding towards their master's vessel, their home of iniquity. They closed in with haste, but still too slowly. Kev and his back-up felt the pull of Gulag's vacuum, their dimensions warping, shrinking, and stretching, all in a split second. They found themselves within the dark, veiny corridors of the hive.

. . .

ACE LAY ON his front, groaning in pain. Clyde found no exit wounds in his back, TREMBLAY and the big number 9 were unscathed, but until he turned him over he wouldn't be able to tell if the bullets had penetrated the front of the armor. He didn't get the opportunity to check. A keyhole opened up below him, and a blur of indecipherable color and texture ran through his eyes during the quick drop through infinity, with everything coming back into focus as he was shot out of another doorway, tumbling across the chamber to land at the feet of Mortis. Clyde rolled away and got to a kneeling position, his rifle useless—if he fired, the bullets would only be redirected towards Ace again, or even to himself. But he knew he was out of options, and the amusement on Mortis' face seemed to verify it. The locksmith didn't even deign walking the several steps over to Clyde; instead, he lashed his hand through a new window, and it reappeared through an exit to Clyde's left, the disembodied forearm and four sharp keys tearing red rivets in Clyde's left cheek before vanishing back through the small portal. The pain and humiliation demanded Clyde pull the trigger, yank the pin on another grenade, even unsheathe his knife and gallantly charge at his enemy, but the jumbled thoughts of how each strategy could backfire on him made him want to scream.

He didn't chance to look behind him at Ace, afraid that he might see him unmoving, dead by his rash actions.

A long, pointy shoe sprung out of another space to Clyde's right, the kick bursting a flash of stars in Clyde's head and knocking him over to a groveling position. The blood flushed in his cheeks with murderous anger, some of it leaking from the cuts in his stinging cheek to dribble onto the stone. He forced himself to his feet, preferring to die in defiance than as a victim on the ground.

'Fucking pussy,' he snarled, still trying to regain his balance from the kick. 'Fight me like a fucking man. No guns, no tricks. You and me.'

Mortis didn't budge from his position near the well's steps, in the shadow of the unmoving Vor Dushi, who was psychically preoccupied. He laughed heartily. 'Who are you? One of those Hourglass fellas?' Clyde didn't answer, but his whole body was jackhammering with adrenaline. 'My boss—ex-boss by now, I suppose—he really dislikes you lot. They all do.'

Like a skilled illusionist distracting the audience's eye, Mortis shot his left hand through a hole that opened above Clyde's head while his right hand appeared through another and backslapped him. 'Killing you and your friend over there might have gone in my favor with the club. But I finally woke up.' Another sleight of hand, and another smack. 'I'd never move beyond the position of shoe-shiner in their little world. I'm of lower caste. Expendable. Well, look at me now. I wish I could have seen the look on their faces when Gulag crashed their soirée.'

Clyde didn't know what Mortis was talking about, and he didn't care. The psycho was cocksure, drunk on his new power. Clyde's hands slowly, carefully reached for something on his person, but his eyes stayed on Mortis, provoking him to continue his petulant victory. Mortis tried his degrading party trick one more time.

Clyde was ready.

The distracting hand waved past Clyde's face, while another hard-soled shoe came out like a piston, about to smash Clyde's nose. Clyde caught hold of the leg, his grip straining to keep hold of the bony ankle. He had a grenade in one hand, the pin already out. Even across the distance Clyde saw the shock and fear register on Mortis' face. Clyde flipped the grenade between the trapped leg and the rim of the portal, watching it fall out the other side, clinking and rolling a few inches in front of Mortis' panicked, hopping form. Reacting without thought, his other leg still caught and unable to break free of Clyde's grip, Mortis closed the tunnel in a desperate hope to hop away from the ensuing destruction. The closure severed his leg at the shin, leaving Clyde holding the loose end of shoe, trouser leg, and slender gushing limb. Mortis shrieked in agony, fought for balance and still tried to bounce away on one foot, but a full second later the boom of super-heated air and shredding metal sent him hurtling backwards, up the shallow tiers of steps, leaving him dazed and seriously wounded beside the wide mouth of the well.

Clyde wasn't taking any chances. He dropped the severed leg, drew both of his semi-automatic pistols, and slowly moved forward, about to gun down the bleeding and dazed Mortis. Mortis was so out of it that he didn't have the wherewithal to climb through an escape hole to anywhere else. Clyde had no mercy. His guns rained down a torrent of death, the barrage of bullets punching straight through Mortis' body.

Then he was falling through space again, the floor having vanished beneath his sneakers, his stomach lurching from the pull of gravity. His eyes couldn't make sense of the interstitial corridor he fell through, but he saw what was waiting for him below when the exit opened directly above the dark, wide well.

Clyde dropped the guns in blind panic and desperately flailed out towards the bas-relief rim of the well, his fingers scrabbling for any type of purchase. They dug in, his arm sockets blazed with strain, but his intense need to survive blocked out the jolting pain and allowed his fingers to grip onto the engraved ledge. But he didn't know how long he could hold on. His sneakers scraped and slipped against the damp stone blocks of the well, but his toe found a crumbling gap between two blocks. His forearms and triceps trembled as he awkwardly pulled himself upwards with scant leverage.

Mortis reared up over the rim of the well, his two sharp and clammy hands seizing Clyde's wrists. Clyde didn't know how Mortis was still alive, whether it had something to do with his preexisting abnormalities or was the demon's doing, but his grip was still strong, despite the wounds. That hideous, troll-like face popped into view, rising over the well's edge, his teeth bared in utter hatred. The keys awkwardly scraped and dug into Clyde's wrists, and he knew he had no way out of this. He was dead. Soon to be another spirit trapped here as fresh game.

'I'm going to send different pieces of you to the four corners of the Earth.'

Clyde was petrified, imagining his forearms being cleaved off by a teleportation guillotine, then how he'd fall, not to the whirlpool far below but into another portal, or a series of them, each opening and closing like an inter-dimensional mouth, pieces of him landing in China, India, and South America.

A large pair of mitts came down from above, latching onto Mortis' own wrists, an arctic blast of icy vapor and intense cold spilling down to buffet Clyde's face. Squinting through the heavy white swirl, he saw Ace crouched over Mortis' back, his hockey mask still hanging over his face. Mortis' scream had been shrill but brief, the numbness of the cryogenic shock rendering him effectively dazed. Those hands and long, awful, freakish fingers were dropping in temperature quickly and starting to chill Clyde's wrists, but the true severity of the ice blast remained focused on Mortis' wrists and forearms, the flesh, bone, and blood turning a bluish-white like midnight snow, studded with frozen crystals. Mortis managed to roll onto his side, eyes glazed, body in hypothermic shock. He'd lost all control of his hands, but his inarticulate grip had slid over Clyde's wrists like wintery twigs, leaving him to pull himself up from the well.

Mortis didn't seem to know where he was from one second to the next; in his eyes he was there, then gone, there, then gone, lucidity lost amidst his physical agonies.

Clyde and Ace stood over him, watching him fumble up onto his knees, his missing foot and shin throwing off his balance. Mortis stared at them both, white eyes wide and packed with loathing and fear. Clyde made a hammer with his fist, tensing the muscle of his forearm, and swung, his arm smashing through Mortis' wrists like they were made of cheap glass. The key maker's hands slapped to the ground between them like frozen meat. Mortis could only stare at his ice-jeweled stumps in blunt acceptance. Clyde kicked him in the chest, sending his body tipping over the edge of the well, all the way down to that swirling thunderous whirlpool in the depths below.

Clyde looked at Ace's armor, searching for bullet holes. 'You okay?'

'I've had worse,' he grumbled. He pushed his mask up. 'You shoot me again, though . . . I'll beat your ass like it's my job.' Clyde nodded solemnly. 'Good job, rook.'

'You saved my ass.'

'You saved us both by crippling that asshole.'

They remained standing, staring into the phosphorescent depths below, feeling tired and sore. Clyde wiped blood away from his sliced cheek.

'Rose and Kev?' Ace couldn't hide the concern in his voice.

'Dealing with it. What about us? How much longer until the hourglass runs out?'

Ace checked his watch. 'About twenty minutes.' He sat down on the top step, his back to the well but keeping a close eye on the entranced figure of Vor Dushi.

After some consideration, Clyde joined him. He stared untrustingly at Vor Dushi for a minute or two, then let his attention settle upon those icy key-fingers. 'What do we do with those?'

46

The Arkhitektor had spread his oily tendrils throughout the hexagonal chambers and corridors of Konstantin's insides like a tar jungle, foul necrotic vines glistening in the burning orange light. Kev made damn sure not to touch any of the horrid growth. His plan had hit a snag: now that he was in here, he wasn't sure where he was going. But Konstantin must be here somewhere. The sanctuary had become a temple of misery, a prison for the clean and noble. Faces of innocence cowed and huddled away from the violent inky smudges imposing themselves in the corridors like a power-drunk militia.

'Incoming.' Sarge spotted one of the shadows disentangle himself from the oily netting creeping across the wall and rush towards them.

Kev and Sarge, in the lead, braced for a fight, but suddenly the attacker stopped. A whispery voice carried through the whole hive, a voice that rasped with a nasty quality, sounding indifferent to violence and grief.

'This way,' Vor Dushi's voice beckoned.

The shadowy thug still seemed braced for a fight, but he relaxed and led them down the corridor.

'I don't think we have much choice,' Kev said.

Sarge nodded. 'I think you're right.'

Barros kept her voice low. 'This Russian, or whatever's controlling him, isn't inviting us for a beer. When we get in there—'

'We swing for the fences,' Sarge finished.

'Good, because Rose is all alone out there,' Darcy added.

'She can handle herself.' Sarge drifted forward to catch up with their smoky escort.

They traversed down several strata, turning a blind eye to the brutes throwing their weight around in front of the weak seeking shelter. They reached a larger cell: the product of several smaller ones having had their walls broken down to accommodate the grand importance of its resident. The grave-dirt roots were veined throughout the floor and walls and ceiling, swallowing most of the orange glow, casting the large chamber in a soiled purple ambience with only scant slashes of orange light struggling to illuminate the room.

Two figures occupied the center: Konstantin, subdued and broken, tangled up in a cocoon of binding coils, and another man of similar age and monastic apparel.

Kev didn't know who he was, but he bore no resemblance to the multi-headed demon that had stood catatonic in that subterranean tower. Yet Kev felt a profound, primeval sense of death emanating from this other man. A whitish, wriggling maggot protruded from his chest, the chunky tapering end suggesting that it would be roughly the size of a fist at its largest circumference.

The Arkhitektor gave them a pitying smirk. 'You four must have a strong desire to serve me, charging in here like this.'

Kev and Sarge exchanged a quick side-eyed glance. The four of them slowly circled the possessed Arkhitektor. After a moment of silent preparation, they converged on him like a wild mob. The Arkhitektor beat them back with ease. Digging his fingers into Kev's throat like a talon, he raised a bunch of the grounded vines, creating a series of tough, leathery whips to lash and choke Sarge and Darcy. Barros was quicker, and even without her agile legs of the past, her reaction speed had her dodging the thrashing tendrils and slipping behind the Arkhitektor, hooking her forearm into the malevolent spirit's throat. Ghosts may not need to breathe, but Barros did a good job of weakening the monk's position. The fingers around Kev's jugular hadn't slackened, though, and they could still tear a chunk out of him, which might finish the job.

Hanging there, unable to pry the fingers away, Kev stared at the fat maggot circling about in the Arkhitektor's chest burrow, the elder monk arching backwards as Barros fought to pull him off balance. Focusing his thoughts, his hand angled towards the gluttonous glob, Kev began to pull, imagining himself ripping it out and crushing it like spoiled fruit in mid-air. It was dug deep, resisting him; however, the anger in the Arkhitektor's eyes told Kev that he was on the right track. Sarge and Darcy were up again, beating away the tentacles as best they could, trying to get in close.

'Kozlov!' Kev shouted around the stricture on his neck. He kicked a leg towards the vine-cocooned monk lying unconscious on the viscous altar at the side of the room. 'Free Kozlov!'

Sarge and Darcy ducked and pirouetted away from a score more of the cracking tentacles but were stung by just as many. Yet they made it across.

'Cover me,' Sarge grunted, hands tearing at the rigid ropes crushing Konstantin Kozlov.

Darcy was instantly beset by more of the foliage, slices opening up across his face and large, warding hands. A muscular bind found Sarge's ankle, but Darcy stamped down on it, grinding his heel until it burst along the seams. Sarge was tearing away handfuls of the greasy wires now, black ichor seeping between his fingers, but the captive was under too many layers.

Kev felt the sharp nails beginning to cut into the ghostly flesh of his neck. His strength was failing him fast, and his right shoulder was screaming. Still, he bent his right arm at the elbow, his hand once more becoming a focal point to make another attempt at removing the bloated soul maggot. Something slithered and slipped around Barros' neck, the snaking appendage writhing its way up to cover her chin, her mouth, nose, and eyes, then her entire head was shaking, unable to break free from the slick, controlling limb. She held tight, though; even blind, she refused to relinquish her own control of the thrashing Arkhitektor.

Kev channeled his energy, his arm wobbling from the strain. The maggot began to shift about in its hole, slipping out several inches. A bellow of fury echoed throughout the hive, but it didn't come from the Arkhitektor's mouth. His face had become blank as a sleepwalker, open eyes expressing nothing. The tight band around Kev's throat slackened a little and he broke free, exhausted. A figure stepped beside him, its details hazy in his periphery. Turning to get a better look, Kev found Konstantin's spirit, bitter, wounded, but now unchained.

Like a wild animal, Konstantin dove at the Arkhitektor, sinking his fingers into the doughy but strong flesh of the maggot. Twisting and turning, he fought to tear the monstrous seed from his master's soul, finishing the job that Kev had started, needing to emancipate himself and the Arkhitektor and every good soul in here from the thrall of Vor Dushi's tyranny. Little by little the maggot gave while Sarge and Darcy fought to restrain the afflicted elder monk's intractable arms.

With what little strength Kev had left, he used it to help Konstantin rip the maggot free in a splash of viscous, clotted muck.

• • •

ROSE WAS SURROUNDED by cooling corpses with impeccable dress sense. She recognized one or two of the faces: a senator from a state she couldn't quite recall; a former secretary of defense; and a former British prime minister. But most were just strangers who had the look of politicians, delegates, or wealthy cabalistic assholes. She was crouched behind a table, having no way of fighting any of those soot-smudged specters thirsty for violence. In the last few moments, she had watched as their territorial swagger had given way to uncertainty and then confusion. It started when that Gulag guy fell to his knees, slapping a hand to the buffered, hard wooden floor of the dining room. He gasped, a trail of saliva drooling from his clenched jaws, in what must have been tremendous pain. The patrol of dark souls exchanged looks, attempted to take a step towards their new flophouse before deciding against it. Then, one by one, they took flight, phasing through walls, ceiling, and the tall, arching windows into the unsuspecting environs of Manhattan.

Not wasting a second, Rose got up, necronaut armor clutched under her arm, and ran the gauntlet of the dead splayed limbs as though it was an agility course in the military. Konstantin paid her presence no mind, if he was even mentally aware of her, and Rose quickly put the armor about the passive body of the necromancer. An exodus of more unclean individuals escaped through the closing joins in the armor before it was too late, lighting out into the city just like the others, though a few of them flashed by her and returned to their still-warm bodies scattered about the place. She began to shove Konstantin's limp arm into the first gauntlet, hoping her team would hurry the fuck up and get out of there before they all found themselves stuck in the middle of a federal and media blitz.

· · ·

KONSTANTIN STARED WITH repugnance at the fat grub wrestling about in his hands, the extension of Vor Dushi's will. 'You ... you've been a pestilence to me, and my brethren, for long enough. Where's the Firmament Needle?'

A spiteful laughter filled the entire hive. Vor Dushi's essence was wasting away, weakening slightly under the blessings of the armor once more housing Konstantin's body. 'You'll never know.' The laughter was a chorus of wet hacks, like seven water-swelled gullets.

The Arkhitektor blinked away years' worth of confusion, a look of great shame dawning on him at the pawn he had become for his nemesis. The black swamp of attacking vines had ceased, releasing Barros one coiled wrapping at a time, and in turn the soldier released the archmonk's throat.

The Arkhitektor placed a hand to his chest wound, surprised to find the soul maggot hadn't done any further damage. He stared quizzically at the corpulent grub still trying to slip from his student's pressing grip. 'He'll never tell. His king would do far worse to him than we could.'

Konstantin seemed to have accepted this already.

'If you destroy me, you'll never know peace,' the seven voices lapped over each other. 'The Order of Terminus will make you suffer in ways you can't imagine.'

'Allow me.' The Arkhitektor proffered his hands towards Konstantin, waiting to receive a gift. He took the wriggling mass of the maggot, listening to its unholy shrieks. 'I've been as good as damned since that day. And your word doesn't count for much.' With a frown of effort, he crushed the foul larvae between his hands, the seven voices cutting off mid-squeal. He dropped the sludgy pulp to the filthy ground of the chamber, staring disgustedly at his hands before wiping them on his stained robes.

· · ·

Inside Vor Dushi's temple, Clyde and Ace were counting down the minutes to their exfiltration when the great hydra's body began to melt. Slowly at first, then rippling down like sheets of thick tallow, some of its mess dripping down through the grates in the chamber floor, into the rushing waters of the Eidolon Trench.

'Did Jack Kirby really work with Hourglass?' Clyde asked, wanting to take his mind off his physical pain and exhaustion.

'Maybe,' came Ace's infuriatingly vague reply. He was toying with Mortis' severed hands. 'Maybe I just thought it would keep you around a bit longer.'

Clyde snorted mirthfully, glancing at the whole other world he was currently sitting in. 'Thanks for that.'

He felt a pulling sensation inside of himself, ticklish, bordering on a slight nausea. Then he felt lightheaded as the tunnel of white light bloomed open before him. The hourglass had dropped its last grain.

. . .

'**You need to** carry on our work,' the Arkhitektor spoke to his pupil in a solemn voice. 'I was right to put my faith in you, Konstantin. You must continue our search. You find it, you undo all the senseless horror of the dead lands.'

'I've lost everybody.' Konstantin's voice was all doubt and anger.

'Crusades are never easy. More will die before this one has been seen through to the end, but great change requires great sacrifice. And this will be the greatest of changes. The will of the holy warrior of light, fallen from the sky.'

Kev saw the conflicting drama play out on Konstantin's face. 'You don't know who we are, but we came here to help you,' he said.

Konstantin regarded him for a moment. 'I appreciate what you four have done here. It was a great thing, and I fear I am in your debt... but I won't be allying myself with outside forces.' His rejection was firm, and Kev knew there would be no way to convince him otherwise under these circumstances.

'Thank you,' Konstantin added. 'Now the four of you must leave this place.'

Kev watched as Sarge vanished, back to the half-dead party, followed by Darcy. 'Wait,' Kev threw his hand up. 'There are people out there ready to take you in. They might already be in the process of doing so. We can help you. Please, let us help you.'

Konstantin paused at this, and the Arkhitektor also seemed a little troubled at the prospect of his best student being forced to waste more years, perhaps the remaining decades of his life, in a military or federal prison or some government think tank.

Konstantin didn't reply to Kev; he stared meaningfully into his mentor's eyes. 'Zarptica root. I have some in my pocket.'

The Arkhitektor instantly followed his logic but sounded cautious. 'I'm feeling weak,' he said. 'If I do this, you won't have a soul anchor to guide you back to the living world. You'll remain in Erebus. Are you prepared to make a final trip?'

Konstantin smiled. 'It's what I was born to do.'

Pride swelled through the Arkhitektor; he slapped a hand to Konstantin's shoulder. 'Then one more time, the last time, back to the Shore.'

Konstantin shot a quick look at Kev and Barros. 'Thank you both.'

Before either could object further, they felt an insurmountable current pulling them, and a second later they were back in the Ivy Lounge, standing around Konstantin's meditative form, surrounded in a loose circle by Rose, Sarge, and Darcy. Most of the dignitaries and power players were back on their feet, seeming remarkably calm about the previous proceedings and the four ghosts occupying the center of the room, though a fair number of them were physically frail and were being fretted over by aides or security. No police or additional private security had arrived yet, but they would certainly be en route.

Konstantin opened his eyes halfway, dazed or in deep concentration, and slowly stood up, his bas-relief armor glinting gently under chandelier light. A stormy passage opened chaotically behind him, its structure not as neat and well-engineered as those of Mortis. With a farewell nod, he patted the contents of his pocket as if for good luck and stepped through. The swirling vortex closed quickly, leaving his temporary allies in the living realm.

Rose calmly brought their attention to the hostile looks they were receiving. 'I don't think these assholes are friends of ours.'

Kev snarled back at them, giving them a look that would assure them that if he was still alive, he wouldn't piss on them if they were on fire.

God, his shoulder hurt, and his throat, and he ached, and he was exhausted. He pointed at the wall of mullioned glass balcony doors as he addressed the three dead GIs. 'Rose, pack up your Intensive Scare Unit; I'll give you a boost a few rooftops over, then we'll get to street level.'

Sarge and Barros filtered into her, then Darcy, but not before he spat on the floor of the Cairnwood Society get-together.

'We just saved your shitty little lives,' Rose said. 'That won't happen again. Have a great night; I hope you choke on shit.' She picked up a dining table and launched it through a set of arched glass doors leading to the balcony. 'I'll call in a pick-up to meet us on the street.'

Kev silently followed her outside and, with a tired sigh, flew her across several blocks of Manhattan, roof to roof. He was pained, exhausted, and concerned for Clyde, still stuck over in the Null for the moment. But all things considered, Kev felt a sense of relief, like he had accomplished something tonight. Something he'd never thought he could be capable of. He marveled at the sprawling blocks of big-city light, taking quiet solace in the abundance of life.

47

CLYDE SAT IN THE COOL, air-conditioned diner drinking a strawberry milkshake, which he was delighted to find on the unofficial menu of the Midnight Vulture. The four of them—Clyde, Kev, Rose, and Ace—sat in a red Naugahyde booth by the window, with Director Trujillo, in all his stony glory, sitting heavily on the end like a suited statue.

Clyde sucked on his straw noisily, lost in thought about what Trujillo had just said. 'So, I'm official?'

The rough, weathered stone head gave a single crisp nod. 'If you want it. It was an enlightening debriefing.'

Clyde's eyes went blank, and he tried to suction up those final dregs of flavor from the glass. The key cuts on his cheek still burned, but the medics at Indigo had assured him that they were only cosmetic.

Rose grew fidgety in the long pause. 'Jesus, nerd. How comfortable is that fence you're sitting on? Nobody made you turn up at the warehouse last night. You did it to help Kev. Well, what about the next time he's under fire? You going to be a civilian who just keeps popping up in times of crisis?' Something dawned on her. 'Christ, is that what this is? Is this some superhero fantasy trip you're on? You going to spring out of a phone box with a mask to help when Kev gives the signal?'

Straw still in mouth, Clyde tried to suppress a smirk, amused that she probably did believe that he was so contrived. 'That's not the plan, no.'

'And you can't use this little event as source material for your comic-book. NDAs.' Ace finished his beer and crushed the can; Trujillo nodded agreeably at this last point.

So much for Guns of the Metronome, Clyde thought. How vague would he have to make the comic-book to avoid litigation troubles? He gently set his empty glass down and watched a military truck cruise past on the shimmering black ribbon of privatized road.

'Okay... I'm in. So long as my mom is protected, and I mean completely insulated from all of this.'

'Standard policy,' Trujillo assured, his face impassive. 'For all intents and purposes, you're a ghost.'

Kev smiled and raised his left fist just above the rim of the table. Clyde sighed, his hesitance and doubt melting away under a smirk, and he bumped it. Kev's right arm was slowly mending itself. The technicians at the New York base, the Madhouse, had examined some of the collected Exorcist rounds scattered all about the Brooklyn warehouse and had confirmed their supernatural properties. They had yet to track down the source of their manufacture, and if it wasn't for the video-recorded evidence of Talbot and the corpses of Citadel Security forces on site, they wouldn't have even been able to confirm the ownership of the property. Many layers and much obfuscation. Regardless, the Cairnwood Society were not adversaries to be fought with legal entanglements and high court proceedings. They were to be fought in the dark, behind the scenes.

Ace punched Clyde in the shoulder. It was probably meant to be a friendly gesture of moral support, but it still stung a little.

Rose slammed the table in excitement, forgetting her strength. 'Good call, nerd.'

Trujillo had something else. 'One more thing, Clyde, Kev. I'm transferring you to the Madhouse. They've had a bad run of late, losing their strike team. They need fresh assets for the heavier stuff, especially now that we know Talbot and his Cairnwood handlers have been increasing their presence and power base along the East Coast. Tampering with Erebus, trawling it for potential resources... This can't be allowed to continue. I want some good people in that region to keep a close eye on them.'

Rose seemed as surprised as Clyde and Kev at the relocation. She glanced at Ace, then back to Trujillo.

Trujillo picked up on her forthcoming question. 'You'll be going with them. I assured Deputy Director Meadows that I'd also supply him with a few senior agents to help round out the formation of a new local strike team. Rose, Ace, you'll both be operating from there until told otherwise.'

Ace cracked the tab on his second cold can of imported Moosehead. He took a long gulp. 'Great. Whatever gets me out of the desert. But you do remember I'm originally a Canadian agent, right, Chief?'

Trujillo was clearly used to such informal conversation from subordinate agents, but Clyde believed it would still be a good while before he felt comfortable with such expression.

Trujillo crossed his blocky stone hands. 'I've spoken to your team at Igloo. They can spare you for now until further notice.'

Ace raised his can. 'I'll hold you to that.'

'And I was just beginning to feel at home here.' Kev sounded wistful. 'Work on my tan, good dusty air for my lungs. So is the Madhouse actually a—'

'It's a decommissioned mental asylum,' Trujillo interjected with a crisp nod.

Kev didn't seem thrilled at the sale. 'Cozy.'

'Well, I think you all have bags to pack.' Trujillo slid his dense frame out from the booth, and the agents followed, gathering near the entrance to the diner.

Something occurred to Clyde. 'What did you do with Mortis' hands?'

'They're under strict supervision,' Trujillo answered. 'It may sound hypocritical, but I'm only comfortable with the hoodoos and me having such access to Erebus.'

'At least we can cross Mortis off the list. Even if he somehow survived, he'll be hopping around, unable to so much as jerk himself off,' Ace added.

Clyde nodded in thought, feeling a little comforted by this but still not entirely on board with anybody striving for such a monopoly on passage to and from the Null.

'Have the hoodoos found anything on Konstantin's whereabouts?' Kev asked.

Trujillo's mouth formed a tight line, a crack in granite. 'You're going to be very busy shortly, Agent. I recommend you set your sights on tack-ling problems this side of the grave rather than worrying about unsubstantiated myths and fanatical cultists.'

Kev slowly tilted his head back, and Clyde knew that that answer had failed to satisfy him. But Kev left it alone for now. Ace finished his second beer, crushed the can, gave a relaxed salute to Trujillo, and pushed through the glass door of the diner, into the pristine blue sky and orange desert lands.

'I'll start the Jeep,' Rose said, heading for the door. 'I'll be in contact before we fly out, sir.'

'Thank you, Rose.'

Clyde and Kev offered the director their humble farewells and were about to exit into the parking lot when Trujillo stopped Clyde at the diner's door, the threshold of fantasy and reality, life and death, scorching heat and chilly air-conditioning.

'Sir?' Clyde asked.

'I never got around to saying it before.' Admiration shone in Trujillo's deep-brown and wholly human eyes. 'Welcome to Hourglass.'

'Thank you, sir.'

Kev raised a fist with an easy smile. Clyde bumped it, and they exited the Midnight Vulture, hopping into the Jeep with Ace and Rose. Ready to return home. New York City.

EPILOGUE

Edward Talbot crossed the immaculately tended lawns of the Westchester mansion, the green cut neatly into precise lanes like a rugby pitch. The armed guards stationed about the grounds didn't pay him any mind, like the good little automatons they were. Nice suits, though, smartly pressed. He approached the owl sanctuary built within the large wood like a fairy-tale castle of wood and glass. The boss was back from abroad. A shame really, as Edward had enjoyed having the run of the place in his stead. Still, he had no shortage of his own luxurious bolt holes scattered across the continents for his seasonal whims. He mainly hoped the Curator hadn't noticed one of his owls was missing. But of course, he would; they were his prized court.

Stepping into the fragrant shade of the wood, Edward opened the pleasantly designed pine door to the sanctuary, seeing the old whipcracker through the door's inset of glass. 'Mr. Gabriel?' All pleasantries.

'Edward.' Nothing more, but Edward detected the characteristic chilliness of the Curator's tone. A man who valued objects much more than the flesh-and-blood complications of people. 'I've been informed of what transpired at the Ivy Lounge. No hard feelings from our guests, not really, though the general consensus is that the collapse of our proposed new energy plan is a tremendous disappointment.' He held out his gloved arm, a welcome perch for a willing feathered friend. Gabriel somewhat resembled a bird in a revolting sort of way: razor thin and light of bone, beak-nosed, with a bald dome surrounded by a nest of wild, unruly hair, and his eyes were startlingly large and cunning, like those of his favored pets.

A great horned owl swooped down, majestic and placid, settling on Gabriel's arm. Talbot hated their eyes, unnerving, never missing a trick. And who could trust an animal that could rotate its damn head around like a swivel?

'And to think, that lucrative project actually might have been a benefit to this ailing world.' The Curator made a soft clucking noise at the owl. 'It's a funny old world.'

Edward felt like he was at a loose end. A naughty schoolboy called into the headmaster's office. 'Mortis was only a tool. Plenty more where he came from. We can put a pin in the energy proposal, revisit it in due course.'

Gabriel, the Curator, looked at him, his head rotating at an almost impossible angle, his wide, hungry eyes fixed on Edward like he was a fat field mouse. 'I concur. Another time. For the moment, the rest of the inner circle want somebody to be held accountable. They believe it would be judicious to satisfy not only our own ends, but the wishes of our outraged benefactors from the party.'

Piss on this, Talbot thought. *I'm the bloody sacrificial offering.*

'It was Hourglass who interfered, was it not?'

Talbot almost exhaled in relief but didn't dare. 'It was ... again.'

'Exactly.' The Curator held up a finger to make a point. 'Again, again, again. This dance is almost as old as time itself. I heard that this new brute of yours, your first test subject, recently disposed of their New York team's big hitters. Butchered them, I'm told.'

'The Hangman.' Talbot nodded. 'Correct.'

'Well, like termites, they get deep inside the woodwork. Hourglass' local office will only replace their losses with a new strike team—perhaps they already have with these latest pests. Either way, I want your man to do the same thing to them. And I want you to use that trinket you brought back to make more like him.'

Talbot couldn't help but grin; not only was he free from blame, but he could really put that relic to work. Optimize his workforce. Dare he create another local leg-breaker like the Hangman? Could he even? Dare he dream? He felt almost giddy. Oh yes, he would dream.

'Certainly, but it'll take a little time,' Edward said. 'Hangman was a smashing debut, as were Captain Agua and his lieutenants in the successive trials. Alas, not everybody responds so well to the change. Many don't even survive.'

'You already have the framework and the resources in place. Be industrious. Large sample sizes, by hook or by crook.'

'I'll be salesman of the year, sir.' A sycophantic smile stressed Talbot's dimples. 'It's a shame about our energy project setback, but I think Churchill said, "An optimist sees the opportunity in every difficulty." Perhaps finding that "trinket" on the shoreline was a better find than we first tipped our hat to. A boon.' He had taken the credit for Mortis' find, the key maker having chanced upon the mysterious artefact poking out of the hard, wet sand of the stormy beach during his first trip. But Talbot didn't see any need to throw posthumous praise on Mortis now. 'We have all of eternity to make more money. In the short term, perhaps we can make an army to help us bury Hourglass permanently.'

The Curator made a noncommittal hum. Feeling the silence settling over them, Talbot decided the man wanted to be alone with his birds. But as he turned to leave: 'Edward?' Talbot glanced over his shoulder. 'If you ever so much as harm a feather on one of these heads again, I'll nail you down and have them peck your guts out.'

Talbot nodded. He liked his guts where they were and knew it'd be stupid to act dumb or remorseful. He'd been caught with his pants down: accept it, move on, and get the hell away from here. He moved with a brisk step and a look of many rewarding tomorrows on his face, crossing towards the gravel courtyard and his British Racing Green Jaguar F-Type. He had phone calls to make and a new job to do. This would help him reach that next rung on the ladder. He'd make all of New York City a no-go zone to the entire Hourglass agency. Punishable by ugly death. He was looking forward to a nice long drive into the city.